REA

P9-AFR-909

"Hey, Parker, wait up!"

Miranda called to the man who barreled on ahead like a steam engine. "I'm going to give the dog this bit of steak I saved from dinner."

Stopping midstride, Lincoln Parker turned and noticed the mist from Randi's breath curling around her head. "Okay, but make it snappy. If we stay out too long we'll freeze."

Smiling, she peered up from where she'd knelt to feed the shivering dog. "I love cold, crisp autumns. Reminds me of home."

"Really? Where's home?" Linc pounced on her statement.

Miranda felt the color drain from her face. She felt exposed. Trapped. "I can't tell you that, Parker—Linc. Please don't send me away. I'm…ah—"

"What? On the lam from the cops?"

"No, no, nothing like that." Stronger now, she didn't fumble so much for words. "There's some…one I'm running from."

Linc drew back and studied her pale features. "A man?"

Looking stricken, Miranda nodded. She waited for the logical next question and then for the ax to fall.

"You're running from a husband, then?" he asked harshly.

She shook her head, not trusting herself to speak.

@ROMANCE

FEB 2 4 2004

Dear Reader,

The heroine of this story, Miranda Kimbrough, has lived inside my head for several years. She came to me one day when I overheard a well-known singer telling a companion that life at the top of the music charts isn't always rosy.

Since then, I've listened to interviews with singing sensations from a variety of musical fields. Many hinted at what the first woman had said. Life at the top means hard work, sleepless nights, endless days on the road, constant pressure from managers, promoters and fans to keep producing hits. As the pressure builds, one singer said, "You lose pieces of your life and almost all of your heart."

The love stories we write are about healing and redemption. It's taken me all this time to find my exhausted country singer a fitting mate. But because love itself isn't easy, and because I wanted to make Miranda's love everlasting, I needed Lincoln Parker to have fought his own battles. So that when he commits himself to Miranda, it's with all his heart.

I hope readers will come to appreciate, as I have, the long road to love embarked on by "Misty" Kimbrough, country legend, and Linc Parker, emotionally scarred former Hollywood financial wizard. And I hope you'll take to heart the ragtag mix of homeless kids who help show them the way.

I love hearing from readers. You can reach me at P.O. Box 17480-101, Tucson, AZ 85731 or e-mail me at rdfox@worldnet.att.net.

Best,

Roz Denny Fox

A Cowboy at Heart

Roz Denny Fox

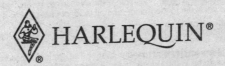

TORONTO • NEW YORK • LONDON
AMSTERDAM • PARIS • SYDNEY • HAMBURG
STOCKHOLM • ATHENS • TOKYO • MILAN • MADRID
PRAGUE • WARSAW • BUDAPEST • AUCKLAND

If you purchased this book without a cover you should be aware
that this book is stolen property. It was reported as "unsold and
destroyed" to the publisher, and neither the author nor the
publisher has received any payment for this "stripped book."

ISBN 0-373-71184-0

A COWBOY AT HEART

Copyright © 2004 by Rosaline Fox.

All rights reserved. Except for use in any review, the reproduction or
utilization of this work in whole or in part in any form by any electronic,
mechanical or other means, now known or hereafter invented, including
xerography, photocopying and recording, or in any information storage
or retrieval system, is forbidden without the written permission of the
publisher, Harlequin Enterprises Limited, 225 Duncan Mill Road,
Don Mills, Ontario, Canada M3B 3K9.

All characters in this book have no existence outside the imagination of
the author and have no relation whatsoever to anyone bearing the same
name or names. They are not even distantly inspired by any individual
known or unknown to the author, and all incidents are pure invention.

This edition published by arrangement with Harlequin Books S.A.

® and TM are trademarks of the publisher. Trademarks indicated with
® are registered in the United States Patent and Trademark Office, the
Canadian Trade Marks Office and in other countries.

Visit us at www.eHarlequin.com

Printed in U.S.A.

To my daughters, Kelly and Korynna. I'm so proud of you for your patience in dealing with children, and for the loving moms you've both become. This book's for you.

Books by Roz Denny Fox

HARLEQUIN SUPERROMANCE

Don't miss any of our special offers. Write to us at the following address for information on our newest releases.

Harlequin Reader Service
U.S.: 3010 Walden Ave., P.O. Box 1325, Buffalo, NY 14269
Canadian: P.O. Box 609, Fort Erie, Ont. L2A 5X3

CHAPTER ONE

Los Angeles, California

HIGH ON A HILLSIDE above a posh Hollywood community where he served as financial adviser to a wide array of successful movie and rock stars, thirty-two-year-old Lincoln Parker stared absently down at the six-month-old grave of his kid sister, Felicity. Sinking to his knees, Parker anchored a small bouquet of yellow roses to the stone. He paid scant heed to the gusty Santa Ana winds tugging at his suit coat. Pretty as the roses were, Linc considered them a sad commemoration on what should have been his sister's seventeenth birthday.

"Felicity, I, uh…I'm trying to make good on my promise. The one I…made far too late to help you." Pausing, Linc scrubbed at tears that spilled over his cheeks. "Just…maybe I can save other kids from suffering your fate. God, honey, I hope you know how sorry I am that I didn't s-see you were serious."

Heaving himself up, Linc thrust shaking hands deep into the pockets of his pin-striped pants. Gazing across endless rows of flat, gray headstones, he swallowed the huge lump in his throat and clamped his teeth tight against further apologies his sister would never hear.

Damn, he'd tried to provide for her after their mom died. His sister had been a change-of-life baby for their movie-star mother and a much older director. Olivia Parker hadn't wanted a second kid, and Felicity's father reportedly still had a wife. Linc's own dad was also in the film business, but he'd long before succumbed to alcohol and had never been part of Linc's existence. At the time their mom ended her messed-up life, Linc had just finished high school. Because he'd been awarded a full scholarship to U.C. Berkeley, the family-court judge had asked his maternal grandmother to take charge of the Parker household.

Looking back, Linc saw that Grandmother Welch had been far too permissive a caretaker for an impressionable growing girl. At the time, though, he'd gone blithely off to university, glad to be liberated from the daunting task. After all, what had he, at eighteen, known about raising kids? "Not a damn thing!" Linc shook his head.

After a last grim perusal of his sister's grave, he turned and strode briskly toward his silver Jaguar.

In the years between Grandmother Welch's death, thanks largely to her hedonistic lifestyle, when he was twenty-five, and Felicity's—of a street drug overdose, the cops said—Linc had committed sins of his own. Overindulgence of his sister was clearly uppermost among them. He accepted the blame. Hell, he'd burst onto the Hollywood scene with a shiny new MBA, and he'd obviously worn blinders when it came to anyone's excesses. Including his sister's... Still, he believed that his belated decision to atone for past transgressions was the right thing to do. The *only* thing to do.

As if his musings triggered a response, his cell phone began to vibrate in his pocket. He retrieved it and flipped open the case as he slid beneath the car's wood-grained steering wheel.

It seemed fortuitous to hear John Montoya's voice. "Hi, Linc. I'm up north, at the ranch you asked me to check out."

"I'm afraid to ask, John. Is the place a disaster or is it anything like the ad in Sunday's paper?"

"Basically it meets your requirements—unless you count the fact that it's twenty miles from anything resembling a town," Montoya said with a chuckle.

"Good. Perfect. I've been reading up on ranching and on teen refugees, plus talking to people. So there's a livable bunkhouse and main residence, as well as a parcel of raw land?"

"Uh…yeah. Three hundred or so acres. You'll want to change the name, though. Rascal Ranch doesn't seem appropriate for what you've got in mind. According to the representative from the Oasis Foundation—the current owners—the ranch has been used for various social-development programs over the past five years."

"For instance?"

"Uh, a summer camp for underprivileged kids. A horse-therapy program for amputees that Oasis funded for a couple of years. Their last project, I think he said, was stopgap housing for kids awaiting adoption."

"Why is Oasis dumping the ranch now?"

"Ted Gunderson said it's difficult to get and keep houseparents way out here. I tell you, Linc, the property is smack in the middle of nowhere."

"In the middle of nowhere suits me fine. A haven for ex-druggie street kids is better if it's less accessible to temptations. Okay, John, you have my permission to start dickering. Now that I've made up my mind, I'm anxious to get going. If Oasis is willing to negotiate, I'll go as high as the top figure we discussed. Oh, and John, if you close a deal, will you swing past the county courthouse and apply for whatever licenses I'll need to house a dozen or so kids?"

"I almost forgot—that's the big plus. Oasis will transfer their group-home license to you."

"That's permissible?"

"Must be. Gunderson seems to know. He says they have a year left on their state contract, but you'll need to undergo a Social Services inspection. Gunderson claims it's a mere formality. He implied there's nothing much to qualifying as a bona fide shelter."

"Well, that's a relief." For the first time since the idea had struck him, Linc felt the heaviness around his heart lift just a little. "I'm headed back to my office. If you work a deal, contact me there. Then I'll put my house in Coldwater Canyon on the market and start notifying clients that I'm turning them over to my partner until I get the shelter operating. Thought I'd allow at least two years. By the way, Dennis has promised he'll retain your firm for all the legwork I currently have you do."

"I appreciate the vote of confidence. I only hope I can work with Dennis. I realize you like the guy, but frankly, Linc, I hope you know what you're doing. Rumor has it he's pulled some shady stuff to get accounts."

"You've been in Tinseltown long enough to know you shouldn't listen to rumors."

"I tell you, Dennis Morrison doesn't have the same standards you do."

"Name something he's done besides drop a couple of going-nowhere B stars to make room for a few up-and-comers. I wouldn't have done it, but our competitors do it constantly. I trust Dennis enough to hand him my personal portfolio. I doubt I'll have time to follow the market for a while. Running a teen shelter is going to be a new experience for me. Once it's up and running smoothly, I figure I can step back and just do the fund-raising for it. By then I'll be ready to get back into the business."

3 1822 04526 8021

"Why risk your career at all, man? You've got it made where you are."

"I'm doing it for Felicity."

"I gotta be honest here. You're putting your life on hold because you feel guilty about something no one could've foreseen. You gave that kid a life anyone in her right mind would grab in a minute. Felicity blew it, Linc. That's the unvarnished truth."

"She was sixteen, John, my responsibility any way you cut it. I spend part of every single day in the Hollywood trenches. I knew she didn't have the talent to be a rock star. Instead of taking the time to try and steer her in a better direction, I shelled out bucks whenever she found some new bloodsucker to give her voice or music lessons. I guess I hoped she'd eventually see for herself. That was a big mistake. *My* mistake."

"Yeah," John muttered. "You think your crystal ball should've told you one of her so-called mentors or rocker pals was a drug dealer on the side."

"According to the cops, not all street kids are losers. I can't save all of them from Felicity's fate, but maybe I can redirect one or two. All I know is that I'll never be able to live with myself if I don't try. Call me with a final deal, all right?"

There was an uncomfortable silence until Linc added, "This Gunderson guy you're dealing with—he verified that there are no restrictions on the land against farming, right? I mean, part of my plan is to have the kids invest a little honest sweat plowing, planting and harvesting crops that'll eventually pay for their upkeep. I'm not offering any other kid a free ride like I gave Felicity. That's where I really fouled up."

"You'll have the land, Farmer Parker. Jeez, I have a

hard time envisioning you with blisters on those Midas hands of yours. But if you're serious, I'll go dicker.''

"Hear me, John. I am serious. Never more so. I'll be waiting for your report at my office. So long for now.''

Nashville, Tennessee

PHONY FOG hissed from canisters strategically placed behind a row of footlights. A single spotlight faded by degrees until it left the twenty-six-year-old country singer swallowed in darkness and her signature mist. Her body cringed away from a rolling swell of whistles and stamping feet.

Unsnapping her guitar strap, she passed the instrument to a stagehand who'd materialized from the wings. Her mind was fixed on the solace waiting in her dressing room.

"Awesome performance, Misty!'' The stagehand's shout was drowned out by the thunderous din from the auditorium. "Hey, where ya goin'?'' The kid's lanky frame blocked her passage.

"I'm fixin' to go change out of this hot costume.'' The singer blotted perspiration from her forehead with a satin sleeve. Eyes made electric blue—by contacts her manager insisted she wear to conceal what he called her blah gray eyes—closed tiredly.

"Wes said you hafta give four encores tonight.''

Her eyes flew open and she shook her head.

"Yep. It's a packed house. Wes says you're to give 'em a taste of your new songs so every fan here will stampede to the lobby and buy a CD.''

"Four encores?'' She sounded dazed, as if he'd asked the impossible. Indeed, he had.

Four fingers were waggled under her nose. The crescendo beyond the stage had escalated to a degree that caused the young man to give up attempting to communicate. He pressed the guitar into her midriff and shoved her back toward center stage.

Miranda Kimbrough, known to country-music fans simply as Misty, dragged in a deep breath. Plastering on a smile as she'd done so many times, she edged into the bright spotlight. She was a corporation. A multimillion-dollar star to whom a host of folks had hitched their wagons. So many people now depended on her that she was afraid of cracking under the burden. Besides back-to-back concerts at home and abroad, there were charity events scheduled and a growing number of photo shoots. Recently, subsidiary companies using her image had marketed T-shirts, look-alike dolls, posters and glossy notebook covers. She needed a break. She felt weighted down. Yet no one heard her plea.

When the theater again fell silent, Miranda adjusted the microphone with a trembling hand. It took a Herculean effort, but finally the music transported her to a place where singing songs had been a joy.

Her newest piece, one she'd entitled "A Cowboy at Heart," flowed easily from her husky voice. As well it should. She'd written it for her dad. And then she sang "A Last Goodbye," which paid tribute to both her parents. Frankly, Miranda doubted anyone in this faceless audience knew or cared that eleven years ago on this very night, her father and his band had perished in the wicked storm raging across his beloved Tennessee hills. The new songs poured out her heartache for a dad she'd lost five days after her fifteenth birthday, and for a mom who'd died of pneumonia when Miranda was four.

Even the most cynical among her production crew considered these ballads her very best. Who'd have guessed they'd be her last? Certainly not Wes Carlisle, her manager, a soulless man who'd hustled her into a one-sided contract during the confusing days following her dad's death.

Wes would be livid when his caged bird flew the coop, and that made her smile.

Her band? A different story. She regretted not confiding in them. Her piano man and steel guitarist were dedicated. And Colby Donovan, her arranger, was the only one left of her dad's friends. It was a good thing he was home recovering from surgery. When she'd attempted to tell Colby how she felt, he'd dispensed his usual bear hug and said Doug would have been so very proud of her. She'd achieved the pinnacle of success that her dad's band had almost but never quite reached.

Despite regrets, she'd planned her flight. It would be complete. And it would be tonight—while Carlisle and his henchmen licked their chops, counting the proceeds they raked in from her sold-out concert. Wesley pushed and pushed and pushed her to write more and better chart breakers. *No more, no more,* Miranda thought with astonishing relief as the audience went still. Perhaps the fans had seen her tears. She couldn't stop them from running down her face.

One last bow. One last wave. She had nothing left to give.

Look at them. They all envied her fame and fortune. None would understand she'd never wanted to be a star. She loved singing, but...

This time when Misty passed her guitar to the kid holding Wes's clipboard full of must-dos, he obviously sensed steel in her backbone. Still, he cautioned, ''Wes won't like that you only gave two encores.'' Jogging to keep up with Miranda's long strides, he panted. ''Wes has you timed to the second. Now you'll hafta sit in your dressing room until he frees up a bodyguard to escort you to your bus. So I better stay with you.''

Miranda's steps faltered as she neared her dressing room. ''Remind Wes I said at rehearsal that this sequence would drain me. I need to have some time to myself. He'll recall the conversation, uh…Dave, isn't it?''

''Hey, you know my name. Cool! Wes hired me for this tour, 'cause your new CD's gonna be a smash. He gave me strict instructions, but hey, you're the star, Ms.… Mis…Misty,'' the smitten kid stammered.

Miranda hated that Wes would fire this boy for losing her. But it couldn't be helped. Dave's very inexperience played into her hands.

As IT HAPPENED, her escape turned out to be ridiculously easy. Inside her star quarters, Misty meticulously transformed herself back into the nondescript persona of Miranda Kimbrough. First, she hacked her long blond hair into a short spiky mop—carefully storing the cuttings in a plastic bag to be tossed later. Then she dyed her hair black. Without her blue contacts she barely recognized the woman staring out from the full-length mirror. Add ragged jeans, a faded blouse and a denim jacket straight off a boys' rack, plus run-down combat boots and an old army backpack she'd scrounged from a thrift shop, and her getaway ensemble was complete. Inside the pack, she'd squirreled away cash withdrawn from one of her accounts. Considering she had millions, it was a pittance.

She worried that the meager funds wouldn't last. But because Wes scrutinized her bank statements, she'd been afraid to take more. Miranda hoped what she had would keep her fed and on the road until her disappearance became yesterday's news. For good measure, she'd sewn a pair of diamond earrings into the lining of her jacket. She didn't need diamonds. Only freedom. A chance to be herself.

While Dave guarded the front entry of her dressing room, Miranda slipped out a rarely used back door. Head down, she sped down a hall and merged with a teeming horde purchasing CDs from Wesley's hawkers. Rick Holden, Wes's right-hand man, even tried to sell her a compact disc.

Shaking her still-damp curls, Miranda popped a stick of sugarless gum in her mouth and blended with a group of boisterous teens leaving the arena. Once free of the building, she ran for six blocks. Only then did she haul in a lungful of crisp October air. But she didn't relax until a Greyhound bus bound for Detroit left the glittering lights of Nashville behind.

Starting in Detroit, her plan was to hop a string of buses that would eventually deposit her in far-off L.A. She reasoned that if one small woman couldn't lose herself on the streets of Los Angeles, she couldn't find anonymity anywhere.

IT TOOK THREE WEEKS after she pulled her disappearing act for Miranda Kimbrough to reach her destination. She hadn't reckoned on Wes suggesting to police that she'd been kidnapped, possibly for ransom. The band, all the staffers and roadies, *everyone* had heard her beg him for time off. But when her bus hit Kansas City, it was a shock to see headlines screaming KIDNAPPED! above her most recent promo photo now plastered on the front pages of major newspapers and magazines.

Panicked, Miranda had taken refuge on the streets with the homeless. Luckily she'd met some kind folks. And vowed that if she ever managed to access her bank funds again, she'd help the homeless in some manner.

When temperatures dropped into the twenties, Miranda began to feel guilty for taking up space at the cramped shelter. And guiltier still accepting a handout of food, knowing all the while that she could, with one phone call, return to a life of privilege.

Could. But she didn't make that call.

Wes virtually owned her. He pointed out often enough that she'd signed an ironclad contract. He'd find a way to turn her disappearance into a windfall. Going back would change nothing—except that she could expect to be watched twenty-four hours a day.

In the aftermath of her dad's death, Miranda learned that few people in the industry performed for the sheer pleasure of it. Her dad had been a rarity. Doug Kimbrough had placed family at the top of his priorities. He'd loved her mother and Miranda and successfully juggled work and his home life.

Since Wes had signed her, she hadn't spent more than two nights in a row in her own bed at home. And she'd like to make just one friend who didn't eat, sleep and breathe music at warp speed. Someday she'd like to meet a man who could see beyond her voice. Someone who really cared about her likes, dislikes, needs and fantasies.

Her murky thoughts turned inward as Miranda hitched her backpack higher and trudged out of the busy L.A. bus terminal, and headed for an inner-city park she'd scoped out on a seat companion's map. Another helpful tip she'd picked up in K.C. was that the homeless congregated in parks. By mingling with them, a newcomer could glean information vital to survival. This particular park was maybe a ten-block hike away, but Miranda didn't care. L.A. was much warmer than Kansas.

Pausing a moment, she slipped out of her lined denim jacket.

"Hi. Is that your dog?" A breathy voice spoke directly behind Miranda, causing her to whirl and duck sharply. A savvy homeless woman in K.C. had repeatedly warned Miranda about not letting anyone come up too close behind her.

"Uh…no. I don't have a dog. I just got off a bus."

"Oh."

"Do you live around here? If so, maybe you can help me get my bearings." Miranda extracted a pack of gum from her pocket and offered a stick to the unkempt brunette—a young woman probably not even out of her teens. With her face free of makeup, Miranda thought she probably didn't look much more than a teenager herself.

"Thanks for the gum. I'm Jenny, by the way." Shrugging, she said, "I guess you could say I live here. I caught some z's last night at the bus depot. Sometimes the cops run us out. Last night I got lucky." She stripped the paper off the gum. Both women cast sidelong glances at the scruffy black-and-white terrier now sitting placidly at Miranda's feet.

"If he's not yours or mine, then whose is he?" Kneeling, Miranda ran a hand around his neck in search of a collar. She and Jenny were alone on either side of the street for at least a block. "He's not tagged."

"Big surprise. He's been dumped. This area's well-known as a dumping ground for homeless people and strays."

"So are you, uh, homeless?" Miranda asked hesitantly.

The girl's grin softened otherwise hard features. "Depending on who you ask, I'm both homeless and a stray. You by chance got any smokes?"

"Sorry, it's not a habit I ever picked up."

"Lucky you." Jenny continued to stare. "You have a

smoker's voice. Unless it's your accent. Are you from down South?''

"Used to be.'' Miranda rolled one shoulder. Preferring to change the subject, she straightened and said, "I may not have cigarettes, but I have two sandwiches. A guy on the bus took pity on me at the last stop. I wasn't hungry then, but I'm fixin' to be now. He said one's roast beef on wheat. The other's tuna on rye. I'll give you first pick.''

"Cool. How about we split fifty-fifty? I haven't eaten since yesterday. Eric, he's my buddy, lucked out and got a gig playing at a wedding reception last night. He promised me he'd nab leftovers. Anyway, he'll come away with a chunk of change. It won't be that much, though. And Eric needs new strings for his guitar.''

Miranda's stomach sank. "Oh, your friend is a musician?''

"Yeah. Me, too. Well, not really.'' She pulled a wry face. "Me and a girlfriend tried to break into rock and roll. But Felicity—that's my friend—she, uh, died.'' Sudden tears halted Jenny's explanation.

Miranda's sympathetic murmur prompted the girl to continue. "Felicity and me had a real scummy audition, see. They're all hard. Some are really bad. The jerk in charge made us feel like shit. And my friend had her heart set on getting that job. Felicity's brother is, like, some finance guru to big-deal stars. She wanted to impress him. So it, like, hit her super hard when the guy said we were totally awful. Felicity must've gone straight out and bought some bad dope. Eric and me, we found her and carried her to County Hospital straight away. But it was too late.''

"I'm sorry.'' Miranda's temples had begun to pound, if not from trying to follow Jenny's narrative, then from hunger. She took out the sack of sandwiches and sat on the low brick wall fencing an empty lot.

Wasn't it her bad luck to run into a wannabe songbird? And did this girl take drugs? Still, how could she renege on her promise to share her sandwiches? Handing over half of one, Miranda asked casually, "Is rock and roll all you sing? What about rap, or…uh…country?"

"Bite your tongue. Don't say a dirty word like *country* around my crowd. They'll run you out of town on a rail."

Relieved, Miranda looked up and realized the dog had followed her. He gazed at her hopefully, his liquid brown eyes tracking her every move. "Okay, mutt. Jeez. I'll give you the meat out of my sandwich."

Jenny was already wolfing down her portion. "I hope you wanted a pet…uh… What's your name, anyway? Just a warning, but if you feed him, he's yours forever."

"I've never had a pet," Miranda confessed. "I wouldn't mind keeping him. For…companionship."

Jenny bobbed her head. "I hear you. I would've loved a dog or cat, but my mom couldn't feed her kids, let alone pets."

"My dad fed me fine. It's more that we traveled a lot. More than a lot," Miranda admitted, tossing another thin slice of beef to the dog. The poor starved beast didn't gobble it in one bite as one might expect. Instead, he thanked her with his eyes, then sank to his belly to take small, dainty bites.

"Would you look at that." Jenny paused to smile. "I still didn't catch your name. I can't be calling you, *hey you.*"

Just in case the girl read the newspapers, Miranda stammered a bit and then settled on a short version. "It's…Randi."

"Cool. I wish my mom had come up with a classier name than Jennifer." The girl frowned.

"I spell Randi with an *i*, not a *y*," Miranda said for lack of a better comment.

Jenny raised a brow. "Doesn't matter how you spell it down here. Only time spelling's an issue is if a cop hauls you in or you end up in the morgue."

Pondering that chilling statement, Miranda halted in the act of feeding the last of her sandwich meat to the terrier. As if to punctuate Jenny's words, a police car rounded the corner and slowed. Both women stiffened. "Cripes, now what?" Miranda muttered.

Jenny swallowed her final bite, wiped her mouth and said, "It's okay. That's Benny Garcia. This is his beat. For a cop, he's cool. All the same, let me do the talking."

Miranda noted that the uniformed man and Jenny exchanged nods. But her blood ran cold as he pulled to the curb and stepped out of his cruiser. What if he recognized her from the flyers that had surely circulated through major police departments?

He didn't. He gave her only a cursory glance, frankly taking more interest in the dog. "Cute little guy." Bending, he rubbed the wriggling animal's belly. "If you're planning to stick around here, kid, you'll need to leash and license him."

Opening her mouth to deny the dog was hers, she stopped abruptly at the cop's next words. "If he's lost or a stray, I'll phone the pound to pick him up." The man stood and reached for a cell phone clipped to his belt.

"I'll get a license." Miranda scooped up the black-and-white bundle of fur. "Where do I go? I'm new to L.A."

"Thought so. Hmm. The bad news, kid, is that you've gotta supply your full name and home address to get a dog license."

Miranda bit down hard on her lower lip.

"Figures." Garcia let out a long sigh. "Why can't you kids just stay home? Running away solves nothing. Trouble always follows. What kind of way is that to live?"

"The cops couldn't stop my mom's drunken rages," Jenny snapped. "Out here, I have a fighting chance. My friends and me do fine."

"Weather bureau says it's gonna be a cold winter. You and your friends should reconsider moseying up north to that new ranch for teens. I gave Eric a flyer for it yesterday. A guy I know, John Montoya, he's seen the place. Says the owner's ordered cows and chickens. Imagine—fresh milk and eggs every morning without having to scrounge for leftovers from restaurant Dumpsters."

With one holey sneaker, Jenny scraped at a weed struggling up through a crack in the sidewalk. "Eric'll want to stay near the action. He's got some contacts. Any minute he could land a gig that'll make us stars."

The cop eyed her obliquely. "How many times have I heard that one? At least think it over. Like I said to Eric, Montoya tells me it'll mean hot meals and a solid roof over your heads through a bad winter. Weigh that against the scuzzy shelters around here. The owner isn't asking much in return. Help tilling a few fields so there'll be produce to eat in the spring. Eric can drive a tractor, can't he?"

"He grew up on a farm in the Sacramento Delta, so of course he can. Question is, does he want to? Here, he gets an occasional chance to play, like last night. I don't imagine there'll be many opportunities for a guitarist on some dumb ranch."

Garcia removed his foot from the low wall. "Suit yourselves. I've got a month's vacation due. I can't promise my replacement will be as easy on vagrants as I am."

"We're not vagrants," Jenny blustered. "Me, Eric, Greg and Shawn are down on our luck is all. We'll get work for our band soon. You'll see."

"Yeah, yeah." Shaking his head, the cop started to walk away.

"Wait," Miranda called. "It's been a while, but I've lived on a farm. You think this ranch owner might let me keep, uh, Fido?" Her gaze swung from the cop to the terrier.

"Maybe. Hop in and I'll give you a lift to the precinct. I left the extra flyers in my desk. There's a map on the back showing how to locate the ranch."

Miranda's uneasiness about visiting a police station came to the fore.

Jenny correctly read her discomfort. "Hey, Randi, I'll give you Eric's flyer. I owe you for lunch. That'll be a fair trade."

"Sounds good. That'd be better, Officer. I've got no idea how well the mutt does in cars. Wouldn't want him to pee on your upholstery."

Garcia laughed. "Wouldn't be the worst my upholstery's had done to it. But I know you kids are leery of visiting the station. You say you're new here? Can you promise me there aren't any warrants out for your arrest?"

Miranda blanched. Wes Carlisle would use every means at his disposal to get her back under his thumb. Everybody in the business said his contracts were airtight. If a warrant was necessary, there might be one. But because Garcia's eyes hardened in the fading sunlight, Miranda declared firmly, "No warrants. My folks are…both dead. I just decided to see the country before I settle down to work a day job."

"Tough life. There's lot of thugs on back streets ready to prey on skinny little girls like you."

A ripple of unease wound up Miranda's spine. It was Jenny who waved Garcia off. "We're not stupid, you know. Come on, Randi. Let's go."

LINC DROVE his new Ford Excursion along a lumpy path that led to his new home. At this moment, everything in his life was new—right down to this gas-guzzling monster vehicle he'd bought to replace the silver Jag. There was growing resentment in the U.S. against purchasing gas hogs, but he'd let the salesman talk him into this one because it would carry a bunch of kids into town in a single trip. Now, after seeing the condition of the road, he knew buying a workhorse SUV had been smart. *Rascal Ranch?* "Ugh." Linc grimaced as he drove beneath the arch bearing the ridiculous name.

First to go would be that sign, he mused. Linc recognized the house from a picture John Montoya had taken. It was the photo Linc had copied onto his flyer. In two weeks, John had promised he'd pass the flyers to a cop friend who knew street kids. Two weeks ought to allow Linc enough time to set up the basics.

An old car stood inside the carport where he'd planned to park. Staring at it, Linc swung around and stopped in front of the house. Surely a rep from Oasis didn't own that rusty monstrosity. But then, Linc had only ever dealt with the firm via phone, fax and John Montoya. Perhaps the former owners felt compelled to transfer licenses and keys in person.

Sliding off the leather seat, Linc started for the steps. The day was waning, and he saw that a light burned inside the house. Torn and stained lace curtains rippled as if someone was watching from within. The next thing he knew, the door flew open. A bald man dressed in overalls and a dumpy middle-aged woman squeezed through the door simultaneously.

"About time you showed up. Lydia and me went off Oasis's time clock at noon. Nobody asked us to stick around an extra six hours to look after the brats. You owe us a hundred bucks. Or…we'll settle for eighty since Lydia didn't cook them no supper."

"Them?" Lincoln gaped at the couple. "Who are you, and who are you calling…well, brats isn't a term I'd use under any circumstance."

"I would've thought your man, Montoya, would've passed along our names. We're George and Lydia Tucker. We spent the last four months as houseparents for Oasis Foundation. Never been so glad to get done of any job. So if you pay up, me and the missus'll be on our way."

Linc withdrew his booted foot from the top step of a porch that wrapped the weathered house. In doing so, he glimpsed three ragtag children on the porch, ranging in age, he'd guess, from four to eight or nine. All peered at him distrustfully.

"Oh, you have a family." Lincoln reached for his wallet. "I don't think I owe you, Mr. Tucker. But rather than hold you up, I'll give you the money and settle with Oasis later." He handed over the bill, which Tucker snatched and shoved in a pocket. Without further ado, he and his wife shot past Linc and jumped into the dilapidated car. They'd shut their doors before Linc realized the children, one of whom sat in a wheelchair, remained on the porch as if glued there.

"Hey. Wait!" Feeling as if he'd missed some vital part of the conversation, Linc rushed to the driver's door and pounded on George Tucker's window.

The man rolled it down an inch or so. He'd already started the engine and the car belched blue smoke. Coughing and waving the smoke away, Linc gasped, "Aren't you forgetting something? Like your kids?"

"Ain't ours," George declared. "Top dog from Oasis came last night. He left the foundation's Social Services contract with the state on the kitchen table. Said it lets you continue on the same as before. Ted Gunderson's his name." George fumbled a business card from his shirt pocket and passed it to Linc. "The area's getting a new Social Services director, a Mrs. Bishop. Ted said she'd be by one of these days to see how you're doin'. Step aside, son. This buggy don't have much gas."

Aghast, Linc shouted, "But...but...what about those kids?" He stabbed a finger toward them, not liking one bit how they all cringed and drew closer together.

"They're your problem now. The nine-year-old swears like a trucker. Oh, and he bites somethin' fierce. Outside of that, cuff 'em upside the head a few times and the others won't give you no lip."

"*What?* No, George. You don't understand. My facility's a haven for street teens. I won't be accepting young children. And special-needs kids...well, absolutely no way," Linc added, frowning at the wheelchair.

"You're the one who don't get it, mister. The kids are wards of the court. Oasis left the lot of 'em to you. Good luck findin' houseparents. We're the third set in less than a year. Too far from town for most folks." George took his foot off the brake and the old car started to roll.

Linc latched onto the side mirror. "Hey! Hey, give me ten seconds. Just until I contact my liaison who dealt with Oasis. I'm sure we'll clear this up. There are probably foster parents in town where Gunderson intended for you to drop the children."

"No. But fine, call. Just make it snappy."

Linc already had his phone out and was furiously punching in John Montoya's number. "John, it's Linc. Yeah, I've arrived. What's the deal with the kids? Three of 'em," he yelled. "Little ones." Then, because three sets of wary eyes unnerved him, Linc turned his back to the children and lowered his voice. "No, you most certainly did not mention them to me, John." Hearing his voice rise, Linc took a deep breath. "I don't just *sound* pissed off, pal. I *am* pissed off. You know this place is for teens. What am I supposed to do with three little kids?" His frustration peaked. Linc stood his dark hair on end by raking one hand through locks that needed more than a trim. "This isn't funny. How could they—Oasis, or for that matter, you— how could you foist off innocent children? They're not livestock included in the transfer, for pity's sake!"

Linc slammed a fist down on the rusted car trunk. "Kids are not *just kids*. Okay. Okay, you didn't know I'd freak out over it. But you haven't heard the last from me about this, that's for damned sure!"

Linc snapped his phone shut, took another deep breath and dredged up a semblance of his old self. "Mr. Tucker, uh…George. Er…Lydia…" Linc's usual aplomb faltered. "I'm the last guy equipped to deal with small kids. Won't you please stay? Just until I straighten out this mess with Oasis. Shouldn't take a day. Two, max."

"Forget it," George snarled. "We stuck it out long enough. As far as my wife's concerned, four months was too long. They're yours, with our blessing. Oh, the wife says there's meat in the freezer. Should last until you can get to town." With that, the old car rumbled off in a trail of blue smoke.

Linc felt as near to breaking down as he had since losing Felicity to a life he desperately hoped to change for other teens. *Teens!* That was the operative term.

Then, as if his day wasn't already in the toilet, Linc saw

a band of scraggly teens ambling toward him along one side of the rutted lane. Five in all, preceded by a yappy dog of indeterminate origin. This couldn't be happening! He needed at least two weeks to ready the place for occupation, as John had been well aware. Clearly he'd jumped the gun. John must have contacted his cop friend. How else would these kids know to come all the way out here?

Linc unleashed a string of colorful curses, which he bit back the instant he caught a huge grin lighting the dirty face of the boy on the porch. *Had to be the biter.*

Squeezing his eyes shut, Linc smacked his forehead hard with the heel of one hand. This was definitely not turning out to be his finest hour. What in hell was he supposed to do now?

A ray of hope glimmered and he snatched up his phone again. The solution was simple, really. Ted Gunderson from Oasis would just have to come and collect these left-over children. Tonight. That was all there was to it.

CHAPTER TWO

MIRANDA ADJUSTED her heavy backpack on already aching shoulders. Several miles back, she'd ceased having any feeling in her blistered heels. No matter what negative things people might say about street kids, somewhere around Fresno it became clear to her that they couldn't be faulted for lack of stamina.

She, Jenny and her pals had been on the road for more than a week. Sometimes they hitched rides, but because they refused to split up, mostly they relied on shank's mare, as her daddy used to call hoofing it.

Eric, Shawn and Greg had started complaining in earnest after the last town disappeared and they'd entered this desolate road. If not for the fact that the nights were pitch-black and cold, Miranda would've been content to let the others turn back. She felt most sympathetic toward Jenny, whose thin jacket was no barrier against the weather. Midweek, long-haul truckers they encountered at a rest stop said it was spitting snow atop the Siskiyou mountain pass. Practically overnight, Mount Lassen, visible in the distance, looked like a vanilla ice-cream cone sparkling in weak sunlight.

"Hey, look over there!" Miranda's excited voice rose above Shawn's griping about the driver who'd just passed. "Shh!" Again she tried to compete with Shawn's swearing and the barking dog. They'd voted to name him Scraps to depict his throwaway status.

Making little headway, Miranda placed two fingers between her teeth. Her whistle garnered the attention of all but the dog. Sparing the dog a last exasperated glance, Miranda pulled out the battered flyer she'd kept as a guidepost. "I think we've found it. The ranch. Doesn't that house at the end of this lane look like the one pictured here?"

Scraps scampered on ahead while the road-weary teens circled around Miranda to peer at the badly crumpled paper.

"It's about time," Eric grumbled. "Jenny's got one sneaker worn all the way through."

Shawn, the heftiest of the three boys, rubbed his belly. "I hope they haven't already eaten. I'm starved."

Greg punched his arm. "You're always starved. You think we didn't see Randi slip you half a pack of the hot dogs we bummed off those hikers yesterday?"

The always-hungry boy glanced guiltily at his companions. "I can't help it that my bones weigh more than your whole body, Greg. We didn't all have itty-bitty Korean moms. And for all we know, your dad could've been a squirt. Not all sailors are bruisers, you know."

Miranda uttered a cranky sigh. A guaranteed way to create dissension was for anyone to bring up the shortfalls of a parent. Before starting out, they'd made a pact, agreeing that attacks of this nature were taboo, which had suited Miranda. Eric, who obviously had mixed-race parents, and Greg, who admittedly did, were touchiest. Before Miranda joined their ranks, Greg had confided to the others that his mom had made him learn English and had sent him to California, hoping her great-uncle would help Greg find the sailor who'd left her pregnant and alone in Seoul. But the relative, an elderly man, had passed away. And Greg soon ran out of cash. Alone, he'd had no luck locating the sailor in a grainy snapshot. His only clue other than the photo was the name Gregory Jones, which might or might not have been valid. The navy had a plethora of Gregory and G. Joneses, none of whom claimed to have fathered a child out of wedlock. But thanks to his early experience in Seoul, Greg was adept at street living. Even so, he was defensive as hell about almost everything.

Shawn, by contrast, was apparently the product of a wealthy but abusive dad and an actress who'd flown the coop. Miranda would have thought he'd be more sympathetic toward poor Greg. Instead, the boys bickered constantly, and she was getting fed up.

"Guys," she cautioned, "let's try and be on our best behavior when we meet the ranch owner. I, for one, am too beat to want him kicking us out of his program."

"What do you mean, program?" Eric narrowed perpetually angry dark eyes. "The flyer didn't say we had to join any program to stay here."

Jenny curled a hand around Eric's suddenly rigid forearm. "I'm cold, Eric. And Shawn's starved. Can we quit arguing long enough to check out this guy's gig? Back in L.A., we agreed Benny Garcia was right when he said we'd be happier bunking here than hustling cots at fleabag shelters."

"Who agreed?" Eric, his thin face framed by shoulder-length dreadlocks that tended to make people view him as a hoodlum, grimaced. "I let you talk me into it."

Miranda hadn't witnessed more than a close friendship between Eric and Jenny—certainly not a romance. He was prone to fly off the handle, and the younger girl provided a calming influence for the boy. But she'd discovered that all small homeless pods had a leader, and Eric, despite his moods, was theirs. So she was doubly relieved when, by tacit agreement, they moved in the direction of the sprawling ranch.

The barn, which they passed first, looked sturdy, even though it needed paint. Two long outbuildings flanking the main house were equally weathered but appeared to have new roofs. One, if not both, could house teens and/or serve as sleeping quarters for ranch workers. Miranda doubted Jenny and the boys had taken notice of the amenities, and she wouldn't bring it to their attention. Being older, and possessing a great deal more travel savvy that she needed to conceal, she took care during this trek not to preach—a trait that ranked low with street kids. Nor did she want them speculating that she wasn't really one of them.

When they'd passed through the town of Chico, Miranda had managed a good look at a Sunday newspaper someone had left at a rest area. The story of her disappearance, while no longer front-page news, still rated a two-inch column in the entertainment section. She needed a place to lie low until there was no mention of her at all.

It shook her to see Wes Carlisle pretend to mourn her publicly, when she knew how fraudulent it was. The article mentioned a deal Wes had worked to reissue all volumes of Misty's back albums—to keep her memory alive, he claimed. Ha! Nothing but pure greed and ambition lay behind Wes's rerelease of her hits. He would exploit her absence for all it was worth. And once her name ceased being profitable, he'd cut his losses and find some other naive singer to "manage." Then she could go back and, with a clearer head, finally confront him.

The group stopped within a hundred yards of the house, where they could see a man stalking back and forth in front of a wide, inviting porch.

Miranda fell instantly in love with the porch. Her dad's house had boasted one roomy enough for a swing, and the band had often gathered to make music there. Instant warmth toward this ranch began to replace her weariness.

That wasn't the case for Eric. He stopped to squint at a rusty wrought-iron arch. "Rascal Ranch? How hokey can he get? Does the dude expect us to be wannabe bronco busters, or what?"

"Maybe this is the wrong ranch." Jenny pointed at the front porch. "Look at all those little kids."

Miranda followed Jenny's finger. Indeed, a young boy and a smaller girl hovered around a third child in a wheelchair. The hope that had begun to mount in Miranda suddenly plummeted.

"This obviously isn't the teen retreat we're looking for," she murmured. "But…the architecture's so similar, we must be near the place. Eric, take our flyer and go ask that man if he knows this ranch. It may take a minute, since he's on his cell phone."

"I'm surprised there's cell reception out here in Nowhereville," Eric responded. "Damn, look! Scraps is attacking the guy's pant legs. Wow, is he ever pissed off."

"Let Randi go," Shawn said. "Scraps is her mutt."

"Shawn's right." Eric nudged Randi forward. "I'll stay and do what I can to plug Jenny's shoes. Especially since we've probably gotta hike who knows how many more friggin' miles. Just everybody remember—I voted to stay in L.A."

The others groaned and plopped down on the ground, heedless of the damp. Miranda reluctantly took the flyer and set out, girding herself to be yelled at by the rancher.

The first thing that struck her as she drew near was that the man shouting at someone on the phone was younger than she'd judged him at first glance. Mid-thirties at most. But regardless of age, he was furious. The cords in his neck bulged as he stomped around, gesturing wildly. A lock of sun-streaked light-brown hair fell stubbornly across his forehead, in spite of the fact that he kept shoving it back. Mad or not, he was fine to look at, Miranda thought, slowing her approach. And if that was his Excursion with a vanity plate reading BAD SUV, it showed he had a sense of humor.

"Hold on a minute, Gunderson." The man whirled and glared at Miranda. "If this barking beast belongs to you, shut him up. I'm trying to have a serious discussion, and I can't hear a damned thing."

Oops. So his disposition was nowhere nearly as fine as his looks. And forget what she'd said about his sense of humor. Miranda scooped up Scraps, who obviously felt that snapping at the man's shiny boot heels was great sport.

The minute the dog stopped his incessant barking, Linc Parker felt the pounding in his head slowly begin to subside. He flashed a thank-you with his eyes toward the woman responsible for the pest's capture. Linc intended to get immediately back to dickering with Gunderson, but words failed him momentarily as—both fascinated and horrified—he watched the newcomer let that damn dog lick her nose and lips. Yuck! Did she know her pet had just been sniffing a pile of cow pucky?

"What? Yes, I'm still here, Ted." But Linc, affected by the sultry laugh of the dog's owner, had to tighten his grip on the phone. Eventually he shook himself back to the present. "Like I said, the situation you foisted on me is totally unacceptable. *Why?* You have the nerve to ask?" Linc flung an arm toward the three youngsters huddled in a knot on his porch. "I've explained twice. I don't know squat about little kids. Plus…well, you leaving them here isn't right."

He swallowed what he might have added, noticing that the gray eyes of the woman darted sympathetically to the cringing children. He also noticed that she clutched one of his flyers.

Feeling guilty, Linc let his voice trail off and his arm drop. "Look, I've got other problems on top of this one. I agree, John Montoya missed a lot. Apparently he also passed out flyers in L.A. inviting street kids to my facility before I planned on opening, so why am I surprised he loused up with you?"

Linc paced several steps to the open door of his Ford Excursion and rummaged inside until he came up with a notebook and pen. Anchoring the phone between his chin and shoulder, he said, "If you insist there's nothing you can do today, give me the name and number of that social worker again." Listening intently, Linc scribbled on his pad. "I *know* you said the agency is in disarray. I understand she's not available until after the Thanksgiving holiday. But surely *someone* in her office can deal with this problem. What? Yeah, I guessed it was a small agency. I also guaran-damn-tee I'll start there and climb up the chain of command until I reach someone in Sacramento if I have to. For one thing, I intend to report those houseparents of yours. The Tuckers should be barred from ever working with kids again. George claimed the way to keep them in line was to slap them around. Come to think of it, where's *your* organization's responsibility?"

"Gunderson? Ted?" Linc made a disgusted sound and threw his cell into the front seat of his vehicle as he ripped the sheet off the pad and stuffed it in his pocket. The Oasis rep had flat-out hung up on him.

Lincoln didn't like that the woman holding the dog was scowling at him as if he'd just crawled out from under a rock. Hell! Judging by the storm gathering in her eyes, she could well be another of his mounting problems. All he needed to cork his day was a spitfire street kid with a temper—if that was actually what she was. Oddly, she struck him as older.

He smoothed a hand down over a chin grown prickly with late-in-the-day stubble. ''I'm sorry, uh…Miss, er Ms.? I'm afraid you've caught me at a disadvantage. I'm Lincoln Parker, new owner of this facility. I, uh, see you're in possession of a flyer I'm assuming you picked up down south?''

Miranda nodded as she pushed Scraps's nose out of her face. ''L.A. My friends and I have been on the road awhile. We're tired and hungry.'' She extended the creased flyer. ''So, are you open or not? I wasn't purposely eavesdropping, but I couldn't help overhearing part of your conversation.''

''Not!'' Linc snapped. ''Open,'' he added with less force as he saw the defeated slump of her slim shoulders. Shaking his head, he dropped his gaze to the toes of her battered army boots. ''I just got here myself. Not only did I expect to have time to fix things up before any teens arrived, but the previous owner threw me a curve by leaving behind three former tenants.''

Lincoln pinched the bridge of his nose between thumb and forefinger. He didn't know why he was confiding so much in this stranger who clearly expected a haven for herself and the friends she'd left at the side of the road.

''Look, what's your name?''

''Randi,'' she supplied. ''And this is Scraps.'' She jerked a thumb toward the road. ''Out there are Jenny, Shawn, Greg and Eric.''

''Jenny? Eric?'' Linc spun around and strained to see through the waning light. Even now, hearing the names of Felicity's so-called friends, who'd dumped her at the hospital and then taken off, made his stomach churn.

''Do you know them?''

"Uh...those were the names of two of my kid sister's friends. Police said they..." Linc broke off suddenly. "They're common enough names. Merely coincidence, I'm sure. Look, I can offer a place to crash for tonight. I...think," he added, frowning at the two units flanking the house. "To be truthful, I've got no idea how many beds are in those bunkhouses. Nor their condition. As you might have gathered from my phone conversation, I didn't get a positive impression of the houseparents the Oasis Foundation had in charge here."

"I don't understand any of what you're saying," Miranda said. "But the gang and I can make do. Sleeping under a roof will be a bonus. But we'd sure like a hot meal. We last ate yesterday when some hikers gave us a leftover pack of hot dogs and a few buns." Again she waved a hand toward the four hunkered some yards away.

"Food? Damn! Wait—Mrs. Tucker mentioned meat in a freezer."

"That sounds encouraging. If there's a microwave, we can thaw it out. So, if you don't mind my asking, why are you conducting business out here in the wind and cold? Why aren't you inside fixing supper for those poor kids?"

"Well, I..." Linc stopped, panic swamping him. "For one, I can't cook. I've lived and worked in the city all my life. I either order in or eat out."

Miranda waved the flyer in his face. "Did you think street kids don't eat?"

"For your information, I intended to hire a cook and a housekeeper before any kids showed up." Linc glared. "Not that I owe you any explanation. And let me guess, your smart mouth has landed you in trouble before."

Miranda ground her teeth to keep from lashing back. Here she was again, responding like a twenty-six-year-old, instead of the way someone like Jenny would. "Sorry," she mumbled, biting her lip.

"Forget it." Linc shook back a lock of dark hair and offered a tentative smile as he glanced at his watch. "Well, it's too late to rectify the cook-housekeeper issue today. Whistle up your friends. For now, we'll all have to make the best of a situation none of us invited."

The smile altered his stern features, and Miranda responded accordingly. "Hey, great! Jenny's worn a hole in her shoe, and the guys stayed behind to try and fix it, in case we had more walking to do."

"Do any of you have injuries?"

"No, we're just tired. I'll go fetch them. Then maybe Jenny and I can check what's in your freezer. I'll bet we can toss together a meal of some sort."

"Really?" Linc felt more grateful for that one simple statement than she could know. His life lately had been hectic. He'd been involved in selling his house and storing the furnishings, as well as studying ranching techniques. He probably should've asked John to make a cursory inventory of what was needed here. Under no circumstances, however, would it have occurred to him to take a crash course in cooking. "Damn John—and Gunderson," he muttered, swinging his fierce gaze back to the three young children he had yet to deal with.

"Don't swear at them," Miranda said testily, again forgetting herself. "Can't you see they're scared?" She didn't care if this jerk took his anger out on her, as long as he left those poor kids alone.

"I'm not swearing at them. My anger's directed at the guy who got me into this mess, and at the Oasis rep who sold me a pig in a poke. What makes you even imagine I'd swear at children?"

"Oh, I don't know, probably the way you're glowering.'' Miranda stopped and slapped a hand over her mouth. ''Excuse me. I'll just go get my friends.'' She hugged Scraps to her chest and sidled around Linc. Once past him, she broke into a run.

Staring after the young woman, he noticed her shapely backside and quickly controlled a punch to his gut that he shouldn't be feeling. He turned his attention to the problems on the porch.

John Montoya thought he was crazy to leave his old job. But in the past few years, Linc found himself growing more short-tempered and less tolerant of people. No doubt the dog's owner had glimpsed and had wrongly assumed he'd swear at little kids. Well, the red-haired boy wasn't so little. He must be the one George Tucker had said was the biter.

Linc approached the trio slowly. ''Hi. My name is Lincoln Parker. Call me Linc.'' He mustered a smile. ''Sorry about the phone call and the time I spent talking to the lady with the dog,'' he added for good measure, as he'd seen the kids' interest in the dog. ''Let's go inside and you can give me your names. Hey, hey, relax. I don't know when I'll be able to reach your social worker—this…Mrs. Bishop.'' Lincoln unfolded the paper and read the woman's name. ''What I'm saying—'' he spoke through a thinning smile ''—is that we may as well be on a first-name basis because it looks as if we're stuck with each other for a while.''

''Screw you,'' sneered the boy. Linc stiffened when the kid barreled off the porch straight at him. He didn't relish getting bitten; Tucker hadn't warned about kicking, though. The little monster landed a bone-breaking blow to Linc's left shin. ''Damn, damn, damn!'' He swore and hopped around holding his ankle as the kid disappeared in the thickening dusk.

"Wolfie!" The girl not confined to the wheelchair cried out and stumbled on one of the wheelchair foot plates. She fell flat at Linc's feet, sobbing too hard to get up right away and follow the boy.

"Easy, easy." Linc reached for her gingerly.

"Wolfie is Hana's brother," said the round-eyed girl in the chair. "His real name's Wolfgang, but he hates it, so everybody calls him Wolfie."

Bending, Linc gently lifted the hysterical child. He was amazed by how fragile her bones felt under his hands and was reminded of a frightened bird he'd rescued from a cat once when he couldn't have been much older than Wolfie. "It's okay," he murmured softly. "You girls go in out of this wind. I'll find your brother, I promise," he told the child who shook violently and watched him in abject fear.

Linc set her down and at once limped off. He could no longer see the boy, but he'd heard a door slam in the distance, in the direction of an outbuilding. Linc supposed he'd find Wolfgang in the bunkhouse. At least, he assumed the low structure was one of the two bunkhouses John said came with the ranch.

Afraid the little hellion might have time to rig some kind of trap at the door, Linc stood well to one side of what appeared to be the only way in. Cautiously, he shoved the door open with a toe. The interior, dark as a cave, smelled of urine and decay. Wrinkling his nose, Linc called, "Wolfie, either turn on a light or come outside so we can talk."

The silence stretched, but Linc felt the boy's presence.

"God, this place stinks like a sewer. Please tell me this isn't where you kids sleep." He reached inside and felt the wall for a light switch. Finding one, he flipped it on. A single bulb in the center of the room sprang to life, barely illuminating the area directly beneath the fixture. Not so much as a glimmer reached into any of the room's four corners, but the bulb gave off enough power for Linc to see two sets of bunk beds. A cracked mirror hung over a single dresser with a broken leg. The mirror reflected the filament inside the bare bulb. As his eyes adjusted, Linc made out the boy crouched against the wall between the two sets of beds.

His heart lodged in his chest. "Look, son," he said, attempting to calm his voice in spite of the fact that it remained rough with emotion. "I can only guess what you've put up with in the past. I promise you here and now, for however long you're in my care, you won't be hit—and your sleeping conditions will darned well improve."

Freckles stood out on the boy's pale cheeks. Wide blue eyes under a shock of sandy red hair warily assessed the man who barred the room's only door.

"Do you understand what I'm saying?" Linc tried again to reassure the boy. "I only took over ownership of the ranch today. I can't make instant changes. But I wouldn't let a dog sleep in this rat hole. I hope the house is in better shape. If so, we'll all bunk there tonight." He shivered and stopped speaking to rub his arms. "What's the heat in this building set at?"

"Ain't no heat," the boy growled. "But even if I gotta take the girls and run away in the dark, ain't none of us sleeping with you, creep. So get that in your head."

"God! That's not what I meant by all of us sleeping in the house." Shaken, Linc withdrew fractionally. "Did you see the older kids by the road? I simply meant it's unacceptable to think anyone would have to sleep here with no heat. I trust the main house has a furnace. It's probably big enough for everyone to stake out a sleeping spot for one night. Tomorrow, we'll clean this place and locate a hardware store where I can buy baseboard heaters. To say nothing of mattresses that don't sag or smell." Linc eyed the definite bow in the beds.

"Why would you go to all that trouble before you get hold of Mrs. Jacobs?"

"Who?" Linc's ears perked up at a new name tossed in the mix.

"Our social worker. I heard you talkin' on the phone about her."

"Jacobs isn't the name I was given. But I gather Mrs. Bishop is new at the agency. I have no idea when we'll be able to connect. So while you're in my care, I want you kids sleeping on clean sheets and mattresses."

"Hana wets. She don't do it on purpose. The house mom said she wasn't washin' sheets for no brat big 'nuff to get up and go to the outhouse. I used to have a flashlight, but it broke. Hana's scared to walk the trail by herself. I told her to wake me up, but she says I sleep too hard."

"You mean…this bunkhouse has no bathroom, either?"

The boy's stringy red hair slapped his ears as he shook his head.

"Where do you kids shower? Or bathe?" Linc amended his statement when the word *shower* drew a blank look from the boy.

"Fridays, Lydia used to toss me and Hana in the creek with a bar of soap. Before she took over from Judy Rankin, we got to wash in a dishpan Miz Judy set on the back porch. After the Tuckers came, they only let Cassie use the pan. On account of her not being able to get in the water 'cause of her twisted hip."

A rough expulsion of breath left Lincoln's lungs. "The news gets worse by the second. I can't listen to any more. Except… Wolfie, how often did Mrs. Jacobs come to inspect the place? What agency worker would approve of kids living in such squalor?''

"She ain't never come that I know. Not since she brung me and Hana here to live. Cassie and some others were already here. One house mister griped to Oasis, and somebody came at night and took the other kids away. That was before Rob Rankin. He said Oasis put them in another group home.'' Climbing to his feet, the boy hiked a thin shoulder. "They coulda kilt 'em. That's what Hana thinks.''

"I doubt that.'' Although… Linc swept the room with a scowl. "How any adult could visit this mess and close his or her eyes to conditions here is beyond me. Look, I'm sure you have few reasons to trust anyone, but I wish you'd give me a chance. At least come back to the house and let your sister see that you haven't run off without her. She was crying her eyes out when I left to find you.''

"Hana bawls a lot, but she's only four. Don't hold it against her, okay?''

"No, I wouldn't hold crying against a child. How old are you, Wolfie?''

"Ten. I had my birthday last month. Lydia Tucker said I was just lying so she'd bake a cake. She never did, so Hana and Cassie think I'm still nine.''

Linc couldn't even bring himself to comment on the Tuckers' callous treatment of the children they were supposed to care for. He met the guarded eyes of the shivering boy. "Will you walk with me to the house?''

"O…kay,'' Wolfie agreed, a catch in his voice. "But if anybody lays a hand on me or Hana, they'll wish they hadn't. I have sharp teeth and I can bite hard.''

"So George Tucker told me.'' Linc waited to smile until he turned his back on the ten-year-old. "Biting's not the way men solve things, Wolfie. Not even if they're bad things. So before you go biting any of the folks up at the house, I'd like you to promise you'll talk to me first. Trust me to handle the problem. Will you do that?''

"I ain't makin' no promises till I see."

"I guess that's fair enough. I've never met the older kids. But I suspect life's been no picnic for them, either. I'll start by giving them my house rules."

"Rules?"

"Dos and don'ts. They're pretty simple."

"Oh." The boy tucked his chin against his thin chest and tried to match Linc's longer stride while leaving plenty of space between them.

Entering the ranch house provided instant respite from the stinging wind. The room was well lit and warm. The little dog dashed up, barking its head off. But otherwise, if Linc expected to walk into a beehive of activity, he was doomed to disappointment. Each teen appeared to have staked out his or her wedge of real estate. The three boys sat on the floor, propped against their possessions, which included backpacks and guitar cases. Randi and the other girl sat on a raised hearth in front of an empty fireplace. Hana and Cassie did their best to melt into a dark corner as far away as possible from the teens. To the last kid, all tensed visibly when Linc walked in with Wolfie.

Linc homed in on Randi. "Was Mrs. Tucker wrong about there being meat in the freezer?"

"I, uh, we didn't check. Eric said we shouldn't rummage in the kitchen without you. That way you can't claim something ought to be there that isn't." At Linc's vacant expression, she added a qualifier. "You know, in case you try to tell the cops we stole from you."

"Oh, for Pete's sake!" Lincoln loosely bracketed his hips with his hands. He studied the room's occupants. One older boy wore a long, ratty velvet coat over holey jeans.

The baggy pants of the other two dragged on the ground. One wore leather wrist bands. All had numerous earrings in both ears, and the girl with the lighter brown hair— Jenny—had her lip, eyebrow and, Lord knew what else, pierced. Distrustful expressions, identical to Wolfie's, were mirrored five times over.

He slowly released a pent-up breath. "It's safe to say the ranch doesn't meet any of our expectations. I counted on having time to spruce it up and lay in supplies. And you thought you'd walk into an operating shelter." Linc's gaze shifted to Wolfie, his sister, and Cassie in her pint-sized wheelchair. "On top of that, I never planned on hosting…small children. But they're here and will be until I reach the new director of Social Services."

"None of us formed any preconceived notions," Miranda muttered. "Why don't we start over? Introduce ourselves, and then food can be our next priority."

"Right." Linc rubbed the back of his neck, beginning to feel overwhelmed by everything facing him. It embarrassed him that the girl, Randi, was the first to voice a mature approach. He was, after all, the adult in charge. Although it struck him that, as John Montoya had said, he'd jumped into this venture without a shred of actual experience.

"I'm Lincoln Parker," he said. "Linc, if you like. Until a few weeks ago I lived and worked in Hollywood. My aim in starting this retreat is to provide a safe, substance-free home for up to a dozen teens who've lived hand-to-mouth on city streets."

"Parker?" Jenny gasped. "You're not Felicity's brother, are you? I mean, you couldn't be *that* Lincoln Parker." She shot Eric a funny look and they both uttered uneasy choking sounds.

"As a matter of fact, I am that Parker." Linc's eyes

clouded. He was getting a bad feeling about these kids again. "No. It's too unbelievable to think you'd be... Not even the cops were able to find the kids who dumped my sister at an inner-city L.A. emergency room and then ran off."

"We didn't dump her," Jenny sputtered. "Two cops at the ER told us to get lost."

Eric scrambled to his feet. "Yeah, I went back the next day and nobody would tell me a thing. We heard later she'd OD'd. Felicity was our friend, you know."

"I spent weeks combing backstreets, asking information of anyone who might have seen where you were."

"Gosh, didn't Felicity ever talk about us? When you were out of town, she let us crash at your place," Jenny said edgily, beginning to chew her nails, which was something Miranda noticed the girl did in tense situations.

"You brought drugs into my home?"

"No!" Jenny seemed horrified.

"Don't lie. I have an autopsy report that shows alcohol, marijuana and embalming fluid in my sister's blood, for God's sake. Oh, what's the use of talking to you? The police were adamant that even if I found you, you wouldn't rat out a dealer." Linc's dark eyes glittered as his anger centered on Jenny. "I won't tolerate drugs here. Maybe you'd better move on." His voice shook with anger.

Eric stepped protectively in front of Jenny. "You've got no right to yell at us, man. Me and Jenny tried to help Felicity."

Jenny's white face bobbed out in the open as she grabbed Eric's arm. "It was wet, Eric. That's what made Felicity act so crazy."

Linc's scowl returned to the girl. "What are you yammering about? The night you took Felicity to emergency, the city hadn't seen rain in months.''

''Not rain, stupid,'' Eric spat. ''Wet's a street name for weed—marijuana—laced with PCP, soaked in embalming fluid and dried. Felicity knew—we all know that's evil shi—er, stuff,'' he finished lamely, watering down his language when Miranda jabbed him in the ribs and rolled her eyes at the children still huddled in a corner. Wanting to defuse the situation, she hauled Jenny toward the kitchen.

''Today has turned out to be a shocker for everyone, Mr. Parker,'' she said. ''My dad used to say trouble's better met and dealt with on a full stomach. Why don't Jenny and I see what we can find to make for supper? Y'all can talk afterward.''

Linc leveled a frown at the girl with the too-dark hair, pale skin and smoke-gray eyes. ''If you have a dad worthy of quoting, why are you hanging out with this riffraff?''

Miranda's chin shot up. ''My dad died. And we're not riffraff. If that's your attitude, and if you want kids with pedigrees, why advertise this place as a haven for homeless teens?''

Her barb struck Linc in an unprotected spot and triggered a load of guilt. Why had Felicity, who had access to a nice home and best of everything money could buy, chosen friends among druggies and derelicts? He obviously wouldn't find out by attacking the very kids he hoped one day to wrest answers from.

Still gruff, he waved the two girls away. Wheeling abruptly in the direction of his youngest guests, Wolfgang in particular, Linc rattled off their names by way of introduction. ''Wolfie, you go help Randi and Jenny. You know better than I do where cooking supplies are kept. Eric and company can help me inventory the rest of the house. Between now and suppertime, we'll sort out equitable sleeping spots for the night.''

Wolfie, mulled over Linc's words. ''What's equit…that word you said. What's it mean?''

''It means fair. Elbow room for everyone, like we discussed earlier. I don't want anyone encroaching on his or her neighbor's sleeping space.''

''I guess that's okay,'' the boy muttered. ''You sure use big words, mister. Me, Cassie and Hana ain't no walking dictionaries, you know?''

The kid sounded so serious, Linc laughed. ''Okay, I'll watch the four-bit words.''

Even the older teens broke out in approving grins. For the moment, the strain that had permeated the room evaporated.

Greatly relieved, Miranda picked up Scraps and nudged Jenny into the kitchen.

''Remember to wash your hands before you touch any food,'' Parker yelled after them. He didn't really expect an answer and wasn't surprised when none came. But he realized that John Montoya had been more right than wrong. He might be in over his head here.

CHAPTER THREE

JUST BEFORE RANDI found the light switch and spilled light into the dark kitchen, Jenny grabbed her. "I'm no cook, are you? What if Lincoln Parker hates what we fix?"

Miranda didn't answer. "Eew...ew!" Pinching her nose closed, she surveyed a mountain of dirty pots, pans and dishes stacked haphazardly on every surface of an equally dirty stove, sink and counter. "Not only were those house-parents despicable," she said in a nasal voice, "they were pigs."

"Yeah, this is disgusting." Jenny covered her nose and mouth with one hand.

"Jenny, go find Mr. Parker. Tell him we can't do any-thing about starting supper until we've made a dent in cleaning up this mess. Warn him that some of these pans look so corroded they'll have to be trashed. Beginning with this one." She gingerly picked up a saucepan with moldy macaroni and cheese burned to the bottom and sides.

Jenny wasted no time hightailing it out of the smelly room.

Not caring how chilly it had grown outside, Miranda flung open what windows she could budge. She sucked in great gasps of fresh air and wondered how anyone could live this way.

She returned to the sink and began emptying it of un-washed dishes when she heard heavy footsteps coming closer, followed by a partially muffled, "Good Lord!"

Miranda couldn't help laughing. "My sentiments exactly."

"This kitchen's a pigsty. No wonder your dog's out by the door hiding his head. I thought the bedrooms were bad. They're the Ritz compared to this." Linc made a slow circuit of the room. "The boys are bagging rubble from the four bedrooms. God only knows what condition the sleeping bags are in. I unearthed them from a back closet." Linc felt his burgeoning headache begin to pound in earnest.

"At least we have hot water," Miranda said brightly. Steam rose from the sink she'd plugged, but her attempt to find dish soap in the cabinet below met with no luck. After searching several more places, she puffed out a breath. "I can't find any soap. I guess they ran out. Maybe that's why they stopped washing dishes."

"A kitchen in a home for kids and no dishwasher? That's idiotic. Shoot, heck and damn. The minute I set eyes on this unholy mess, I figured it'd be midnight or later before we could reach a point where cooking was possible. But without soap and disinfectant, I doubt it'll happen at all."

"So, we'll, uh, tighten our belts again tonight." Miranda knew her friends had hoped to have a decent meal. But it wouldn't be the first night they'd gone to bed hungry. "At least we'll be sleeping out of the cold. That's something."

Known in the world of finance for making quick decisions, Linc made one now. "Look, Randi—that is your name, right?" At her nod, he continued. "I don't see that we have a choice but to load everyone in my Excursion and go in search of a restaurant. And if there's a motel with vacancies anywhere in town, two rooms should do us, I think. Tomorrow, before we head back, I'll buy supplies. I'd appreciate it if you'd make a list of what's needed for this kitchen to be operational.''

''A shovel?'' Her smile brought out a dimple in one cheek.

Once again Linc felt a tug that was almost physical. Frowning, he said, ''Put a case of jumbo trash bags and a new set of cookware on the list.'' He took a giant backward step toward the door. ''While you work on that, I'll round up the others. I'll see if the little squirts have nightclothes and clean clothes for morning. If I ever saw kids in need of a good scrubbing, it's them.''

As he turned to go out, Linc almost fell over the gumchewing girl who'd purportedly been friends with his sister. Given the circumstances, it was all he could do to mutter a civil, ''Excuse me.''

Jenny, who'd overheard part of his and Randi's discussion, blocked Linc's exit. ''You really intend for us to eat at a restaurant and then go to a motel?''

''I see no other choice. Help put those pans in to soak, please. By tomorrow, steel wool might get some of them clean. Right after heat for the bunkhouses, I'm adding an industrial-size dishwasher to my list.''

Linc made a second attempt to leave the kitchen, but something in the way Randi studied him through narrowed eyes gave him pause. ''If you've got a problem with my solution, spit it out. From what I saw of the towns I went through on the way here, they're liable to be the type that roll up their sidewalks at nine o'clock.'' To keep from reaching out and giving her arm a reassuring squeeze, he glanced at his watch.

''I think Jenny means money's an issue,'' Randi blurted. ''We may be able to pool our pennies and buy burgers. But…well, we can't begin to cover the cost of a motel.''

Miranda still had her diamond earrings, but since throwing in her lot with Jenny and the boys, she'd found no opportunity to visit a pawnshop. And she dared not risk the kinds of questions that would crop up if any of her new friends got a glimpse of the rocks she had sewn in the lining of her jacket.

"You think I'd expect you kids to pay?" Linc exploded. "Like any of this is *your* fault." He swept an arm to encompass the mess. "It's a damned good thing I'm not within reach of my buddy who negotiated for me on this place. All I can think is that John Montoya never set foot inside the house, or else he's blind and missing his sense of smell."

Linc wrung a low laugh from Randi. A husky sound that slid up his spine the way her voice did. Her voice made him think of a piano bar and mellow scotch.

Suddenly Linc found himself wondering why, if she hung out with Felicity's starstruck groupies, some producer hadn't seen her potential? True, her skin tone and unusual eye coloring were at odds with hacked-off, too-black hair. But a hairdresser and color could remedy that. It flitted through Linc's mind that black wasn't Randi's natural shade. Probably a phase she was in. A few years back Felicity had dyed her rich brown curls a dull black, too. She'd also worn black lipstick and nail polish. She described the style as "goth" and refused to speak to him for weeks when he'd objected to her appearance.

Though he couldn't say why, Linc was glad that Randi saw fit to leave her lips and nails bare. Of course, she and Jenny wore too many sets of earrings. And like his sister, Jenny sported tattoos. If Randi had any, they weren't visible.

He didn't even want to recall the argument he'd had with Felicity the evening he'd come home from a road trip and discovered her first tattoo. Had his failure to understand her need to look bizarre been the beginning of their estrangement? He erased that thought from his mind and returned to his evaluation of Randi. Why had she landed on his doorstep, instead of on her way to being a new soap or big-screen movie star?

Because she was short? About five-three. Otherwise she had that look producers liked. And she walked as if she owned the world. Linc would bet his bottom dollar that before Randi whatever-the-hell-her-last-name-was ended up living on the street, she'd known a better life, too.

"Are you changing your mind about going to town, Mr. Parker?"

Jerked back from his meandering thoughts, Linc all but snapped at Jenny. "No, I haven't changed my mind. And, Randi, start writing that damned list, okay? Here, take my pen," he said roughly, extending one he yanked from his shirt pocket. "Tear a piece of paper off one of the hundreds of grocery sacks piled around here. Jeez, add all this junk to what we found in the bedrooms and it's a miracle the place didn't burn down. Come to think of it, I want a lot of answers from Oasis."

Miranda, who had no idea what she'd said or done to bring a return of Parker's bad humor, immediately set about starting a list.

And this time Linc lost no time in stomping out.

He should've guessed Wolfie would be next to object to his proposal.

"Hana and me ain't goin' nowhere," the boy declared flatly, not caring that the older kids were already moving toward the door.

"Mind telling me why?" Linc inquired mildly.

"'Cause you'll make all nice, and then take off and leave us there. You think I'm stupid, mister?"

"Good grief. You have a wild imagination. I already

explained that you'll have a home here until I can get in touch with the area's new social worker. Not only that, I intend to grill her about a system that leaves children living in squalor.''

"Yeah, I know that's what you said. But you don't want us. We're—'' the boy screwed up his face and hesitated "—we're a comp…comp—something I heard the fat dude say.''

"Watch who you're calling fat.'' Shawn's face erupted in fury as everyone swung toward him. "So shoot me for thinking the kid had left the room before I said those little farts were a complication for you, Parker. They are. I didn't say anything that's not true.'' He thrust his jaw out pugnaciously.

"Are not…whatever you said!'' Wolfie yelled, descending on Shawn with fists flying and teeth bared.

"Are, too,'' Shawn shot back, holding the wiry boy off with a stiff arm.

"All right! Enough!'' Flinging out his own hand, Linc hooked Wolfie around the waist and easily dangled the fist-swinging boy three feet off the ground. "Hold on there, pardner. Remember what I told you earlier about biting not being how men solve things?''

For a few seconds, Wolfie actually looked chastened. "You didn't say nothin' about kickin' or hittin'.''

"I didn't then, but I am now. And, Shawn, I don't want any pissing contests going on, understand?'' Linc leveled a stern glare at the older boy as he turned Wolfie loose. "Everyone, go climb into my SUV. You'll have to keep quiet during the drive so that on the way to town, I can tell you my house rules.''

Shawn led the charge to the door. He stopped and said to Linc, "The kid calls me a fat dude again and I'll kick his ass.''

Linc took a moment to study the unkempt overweight teen with a face full of zits. Cutting through the bluster, it wasn't hard to see the unhappy boy underneath. "Look, Shawn. I know the kid's abrasive, and you're tired. We all have our hot buttons. I'm not planning to implement a lot of rules. But number one is respect. Respect for the other guy's person and his space. The rules apply equally across the board. Anyone who can't live with them can hit the road."

Shawn nodded shortly and stalked out.

Linc eyed the next two boys getting ready to pass him. Eric and Greg. They hunched over their packs. Eric clutched a guitar case, while Greg carried a narrower case that obviously held a keyboard.

"No need to lug that stuff along. We'll only be gone one night. And I'm locking the house."

Greg leaned his keyboard up against the couch. Eric elbowed him sharply. "Me and the guys don't go nowhere without the tools of our trade, man."

"Tools of your trade?" Linc all but sneered. "Like you're such frigging successes."

Miranda sensed a fight in the making. And although it'd suit her if music was downplayed here at the retreat, she'd had her fill of bickering. In an effort to distract the participants, she tucked Scraps inside her partially buttoned jacket and stepped between the combatants. "Do you think they'll mind if I have a dog in the motel?"

Linc's eyes shifted away from the hostile kid with the awful dreadlocks. He wasn't at all prepared to see that scruffy dog nestled against his young charge's generous breasts. For a moment, his tongue tangled with his teeth. What came out sounded like a stutter.

Randi waited, not sure what Parker was trying to say.

"Hell, take the dog! Take everything," he finally man-

aged to spit out. Afraid he was in deep trouble when it
came to playing houseparent to this particular group, Linc
put some space between himself and Randi. He waved a
hand toward the open door, through which the heavyset
boy had already disappeared.

Linc disliked starting his new endeavor by losing control. Especially since turning a blind eye and deaf ear to
Felicity's behavior had been his big mistake. One he didn't
intend to repeat. But maybe after a meal and a good night's
sleep, he'd be on more certain footing.

Pocketing his house key, he made directly for the
driver's door of the Excursion. He veered off course when
it appeared no one was helping Cassie. Linc lifted her out
of her wheelchair and set her gently down in the middle
row of seats, buckling her in. He folded her pathetically
small chair, then went around and tucked it in the space
behind the last row of seats. Wondering what had caused
her condition, he slammed the door and returned to watch
as the others climbed inside.

Earlier, when he'd convinced Wolfie to leave the bunkhouse, Linc had considered that his first small victory. But
now, as Eric knocked into him with his guitar case, determined to sit in the very back of the big SUV, Linc tasted
the bile of defeat. He foresaw his tussle with Eric as the
first of many. After learning these kids were bent on becoming rock stars, the way his sister had, he could no
longer stand the thought of listening to their music. John
Montoya had intimated Linc was deluding himself to think
he had a prayer of guiding kids like these away from the
fickle field of music or acting into other less risky pursuits.
Once again, Linc was afraid he'd been right.

After they were all seated in the SUV, Greg demanded
a rundown of Linc's rules. Eric dissented loudly at Linc's

order that they needed to buckle their seat belts or the Excursion wasn't going anywhere.

"Wearing seat belts isn't *my* rule." Linc raised his voice over their grumbling. "It's California state law. And while I'm in charge, we will obey the laws of the land." He segued right into his vision for the group. "Being law-abiding citizens is in sync with my idea of rules to live by. I assume you're all too young to drink alcohol and buy cigarettes. Weed and other drugs are against the law. Those head my list. It goes without saying that I expect everyone to pitch in with the chores. I'm not going to harp at you or mete out punishment. Shirkers will, however, get privileges taken away. That's about the extent of my rules for the moment, especially since we already touched on respecting the personal privacy of your neighbors."

Jenny let silence settle inside the vehicle before she spoke. "What kind of chores, Mr. Parker? I already told Randi I can't cook."

"Asking you girls to cook tonight was because of our unusual circumstances. I plan to hire a cook-housekeeper. In fact, I'll look into it tomorrow."

"What chores, then?" Shawn persisted.

Linc glanced into his rearview mirror. "I've ordered a tractor and all the attachments needed to plow enough acres to grow a vegetable garden, plus olives and walnuts, which I hope will help defray some of the operational costs. I plan to keep a few head of beef, mostly to teach responsibility. And chickens, for eggs. Don't you agree a little honest labor ought to rid us all of our city pallor?" He shot them a smile via the mirror.

"We're only staying here through the winter," Shawn said, breaking off suddenly when someone—Eric, Linc saw—cut the heftier boy off with a solid jab to his solar plexus.

"I'm figuring kids will come and kids will go," Linc said with a shrug, looking forward to the day this particular group would pull up stakes and leave. "I've arranged to have cattle feed delivered for the winter. The guy who sold me the farm implements was very helpful. He said there should be enough nice days before the snow hits to till the soil and plant the olives and walnuts."

"How many acres?" Eric asked as if he'd taken an interest.

"Three hundred including where the buildings sit. I have a guide in my briefcase that shows how many acres need to go in sweet grass, how many in grain, walnuts and olives. The folks I consulted said ten acres of garden ought to feed the dozen or so mouths I'm licensed to take in."

"You're licensed?" Randi threw out casually.

"Certainly. Oasis transferred its permit to my name. The rep said the same state regulations apply to housing teenagers as little children."

"Yeah, well if you're relying on the folks who were in charge... It's a wonder they weren't shut down ages ago."

Linc hadn't noticed Randi's Southern drawl so much before. Just now it was quite pronounced. "What brings you out West, Randi?" Linc cast a glance over his shoulder. "I have...er, had a client from North Carolina who sounds exactly like you. Is that where you're from?"

Miranda cursed silently for drawing attention to herself. Because now the others appeared interested, too. "Don't all Southern accents sound alike?"

"No," Linc said. "I recognize when someone's from Mississippi or Alabama as opposed to Texas or the Carolinas."

"The day we met, Randi said she'd moved around a lot," Jenny put in.

"I like how she sounds when she talks." Cassie spoke

up for the first time. "And I think she's real pretty. Don't you, Hana?"

The smallest child sucked her thumb and battled against falling asleep, tucked tight against her brother's skinny side.

Miranda noted that tough as the kid, Wolfie, tried to act, he frequently combed comforting fingers through his little sister's curls. Washed, Miranda thought Hana's hair would probably be strawberry blond. The girl and her brother were both freckled redheads. She flashed the kids a warm smile.

Hana took her thumb out of her mouth and whispered to Cassie, "Yes, she's pretty. She looks 'xactly like the Barbie doll Mrs. Tucker taked away from Cassie and frowed in the trash."

Then, because the older boys chortled and poked fun at Miranda—calling her Barbie—Hana shrank against Wolfie, as if fearing the noisy teens might attack her.

"Stop," Miranda ordered. "You guys are scaring Hana."

"Yeah, dickheads, tone it down." Jenny batted at the boys nearest her, defending her newest friend.

"Who're you calling a dickhead, Jen?" Eric pouted. "The little kids had better toughen up. If name-calling is all they encounter in three outta five foster homes in this state, they'll be lucky."

Linc couldn't resist commenting. "You're not being fair in your assessment of our foster-care system, Eric," he said.

The teen snorted. "That's because there's nothing fair about the system. Why do you think so many kids opt to go it alone on the streets?"

"I honestly have no idea. Care to enlighten me?"

"Man," Shawn broke in, "it's because most foster homes suck. Those people are in it strictly for the cash."

"It's words like *most* I take exception to," Linc responded. "Instead of rushing to hang out in street packs, maybe kids ought to complain to someone in a position to make their homes better and safer."

"Like, who would that be?" Jenny blazed, leaning forward.

"In the case of foster homes, it'd be the social worker in charge."

The interior of the SUV filled with hoots. "Get real, dude. And don't lecture *us*. You and Shawn's dad are so like…twins," Eric said. "You're both so blind, you think tossing money at a kid or handing him over to somebody with a slew of letters after their name is an automatic cure. Felicity told us how you sent her to shrink after shrink. They're about as far from the truth as this planet is from Mars."

"Our grandmother sent Felicity to counselors, not me."

Jenny sat forward in her seat. "She said you shelled out the bucks for everything, including her music lessons."

"I was the only one in the household who was employed. Not that I owe you any explanations. Felicity should have listened to what the counselors said. If she had, maybe she'd still be alive."

"Or maybe she would be if *you'd* listened to her, man," Eric murmured just loud enough for everyone in the vehicle to hear.

A red haze interfered with Linc's ability to see for a fraction of a second. Then, remembering he was dealing with kids who had a skewed perspective on life, he kept his mouth shut and promised himself he wouldn't be drawn into pointless discussions like this in the future.

"Hey," Greg called after they'd bounced and jounced

in silence for a time, "can you turn on the radio or something?"

Linc pushed the start button on the CD unit and shoved in the disc he'd been listening to on the last phase of his journey to the ranch. Soon the dramatic sounds of an orchestra filled the vehicle's interior.

Eric leaned as far forward as his seat belt would allow and shouted over the music, "What the hell kind of tune is that you're playing, Parker?"

"That, young man, is Wagner." He pronounced it with the German V. "It's the overture to *Tristan und Isolde*."

"Never heard of those dudes," Eric muttered. "Are they on the charts?"

Miranda waited a heartbeat for Linc to explain. When he said nothing, she rattled off a brief description of the opera. "The opera depicts a beautiful but tragic love story set in medieval Ireland. Isolde nurses Knight Tristan back to health, only to discover he killed her fiancé in battle. To make matters worse, Tristan is sworn to deliver Isolde as a bride for his uncle. She mixes a potion to kill him, and he offers her his sword, instead. That's when they discover they really love each other. So they kiss.... A lot happens in the next scenes. The king brands them traitors. A battle takes place where Tristan is badly wounded. Isolde believes if she can get to him, her magical powers will heal him. When they're reunited, Tristan declares that, as a knight, he cannot bear to live as an outcast. He falls dead at her feet. She drinks her potion just as a courier arrives from the king ready to pardon her and Tristan. The last scene of the opera is her collapsing across his body. It's difficult to describe quickly, but if you listen to the entire score, you can feel the scenes unfold. 'Liebestod' is probably my favorite piece."

The other teens gaped at Miranda, as did Linc.

"Wow," Jenny said, continuing to bite her nails. "That sounds so cool, Randi. I wouldn't have believed it, but you *can* feel grief in the music. Except…I thought you told me you didn't know much about music."

Linc found himself straining to hear Randi's reply. Something about her was out of step with her companions. And he doubted that opera was normal fare for street kids.

Miranda couldn't deny the knowledge that had obviously caused the others to regard her suspiciously. She shrugged. "Funny how things can slip your mind. I totally forgot about picking up that community-college class. The prof who taught basic music appreciation was an opera buff. He took us to see Puccini's *La Boheme* and Verdi's *Rigoletto* and *Aida*. Oh, and Bizet's *Carmen*."

"You went to college, studied highbrow music and it slipped your mind?" Shawn roused himself from his slouched position in the far back seat.

"Intro to Music sounded like an easy class." Miranda felt herself being drawn deeper and deeper into revealing bits of her past. Maybe she should just admit her age. But then what? "Gee, guys, why the grilling?"

"So you're how old?" Linc asked offhandedly.

Miranda's heart thumped hard and fast. "Old enough. I, uh, graduated from high school at sixteen." And that was the truth. Still, she didn't like the way Parker kept staring at her in his rearview mirror. It seemed the more she said, the farther she put her foot down her throat. *Please, someone change the subject.*

Eric did just that when the Excursion bounced off the last few feet of rutted lane and Parker swung onto the smoother highway. "Why turn east? Don't you go west to get to town? That's the direction we came in from."

"According to the friend who scoped out the ranch for me, Susanville is really the closest town to the property.

Because there's national parkland in between, it's not the most well-traveled stretch of road. But, John, my friend, is an avid outdoorsman. He said the streams and lakes are stocked with several kinds of trout. Do any of you fish?''

Wolfie perked up. "I ain't never fished with anything but a skinned tree branch with a string and a safety pin. The houseparents before the Tuckers used to let me fish our creek. But Mrs. Tucker said she wouldn't eat no fish from where us kids took baths. And Mr. Tucker, he said fishing was a waste of time. He only wanted me to chop wood for their fireplace.''

The more Linc heard about George and Lydia Tucker, the angrier he became. What kind of man sent a boy Wolfgang's age to tackle a dangerous job?

He mustered a smile he didn't feel. "Fishing season here runs from Memorial Day to December thirty-first. Since it's early November, we might find time to fish, even with the work I want to accomplish. It's something I've always wanted to try, but never had the opportunity. If you're our resident expert, Wolfie, I'll buy rods and you can teach the boys and me how to catch trout.''

"What's resident…whatever you said?" the boy asked, puckering his brows.

Jenny heaved a sigh. "Man, are you dense. Resident expert means you're the best person to demonstrate a skill. Fishing, duh! What I want to know is why only the boys get to go. Why not Randi and me, too?''

"If you girls want to slog through underbrush for hours on end, I've got no objection.''

"But you're gonna make 'em put their own worms or bugs on their hooks, ain't you, Mr. Parker?" This gleeful addendum from Wolfie was the most animated he'd been. His smile showed two teeth in different stages of coming in.

Jenny recoiled at the very mention of baiting a hook. Miranda said nothing at first. She'd learned her lesson about jumping in too fast. You could give away too much that way. From here on, she'd weigh everything she said. "My dad liked to fish." It was true. "He took me a time or two when I was Cassie's age." Also true. "You're about eight, aren't you, Cassie?"

"Seven, I think."

"You think?" Greg scoffed from behind the girl. "Don't you know?"

The child blinked owlishly, and large tears welled up behind her smudged lenses. Miranda reached out and clasped the child's hand. "It's okay, Cassie. Mr. Parker can find out. There must be school and health records on each of you back at the house. Do you know why you can't walk?" Miranda asked softly.

The girl nodded. "Because my spine's twisted at the bottom."

Wolfie cleared his throat. "We heard Mrs. Rankin, one of the house moms, say Cassie's mama had a boyfriend who threw Cassie down the basement steps."

Jenny sucked in her breath. And Scraps emitted what could pass for a sympathetic growl. Miranda merely tightened her grip on the child's fingers. "But, honey, you probably don't remember the details of the accident."

"I do sorta," Cassie said solemnly. "I remember being cold for a long time. And I remember some policemen took Joey and Mama away. Then I was in the hospital for a lot of days and nights. I've lived a lotta places since. Nobody ever wants me to stay, 'cause it's hard having a kid around who can't walk."

A heavy silence descended on the vehicle. Miranda stroked the girl's small hand as her gaze met Linc's in the mirror. She could only guess that her horror matched the sick expression she saw in his eyes.

"Look," Eric announced, a catch evident in his voice, as well. "We're coming to some lights. That must be the town up ahead."

Gladly latching on to a chance to avoid what he read as censure in Randi's cool gaze, Linc switched his attention to the glow Eric pointed out.

"Get outta here," Shawn said. "If that's the town, I'd say we're in deep shit when it comes to finding a motel. Looks like nothin's goin' on here."

"Please watch your language, Shawn." Miranda cast her eyes toward the younger members of their group.

"Come on, kids." Linc injected a cheery note in his voice. "Susanville is the county seat. Montoya said it's a hub for serious hikers, sport fishermen and mountain bikers. There have to be motels to accommodate those groups. And it's not so late that there won't be a choice of restaurants still open." Even as he spoke, they passed a well-lit café.

The kids all clamored for him to stop, but Linc drove on. "I think we should book a motel before we eat. Let's get our sleeping arrangements nailed down, and then we'll worry about filling our bellies."

There was a lot of grumbling, but in the end the kids capitulated.

At the first motel with a vacancy sign, Linc swung in. He told everyone to stay put, but no one listened and they all got out and trooped into the office behind him.

The clerk took one look at the kids and immediately informed Linc she couldn't accommodate his party.

"That's odd. I only saw three cars in your parking lot. And you have two floors of rooms," he said, smiling as he leaned an elbow on the counter.

"Uh…it's the dog. We don't allow pets," the woman said, almost happily trumping Linc's ace.

He recognized her shallow ploy for what it was, and while he wouldn't stay here now if it was the last motel in town, he didn't intend to go without leaving her something to think about. "That's too bad for your establishment. This dog is a movie star. We've had a long drive today—up from Hollywood, haven't we, kids? I told my cast this looked like a perfect spot to film." Turning, he motioned them out. "That's okay. We'll take our money down the road."

Even though the woman sputtered behind him, Linc steadily moved everyone outside. As they reloaded the SUV, silence reigned. Then Eric crowed, "That was sweet, man, how you made her look at us with respect."

"Let that be a lesson, Eric. All people are worthy of respect. Note that I wasn't disrespectful to the clerk. The choice was hers. And she's entitled to her beliefs no matter how much I disagree with her."

"But you flat-out lied," Miranda said. "Scraps isn't a movie star. And we don't even know that he won't mess in a room. I mean, we'll have to leave him in there with a bowl of water while we go eat."

"I bent the truth. Jenny said you found him near Burbank. You don't know that he hasn't been in films. And he won't mess up the room if you walk him before we go eat and again before you turn in."

The kids mulled over Linc's words as he drove down the main street to another motel. This time when he asked them to stay put while he booked rooms, no one objected. They gave high fives all around, however, when he came back a few minutes later wagging three keys. "And Scraps is legally in."

"I thought you said two rooms earlier," Miranda said.

"Yes, but I have to make some phone calls. I booked a single for me and two doubles. Splitting up the boys and girls means everybody has more space."

"Uh, that'll be great." Miranda capitulated fast enough. "It means an extra shower. I could almost skip eating to enjoy a hot shower. How about you, Jenny?"

Before she could answer, Linc interrupted, "Do you girls mind bathing Cassie and Hana tonight?"

"They'll be glad to." Shawn readily volunteered them. "Now can we please go find a burger joint? I'm starved."

With moods greatly improved, they all laughed.

"I'm three steps ahead of you, Shawn." Linc handed out the room keys and then went to unload the packs. "I told the clerk I had eight hungry mouths to feed. Taking pity on me, she drew a map to the closest steak house."

"Steak?" The older boys chattered excitedly among themselves as they dropped stuff in their rooms and Miranda prepared to leave the dog.

Linc had never gone hungry in his life. And this one night, steak was the least he could offer pathetic kids whose stories had shaken him more than he cared to admit.

CHAPTER FOUR

LINC RESENTED the surreptitious looks they got from other patrons as they ambled in. They were seated at a large oval table near the back of the restaurant, shown to their seats by a hostess wearing a red-checkered dress that matched the décor. He dismissed her look of pity as he took the stack of menus she thrust into his hands.

Miranda waited for Parker to request booster seats for Cassie and Hana. Not that Cassie wasn't old enough to sit in a regular chair. But these were wooden ones, built low, probably for big men—the sportsmen Linc had mentioned earlier.

In gentlemanly fashion, Linc pulled out Jenny's chair, then Randi's. "We got enough chairs?" He glanced around the table and counted.

"Don't you think we need boosters for the little girls?"

"High chairs, you mean?" He frowned, letting his mind drift back to when his kid sister had needed a chair that had its own tray.

Miranda rolled her eyes. "Boosters are molded plastic seats that go on regular chairs."

She didn't tack *stupid* onto the end of her sentence, but she might as well have, Linc thought. "Does this restaurant have such an item?" He squinted to see into the dimly lit corners.

"We do have boosters, sir," the hostess assured him

with a broad smile. "How many do you need for your family?"

"Oh, they're not mine," he said, refocusing on the woman who looked as if she belonged at a square dance.

"Two, please," Miranda rushed to say. Turning, she followed the hostess to where the multicolored seats were stacked. Miranda selected a blue one and a red one. The red had a cushion made of fabric like the woman's dress. It turned out to be oilcloth, more like the tablecloths. Regardless, she judged the cushion better for Cassie and had barely started back to the table when the seats were whisked from her hands. Glancing up in surprise, she discovered Parker had relieved her of them.

"Give Cassie the red one," she said quickly. "It was the only one with a cushion. I think it'll be softer on her poor back."

"I'm not dense, Ms—what in hell *is* your last name?" Linc demanded, suddenly perplexed.

"Ah...uh...according to Jenny, street people never give their surnames to anyone. It's for protection," she said when Linc stopped to stare at her.

"So does that mean you weren't a street person before you hit California?"

"No. I mean, I was...for a while. In Kansas City," she blurted, trying to stick as close to the truth as possible.

"Kansas City." Narrowing his eyes, Linc turned that tidbit of information over in his mind. "You didn't get that thick drawl there. Where did you live before K.C.? And why did you leave?"

Miranda drew herself up to her full height, yet she was still woefully shorter than the man studying her like a specimen under a microscope. "My past is my own business. And your silly interrogation is holding up the waitress who wants to take our drink orders."

Feeling smartly put in his place, Linc set the booster seats into the chairs. He gently lifted the little girls into them. The only two empty chairs at the table were quite far from each other.

Damn, he'd wanted to probe deeper into the mystery that came packaged as a woman calling herself Randi with no last name. If Randi was even her name... Why he cared about her history, Linc didn't know. After all, he'd been warned not to expect the truth out of street kids. Yet Randi managed to irritate him while simultaneously giving him pause. Linc vowed he'd unravel her story or know the reason why.

"Are you kids ready to order?" Linc asked as the waitress stood patiently by his chair.

"We don't know how much you are letting us spend," Greg said, his English showing traces of his Asian background. "Have you looked at the cost?"

Linc opened the menu, expecting to see something outrageous. In actuality, the steaks were cheap. "Order whatever suits your fancy. Let me worry about the bill."

There wasn't one person at the table who didn't show shock at that news. Miranda alone noticed how Parker had softened his tone so that his statement, which might have sounded as if he lorded it over them, held no patronizing inflection.

She imagined her former manager in a situation like this. Wes Carlisle would have found a way to put everyone at the table in his debt. Which was how Wes had operated from the minute he'd stepped into a job previously handled by her father. Throughout the years that Doug Kimbrough had made decisions for her, she'd remained blissfully ignorant about the working end of her singing career. The rude awakening came the moment Carlisle stepped in. It hadn't taken Miranda long to figure out that she'd made a horrible mistake in signing an open-ended contract with Carlisle's agency.

As they awaited their food, Miranda recalled something Jenny said the day they met. She'd said her good friend Felicity's brother was some guru who worked with movie and singing stars. Miranda couldn't help wondering if Parker managed his stars in a manner similar to Carlisle's handling of country singers. Try as she might, she couldn't picture Wes giving up his rich lifestyle to go to some remote locale and set up a safe house for street kids. The two types of personalities—manager to the stars and socially conscious benefactor—weren't mutually compatible. So maybe Jenny was wrong about Parker's occupation.

After everyone had their drinks, Miranda lent a hand to Hana so the girl didn't spill her milk all over the place. Catching Parker's eye, she asked casually, "What did you do before you bought the ranch? I know you worked in Hollywood. Did it involve teens? You're not the type to have been a cop." Miranda pretended she knew nothing about his background.

Jenny frowned. "I thought I told you about Felicity's brother."

"Unlike some people," Linc said, aiming a pointed stare at Miranda, "I'm not secretive about my past. I graduated from a California college with a master's in finance. I became a CPA and then set up a partnership with a guy I met in grad school. We invest our clients' excess capital and do their quarterly taxes."

"Felicity said his clients are top movie and rock stars," Jenny said in a tone filled with awe.

"No kidding?" Greg's face was a mask of envy. "I guess I joined the group after Felicity mentioned that," he whispered to Jenny. "Anyway, I didn't know her as well as you guys did. But the house...wow! Megabucks."

Linc sliced an impatient hand through the air. "A firm doesn't start off working for big names. It takes time to earn respect in any field."

"There's that word again," Eric pointed out. "Respect's a big word in your vocabulary, isn't it, Mr. P.?"

"No more than honesty, reliability and diligence."

Wolfie, who now had a white mustache after draining his glass of milk, asked in a small voice what diligence meant.

"Sorry," Linc said. "I know you aren't a walking dictionary. Diligence is a high-priced word for hard work."

"Well, why didn't you just say hard work?" Wolfie sighed, then launched another question. "I guess you gotta go to school to learn big words, huh?"

Linc flashed him a grin. "Don't worry about it, kid. Learning anything takes time. You're only in what—fourth grade?"

"No grade. Well, I used to go to school before the Tuckers came to Rascal Ranch. They didn't like to drive me and Cassie out to the highway to catch the bus. And Miz Lydia never liked taking care of Hana by herself."

Miranda exhaled loudly. "You mean they arbitrarily stopped sending you to school?"

When all three kids gaped at her without comprehension, she hastily rephrased her question. "Arbitrarily means the Tuckers took it upon themselves to take you out of school. Is that what they did?"

Wolfie thought a minute, then nodded.

"Nothing about that couple would surprise me," Linc exclaimed when Miranda telegraphed him a look of outrage.

"Before we head back to the ranch, shouldn't we, uh,

you find out how long this has gone on? Surely you can reinstate them in school.''

''Yes, if they are going to remain with me. Tomorrow, though, among other things, I hope to contact a living breathing soul who knows what agency ought to be taking responsibility for them.'' Fortuitously, in Linc's estimation, their meal arrived. Otherwise he was certain Randi would have given him hell. She'd made it plain in a glance what she thought of him for shucking off what she mistakenly considered his responsibility for the children's welfare. But why in hell should he care what a woman, who had no apparent direction in her own life, thought about the way he chose to manage his contribution to charity?

The answer was, Linc didn't care. Or rather, he *shouldn't* care. It so happened he did. Because throughout the meal, she sent him darting looks that penetrated deeper and deeper into his fairly thick skin. Why couldn't she attack her steak with the same fervor showing in those expressive gray eyes?

If she thought he'd embroil himself in a battle during mealtime, she was sadly mistaken. Linc intended to enjoy his steak.

He might have succeeded if he'd kept quiet. But no, he had to be the one to reopen the can of worms with a simple sentence. ''Wolfie, Cassie and Hana, stop stuffing dinner rolls in your pockets.''

The girls froze immediately. The boy continued calmly filling his pockets.

''I said quit that, Wolfie. It's unsanitary and unnecessary. Why are you taking more food than you can eat here and now?''

''Because tomorrow we might be hungry.''

Linc's brows drew together. ''Good grief. Tomorrow you'll be fed.''

Randi stopped cutting her steak. "How can you guarantee them that? Doesn't the history of the welfare system speak for itself? You as much as said you're dumping them back—like...like too-small fish in a pond."

Her verbal spear penetrated all the way to Linc's heart and made it skip a beat. He cast a furtive glance around the table and saw that the bigger boys kept shoving food in their faces. Jenny, Randi and the little kids all impaled him with expressions of distrust. Well, if not outright distrust, something damned close to it.

"Look, I guarantee that tomorrow there'll be plenty to eat. Beyond that, I'm not sticking my neck out. Yes, the system appears to be broken. Can I fix it? That I can't promise. I will go to the authorities and try to make waves."

Banking her hostility ever so slightly, Randi deliberately sliced up a few pieces of meat and wrapped them for her dog. "Kids, we'd better eat up before our meat gets cold. Meat has protein, and protein gives you strength and energy. Hard, stale rolls will only fill an empty hole in your bellies."

Linc didn't know why the statement made him feel like a jerk. He'd set out to help wayward teens maybe get back on track and find a new direction in life. He hadn't promised to save the whole damned world. Or even this corner of California. At Felicity's funeral, he'd pledged to put his life on hold for a couple of years. He'd devote personal resources toward derailing youth headed down the same path as his sister, and once the shelter ran well, he'd hire people to keep it going. "I'm not a miracle worker," he muttered. "I'm just one man, after all."

"You're one of the power brokers," Jenny pointed out. "Felicity said it'd only take a word from you in the right ear, and she, uh, we would've been on our way."

"Way where?" Linc arched a brow.

"To the big time. Our band." She swung her fork in an arc, gesturing at herself and the boys.

Linc looked pained. His steak had turned to ashes in his mouth. "Do you have any idea how many truly talented artists are down and out in Hollywood? Hundreds. Thousands, even. They flock there because someone has filled their heads with unrealistic dreams of becoming rock stars. They're caught in an insidious web and some end up selling their bodies—and their souls. The majority don't come close to the pinnacle they're seeking." Linc balled his napkin. "I'm sorry, but Felicity had zero talent. I...I believed that by continuing to subsidize her lessons, I was giving her time to come to that realization herself. I was wrong."

Randi understood his pain. Furthermore, she understood what he was saying. Nashville wasn't Hollywood, and the people who flocked there didn't dream of being rock stars, but of being hit country singers. She wanted to say that, even if a person reached that coveted pinnacle, stardom wasn't what people thought. She sealed her lips, instead.

Jenny, however, wasn't to be deterred. "All Felicity needed, all any of us need, Mr. Parker—" she included Eric, Shawn and Greg in the sweep of her defiant eyes "—is a break. We're as talented as any of the groups who paid you to make them teen millionaires."

"I didn't make them teen idols. I help shelter some of the money they make. That's all." Lifting his head, Linc saw Randi staring at him. "You're remarkably silent all of a sudden. What's wrong?"

"I...I didn't know Felicity. And I don't know anything about what makes a rock star," Miranda said, carefully crossing her fingers under the table.

"Well, that's a relief." Linc picked up his knife and cut

another piece of steak. "I'm giving fair warning. The subject of star-building is permanently closed. If you came here hoping I could do for you what I never did for my sister, it's not going to happen. The subject of rock music and rock stardom is going to be taboo. Understood?"

Eric laid his fork aside. "We came to get off the streets and out of shelters for the winter. But rock music is a big part of who we are. We ain't gonna change that for you, man."

"Yeah," Shawn added stiffly. "Until you told us your name, we had no idea it was Felicity's brother who'd opened this retreat."

Linc realized belatedly that was correct. He'd seen Jenny's shocked expression when he'd announced his name. "Okay, but another word to the wise. The program I have in mind won't allow you time to bang away on your guitars. And when I come in dog-tired from tilling and planting fields, the last thing I want is to be assaulted with earsplitting rock music. I won't have your radios or CD players shaking the bunkhouse walls. Are we all clear on that point?"

Randi nodded at once. The others turned to Eric and awaited his response. He scowled and grunted a couple of times. Eventually he shrugged. "What the hey. For food like this and a real bed, we can use earphones between now and spring, when we head back to Hollywood."

Something about the kid's half-assed truce bothered Linc. But since he was going on the advice of people long on theory but short on experience, he'd just have to play this by ear. As other teens heard about the ranch and joined this group, a change in the dynamic might test Eric's leadership role. These kids could simply choose to move on.

In fact, Linc had been warned of that by a friend, a psychologist who worked with wards of the court. He'd told Linc repeatedly that working with teens was a roller coaster of wins and losses. And that Linc shouldn't let the losses become personal.

Although Linc wasn't totally comfortable with this first batch of teens, he didn't like failing at anything. That was one reason his inability to provide Felicity with a happy, secure home had hit him so hard. He had to at least go into this with the intention of succeeding.

The waitress appeared and began collecting plates. "Anyone save room for dessert?"

Shawn raised his hand. "What have you got?"

The waitress answered. "Tonight we have apple pie or ice cream."

"Not both?" Shawn looked crestfallen.

"Yes, both if you'd like." She laughed heartily.

"Just coffee with cream for me," Linc said as the waitress took out her pad and started with him.

Miranda debated ordering a coffee, too, but declined when the waitress reached her. Instead, she carefully collected all the leftover bits of steak, explaining it was for the dog.

Jenny poked her in the side. "Why would you turn down a chance to have pie à la mode? I don't know about you, but it's been ages since I've had a treat like that."

"It sounds good, but I'm full. Dinner was great. Thanks, Par...Parker."

The rest of the kids chimed in their thanks, too.

"You're welcome. Keep your fingers crossed that I can hire a cook who's able to keep us as well-fed."

Whenever the topic under discussion was food, Shawn had things to say. "How long do you think it'll be until you hire a cook? Will you have to advertise and interview and all that stuff?"

"I suppose. If what the Tuckers said about the ranch

being so remote that no one stayed on for long is true, I may have to go farther afield and offer incentives. No matter, I'll be checking references to avoid getting someone like the Tuckers.''

''Good,'' Cassie said meekly. ''They were the worst houseparents we ever had.''

Miranda gazed at her pinched features. ''I can believe that from the shape of the kitchen. If you had to guess how long it's been since you saw a social worker, Cassie, would you say days, weeks or months?''

The girl shook her head until two or three stringy blond curls fell into her eyes. Miranda couldn't wait to get this girl into a tub of warm soapy water. Cassie's long curls held the promise of being flaxen gold. ''I don't know how to read a clock,'' she said.

''Because you never got to attend school?'' Miranda's eyes snapped. ''That's okay, sweetie, it doesn't really matter exactly how long it was since you saw someone from Social Services. I just thought knowing a definite time might be useful to Mr. Parker when he gets hold of your new caseworker.''

Jenny, who'd been served her dessert first, raked furrows in her ice cream with her fork tines. ''We don't—I mean, the rest of us kids don't have to be assigned a caseworker, do we? I've never met one of those do-gooders who isn't itching to send street kids straight back to their folks.''

''Yeah,'' Eric agreed. ''It's like…don't they *get* why we left home?''

''Why did you?'' Linc inquired as he stirred cream in his coffee.

''Are you kidding, man?'' Shawn spoke through a mouthful of pie and ice cream. ''In my case, the word *home* is a farce. According to the dictionary, home means a place that's the center of domestic pleasure. No pleasure in gettin' the shit kicked outta ya.''

Linc winced, lifted his cup and covered his shock by taking a long drink. ''So, uh, were you all abused?''

''Naw, not me.'' Greg retold his story. ''Even if I had the money to go back to Seoul, I can't face my mom. So I'll hang out with these guys until I figure out how to earn enough to start another search for my dad.''

Linc's gaze skipped again to Eric.

''I had my reasons for leaving home,'' the boy snarled. ''Nobody's business but mine. As for Jenny, her mom drank like a fish and still kept havin' babies she expected Jenny to take care of. Caseworkers didn't put a stop to that. What good are they?''

Linc honestly didn't want to debate the issue with Eric, and he didn't have to because Jenny took the boy's hand. ''Hush, Eric. I did what I did to help the younger kids. And after I took off, the authorities finally paid attention and took away my brothers and sisters.''

Waiting to see what could top that unsettling account, Linc cocked an eyebrow at Randi. ''I assume you have a story, too.''

She was caught off guard, although Miranda didn't know why she hadn't expected Parker to get around to her, too. She turned her head, scrabbling for something to say. ''My mom died when I was about…Hana's age. Dad traveled a lot for his work. He took me with him. After I reached school age, he home-schooled me. I didn't like the travel, and one weekend when I didn't go, his airplane crashed.'' For an awful few seconds she relived the tragedy. With a catch in her voice, she eventually continued. ''My life fell apart. I…realize I can't just keep drifting. I hope time will, uh, let me eventually get my act together.''

''No aunts, uncles or cousins who'll help you through

this crisis?'' Linc asked after draining his cup. He wasn't sure why, but something about the girl's story didn't ring true. Maybe she was a consummate actress. But there was some fact, some detail she was holding back. Linc trusted his judgment. He'd developed a reliable sixth sense in dealing with the Hollywood crowd, many of whom couldn't separate reality from fantasy.

Miranda sighed, wishing he'd move on to Wolfgang. ''My parents were both only children,'' she murmured. ''My grandparents are gone, too.'' Rather than let Parker dredge up more questions, she moved on for him. ''Wolfie, how did you and Hana end up alone?''

The boy jerked spasmodically and clapped two hands over his little sister's ears. ''Pa kilt our ma,'' he muttered, face drained of color. ''I knew it was gonna happen, 'cause he hit her lots. But Hana didn't see. I sneaked her into the closet and stayed with her till the cops showed up. Pa's on death row. The relatives didn't want no part of raising his kids, but a judge made him sign so Hana and me could be adopted.'' The boy slowly removed his hands from Hana's ears, then slid an arm around her small shoulders. ''A family took Hana. But she wets the bed and cries lots. The woman brought her back to the group home.'' He shrugged. ''It was an okay place.''

Aghast, Miranda asked him how they'd ended up at Rascal Ranch.

''Oh, a neighbor pitched a fit. He said the group home was falling down, so Oasis moved us. The woman who brung us said somebody would adopt us together. I knew she was lying. Nobody wants a kid my age. And Hana still has problems at night.''

The waitress reappeared. ''Anything else, sir?'' She hefted the coffeepot.

Linc realized the turn of their conversation had stolen

everyone's appetites. "We're ready to leave. No more coffee for me, but thanks."

Smiling, the woman took the check out of her apron pocket. "Pay at the register up front."

Accepting the check, Linc stood. Digging in his jeans pocket, he pulled out a money clip. A quick perusal of the check showed she'd added it correctly, and he peeled off a couple of hundreds to cover the bill, plus the tip. That was when he noticed the older kids staring, openmouthed, at the wad of cash he had in his clip.

Unsure as to whether any of them had police records, he decided that carrying so much cash might have been a dumb move.

But John Montoya had said not all merchants in the small towns bordering the ranch were set up to take credit cards. And because Linc knew there'd be things he'd have to buy right away, he'd brought five thousand in cash. Of course, he'd never dreamt the ranch would need big-ticket items like baseboard heaters or a commercial dishwasher. The very thought made him pause and wonder again if he'd been crazy to plunge headlong into this project without any experience or even an apprenticeship.

Figuring he might as well test the kids' honesty straight away, Linc handed his car keys to Eric. "I'll go square our account at the register. Will you see that everyone gets loaded and buckled up? Oh, and start the heater. Those last people who came in said it's gotten cold outside."

For a minute, Eric acted stunned, as if he couldn't believe Linc had singled him out. The kid even shot a wary glance over each shoulder. "Me?" he finally managed to croak. "You want *me* to start your Excursion?"

"Yes. You seem like a guy who's done his share of tinkering with engines and such."

Eric straightened visibly. "I got my license. Both me

and Shawn do.'' Snatching the dangling key chain, he turned to the others. ''You heard the man. Let's go load up and get some hot air rolling besides what's coming out of your mouths.''

Linc allowed himself a second or two to marvel at how the rest of the kids fell meekly in line with Eric's orders. Including Ms. Sassy Randi, who lingered to help Cassie into her wheelchair. She settled the injured child and maneuvered her over the doorjamb—like a regular little mother. He mulled that over as the others filed out after her.

That was it—the major thing that set Randi apart. As a rule, teens were self-centered. Randi looked out for others first.

Speaking of looking out for others, Linc sent up a silent prayer that he'd still have a vehicle parked in the lot when he exited the restaurant.

To his relief, it sat in the exact spot he'd left it.

As he sprinted toward the SUV, Linc could see his breath in the night air. ''Whew, it's colder than a witch's, uh, tail.'' He hurriedly changed what he'd been about to say as he jumped into the SUV. With the little ones, he'd have to learn to watch his mouth. Hollywooders weren't known to use the best language. And old habits died hard. Turning, he dumped a handful of mints in Jenny's lap.

''What are these for?'' she asked, scrambling not to let them fall off her lap.

''For…because you all behaved yourselves, I guess. The cashier complimented me on my children's good manners.'' He wondered how they'd react to that statement.

''Didn't we act how you're supposed to?'' Shawn stopped blowing on his hands and frowned at Linc.

He kicked up the heat a few notches before responding. ''You did. Apparently they've served a few families lately with really rowdy kids. You did us proud in there, guys, but frankly I thought the fact that she referred to you as 'my children' would get a rise out of at least some of you.''

"She couldn't see half of us *aren't* children?'' Eric snorted sarcastically. "Or was she blind? Like you'd be my dad, or Greg's.''

"If Mr. Parker was ever a sailor, he could be my dad, you know,'' Greg said tartly.

"Sorry, Greg, I never served in the military. For the record, I don't have any kids floating around the country.''

"That makes it even weirder that you'd be the one to open a shelter for street kids, don't you think?'' Miranda had little inflection in her voice. Nor did she look directly at Parker. She was busy checking Hana's seat belt as she made the comment.

"Or maybe it makes him gay,'' Eric said defiantly. "A lot of guys in Hollywood are.''

Linc could let both remarks slide. He probably should. On the other hand, maybe they deserved to know his reasons. In a voice fraught with emotion in spite of his effort to sound matter-of-fact, he said, "Jenny hit the nail earlier when she implied I'd let my sister down. At her funeral, I looked around and saw that everyone there was either my friend or a business acquaintance. That's when it struck me how little I knew about Felicity's day-to-day activities. So I started asking myself some hard questions. The answers I got didn't exactly nominate me for guardian of the decade.'' His deep voice trailed away into silence.

Miranda tried to read between the lines. "You mean you felt guilty, so that's why you quit a lucrative job to come and do penance in the back of beyond?''

Linc let his eyes locate hers in the mirror. Who was this woman he hardly knew—a woman who could cut to the heart of the massive guilt he'd been burdened with every day for the past six months? "I don't consider it penance," he corrected. Wishing himself anywhere but here, he slammed the gearshift into Reverse and backed in a sharp turn so he could peal out of the lot.

If any of them thought his speed was worrisome or even a bit dangerous, no one made a peep about it.

Linc covered the distance to the motel in absolute silence.

CHAPTER FIVE

LINC WAS QUICK to anger, but just as quick to cool down—
a useful ability for anyone who hoped to be successful in
the business he'd so recently left. Stars prone to fits of
temper themselves tended not to work well with anyone
who behaved in a similar fashion. Over the years Linc had
learned to perfect control. And he'd been good at his job.
That was why it irritated the hell out of him that he'd let
Randi rattle him tonight. It wouldn't happen again.

By the time he slowed to make the tight curve into their
motel parking lot, Linc had a lock on his guilt and his self-
contempt. Perhaps that was why he took notice of an all-
night pancake house adjacent to the motel, which he hadn't
seen earlier. The place caught his eye now because of the
group of rowdy young men hanging out near two low-
slung sports cars.

Shawn saw them, too. "Hey, Jenny, do you think we
can bum some smokes off those dudes?"

Jenny pressed her nose to the window. "Go ahead,
Shawn. But not for me. I haven't had a cigarette in a week.
Like Randi's been trying to tell me, food tastes better and
my throat's not so scratchy. I'm going to try and quit for
good." Still, the girl gazed longingly at the red glow being
passed around the huddle of strangers.

Linc, afraid the yokels might offer his kids more than
cigarettes, thought it best to nip Shawn's idea in the bud.
"First person I see approaching those creeps can kiss off

sleeping in a bed tonight. The only rooms available when we checked in were nonsmoking. I promised there'd be none. And before you say you'll step outside, let me squelch that idea. I don't want you mixing up with home-grown hoods. Those guys look about as far removed from the Chamber of Commerce welcoming committee as any-one can get. Tomorrow I'll be doing business with local merchants, and I prefer to avoid a bad reputation before I even start out.''

"Jeez, I wasn't going to fight 'em if they refused me a smoke,'' Shawn muttered.

Eric solved Linc's potential problem. He eyed the group of toughs and said with finality, "Shawn, you dumb-ass. Didn't you see the bloody daggers on the backs of their jackets? That's a trademark of the Steel Blades. They're not from here. At least, this didn't used to be their territory. They're from up north around where my pop grows olives. Word is, they'll carve a dude up for lookin' cross-eyed. I say, let 'em be.''

Linc sneaked a second peek. "Sound advice. Let's see how close I can park to our rooms.'' It was his good for-tune to spot someone backing out, four doors from the rooms he'd booked. Linc assumed Eric had warded off danger until the nine of them split up to go unlock their rooms and he overheard Randi talking to Jenny.

"Jen, will you fill the tub and stick Hana and Cassie in to soak while I walk Scraps? He's lunging at the window with that anxious look that says he's gotta go outside *now*.'' She removed a coiled leash from her pocket and transferred Cassie's wheelchair into Jenny's hands. "Sorry, I know I said I'd bathe the girls. I promise I'll take over as soon as Scraps is finished doing his business.''

Linc didn't stop to consider that Randi and the others had been on their own throughout their journey. He only conjured up a vivid picture of how futile that nothing of a dog would be as a bodyguard against hoodlums who had bloody daggers stitched on the backs of their black leather jackets.

"Here, give me the leash. You carry out your original plan. I'll walk the damned dog."

The words had no more than left his lips when Linc managed his first good look at the leash—a psychedelic fuchsia strap attached to a narrow band of garish purple sparkling stones. "I can't believe you bought this for a mutt named Scraps." He shuddered to think how many Steel Blades he'd be forced to punch out if he strolled past them with a yapping dog clamped to the end of this getup.

Randi studied him, laughter crinkling the corners of her eyes. "No one asked you to walk him. I can't help it if L.A. has a leash law and this was the only one left in the pet store." She plucked the leash out of Linc's hand. "Scraps is my responsibility. I'm perfectly capable of walking him."

There ensued a tug-of-war on the hot-pink leather that the others found amusing. Eric finally stepped between them and took the leash from both Randi and Linc. "If all you're gonna do is argue about which of you does the honors, it'll be too late, anyway. The dog will have done his business on the motel rug."

The two had the grace to look guilty.

Squaring his shoulders, Linc drew himself up to his full five-foot-eleven, towering over Randi's scant five-foot-three. "Somebody get me the dog," he insisted. "I'm walking him around the building and that's that."

Randi nibbled on her lower lip. She'd seen Parker's gaze dart toward the raucous-looking thugs who lingered by their sports cars. Parker was so transparent. She knew exactly what was going through his head. Zipping her denim jacket, she flipped the collar up around her ears. "Scraps is used to me. He doesn't trust men yet. But I'll understand if you feel the need to walk off that big steak. Scraps and I won't object if you tag along, Parker."

"Damned decent of you," Linc said sarcastically.

Scraps streaked out from between Jenny's legs and danced around Randi's feet. She bent and greeted her pet with a musical lilt—the sound of which caught at something in Linc's chest.

Jamming his hands in his jacket pockets, he reminded the kids to lock up. "You'll hear us return. And I'll check on how you're all getting on. Everyone has half a bed. And there's enough hot water to go around."

"Yeah, yeah, yeah!" Eric waved Linc away before slamming and locking the door to the boys' room.

"Are you sure you aren't a dad?" Randi asked very near Linc's ear. "You have the routine down pat."

He moved aside, giving her and the animal more room on the sidewalk. But he must've made some feeble noise because she began to justify herself. "My dad had a habit of lecturing me to be careful and lock up tight, even if he was only gone a few minutes. I could recite his litany word for word."

Linc might have said nothing about her revelation had the light at the corner not illuminated her face, which revealed the despondency in her eyes and the downward curve of her lips. Her sadness reached so deep inside him, it triggered memories of past losses.

It'd been twenty years since he'd allowed himself to despair over missing what most kids had—parents who cared. When the feeling returned now, swiftly and with deadly precision, Linc was ill-prepared. So ill-prepared, he ran into a post that held up the second-floor balcony.

"Hey, are you okay?" Randi shot out a hand and grabbed his arm.

"I'm fine." He pulled away. "Must've stumbled on a sidewalk crack."

Frowning, she glanced back at where they'd been. Miranda hadn't felt any flaws in the walkway. Nor did she see any now.

"Hey, wait," she called to the man who barreled on ahead like a steam engine. "While we're at this lighted intersection, I'm going to give Scraps the steak I saved. It's not much. Since I'm not sure how rich meat will affect his stomach, I'd rather feed him while we're outside, if you get my drift."

Stopping midstride, Linc turned and noticed the mist from Randi's breath curling around her head. "Okay, but make it snappy. It we stay put too long, we'll freeze into ice statues."

Smiling, she peered up from where she'd knelt to feed the shivering dog. "You and Scraps are thin-skinned Southern Californians. I love cold crisp autumns. Reminds me of home."

"Really? Where's home?" Linc stopped rubbing his palms together and pounced on her statement.

Miranda felt the color drain from her face. In the harsh lamplight, she felt exposed. Trapped. "I can't tell you that, Parker. Please don't send me away. I'm…uh…"

"What? On the lam from the cops?"

"No, no. Nothing like that." Stronger now, she didn't fumble so much for words. "There's some…one I'm running from."

Linc drew back and studied her pale features, then the nervous fingers shredding the bits of well-cooked steak. "A man?"

Looking stricken, Miranda nodded. She waited for the

logical next question and then for the ax to fall. She sincerely doubted a man known as a financial guru in Hollywood would show mercy for a performer cutting out on her contract.

The longer Linc gazed into her wary eyes, the more his brain manufactured worst-case scenarios. He wondered if the dark shadows he was seeing hid scars of mental and maybe even physical abuse. "You're running from a husband, then?" he asked harshly.

She shook her head, not trusting herself to speak.

Ah, a boyfriend, or live-in lover. Linc filled in the blanks himself, feeling a knot tighten in his stomach. "There are laws protecting minors."

"I'm not a minor." She rose, dusted off her hands and then wadded the napkin that had held the meat.

"Not a minor," he repeated. "That means…you're twenty-one?"

"Twenty-six, actually." She stared at her toes. "Please, if you find it in your heart to let me stay, don't give me away to the others. It's easier pretending to be one of them. Easier on *them* and on me."

"Well." Linc didn't know how to react to her revelation. "I guess the age explains your patience at dealing with the younger kids." He scowled momentarily. "You don't have any, do you? Children hidden away, I mean," he blurted, oddly nervous, although it should have been a huge relief to know his instincts hadn't been wrong, after all.

Miranda realized the path his mind had taken. He thought she'd run from an abusive relationship. Well…he was right in a way. Wes Carlisle had a stranglehold on every aspect of her life. It was suffocating her. Why not let Parker think what he wanted if it would give her more time to figure out how to free herself from Wes? "I promise I haven't left a husband or any children behind. I *have* left an untenable situation. I need time to sort through my options. To rebuild my life. If you can see your way clear to give me that time, you won't regret it.''

He shoved his hands deep in his jacket pockets. ''I already do,'' he said in a sandpapery voice that seemed to have difficulty getting past his lips. ''But I applaud your courage in coming clean with me. We'll see how it goes. Has that mutt done his stuff? If so, we'd better be getting back.''

''Yeah. Jenny wasn't happy that I asked her to start the girls' baths. They're liable to resemble prunes if they're left soaking much longer.''

They'd progressed to the far end of the motel and were now adjacent to the pancake restaurant. The young rebels stopped talking among themselves and stared openly at the couple with the dog. One by one, they uttered catcalls and piercing wolf whistles.

Linc latched on to Randi's elbow. ''Don't look at them,'' he ordered. ''What were we talking about before they noticed us? Oh, I know, Cassie and Hana.'' He casually raised one arm and let it drop around her shoulders.

She stiffened, but he squeezed her upper arm and gave a shake of his head. He kept his broad body solidly between her and the pack of young hoodlums. ''Will you wash Cassie and Hana's hair? I didn't find shampoo with their stuff in the bunkhouse. I have a bottle in my shaving kit, if you need it.''

''Uh…I have shampoo.'' Miranda found it difficult to speak. Her heart had begun to race as the warmth from his body seeped through her jacket. He certainly couldn't be feeling what she was, otherwise he wouldn't be chatting so matter-of-factly.

''It's a travesty to call what I found in those kids' dressers clean clothing. Gray is the universal color of their underwear. Makes me furious when I think about those so-called houseparents.''

Miranda hiked a shoulder in an attempt to put more of her collar between her face and Linc's rumbling chest.

"It's a damn wonder those kids didn't freeze last winter. Did I mention there's no heat in the bunkhouses? No bathroom, either. The only halfway clean clothes I found for them are pathetically thin.'' Linc cleared his throat. "If I ever catch up to anyone at the top echelon of Oasis, somebody'll have to bail me out of jail.''

"Are you planning to meet with them tomorrow?'' Miranda couldn't help feeling uneasy at the prospect. She didn't doubt that Jenny and the crew would abandon Wolfie and the girls if something happened to detain Parker.

"I have no idea where their office is. I am planning to contact Social Services for our area. Wolfie and Cassie should be in school. All three of them need the stability of a real home.'' His anger was evident. "Kids their age need a mom and a dad.''

"I agree, but take their cases and multiply by a thousand.''

Startled by Randi's insight, Linc realized with a guilty start that it was inappropriate to discuss the children's welfare with her, even if she was older than he'd first thought. He released her immediately.

"If Scraps has sniffed enough car tires, you'd better go on inside. I'll hang around out here for a bit. Just to make sure those characters don't decide to make trouble.''

If Randi felt his decision was odd or abrupt, she didn't say so. "Scraps will nose around as long as I let him. He had a good home at one time, I think, from the way he hopped up on the bed before we went to the restaurant.

He put his nose on his paws and didn't attempt to follow us.''

"Did you try to find his owner?"

"You wouldn't ask that if you'd seen the shape he was in the day I found him. He'd been kicked. And starved. Still, he had manners. That impressed me. I figure that anyone who'd beat a defenseless little terrier doesn't deserve to have a pet. So Scraps is mine now, aren't you, boy?" Bending over, she rubbed his sides vigorously. The dog rolled onto his back and stuck his feet in the air, begging for a belly rub. Miranda laughed and hauled him into her arms.

Linc watched as the two exchanged kisses. That only seemed to magnify Randi's womanly attributes and stirred the most masculine part of his anatomy, so he pounded on her door until Jenny rushed to let them in.

"Good night," he told her sharply, turning away. Linc rammed his key card in his own lock. Then he waited, because hers hadn't closed. "Why aren't you inside?"

Faint frown lines formed between Miranda's brows. "I, uh, thought you'd check on the boys and then poke your head in and say good night to Cassie and Hana."

"Right." Linc snapped his fingers. "In fact, I have a rain slicker in the wheel well. I planned to put it between Hana's sheet and mattress. If, as Wolfie claims, she has accidents every night, something waterproof may save the mattress."

"Oh. Good idea. So...will you bring it? Or shall I go with you to the SUV?"

"You go supervise the bath. I'll fetch the slicker. I'll tap three times as a signal. That way there's no reason to open the door for anyone else."

"Who else would knock at our door?"

"You never know." His irritation spiking again, Linc

practically bit her head off. "Good grief, Randi, that ought to be common practice for a woman traveling the country alone."

She tossed her head defiantly. "I have Scraps. And friends. I'm *not* alone."

Linc, well aware that he'd overreacted again, excused himself. Damn, what was there about her that raised his protective hackles? As no clear answer presented itself, he took his sweet time retrieving the slicker.

It was Jenny who opened the door and let him in. "That's Hana's side of the bed." She pointed to one of the two queens in the room. "Randi's in the bathroom washing their hair. She asked if you'd spread the slicker over the mattress for us."

"Sure." Linc stripped back the sheet and arranged the yellow slicker across a spot where he thought Hana's bottom might end up. "It sort of crackles," he said after restoring order to the sheet and blankets. "I hope the noise doesn't keep the kids awake all night."

"Is that you, Parker?" Randi called. Her voice sounded hollow, as if her head was underwater.

He stepped into the next room and saw she'd shed her jacket. She'd rolled up her sleeves, showing the curve of pale slender arms.

From the way the two children giggled and splashed in the bubbles, it was no wonder her voice had sounded muffled. Linc couldn't contain a chuckle of his own, watching their antics.

"You mentioned bringing shampoo?" Randi said. "Jenny and I are both almost out. I mixed what we had together for the girls. I don't know when these two last had their hair washed. Not recently, I'm guessing."

"I'll go get you my bottle. It's only a travel size."

''My hair is so short now, I don't need much.'' She ran a soapy hand over her short curls.

Linc envisioned her with long hair and suddenly backed from the room. He made a point of not seeing her the next time. Instead, he passed the bottle of shampoo to Jenny and prepared to withdraw.

She yanked it out of his hand. ''Thanks. I hope Randi hurries up. I'm tired, but I can't shower until she finishes. I suppose the guys are flaked out already.''

''I'm about to go see. Lock up as soon as I leave. Oh, and just knock on the wall if you need me for anything during the night.''

''Like what?''

''Like if Hana has a nightmare. Or if she really soaks the bed, you girls may want someone to run up to the office for dry sheets.''

''I'll tell Randi. I did my time playing mom, Parker. I'm never having kids, you know. They're a royal pain in the ass.''

Linc pretty much echoed her sentiment. However, he drew back politely and watched her close the door without comment. He carried away an image of Randi playing mother. Only in his fantasy, she wasn't acting... Shaking off the alarming thought, Linc all but ran down the walkway. He knocked far too hard on the boys' door.

Wolfie yanked it open. ''Sheesh, be quiet. Whaddaya want? I'm watchin' TV. All those dudes are sleepin'. Is Hana okay? Dang, I knew she'd sop the bed or bawl her head off.'' Sighing, the scrawny kid hitched up his too-large pants and started to step outside barefoot, regardless of the frosty night.

''Hey, hey. This cement's like ice. Your sister and Cassie were happily drying off after a bath when I checked. I came to see how you four are doing. If the others are out for the count, you might follow their lead,'' he said pointedly.

"I ain't sleepy. And this TV's cool. I ain't got to watch any shows in forever. Well, not since I come to Rascal Ranch.''

Linc glanced at his watch. "At this hour there's probably nothing on that's suitable for a kid your age.''

"It's a cop show. It's almost over. Please, can I stay up and see the end? I hardly ever go to bed this early 'cause Hana has trouble fallin' asleep.''

Linc grinned at hearing a tough kid like Wolfie employ the word *please*. "All right. See the end. But then it's lights out. I'm setting my alarm so we can get an early start. Oh, and about Hana—don't worry tonight. Randi promised to look after her.''

"Wow, okay! So what time should I be up? Four o'clock or five?''

Linc's jaw dropped. "More like seven or seven-thirty. The stores won't open before ten. If we get everyone moving by eight, I figure that'll give us plenty of time to eat breakfast next door before we check out.''

"Seven? Are you kiddin'? Mr. Tucker always had me up choppin' the morning firewood by five. I ain't never slept to seven.'' He stared past Linc toward the neon restaurant lights. "Do you think they have biscuits? The house mom we had when we first got to the ranch used to make biscuits once in a while. They was real good.'' He rubbed his thin belly and licked his lips.

"The restaurant's specialty is breakfast. They probably serve biscuits.'' Linc backed away and motioned for Wolfie to shut his door.

A few minutes later, as he let himself into his own room, Linc's mind wandered. Lord, he hoped those poor tadpoles landed in a foster home that served biscuits often. And where no boy of Wolfie's age would be expected to be up at 5:00 a.m. chopping wood. Linc's gut burned just thinking about such gross mistreatment.

Hana's crying woke him in the dead of night. Actually it felt like he'd barely drifted off. He'd stayed up late making phone calls. If it hurt to open his eyes, it was his own fault.

Finally finding the lamp switch, Linc struggled into cold jeans. He half expected a knock on his wall, and he pawed around for his shirt before he recalled wadding it up and stuffing it in his duffel. He'd planned to wear a fresh one in the morning.

Boy, did that kid have a set of lungs. He'd probably have to drag Wolfie out to deal with her, otherwise she'd wake half the motel. Linc had no idea what they'd do if she got the lot of them tossed out at…2:00 a.m.?

Groaning, he heard a toilet flush. Then water ran for a bit. All at once, as he was pulling on his second boot, the crying stopped. He swallowed his yawn while listening to low murmurs on the other side of the wall.

His fingers began closing shirt buttons he was too tired to see. He sat for a moment, waiting. His wall-mounted heater kicked on as Linc strained to hear movement next door. Soon the heater shut off. All seemed quiet next door. He debated whether or not he should go tap on the girls' door to satisfy his curiosity. But he decided to recline against the pillows for a minute first. The last thing he remembered was deciding to stay dressed while he waited for the next siege.

Slamming doors and laughter pulled him once again from sleep. Bolting upright, Linc was shocked to see sunlight filtering in through blackout curtains that didn't quite meet in the middle. He leapt from bed and dragged both hands over a chin scratchy with stubble. He reached for

the curtain to look out, but was halted by a commotion at
his door. "What the hell?" He fumbled with the locks and
yanked it open wide.

Randi stood grinning up at him. Hana—or at least it
looked like Hana with shining reddish hair and a scrubbed
cherub face—hopped up and down next to Cassie's wheelchair. That girl, too, had been transformed into a radiant
child with long dark hair tied up in pigtails with bright
pink bows that matched the shirt peeking from beneath a
tattered sweater.

"Good morning, sleepyhead," Randi chirped. She
passed a steaming, aromatic take-out cup of coffee under
his nose, deliberately looking Linc up and down. "Jeez,
Linc, you look like something Scraps dragged in."

"Good. Because that's how I feel. Give me that coffee."
He lunged for the cup and popped off the lid. Closing his
eyes, he took a long satisfying swallow. "What makes you
all so cheerful at this unholy hour?"

"Not a morning person, are we?" Randi cooed. "Wolfie said you wanted to get an early start. It's coming up on
eight."

"No way!" Linc shot a cuff on his now-wrinkled clean
shirt and went so far as to shake his watch next to his ear.
His expression said he didn't believe his eyes.

Randi merely smiled and nodded her dark spiky curls.
The color shone jet-black next to her creamy cheeks. It
crossed Linc's mind that she'd colored her hair again.

"Where are the boys?" he asked, instead of commenting on her hair, which wasn't really any of his business.

"They're watching some rerun on TV. Jenny begged
for a few extra winks, so Cassie, Hana and I walked up to
the office to get coffee." If there was anything Miranda
loved, it was a huge bracing cup of coffee in the morning.

"I heard you up once during the night with Hana.

Then…'' Linc shook his head. ''That's the last thing I recall.''

Randi ran her fingers through Hana's bright curls. ''We had a visit from those nasty old night monsters. But we kicked them out and told them not to come back, didn't we, honey?''

The child smiled shyly up at Linc. ''Randi did. Kicked 'em out. Then I went potty, and…and…I didn't wake up no more, 'cause I didn't wet my bed.''

''For that, I think Hana deserves a special treat at breakfast. We are fixin' to eat, aren't we?'' Miranda asked.

''Absolutely. Give me a minute to run a razor over my face and hop in the shower.'' Again Linc rubbed the bristles. He felt Randi giving him the once-over, and he saw an altogether too astute appraisal in her smoky eyes.

''You guys go round everyone up. And pack your stuff,'' he added. ''I'll shower fast. Be ready to go to the restaurant in fifteen minutes.'' He shut the door in their faces. However, the calculation in Randi's eyes set off warning bells in Linc's sleep-fogged brain. He needed that shower—a cold one—to shock his brain back on track. Still, he hadn't been out of the dating circuit so long that he didn't recognize feminine interest when he saw it. And that had been interest in Randi's eyes. Twenty-six, she'd claimed to be. *Damn!* That wasn't a complication he needed.

Outside Lincoln Parker's tightly closed door, Miranda stood for a minute with her nose almost touching the wood. She tried to digest what had just happened between her and Parker. Something knee-knocking, that was for sure.

Belatedly regaining her composure, she stepped back, sucked in a deep breath and fanned her hot cheeks.

''What's wrong, Randi?'' Cassie tugged on Miranda's

sleeve. "Shouldn't we wake Jenny? Mr. Parker said we had fifteen minutes. If somebody's late and he gets mad, he might not buy us breakfast."

The worry Miranda saw pinching the narrow little face, coupled with real fear blinking out from behind the round glasses, forced Miranda's mind off what had just happened between her and Linc.

"Oh, sweetie, Mr. Parker told Wolfie we'd get breakfast. He doesn't strike me as a man who'd go back on his word."

Cassie hunched her narrow shoulders. "Lots of people make promises to kids, and then they do somethin' else."

"We will eat," Randi said, staunchly sticking up for Linc.

And they did. He breezed out barely two minutes later than his requested fifteen. All the kids surrounded his door. He deliberately avoided making eye contact with Randi, instead asking, "Anybody in this group hungry?"

A chorus of yes almost bowled him over, Shawn's louder than the rest. "I'm plain starved. I hope I get at least six pancakes."

Linc spared a glance for a boy he already feared was a bottomless pit. Perhaps Shawn had gone without food for so long that his urge to eat his fill when offered the chance overpowered his good sense. "If there's not enough in one order, Shawn, we'll order for a second round. Because after breakfast we're going shopping. It's a fact there's nothing that saps a man's energy more than shopping."

"Girls can shop for hours, even days on end," Jenny said. "It's the most fun to shop for cool clothes and things, though. What are we going to buy today?"

"I have a long list." Linc shooed them in the direction of the restaurant. "We'll divide it up after we put in our food order."

Eric scowled. "Divide the list? How, when none of us has any money?"

"Well, Eric, I plan on giving you some."

"You mean you're, uh, gonna trust us with cash?"

Linc opened the door to the restaurant, holding it to let the kids pass. He looked each of them in the eye before asking Eric softly, "Is there some reason I shouldn't trust you?"

"No. No reason, man." Eric threw back his shoulders.

"What are you gonna be doing if we're buying supplies?" Greg posed the question after they'd all sat.

Linc was glad the usual morning breakfast crowd had cleared out. They had the dining room virtually to themselves. "I have some big-ticket items to order, like baseboard heaters, a dishwasher and new mattresses. Those, of course, will have to be shipped. You kids will purchase the things we'll take home today. Groceries, cleaning supplies, maybe some warmer clothes. Oh, and feed. I have some horses due to be delivered at the end of the week. We'll need grain to get us by until the bulk hay and oats arrive. By spring I'm hoping we'll have fields of sweet grass to turn the horses out in."

"Did you order fertilizer?" Eric shifted in his seat several times, obviously uncomfortable with the tide of the conversation.

"I did. I have a friend who farms out near Bakersfield. He gave me a rundown on what to order and who to order from. If you have experience spreading fertilizer or planting trees, that's a plus I hadn't counted on."

"I can plow furrows and spread cow manure," Eric said. "But I'll tell you what I told my old man. I'm a musician, not a farmer."

"I understand your stay at the ranch isn't permanent,

Eric. In fact, you're free to leave any time.'' He glanced up and greeted the waitress who'd come to take their order.

After she left, Linc pulled out Randi's original list and removed a small notebook from his shirt pocket. ''For those of you who intend to stay and help out at the ranch, I'll split this list among you.''

All but Eric raised their hands.

''Jenny. Shawn.'' Eric scowled at them. ''We made a pact. We're going to spend this winter writing songs and composing new arrangements. Come spring, we'll cut a demo CD somehow. Then we'll make the rounds of producers again.''

Miranda gnawed on the inside of her cheek. She wished she'd known about this plan before she'd hooked up with them. Making the rounds of music studios was the very last thing she wanted to do.

Jenny pouted. ''Eric, you promised we could stay here till spring. You know how scummy the L.A. shelters are.''

''Yeah, Eric.'' Shawn reached eagerly for the plate the waitress held out to him. ''I'm all for going back by April...or so. But if Mr. Parker's gonna let us leave whenever we decide, then I vote we bunk at the ranch and help out with chores for a while.''

Eric brushed aside his dangling dreadlocks. ''You stupid jerks don't have any idea what it's like shoveling a mountain of cow shit into the back of a spreader. It's backbreaking work that can kill a guy young. My uncle kicked the bucket at thirty-three. He fell over in the middle of hooking the harrow up to his tractor.''

Linc waited until everyone had been served before he broke into their argument. ''Eric, the state welfare office wouldn't let me make the ranch a homeless teen haven if I planned to work you kids so hard you keel over. I want this to be a good experience for all concerned.''

Eric glowered as he dug into his pancakes.

"However, I expect you to pull your weight if you want to eat like Shawn prefers to eat. I explained how the ranch will pay its way. Let me be clear on another thing. I'm not running a jam site for would-be musicians. My bunkhouses are to be used for sleep and relaxation. Not all residents will share your taste in music. So I want your word. During the time you spend at Felicity's Refuge, which is what I'm renaming the ranch, I'll expect an honest day's work for a nominal wage and three daily nutritional meals."

"A wage?" Greg's head shot up.

"How much?" Eric reluctantly asked. "I didn't know we'd get paid. Maybe it won't hurt to stick around. We can build a nest egg that'll let us book time in a real recording studio. That'd be cool."

Linc held up a hand. "I don't care what you do after you leave the ranch. But while you're here, I'd rather you spend your free time reading or learning more marketable skills than strumming a guitar."

Eric snorted. He might have objected had Jenny and Shawn not both talked at once. Shawn, being louder, won out. "So, Eric, you're saying we can stay and pool our funds? There'll be time later to put together a plan for our music."

Eric swallowed half his meal and washed it down with a full glass of milk while the others waited, silently darting him glances. They all cheered when he eventually gave his consent to stay for a while.

Linc, too, breathed a sigh of relief. He knew why Greg hadn't said much. The boy had a different goal. But Randi had been surprisingly quiet. Did that mean she was toying with the idea of leaving sooner rather than later?

His breakfast was suddenly hard to swallow.

CHAPTER SIX

LINC PAID for their breakfast. Outside, he gathered the kids to talk about the shopping that needed to be done. "I'd like you older boys to handle buying feed." He peeled off several hundred-dollar bills and told them how much to order. "Ask the clerk to have the bags stacked in the loading bay by three. We'll drive the Excursion over there and load them ourselves."

"Are Jenny and I buying groceries and cleaning supplies?" Randi asked. "Oh, but if we all go, what about Scraps? We can't take him into the store."

Linc glanced over the list yet again and handed it to her with a wad of cash. "You take Cassie and Hana. Leave the dog. Roll the two back windows down far enough so he'll get plenty of air. We'll be coming and going. He'll be fine.

"Jenny, here's what I thought we'd order in the way of bedding and housewares. The department store is directly across from the market. Wolfie, you tag along with Jenny and help her carry things to the car. I hope we can park centrally. I'm keeping one key and I'll give Eric the spare. Once you boys finish at the feed store, give Randi a hand loading groceries. Remember we need to pack wisely, so there'll be room for all of us and our purchases on the trip home."

Accepting the key, Eric shoved it in a baggy pocket near

the bottom of his wide-legged pants. "Man, what are you gonna be doin' while you have us toting and loading?"

"Ordering heaters, mattresses and a dishwasher. I also hope to stop at an employment agency. We need a house-keeper-cook in the worst way."

"We sure do. No problemo. Me and the guys can walk to the feed store. Shawn needs to wear off a dozen pancakes, anyway." Eric gave his friend a poke to the midsection. Shawn cuffed his arm in return.

Linc watched their clowning with some trepidation. He wondered if he'd made a mistake expecting so much from them. But he had a second errand. One he'd rather handle alone. As well as the employment agency, he wanted to drop by the office of Social and Community Welfare Services.

They piled into the SUV with a lot of good-natured bickering. Wishing he had earplugs, Linc drove along the main shopping street in town and easily found a parking space between the grocery and department stores.

"Do any of you own a watch?" Surprisingly, all five of the older ones did. "Good. It's ten-thirty now. Is everyone comfortable meeting here at one o'clock? Maybe while some of you load supplies, someone else can walk Scraps in the park. See it there in the next block?"

"What are we gonna do for lunch?"

Linc laughed outright. No one else seemed surprised at Shawn's focus on his stomach. Except that Greg made gagging sounds.

"Jeez," Shawn complained, "since when is there a law against asking about food?"

Linc studied the clearly disgruntled and overweight boy. "I thought we'd grab a bucket of chicken and some side orders before we leave town. But I think I saw a barbecue on the patio back home. If you'd prefer, we can toss some-thing on the grill. I'm fine with either.''

Wolfie, who'd been remarkably quiet up to now, drew their attention to an ice-cream parlor sign midway down the block. ''I'd give up lunch for ice cream. Hana and Cassie, too. Right?'' He, of course, got the reply he wanted.

Linc noted the sparkle in all three pairs of eyes—an excitement that was dashed when the teenage boys shouted down Wolfie's idea. They were all for the chicken.

''A little ice cream won't ruin your appetites,'' Linc said. ''In fact, if you kids finish your chores before I get back, one of you will surely have enough money left to treat everybody to cones.''

Randi got a collective agreement from the others. Linc could no longer lump her in with the teens, and while he understood her leadership role, he wasn't sure how he felt about it.

He hadn't bargained for the age discrepancies among his tenants. The first thing he had to do after ordering the appliances was find out if Social Services had a solution to the Oasis Foundation's screwup. Those poor little tykes. He wasn't qualified or prepared to work with children that young, so there was no way he could let them stay on at the ranch. But dammit, kids deserved to be wanted.

Randi perused her list again and again, alternately checking the ones Eric and Jenny had. ''We'll never fit us and all these things into the Excursion. There's not a lot of cargo room.''

Linc opened the hatch. He and all the kids eyeballed the area. ''She's right,'' Linc said, slamming it shut again. ''Now what?''

''You've got a trailer hitch.'' Eric kicked it with a toe. ''I bet you could rent a trailer.''

"I wonder if they sell them at the feed store," Linc mused aloud. "I foresee plenty of times we'll need to haul larger stuff. Will you three investigate that possibility? Jot down prices. If you find a decent size for a good price, tell them I'm interested."

"Will do." Eric wrote himself a note.

Linc watched them scatter. He felt good about the way they all seemed to accept responsibility.

It took less time than he'd figured to place his order and arrange for delivery. The employment office was a different matter.

"I realize my ranch is secluded. But I'm offering room and board plus a salary. Surely there's some nice woman around who can cook, likes kids and needs to supplement her retirement income or something."

The counselor had begun to sound as exasperated as Linc felt. "There's more to employing someone in this day and age, Mr. Parker."

"I explained why I can't give two days a week off, Mrs. Sievers. I'll have teens there seven days a week. Kids don't eat just five out of seven days."

"Well, there's also the matter of health insurance. And transportation. Those are perks we guarantee our clients, Mr. Parker."

Linc got to his feet. "It's funny. In all the Western movies I've seen, ranchers hire loyal cooks who practically become part of the family."

"You said you'd lived and worked in Hollywood, so I should think you'd know how much they exaggerate."

"Would you just look at your applications again and see if you missed anyone?"

"I know who's in my files. I'm sorry. Perhaps if you stop at the newspaper and advertise privately, Mr. Parker, you'll have more success. I'm not promising it will be different, though. To be honest, domestic jobs are almost impossible to fill. Most women wanting to work outside the home are seeking a break from kids and kitchen. Hence the high turnover in those jobs. That's the main reason our agency doesn't actively go in search of household positions."

"But you're the only agency in town. Are there no poor grandmotherly types living here?"

"Modern grandmothers are busy playing bridge or golf. Or else they're traveling the world to keep from getting trapped raising their grandkids."

Thinking back, Linc wondered if his grandmother felt trapped when the juvenile-court judge asked her to serve as guardian for him and his sister. Flamboyant, freethinking Grandmother Welch. Money slipped through her fingers with the ease of sand sifting through an hourglass. He didn't want someone like her or the Tuckers. He needed a person who liked kids, had a work ethic and would consider the ranch home.

If the agency couldn't help him, he had no choice but to advertise. The trip to the newspaper office took quite a while. He walked quickly back to the Excursion to tell the kids he had one more errand. All that greeted him was an overzealous dog with muddy paws. He knew the kids had been back. Also, the Excursion overflowed with packages. Grocery bags were stuffed between the rows of seats. He could see a cookbook in one bag, and that made him smile. Yet the kids were missing—unless they'd gone for ice cream. He checked his watch and hoped that would occupy them another twenty minutes. "Stay," he told the dog.

The welfare office was approximately two blocks away. He jogged there and arrived out of breath. Linc peered through the window, smoothing back his wind-tossed hair. He straightened his shirt cuffs before going in. A couple of families sat in wood chairs ringing the waiting area. A very young woman rocked a new baby. A creaky senior citizen occupied a seat across from a stern-looking woman in a glassed-in office. The director, Mrs. Bishop? With any kind of luck.

Another young woman sat behind what must be the reception desk. She wore a hands-free phone headset and chewed gum a mile a minute as she talked to someone on the line.

Linc crossed to stand before her. She was giving someone directions to the office. He glanced worriedly at his watch. He'd used up seven minutes so far.

Finally she said goodbye and turned her attention to Linc.

"I've recently bought a ranch in the area," he said. "A place formerly owned by the Oasis Foundation."

She gave him a blank stare. Linc tried again to forge a link. "Oasis ran a group home of sorts for children awaiting adoption. Little children," he added. "I'm converting the facility to house teenagers, former street kids."

"Yeah? So where is this place? Are you here to apply for a state license?"

Linc delivered a patient smile. "I have a license. What I need is to talk to your director about finding homes for three children Oasis left behind."

"No kidding? You mean they just left them?"

"Exactly. And I'm not providing services for anyone under the age of thirteen. These children are ten, seven and four."

"And your ranch is where?"

Linc withdrew a business card he'd had made up with his name and the address. He didn't list the property as Rascal Ranch since he planned to rename it. Only, he wasn't sure what was involved in that, either. Anyway, at the moment he had more to worry about.

"This property's not in our jurisdiction. Sorry." She handed him back his card.

"But…but…" Linc stuttered a moment before collecting his thoughts. "Susanville is the nearest town."

"Can't help it." The girl cracked her gum loudly and depressed the key on a phone panel, which had begun flashing. "Over on the north wall is a jurisdictional map. The green stars show where the branch offices are. Find the one closest to your address."

Linc whirled to look at the wall. "Uh…thanks." He lost no time making his way there. To reach the wall, however, he practically had to climb over another family who'd come in and taken seats directly below the map. "Excuse me," he muttered.

It took several minutes to decipher which stars designated which service areas. Red lines intersected roads, state parks and recreation land, plus rivers. He wasn't certain, but as near as he could tell, Rascal Ranch sat between a river, a recreational property and a star denoting the Social Services office west of the ranch.

Excusing himself to the family again, Linc returned to the reception desk. This time, the girl was dispensing information about food stamps. When she saw him, she covered the mouthpiece and frowned. "This may take a while. Is there something else you need, Mr. Parker?"

"I think my ranch falls within the boundaries of the service area directly south and west of you. Is there a list of office phone numbers and addresses?"

She ducked down and rummaged in a drawer, eventually coming up with a page of numbers. She circled one, then dismissed him perfunctorily and picked up her conversation where she'd left off. Linc mouthed a thank-you as he folded the paper and pocketed it. He'd call later. Right now, he needed to get back to his charges. He figured he'd left them alone long enough.

AT THE ICE-CREAM SHOP, Miranda took charge of buying cones for the three younger children. Eric paid for the others. Miranda didn't want one. What she did want was a few personal items from a drugstore. Parker hadn't put shampoo, Band-Aids or any health-care products on the grocery list. Nor had it dawned on her until they'd gone back to the SUV and Jenny asked about shampoo.

"Jen, I have money left over after paying for the ice cream. If you'll watch the little kids a minute, I'll dash across to the drugstore and grab what we missed."

"I want to go, too," Jenny said. "I need some, uh, really personal stuff, like tampons," she whispered.

"Tell me what kind and I'll buy them." Miranda started for the door.

"Wait. I don't see why we can't both go. Eric!" Jenny grabbed his arm. "Randi and I are going across the street to the drugstore. If you finish your ice cream and decide to go back to the van before we get back, be sure to take Hana and Cassie."

"I will," Wolfie informed her. "I'm used to lookin' out for them."

"See that you do, okay?" Jenny snapped. "And somebody tell Mr. Parker. We don't want him driving off and leaving us."

"Like I'd tell him to wait for *you*." Wolfie sneered. "I won't let him forget Randi, though."

Eric obviously saw that Jenny was spoiling for a fight. He intervened. "Mr. Parker won't forget. Especially not Randi."

"What's that supposed to mean?" Shawn stopped licking his cone.

Eric acted smug. "Don't tell me you haven't seen how the guy watches her."

"Watches her…how?" Jenny forgot her argument with Wolfie, just as she forgot that Randi stood outside the door waiting impatiently for her.

Eric shrugged. "You know the look. Jeez! I noticed last night at dinner. This morning he showed more interest in our Randi than in his breakfast."

Shawn, who rarely countered Eric, did so now. "You're just trying to make trouble. Mr. Parker knows the score. Why would he screw up what he's trying to build at the ranch by getting too chummy with jailbait?"

Jenny nodded. "Yeah, Eric. I know you don't wanna stay at the ranch this winter. But don't be ruining a good deal for the rest of us. You saw all the stuff Mr. Parker let us buy. He's going to feed us and give us a warm place to sleep."

Greg, not to be outdone, chimed in. "Not only that, Eric. He handed you his car keys and a lot of cash. Name somebody else who'd do that. And you pay him back by calling him a dirty old man?"

Eric simmered. "Go on, Jenny, get outta here. By the way, Shawn and I need disposable razors."

Jenny jerked a thumb. "Randi's the one with money left. I'll tell her."

Armed with the information, Jenny burst out the door. "Have you got enough money left to buy the guys a few things?"

Randi narrowed her eyes skeptically.

"Not what you're thinking," Jenny rushed to say. "Not condoms. Shawn and Eric asked for razors and Greg says they all need deodorant. That's good, especially if we're all going to get cozy in the house until Mr. Parker installs heaters in the bunkhouse.''

Randi laughed. ''I only have fifty dollars. But I suppose Parker—Mr. Parker—would thank us for spending it wisely.'' She broke off laughing abruptly and took a deep breath. To get to the drugstore they had to pass a well-known chain music store. Skidding to a stop, Miranda almost shrieked. In one window stood a life-size cutout of her as Misty. It was an ad for a brand-new CD. The one in the works at the time she left.

Jenny, who'd scampered ahead, glanced back. ''What's keeping you? We probably don't have much time left.'' Jenny stared at Miranda, who had her nose pressed to the window.

Thoroughly shaken, but not wanting her friend to see the likeness, Miranda forced her feet to move forward.

Jenny did notice the store, however. ''Gosh, you wouldn't be considering using Mr. Parker's money on CDs, would you? I mean, he'd shit a brick.''

Miranda hustled Jenny on. ''No, I wouldn't. Use his money that way.''

''I didn't think so. Did you hear Mr. Parker say he'd pay the boys to till his fields?'' She sighed. ''It's not fair to let them earn money and not us.''

Breathing somewhat easier as they entered the drugstore, Miranda feigned interest in the shelves. All she really wanted to do was get what they'd come for and hope to heaven Parker was ready to leave town.

''You're acting funny.'' Jenny had paused at the perfume counter where she tried in vain to capture Randi's attention.

Still shaken, but determined to avoid potential pitfalls, Miranda snatched up a basket and addressed Jenny's remark about earning money. "Maybe he'll hire us to work with the boys. That way we can earn money, too."

"Plowing is hot smelly work, I bet. I'd like to earn some bucks, but I don't think I'd be any good at clearing fields."

"We could cook and keep house. I wish we'd thought of it earlier. Didn't Mr. Parker say he was going to stop at an employment agency?"

"Are you nuts? I told you I can't cook. I mean, I actually burn water. Ask Eric."

"I can cook, Jenny. And I presume you can run a vacuum and make beds."

Jenny wrinkled her nose. "I told you I was responsible for practically raising four brothers and sisters."

"And you didn't cook?" Miranda raised an eyebrow as she scooped a couple of items into her basket.

"I microwaved macaroni and cheese, canned spaghetti and soup. Lots of soup. Oh, and we ate tons of cereal."

"Didn't you ever get tired of eating the same old stuff?"

"Sure, but it was cheap. As it was, I had to fight my mother for her welfare check before she spent it all on booze. Look, I did the best I could."

"I'm sorry, Jen. Living like that must have been rough for you and your brothers and sisters."

"That's why I want to make it as a singer. I'd live on easy street and never have to worry about being cold or hungry. The really hot babes live in million-dollar mansions. They bop around the country staying in five-star hotels. I mean, how hard is singing an hour or so a day, you know what I mean?"

A shiver walked its way up Miranda's spine. "That is so off the mark, Jenny."

"Right. Like you're an authority. Tell me you feel sorry

for Britney or Christina or that rapper, Nelly. They're laughing all the way to the bank.''

Miranda saw deep waters ahead. She ought to shut up rather than plunge in up to her eyeballs. She ought to. ''You've named stars who are at their peak today. Where will they be in five years? In ten?''

''Who cares? They'll have made their money.''

''Maybe a few. What about the singers who crack up, go repeatedly into rehab or even commit suicide? Then there are the performers who are bilked out of their fortunes by crappy managers. Oh, and don't forget the ones who fritter away what they did make trying to remain forever young. It's a tough business, Jenny.''

''I don't care.'' Jenny flounced down the aisle toward the cashier. ''Eric is real smart. Sure, he smokes a little weed now and then to…to help expand his creativity. We've talked about hitting it big, touring for a year or so, then quitting so we can enjoy life. Y'know what I mean?''

''Dream on,'' Miranda muttered, too low for Jenny to really hear.

''Hey, look at this cool nail polish. Silver and gold glitter. Can we afford to buy one of each?''

Miranda turned from unloading the basket at the counter. ''I don't want to use Parker's money frivolously.''

''What's the difference between nail polish and that package of barrettes you grabbed back there? I saw you, so don't deny it.''

''I won't deny it. Those are for Cassie and Hana. The pack was on sale for fifty-nine cents and gives the girls three sets each. Did you see how happy they were last night just to have me wash and brush their hair? Poor kids, they've had precious little attention. This morning when I cut my pink hair ribbon in half and tied up Cassie's pigtails, you'd have thought I'd given her a gold mine. Hana wanted ribbons, too. She looked so resigned when I said I only had one ribbon. I almost cried.''

Jenny set the polish back on the shelf. ''You're getting too attached to the kids, Randi. That's not good. Mr. Parker's gonna boot 'em out as soon as he can. And what if their next foster parents don't spoil them with pretty things? Chances are they won't.''

''Maybe Parker's softer than he wants us to think. I saw he had you buy the girls underwear. I know he was horrified because theirs was so old and gray.''

''Oh, you do live in la la land. Don't forget I knew his sister. She was pathetic in so many ways. Felicity *bought* people's affection. Why? Because her big brother couldn't be bothered. He was too busy hustling a buck.''

Miranda paid the cashier. ''Can't you see how bad he feels about that? It's why he bought the ranch. People change.''

''Eric says guys like Lincoln Parker don't change their stripes. Once a skunk, always a skunk.''

Grabbing her purchases, Miranda headed out. ''It may come as a surprise, Jenny, but Eric doesn't know everything.''

That comment shut the younger girl up. And like a normal teen, she immediately skipped on to another subject nearer and dearer to her heart. ''Let's stop at that record shop we passed.''

''You don't have money to buy anything.'' Miranda couldn't let Jenny go back there. Seeing her cutout had been a shock, especially as it showed her wearing the outfit she'd had on at her last performance. And judging by the pose, the way her eyes were closed and the look of anguish on her face, Wes must've had someone take the photo during her last song, ''A Cowboy at Heart,'' the one she'd written to honor her dad. She'd felt genuine anguish. And who knew what likeness was on the CD cover? Eric was sharp when it came to remembering songs and artists. Even though he threatened to puke at the mention of country, that didn't mean he wasn't up on what was popular.

While she was trying to figure out how to dissuade Jenny, deliverance came in the form of Linc Parker.

The minute they stepped out of the drugstore, he called to them from across the street. "Randi, Jenny. Where are the others? I thought you were all going for ice cream."

Randi waved, grabbed Jenny's sleeve and began pulling her across the street. "We remembered some drugstore items that weren't on the grocery list. The boys are watching the little kids. Look, they're coming out of the ice-cream shop now."

Jenny jerked loose from Randi's grip. "You don't have to haul me along like I'm Hana's age. If you ask Mr. Parker, I'll bet he'd let us browse in the record store," she hissed.

"I'm not asking. It's getting late. You know the mess we left. I think we ought to get under way. Otherwise we'll be up half the night scrubbing."

"That's not up to us. Sheesh, you act like it's our ranch. Yours, anyway."

"I do not. Maybe *you* don't have a problem sleeping in dirty places. I do."

"Sometimes you don't act like the rest of us. Sure, it's a mess, but the house has heat and a roof. That's heaven compared to some of the spots me and the guys have bunked in."

Miranda's mouth opened and shut several times. She had to think about how a truly homeless person might react to Jenny's accusation. "Uh…did you hear me complain on our trek north? I slept at rest stops, on picnic benches, right alongside you."

"I know. I'm sorry for ragging on you, Randi." Jenny scuffed her toe. "Do you ever wish…you could live like normal people? I hate getting yelled at for trying to wash in public rest rooms by someone who has no idea what it's like to go for days without hot water. And there's the looks we get when we hang out at fast-food restaurants, just praying some rich kid will toss out half of a perfectly good hamburger."

Miranda's stomach lurched. The truth was, she *couldn't* relate. But since she'd hooked up with Jenny and her friends, she really was trying to understand. "When Social Services took your brothers and sisters, why didn't you let them help you?"

"Help me how? The caseworker said I'd missed so much school I'd have to go back to ninth grade. And let those rich snots make fun of me for being dumb? Gimme a break."

Having successfully crossed the street without getting run over, they stopped talking when they reached the other side. Parker had gone into the ice-cream shop and now came out pushing Cassie's wheelchair. He joined the others.

"You sure were gone a long time if you only bought what's in that dinky sack," Shawn complained to Randi and Jenny. "We didn't sign on to baby-sit, you know."

Linc relieved Randi of the sack under discussion. He winked at Shawn as he set the sack on Cassie's lap. "Let that be a major lesson about women, fellows. There is no such thing as a quick trip to a store."

"That's because men expect women to handle all their shopping. For food, clothes, gifts and anything else that crops up." Miranda stuffed her change in the breast pocket of his shirt. "Receipts for what I spent are in the respective bags."

Seeing her, Eric dug in his pocket and pulled out cash wrapped in a cash-register receipt. "This accounts for what we spent at the feed store. We didn't get a slip for the ice cream. It came to under ten bucks, didn't it, Randi?"

Linc waved away the explanation as they went back to the vehicle.

"There's no room for us." Randi, who'd opened the door and started to lift Cassie into her seat, put her back in the wheelchair.

"The feed store has a trailer for five hundred bucks. That'll work."

Linc leaned in past Randi. Their bodies brushed as he arranged the bags and sacks. They both jumped apart as if they'd been burned, and Linc actually wondered if some kind of shock had passed between them. One thing was for darned sure: he hadn't stopped to realize that beneath Randi's bulky jacket, she had breasts. Of course he knew she had them, but...

"Hand me that damned chair," he told Greg, who stood nearest the side door. "We'll make do until we can go pick up the trailer." Ordering Randi to take her seat, Linc proceeded to erect a barrier of sleeping bags between them, beginning with two he plopped in her lap. Without so much as glancing at her, he jammed the chair in at an angle that effectively fenced her off from the driver's seat.

"It's a cinch you don't expect Randi to help load the trailer," Shawn noted.

"I wouldn't even if she could get out. Women and kids have no business lifting fifty-pound bags."

"Boy," Jenny exclaimed, "you just burst Randi's balloon. She hoped you'd give us the same deal you offered the boys to earn money."

Miranda glared. "If I'd had any clue Parker was so sexist, I'd never have suggested it, Jenny."

Jenny snickered.

His feathers more than ruffled, Linc slammed his door and ground the engine when he started it. "Too bad no one ever taught you to keep a civil tongue in your head." Linc stressed the point for two reasons. One to shut Randi up and, two, to clamp a lid on his own wayward thoughts. He was far more aware of Randi-with-no-last-name than he should be.

He probably should've told her just to leave. Now the best he could hope was that whoever answered his ad for a housekeeper turned out to be the eagle-eyed sort. *He* might know Randi was older than her friends, but she wanted to keep the truth from them. That meant he had to squelch any feelings of the type he'd just experienced.

Loading fifty-pound bags of fertilizer and feed was precisely what he needed to wear himself out.

CHAPTER SEVEN

RANDI RECOGNIZED the sexual zing that had accompanied her body's accidental brush with Linc Parker's solid muscles. True, in the past, she'd been too busy with her career to develop any significant relationships. That didn't mean her head was always in the sand, or that she was still a virgin.

In spite of working in close proximity with many male musicians and performers, she could count on two fingers the times she'd felt like this. That was more or less her yardstick for what a good romantic response should be. Neither of the other times had the feeling been as strong or immediate as with Linc Parker—of all people.

Oh, this was bad! Not good at all. Potential problems raced through Miranda's head. She tried with unsteady fingers to buckle her seat belt.

"Need some help with that?"

Her fingers stilled. She dropped the belt the minute he turned around. But she saw that he looked annoyed with her.

Embarrassed and afraid her face showed it, Miranda firmly grasped both ends of the seat belt. The loud snap of the buckle felt better than if she'd given in to the childish inclination to stick her tongue out at him.

Parker had just validated something she'd long suspected. Men who'd looked at her with desire in the past only saw Misty, the wealthy, much-hyped country star.

Plain Miranda Kimbrough didn't stir even basic male hormones.

Not knowing whether to be relieved or chagrined, she withdrew into a corner of her seat and let the others talk on the drive back to the ranch. At the lunch stop, when she and Linc might have engaged in small talk, he busied himself helping the little kids with their chicken, biscuits and coleslaw.

Once they reached the ranch, Linc set up a human chain designed to quickly unload the SUV and the trailer. He barked out cleaning assignments to everyone but Cassie and Hana.

Cassie wheeled her chair right up to Linc's leg. She tugged on his jeans. In the middle of telling the boys where to stack the new bedding and where to dispose of the old sheets, Linc's first response to her insistent tug was a sharp, "What? Can't you see I'm busy?" Then he glanced down, and his face lost all its harshness.

"Oh, Cassie." Instantly he knelt to her level, and Miranda witnessed a huge change in his demeanor. She felt another odd twist in her belly.

"Mr. Parker, I wanna help. Hana, too. I'm strong and Hana's fast. I'll bet we can clean out the bottom kitchen cupboards for Randi and Jenny."

Linc stuttered a bit, saying he didn't want them getting hurt, and that they should try to stay out from underfoot. But deep in the girl's eyes, he saw something that quickly made him relent. A subtle message that said she'd been invisible for too long. Straightening, Linc found his eyes meeting Randi's. Her arms were laden with grocery sacks. Jenny had already disappeared into the kitchen with a load.

"Can you and Jenny use four more hands in the kitchen?" Linc's dark-blond brows dove together, practically daring her to refuse.

She'd never hurt Cassie's feelings. The big dummy couldn't tell that about her? Miranda donned a really warm smile. Not for Linc, but for the two little girls, and she made that plain. "I have the very job for two pairs of helping hands. Cassie, remember the rolls of shelf paper I found on sale today? You and Hana can unroll them so Jenny and I can cut pieces to cover the shelves and drawers once they're cleaned."

Wolfie entered the room in time to hear. As Randi herded the girls toward the kitchen, he spoke up. "I'll help with the shelf paper," he volunteered. "I'm done sweeping the bedroom floors like Mr. Parker asked. That way, if anything happens to the rolls of shelf paper, you can beat me, instead of Hana or Cassie."

Linc and Miranda both spoke at once, Linc more loudly, "Wolfie, I thought I'd made it perfectly clear. No one, and I mean *no one,* lays a hand on you kids while I'm in charge."

The boy's chin wobbled. "I know that's what you said. But big people lie."

"No," Linc repeated firmly. "You have my word, son. I don't know how to say it more clearly. You wouldn't know, but where I lived and worked before, well…people knew they could count on my word."

"Yeah, but in town you went to hire a house mom. What if she's like Mrs. Tucker?"

Linc rubbed the back of his neck, warding off tension. His action had Miranda hesitating at the kitchen door. "Does that look mean you hired someone capable of striking a child?" she asked severely.

"Of course not! I, uh, didn't have any luck hiring anyone. I put an ad in the local paper. I'm sure we'll have candidates calling for interviews before the week is out. I plan to scrutinize every single person and every single reference.''

Miranda passed her sacks to Jenny, who'd come back to see what was keeping her. ''Figures,'' the younger girl muttered sullenly. ''We'll get the placed spiffed up, and the woman you hire won't have anything to do but lie in bed all day.''

''Yes, she will,'' Linc declared. ''Caring for a house this size and cooking for a crowd will never be a piece of cake.''

''Speaking of cake…'' Jenny tossed her head. ''What'll we do about eating until you hire this dynamo?''

The furrows returned to Linc's forehead. ''Keep it simple. Since the boys and I will be out plowing and planting fields, we'll be hungry enough to eat anything. And even I'm capable of making a sandwich or popping wieners in a microwave.''

Jenny rammed her elbow in Miranda's side so hard, she jumped and yelped.

''Remember, we talked about Mr. Parker maybe letting us work so we can get paid like the boys? So ask him,'' Jenny whispered to Miranda.

''We realize you won't let us drive a tractor or anything,'' she told Parker. ''But you mentioned horses. Jenny and I can muck out stalls and feed livestock for money,'' she clarified.

''Somehow I doubt Social Services would be overjoyed to discover I'm letting girls muck out stalls. I'm sure they'll want you learning more marketable skills.''

''Can you call Social Services and inquire?'' Miranda pressed. ''Jenny and I would like to earn enough to buy stuff like cosmetics, books or CDs.''

''Yeah!'' Jenny nodded. ''And like…if this was our real home, we'd hafta do that kinda junk and not get paid.''

Miranda found Parker's brown eyes impossible to read. "Okay, maybe not clean stalls. But between now and when you hire a cook-housekeeper, could you pay Jenny and me, instead? We'll split the chores. Surely Social Services won't object to a temporary situation."

"You're right. Okay, you're hired. I picked up a pay scale for housekeepers at the employment agency today. I'll pay a weekly rate, which you two can split." He dragged back a cuff and studied his watch. "Late as it is, I'll have to wait and phone them tomorrow. I found out the Susanville office doesn't serve our area. In fact, our service area is bigger. And I don't know if that's good or bad," he muttered.

Rather than give him an opportunity to reconsider, Miranda delivered a brisk impersonal smile and hustled her crew into the kitchen. Scraps bounded around her feet, but soon danced off after Hana. Miranda liked how the dog gravitated toward Hana. The two would be good company for each other when Wolfie and Cassie started back to school.

"You shouldn't have said CDs were one of the things we planned to use our money for," Jenny hissed at Randi, who'd begun cleaning cupboards. "Did you see the look on Parker's face? That comment of yours almost blew it for us."

"That's silly, Jenny. If you ask me, he's worried about Social Services pulling his license. Parker isn't against music. Look at the tapes and CDs he has in his SUV."

"You call that mortuary stuff music? No way!"

Miranda grinned. "Lucky for him there's music for all tastes."

"You like rock and hip hop, don't you, Randi? I hope so. Otherwise, when you and I earn enough to buy a compact disc player, it won't be cool if we're always fighting over what to play."

"Actually I'm good with silence," Miranda drawled, hoping Jenny would take the hint to stop talking and start working.

"Wolfie's got a radio," Cassie announced. "He hid it in the woods after Mr. Tucker switched him hard for having it on at night when we were s'posed to be sleeping. Wolfie only played it so Hana wouldn't be scared in the dark."

Jenny brightened. "I'm gonna go find the kid and ask to borrow his radio. Will you ask Mr. Parker to let us have it on while we're scrubbing his dumb old kitchen?"

"You want the radio, you ask him," Miranda said, pausing to wipe a lock of hair out of her eyes with a soapy hand.

"Like Eric said earlier, Parker's got the hots for you, Randi. He looks at me and sees somebody he thinks was involved with his sister's overdose. I swear I wasn't even with Felicity that night. I only went to find her after another friend said she was acting crazy. Eric and me were there when she passed out. We took her to the hospital."

Miranda almost didn't hear all of what Jenny said. Shock had paralyzed her brain at the girl's first sentence. "When did Eric say…that first thing? And why would he?" she demanded.

"Jeez, don't get your panties in a wad. When you'd left the ice-cream shop. The subject came up, is all. I don't remember why. Even if Eric's all wrong, it's definitely true what I said about Parker connecting me to Felicity's overdose."

Miranda tried to brush off Jenny's comment, while at the same time vehemently denying the validity of Eric's remark. But the only way Eric would suspect Linc might be interested in her would be if Eric saw through her. Saw through her attempt to pass herself off as one of them. It was bad enough that she'd told Linc Parker the truth. The more people who knew her real age, the greater the chance of someone linking her face to the image Wes had splashed all over the news.

Only now did she realize how desperately she'd counted on this ranch to provide her with a refuge until she figured out how to get her life back. Somehow she had to find a way to get out from under Wes Carlisle's thumb. But he was so huge in the country-music industry, it seemed impossible.

Miranda didn't like deceiving anyone. Maybe kids like Eric and Jenny didn't see the drawbacks of going through months and years using only a first name. Miranda, however, understood that a person had to be able to produce proof of name, address and birth date if he or she hoped to ever live normally. And living normally was Miranda's goal. Hiding as though she was a thief or worse had become even more distasteful than she'd imagined. Yet the alternative—going back to a life in which Wes controlled her every breath, movement and thought—was more abhorrent. One time she'd been speaking to another of Carlisle's clients and had casually mentioned the possibility of breaking her contract. The male vocalist had told her she was crazy. He said Wes would sue her for breach of contract and wipe her out financially. He also warned that Wes would blackball her in Nashville and see she never sang another note or sold another song. Miranda used to daydream about not performing; she'd liked the idea of making her living writing songs for other country stars. The dream had seemed so hopeless.

Bending over the sink, she threw herself into the task of scrubbing pots and pans. Scraps licked the last morsel of food from his new bowl and found a spot to flop down and sleep.

Jenny soon returned with Wolfie's radio in hand.

Miranda blocked out the sound, retreating within herself. Draining the dirty water and refilling her pail with clean soapy water became rote. The repetitiveness of the chore gave her ample opportunity to dwell on her past.

Next thing she knew, she had her head completely inside a bottom cabinet and the screeching background noise had disappeared. Glad that Jenny had apparently departed to another part of the house with the radio, Miranda smoothed out the back corners of the adhesive shelf paper.

Linc Parker's raspy, "What in God's name are you doing?" caused Miranda to lift her head suddenly and crack it loudly against the top of the cabinet. Rubbing the tender spot on her head, she backed out and found herself on hands and knees staring at Lincoln Parker's dusty cowboy boots. Instantly, all the old feelings she'd poured into her song, "A Cowboy at Heart," overwhelmed her. The man she'd written it for, her father, hadn't been a real cowboy, either. But he'd possessed the qualities. A good heart, courtly manners, honesty and gentleness. He had comforting hands. Growing up without a mom, there were so many times Miranda had relied on a soothing touch from her father's broad steady hand.

Linc extended his now to assist her in standing.

Ignoring it, she grasped the cupboard door, instead, and climbed to her feet unaided. "Did you need something?" she asked. "I have one cabinet left to do. Then they'll all be lined and we can start putting dishes and groceries away."

"Who? You and the mouse in your pocket? It's midnight, Cinderella. Everyone else has turned in. I thought you had, too. I came in to see if there was any coffee left."

They'd taken a break for sandwiches at six-thirty and she'd made a small pot of coffee for Linc.

Miranda blinked at the wall clock she'd washed—three hours ago, she saw. "I didn't realize it was so late. Jenny never said she was going to bed." Still rubbing the lump on her head, Miranda moved slowly down the counter. Someone had shut off the coffeemaker and cleaned it. "The coffee's been dumped. I'll make a new pot. Frankly, something hot and steamy sounds great about now."

Linc studied her backside. The same one he'd viewed moments ago wriggling so attractively out from under a lower cabinet. Forcefully jerking his steamy thoughts away from her curves, he focused on her last statement.

"Better not let the kids see you drinking coffee," he said gruffly. "That'll tip them off that you're not one of them."

"You're mistaken, Parker. Street kids beg coffee just to warm up."

"Huh. No teen I've ever met liked the taste."

"Those who live at home have moms who probably nix it. I guess they don't realize there's more caffeine in some soft drinks."

Linc recalled buying cases of cola for Felicity and her elusive friends. Only now did he question the speed with which the drinks and snacks had disappeared. How many street kids had his sister supplied with food? he wondered.

The coffee began to drip, and Miranda knew she couldn't just stand there and watch it. She had to face Parker and make inconsequential conversation. "If you're not too tired, I could use a hand filling the top shelves. Since you're taller than me, it's easy for you to reach the high places."

For maybe the first time since entering the room, Linc glanced around. "Big difference now from the mess it was.

You and Jenny worked miracles. I've gotta admit I didn't expect this much. Especially after Wolfie admitted giving Jenny the radio responsible for the racket I heard blaring from here. The door doesn't close tight, you know.''

Miranda laughed as she loaded his hands with items she didn't think they'd use frequently and pointed him toward the shelf above the fridge. ''Believe it or not, Jenny's work level improved after she got the radio—when she wasn't stopping to play air guitar, that is. I ought to be used to that by now. Eric plays air guitar so often, strangers think he's spastic. Shawn, too. Not Greg, although he's getting into the music more. Greg fell in with them for the same reason I did.''

''Why that group?'' Linc closed the door on a full cupboard and moved on to the next.

''What?'' Miranda turned from lining up cereal boxes.

''I just wondered why you hooked up with Eric, Jenny and Shawn. It doesn't take a genius to see you have much more on the ball.''

''They're decent, kind and generous.''

He grunted, a skeptical sound.

She smacked canned goods into the pantry. ''I'll bet if you dumped them in with kids who have the advantage of daily showers, three square meals a day and access to Daddy's credit cards, you wouldn't see any difference. Or in your case, it'd be big brother's credit cards.''

Her observation stung and Linc didn't like it.

''Don't presume you know all there is to know about me based on Jenny's version of my sister's life.''

Miranda finished storing the clean dishes, except for two cups, which she filled with coffee. It was probably a dangerous preoccupation, but she was curious about Lincoln Parker. She sensed that his life hadn't been all rosy. ''I picked up packets of sugar substitute and nondairy creamer from the motel. Here, use them if you'd like.'' She dug some smashed packages out of her jeans pocket rather than push past him to get to the fridge. Besides, she wanted to prove she and the kids could be frugal.

''Worried about my waistline, are you?''

''Your wallet,'' she snapped. ''Look, it's a habit I've gotten into from traveling with the kids. Take anything that's free.''

Linc ripped the tops off two packets. ''Nothing is free. The motel owner figures these perks into the price of the rooms.''

''So it's yours by right, then, because you paid for our room.''

Linc shrugged, but continued to study her over the rim of his cup. ''I can't figure you out. You've cleaned these cupboards and organized them with precision. While your pals resemble spooks left over from Halloween, you dress normally.'' He stopped and looked her deliberately up and down. ''Something doesn't add up, Randi. You have a natural confidence. Frankly, I find it hard to picture you as a victim. Suppose you tell me the whole truth.''

Miranda's heart galloped in double time. She stood, drained her cup, then went to rinse it out. ''Don't presume you know all about me on the basis of a few short days.''

''Touché.'' He lifted his cup in salute. ''I'll back off for now. I know one thing—you're a hard worker. I suspect you're responsible for way more of this kitchen transformation than Jenny. And I'm sure Cassie and Hana were more hindrance than help.''

''Actually, they were little troupers. I sent them off to find Wolfie when they both started yawning. The truth is, neither admitted to being tired. They're sweet, delightful children. I can't fathom how anyone could have mistreated or discarded them.''

"I notice you're good with them. If you were telling the truth earlier about having some college, maybe you ought to think about finishing. To, I don't know, be a teacher or a nurse or something. A degree would give you more options. Certainly more earning power."

She shrugged offhandedly. *If only he knew how much she'd earned in a job that had nothing to do with her liberal arts degree.*

"There are scholarships for adults with aptitude. For returning students who want to complete their education."

Miranda nodded, thinking to herself that she wouldn't mind going back to school. She loved reading. Studying in general. Of course, she'd been away from formal schooling for more years than Parker could guess. Although, after her dad died, Wes had provided a tutor because the laws governing young performers were strict.

"Going to college would necessitate staying in one place," Linc said, after taking another swig of his coffee.

And therein lay the real problem. She'd have to not only settle in one spot, but a college would demand ID. Miranda hoped she successfully hid her shiver of concern from Linc. "What's on tomorrow's agenda?" she asked abruptly. The silence that had fallen between them was nerve-racking.

"The boys and I discussed cleaning out one bunkhouse. The salesman at the appliance store promised delivery of the baseboard heaters by noon tomorrow. Oh, and the dishwasher, as well. I ordered a freestanding one with a butcher-board top. That way it'll serve as an extra chopping surface."

"What time do you want breakfast, then?"

Linc frowned. "That's right. You volunteered to cook." He paused. "Can you? Cook, I mean."

"Why would I volunteer for something I couldn't do?"

"For money. It's done all the time in the business world, sweetheart."

Miranda's heart kicked over at his casual use of the endearment. Wes called everyone *sweetheart,* too. The way Linc said it stirred up angry memories. "Then I guess you'll have to reserve judgment until you see if I poison you," she countered in a syrupy voice.

Linc laughed, stood and shut off the coffeepot. "Like I said, I have a hard time imagining that you let anyone run roughshod over you."

"I think I'll turn in," she said, stretching and stifling a yawn before heading out.

His gaze followed her curves, where the light outlined her breasts. His last swallow of coffee stuck somewhere in his throat. "Damn!" he spat, not liking the wild flutters in his stomach.

Outside the kitchen, Miranda heard him swear, and she wondered what had happened. Had he spilled his coffee? Burned himself? Jeez, the man unnerved her. She couldn't afford—wasn't in any position—to investigate the interest he sparked in her. So tonight it was better to leave him alone to remedy whatever ailed him.

LIGHT PEEKING through the uncurtained windows woke Miranda the next morning. The others slept on, uncaring of the hour. Always a fairly early riser, she had rarely used an alarm clock unless her studio recording call had been before ten in the morning.

She slipped into yesterday's shirt and jeans. The lack of clean clothing was what bothered her the most in this disappearing act she'd pulled. Back home she had closets bulging with T-shirts in every color, and jeans in thirty different styles. Now the three sets she'd packed seemed woefully inadequate.

The ranch had two bathrooms, for which Miranda was thankful. This morning, she was happy to find the main one in the hallway unoccupied.

But when she exited after having scrubbed her face and brushed her hair, she ran smack into Parker. He'd obviously showered, shaved and, unlike her, had undergone a complete transformation of clothing. He smelled quietly of soap and a classic scent, like fine leather. She caught just a whiff and was tempted enough to step closer. The scent was subtle, not overwhelming as some men seemed to prefer.

"I thought I was the only one up," he said in a sleepy rasp.

Miranda grinned. "A bear in the mornings, are we, Parker? Don't worry, I'll keep out of your way. I'll slink into the kitchen like a good little cook. Wolfie wants biscuits. They take a while to make. Outside of that, I'd planned to fix oatmeal. Stick-to-your-ribs fare for cleaning bunkhouses. That's hard work."

His gaze raked her once, then twice. "Oatmeal must have been in short supply around your house, skinny as you are."

Miranda realized his eyes weren't on her ribs. There was invitation in his expression. In an involuntary reaction, she skimmed her fingers up the snaps running down the front of his Western-style shirt.

Linc grabbed her hand roughly, his eyes suddenly hard.

His knee-jerk reaction surprised her, and his grip hurt. Emitting a tiny cry, she wrenched loose and dashed into the kitchen.

Feeling like a heel for overreacting, Linc followed. When he caught up, she'd already pulled flour and shortening from the pantry and was reaching to turn the stove on to preheat. A stove she'd scrubbed clean last night.

"Look, Randi, I'm sorry for grabbing you. Did I hurt you?"

"Yes. But it's my fault for touching you. I shouldn't have. It's just…you look good in that shirt, Parker. Really good. And I thought…I thought for a minute that, well, we had a mutual-admiration thing going there."

"We did, dammit." He paced and thrust a hand through his still-damp hair. "I'm not going to lie and say I'm not attracted to you, Randi. I am."

"So what's the problem?" She hesitated momentarily before glancing up from kneading the biscuit mix. "You did believe me when I said I'm twenty-six, right?"

"Oh, I don't doubt your age now. It's this situation we're in. I put my career aside to start this teen retreat. In fact, I put my life on hold. I've already had enough setbacks. What with the little kids being abandoned here, teens showing up early and then your *not* being a teen…" He wheeled and faced her with a scowl. "The refuge isn't about me. It's for my sister."

"And I'm a problem for you?"

"Yes. No. It's just…too important. I can't mess this up. Maybe if you'd agree to tell the others…so I don't have to lie to Social Services."

Miranda battled a surge of panic. "I can't. Please…I just need a little more time. A few months. If you can't see your way clear to letting me stay, I'll leave. Tonight. After all the others go to bed."

Linc slashed a hand through the air. "And go where? Back to the streets? I can't let you do that." He watched her cut the biscuit dough and place the rounds in a baking pan. "At the risk of sounding totally selfish, I need you to help me here. At least until someone answers my ad. It's obvious that you're a capable woman, Randi."

Miranda glanced up from the baking sheet. Boy, he did

look good, so good her heart skipped a beat. "Thanks for that, at least, Parker. I knew from the minute I laid eyes on you that you were a cowboy at heart." It was the greatest compliment she could give.

Pausing, Linc appeared disturbed by her comment. He shoved his hands sheepishly in his pockets. "Know a lot of cowboys, do you?"

"No. But I know from movies and novels what kind of men they are. Cowboys are men a woman can count on. They're bighearted and chivalrous. And they have a…a certain walk." She arched an eyebrow. "You've got the walk, Parker." Miranda might have said more, but she broke off, seeing color rise to his cheeks.

"You're talking fantasy. Too many people wreck their lives believing in fantasy. You'd better start dealing with real life."

He left then, giving her heart a one-two punch. And as Miranda measured the oats and opened a box of brown sugar, it crossed her mind that he'd probably spoken from experience. He'd pulled down big bucks in Hollywood, in a capacity similar to Wesley Carlisle's.

But that was dumb. She would never have described Wes as a cowboy even though he liked to dress the part. True cowboys were good men like her father had been.

Miranda did deal in reality. Most men wouldn't give a second thought to tossing her out on her ear she knew. There was more cowboy in Linc Parker than he apparently cared to admit.

That kind of thinking will get you in trouble, girl!

As she popped the biscuits in the oven, Miranda mulled over the advice Doug Kimbrough might have given her in these circumstances. He'd tell her to go with her gut instinct. In his slow drawl, her dad would declare that she had the brains to know if a man was all foam and no beer.

Just remembering his sage advice made her sad. But...
nothing really held her here. She could pull up stakes and
leave anytime.

The kids straggled in sleepy-eyed, following the scent
of breakfast. The moment Linc joined them for the meal,
Miranda held her breath. Would he rat on her?

But breakfast went off without a hitch. He virtually ig-
nored her, chatting instead with the older boys about the
work that lay ahead.

Readying the bunkhouses for habitation couldn't happen
too quickly to suit Miranda. The sooner she moved to one
of the bunkhouses where she risked fewer encounters with
Parker of the type she'd had in the hallway this morning,
the better her life would be.

"Is it okay if I save some of these biscuits to eat for
lunch?" Wolfie asked, breaking the rare silence that had
fallen over the table.

"As opposed to eating them now?" Miranda inquired.

"It's a long time till supper. If we get supper," Wolfie
said.

Linc made an impatient gesture. "As long as you live
here, son, there'll be food on your plate. That is—" he
shot Miranda a worried glance "—if Randi agrees to cook
until I hire someone."

"Why would she quit?" Jenny paused with a buttered
biscuit halfway to her darkly lipsticked mouth. "You're
paying her, aren't you, Mr. Parker? Has something
changed since we struck our deal last night?"

Miranda and Linc shared a fast guilty look.

Linc read in Randi's eyes a real fear that he'd expose
her. It reminded him too strongly of the absence of trust
he'd sometimes seen in his sister's gaze.

Wanting Randi to view him as the cowboy she'd described earlier, Linc stated lightly, "Let's settle first on

everyone calling me Linc, instead of Mr. Parker. As for pay, I'll be fair. And I don't want you working every blessed hour of the day. How does five hours sound? Randi, keep a close tally of your time. If you go over five because of kitchen duties taking longer, we'll renegotiate.''

She nodded, even though merely looking at him scrambled her breathing. Damn, she had to avoid this man for both their sakes. Why did he have to be so decent, so charming, so...attractive? But she knew her response to him was more than simple physical attraction.

''Fine,'' was all she managed to squeak out. Because she'd die if anyone, especially Linc, guessed the way she really felt.

CHAPTER EIGHT

SHORTLY AFTER MIRANDA finished drying and storing the last of the breakfast dishes, a horse van bumped down the lane and stopped in front of the house. Linc and the boys emerged from the bunkhouse as the girls gathered on the porch to watch the unloading process. Linc hurried to help the driver lower the trailer ramp.

"They're beautiful." Jenny sounded awed, even if she cracked her gum so loudly it startled a small dappled mare Linc backed from the van. The mare shied and bucked on the ramp. It took Linc and a second man to subdue the frisky animal.

"We'll put them in the corral for now, rather than the barn, which I'm sure needs cleaning."

"Anywhere you want 'em, bud. We just deliver the goods." The driver extended a clipboard with a bill of lading for Linc to sign.

Miranda heard his deep sigh from where she stood on the top porch step. "Mucking out stalls is our job," she called, indicating herself and Jenny.

"Mucking. Yuck, what a disgusting word." Jenny hung back as Miranda descended the steps.

Hana ran up and slipped her hand into Miranda's, clearly not intending to be left out. It wasn't until they'd nearly reached the horse van and Miranda glanced back that she noticed the disappointment on Cassie's face. "Hana, honey, take Scraps and go to the barn with Jenny.

I'll guide Cassie's wheelchair over the rough spots along the path.''

"Can I really help clean the barn?" Though Cassie sounded unsure, her eyes lost their dullness as Miranda maneuvered her chair behind the others.

"You can keep Scraps out from underfoot. He can be a pest at times.''

"I wish I could ride one of the horses,'' Cassie murmured wistfully.

Miranda, who'd heard of therapeutic riding programs for disabled children, made a mental note to find out more about them. But rather than get the girl's hopes up, she asked Cassie some specific questions about her bad hip.

"I can't remember any doctors saying I had hip pins. What are they, Randi? Like hairpins?"

"Goodness, no. They're small steel rods designed to replace badly broken hipbones. They're hard to describe, honey, and nothing you need to worry about. I was curious as to what treatment you'd had, that's all.''

The subject was dropped—largely because the barn turned out to be a smellier mess than either the kitchen or bunkhouse.

Jenny balked at the entrance.

"This is what Linc's paying us for,'' Miranda reminded her. The prospect of money stirred the younger girl to action. After opening both front and back doors, they swept, hauled, dumped and hosed until well past noon. They might not have taken a break even then, if it hadn't been for the truck delivering the large household items Linc had ordered yesterday.

Miranda led the men who'd unloaded the dishwasher into the house. She scrubbed her hands and stayed to fix soup and sandwiches while the workmen hooked up water hoses and explained how to use the washer. "Thanks,'' she called, as they started out the back door. "Hey, will you tell Mr. Parker and the kids it's time for lunch?"

She expected everyone to be excited over the horses and the new equipment, but no one talked. "Did y'all wash your hands thoroughly?" Her voice blurred with the Southern inflection.

The little kids promptly extended their hands for her to inspect. The others grimaced. "Like, who appointed you mother?" Eric said peevishly.

"Enough." Linc scowled around the table. "Eat. We have a lot to do before we lose daylight."

"Aren't there lights in the bunkhouse?" Miranda passed a plate of sandwiches to Shawn, expecting an affirmative answer, but got none. "Gosh, why is everybody so down? We have new heaters, mattresses, a dishwasher and *horses*. It's like an early Christmas."

Linc cleared his throat. "I told the boys we'll probably have to continue sharing the house until I can get a contractor out here to rewire the lights and add a bathroom to the bunkhouses. It's unbelievable to me, the shape they're in."

"I like sleeping in the house."

All eyes suddenly zeroed in on the tiny speaker. Up to this point, Hana had been as silent as a shadow.

Cassie said conspiratorially, "Me, too. 'Cause last night's the first time Hana didn't have nightmares. And she didn't wet the bed."

"That's right." Miranda ruffled Hana's blond curls. "We're all so proud of you, honey. *Aren't we?*" Her glare elicited a rapid turnaround from the others. It wasn't until silence had descended again that she realized more than weariness caused Linc's brooding. She let the others leave the table and used clearing it as an excuse to hang back. She wanted to talk to Linc.

"Something's bothering you. Have you run out of money?"

"No. I budgeted enough." He shut his eyes, not sure he should involve her.

"If it's none of my business, tell me to butt out. I had an ulterior motive for waylaying you that doesn't concern the ranch."

Linc's eyes opened wide at that admission. She couldn't possibly have guessed how long he'd lain awake last night deliberating over her. Over whether or not to let her stay. Over how to treat her as opposed to the real teens. Over imagining how her lips would taste and her body would feel under his hands.

Ignoring his prolonged silence, Miranda plunged ahead. "Every day that passes without Wolfie and Cassie going to school is a loss for them. I realize you're busy, Parker— Linc. But you need to enroll them as quickly as possible and arrange for the bus to pick them up at the end of the lane. But…they can't go in the clothes they have. The kids at school will eat them alive."

His jaw tightened, then relaxed. Linc jerked his head back to avoid her wild gestures. "Dammit, Randi, why me? Oasis literally abandoned them. That's the larger part of my problem. This morning, when we took a break, I phoned our area Social Services office. I'd already been told they're in the process of getting a new director named Mrs. Bishop. The only person in the office until after Thanksgiving is a receptionist. She's arranged a visit right after the holiday. According to her, the kids aren't even listed on their rolls. Wolfie told me his and Hana's last name is Schmitt, and Cassie's is Rhodes. Apparently those names aren't showing up in the computer."

"How can that be? Unless—do you suppose it's because Oasis is a private foundation? Could they have paid care costs out of their own resources? Can you phone and ask them?''

''I tried to reach Oasis. Their phone's been disconnected. And a bigger headache—the receptionist told me the foundation is under investigation for something like twenty counts of fraud. She said Oasis lost state funding ten months ago, and her records show that all children should have been removed from their care at that time.''

''You're kidding!''

''I wish I were.'' He traced the deep creases that bracketed his mouth with a forefinger and thumb.

''This is ridiculous, Linc. Someone has to be handling this area's needy families until the new director comes on board. They can't have left the office unstaffed.''

''As I understand it, two overloaded caseworkers from neighboring counties come in once a week to authorize services already in place. New cases are being deferred.''

''That's terrible! What if those houseparents had taken off and you hadn't shown up as planned? You said they couldn't wait to be gone. Shoot—that explains the awful conditions here. I mean, if Oasis lost operating funds ten months back...''

''Yeah.'' Linc sounded defeated as he pulled thick work gloves out of his back pocket and began putting them on. ''It appears the kids stay here until after Turkey Day. Or maybe longer. The receptionist promised to put me on the director's list. But, she said, Rascal Ranch sits in sort of a no man's land. She thinks there's been some debate as to which service area we actually belong in.''

''Great! Well, we're getting by okay. And...you really have no choice.''

''My biggest worry is, what if other teens pick up my flyers? I had my contact person tell the police I'd take up to a dozen in my program. I actually thought I could handle twelve to fifteen based on the sleeping capacity of each bunkhouse. I'd been told to expect some kids to come and others to go. My mistake was in not checking the property out myself. How my friend Montoya missed the fact that there's just one broken-down outhouse to serve two bunkhouses…'' He shook his head. ''But in John's defense, I did push him to close the deal fast.''

Feeling Linc's frustration, yet secretly glad for the children's sake that they'd get to stay on a while, Miranda forgot herself and gripped his arm. ''Have a little faith. These kids have overcome far worse. All of them. Why not cut yourself some slack?''

Her face was so close, Linc had to battle an urge to kiss her. He found the changing colors in her smoky eyes compelling. And the faint scent of soap and shampoo clung to her, even after the hard morning she'd put in shoveling out the barn. He saw her chin automatically tilt higher. If he leaned forward like this, in slow motion… It was so, so tempting.

Her eyes began drifting shut. Linc had just tasted the slightest brush of her soft lips when Eric's strident yell rocked them both back on their heels.

''Linc, where are you? Shawn fell when we were taking down old curtains. The ladder broke.''

Taking a last rueful look at Randi's lovely features, Linc threw up his hands and bolted from the room.

Miranda crossed her arms to rub away a smattering of goose bumps. She allowed only one twinge of regret for a moment lost. A moment that shouldn't have happened at all.

Worry for Shawn succeeded in erasing her self-pity. And although she dashed out of the house only seconds behind Linc, his broad back was disappearing through the bunkhouse door as she plunged off the porch in a single leap and took off running after him.

Luckily Shawn had extracted himself from the broken pieces of the ladder. He was sitting, gingerly testing for sprains or breaks by the time Linc and Miranda burst onto the scene. "Did you break anything?" Linc demanded, bending anxiously over the boy.

"The ladder. And I ripped the curtain rod out of the wall."

"I mean, did you break any bones?"

"Naw, I don't think so. Comes from having all this extra padding." Shawn grabbed a fistful of the excess blubber that put a strain on all his shirt buttons. "I feel like an idiot, though."

"Sorry, Mr. Parker. I thought he was hurt bad!" Eric exclaimed. "Otherwise I wouldn't have bothered you."

"It's Linc, remember? And there's nothing to be sorry about. It could've been a disaster. I just realized I have no idea where there's a clinic, or if this area has 911 service." He extended a hand to help Shawn up. "You're sure you're all right? I can find out about a clinic and have you checked over by a doctor."

"My old man hurt me way worse, knocking me across the room. A clinic would probably want his name because he still covers me on his insurance. At least I think I'm still on his policy. Last I heard, his lawyers said he hadda pay premiums until I turn eighteen. That's not for another year."

Linc didn't comment, but he recalled his lawyers making the same recommendation regarding Felicity. Apparently someone in the firm had gotten wind of his sister being served alcohol at a Hollywood nightclub. His lawyers increased his indemnity, saying it could kill him financially if she drank and drove. Especially if she had an accident that took anyone with her. That should've been a wake-up call. Instead, he'd questioned her about her activities, and she'd assured him someone was telling him lies. Yeah, she sneaked into nightclubs, but only to hear the band and the singers. He'd bought her story hook, line and sinker.

Linc growled something indecipherable, followed by, "There'll be no more climbing ladders or anything else unless I'm on hand. Shawn, take the rest of the afternoon off. I'm expecting delivery of our farm equipment in the morning. It's more important that we get those fields turned and planted before bad weather sets in than it is making this bunkhouse livable. I can't let you sleep out here without a bathroom, anyway."

"I feel fine, Linc. I can still paint walls and stuff."

Miranda, seeing Linc was shaken and truly wanted Shawn to rest, attempted to offer an alternative. "Or you can come out to the barn and keep Cassie company. She's frustrated about not being able to help more."

"Yeah, sure. I know how she feels." Shawn shuffled his bulk out after Miranda.

"Or we could go fishin'," Wolfie said hopefully.

"That you could, and I'll join you," Linc said. "Can you cook trout?" he asked Miranda. She was still within earshot.

"If it's in the cookbook I bought, sure," she called back.

SHE WAS SECRETLY GLAD no one caught any fish she'd have to clean. They all had exciting tales of near misses, however. Jenny complained bitterly that she and Miranda had to stay behind and finish the barn so the horses had a place to sleep. Exhausted, everyone yawned over Miranda's supper of pot roast with all the trimmings. Except for Wolfie. He held out his plate for seconds and then asked for a third serving. "I wanted fish for supper, but I've never tasted anything so good," he said, smacking his lips.

Miranda eyed the food disappearing from his plate. "I'm glad you like what I fixed, Wolfie. But don't eat too much or you'll be up with a stomachache tonight."

His gaze swerved between her, his plate and Linc. "I am kinda full. Is it okay if I save this and eat it for breakfast?"

"You may. Or you can let Scraps have it. And in the morning you can share the ham, eggs and hash browns I'll be cooking."

The boy vacillated. The expression on his face would've been comical if it wasn't so heartbreaking to be aware of the source of his indecision. "Really, Wolfie, there's food enough to go around," Miranda told him. "Hey, when you and Cassie attended school, didn't your teachers worry about your lack of lunch?"

"We got a free hot lunch," Cassie said solemnly. "That was the best part about school, huh, Wolfie?"

"Yeah. Me and Cassie tried to save stuff so we could split it with Hana when we got home. But sometimes I just…couldn't."

Linc, recapping the gallon of milk, had seemed content to let the others talk. But when his gaze settled on the youngest child, he asked, "Hana, what did you do while the others were at school?"

"I didn't like them bein' gone. Miz Tucker said I hadda stay inside by my bed. So I cried and cried till I fell asleep."

Linc and Miranda exchanged looks of disbelief. Even the teens made noises denoting shock. But it was Linc who reached out and smoothed away the pinched lines from the little girl's face. "Hana, love, I guarantee no one's going to leave you alone again, even if Wolfie and Cassie go off to school."

The child continued to look apprehensively at Linc for a long moment. At last she said, "Okay," in her soft voice. And for the first time since he'd arrived and discovered that nothing about the ranch was as he'd imagined, Linc actually felt as if he was making progress.

"Do we hafta go to school tomorrow?" Cassie ventured.

Avoiding Randi's accusatory gaze, Linc cleared his throat. "Probably not tomorrow, darlin'. Tomorrow, the boys and I need to decide what we're doing with the fields, since we played this afternoon. But soon. You'll need to go back soon."

If Miranda thought "soon" was too vague, she managed to hide her disappointment as she began stacking dirty dishes. "Jenny, you look totally bushed. It's all you can do to keep your eyes open. If you'll help Cassie and Hana get ready for bed, I'll clean up here. I'll do the dishes and set up for tomorrow's breakfast."

"Deal! I'm beginning to feel aches in muscles I forgot I had." Jenny levered her body out of her chair. "Tell me why the muscles in my butt hurt."

Linc laughed. "Those are the ones you use when you shovel hay."

"Who shoveled hay? We threw it around with our hands, and that was the easy part. Randi and I shoveled horseshit, though, until I thought my arms would fall off."

"Shh," Miranda shushed her, darting meaningful glances toward the little ears.

"Get used to it," Greg told Jenny, making ready to leave the table. "With four horses, I'll bet shoveling manure is a daily event."

Jenny groaned.

"It's not so bad if you clean the stalls every couple of days," Miranda rushed to say.

"We're singers, not farmers," Eric grumbled on his way out.

"Keep telling yourself that!" Jenny exclaimed.

Once again, Miranda and Linc found themselves alone. He stood and carried his plate to the sink. "Maybe this idea I had of a working ranch wasn't so hot."

"Why? Because everyone's complaining about being sore?"

"Because these kids will never see the value in anything except show business."

Miranda paused in scraping Wolfie's uneaten meat into Scraps's dish. "Loving the land takes time. If they can hang in here until spring and see the results of their labor, I predict it'll be harder for them to leave."

"*If* they hang in. Funny, the day they came, I wanted them gone." He paused. "You're very different from them, aren't you, Randi?" Linc murmured from directly behind her. "Is that even your real name?"

She stiffened, feeling his warm breath on the back of her neck. "What's in a name?"

He felt her tense and stepped aside. "Sorry, I didn't mean to crowd you. I'm…just…"

"Just?" Miranda glanced over her shoulder.

"Nothing." He blew out a harsh breath. "I appreciate the way you've pitched in with the cooking and cleaning the barn. Can I…uh…give you a hand with the dishes, so you can follow the others to bed?"

"No. But thanks for the offer. I only have to load the new dishwasher and poke a few buttons. I like having time to myself. It helps me unwind after a long day at work, if you know what I mean."

"I do." He rummaged in a cupboard and came out with a good-size flashlight. "I need to let that farm supper settle." He rubbed his belly, and Miranda had to make a yeoman's effort not to stare at his lazily circling hand.

"I thought hard work called for hearty fare. I can fix more vegetables and less meat and potatoes if you'd like."

"Don't get me wrong. The food was great. I expect we'll burn those calories off, especially the guys, once we start clearing the land."

"Oh. Okay. I'll stick with my plan to serve roast chicken tomorrow night. What are you doing with the flashlight?"

"I thought I'd walk around outside and check to be sure the horses are adjusting to their new quarters. Want me to take Scraps out for you?"

"He's still eating." Miranda debated, though, whether or not to suggest making a pot of fresh coffee. But she debated too long, for she heard him go out and quietly close the door.

She'd tidied up the kitchen, shut off all the lights except the one over the sink, taken Scraps out for his evening constitutional and had just gone into her room when she heard the outside door open and close again, signaling his return. She waited to hear him walk down the hall. She didn't hear his footsteps, but after a moment noticed sounds coming from the main bath. A toilet flushed. Water ran. Not the shower, but more like he was just washing up.

Miranda sat down on her cot. The room was dark, and Jenny and the little girls breathed rhythmically as if all were deeply asleep. Wishing she had a book and a small light by which to read, Miranda ultimately decided she was too wide awake to fall asleep. Scraps seemed restless, too.

Taking care to walk softly, she exited the room. She

grabbed her jacket off the peg by the back door, thinking she'd sit on the porch awhile and look at the stars, while the dog nosed around. It was a beautiful, if rather cool, night. A three-quarter moon sent patterns through the leafless trees, scattering diamondlike sparkles across the floor of the porch.

Miranda leaned against the railing, Scraps beside her, and searched for the Big and Little Dippers. She gave a triumphant sigh as she found the North Star and followed it to the Big Dipper.

"Who's there?" a gruff masculine voice called from the far end of the porch.

"It's me," Miranda squeaked. "Linc, is that you?" Miranda thought so, but she gripped the railing and stayed where she was in case she was wrong. She hadn't heard him leave the house after he'd come in.

He loomed out of the shadows, his broad shoulders blocking the moonlight.

"I thought you'd turned in," Linc said. "The lights were out when I got back from the barn."

"I tried to go to bed. I guess I'm too keyed up from all the physical labor to be sleepy yet. Are you having trouble sleeping, too?" She smiled. "If you'd like, I can go brew a pot of coffee. Or would you like a cold roast beef sandwich?"

"No, I'm still stuffed. Thanks again for dinner." He grinned. "You cooked a roast because you had no faith in our fishing abilities?"

"It was already in the oven when you decided to go fishing. And roast is always good for sandwiches, hot or cold."

"You're right. But I'm capable of making a pot of coffee, Randi. You're not here to wait on me."

"I only meant…well, I offered because you put in a long day."

"So did you."

Miranda gathered her jacket beneath her chin. She eyed him through her lashes, trying to figure out what was making him act so testy. "I'm sorry if I'm intruding on your privacy, Parker."

"It's Linc, remember?" He leaned a shoulder against one of the upright posts. "If I sound guilty, it's because you caught me sneaking a beer. I brought a six-pack from home, but stashed it because I'm not sure if any of the kids have problems with alcohol." To be more truthful, she'd caught him thinking about her. Thinking—and wondering what kind of guy would terrify her so much she'd go on the run.

She laughed, low and sexy.

Her way of laughing tightened Linc's belly.

"I enjoy an occasional beer myself, Linc. But you're probably right to hide it from the boys. There's something about forbidden fruit, so to speak, that attracts teenage boys."

"Yeah." Linc hoisted himself up so he sat on the porch rail facing her. He offered her the bottle and she took a swallow.

"Ah-ha! I knew boys weren't the only ones attracted to forbidden fruit."

"Oh, but I'm legal, so it's not forbidden."

"All the same, it's not something I indulge in to excess. According to Wolfie, George Tucker always had a beer in one hand and a cigarette in the other."

"So you're determined to present the kids with a better role model."

"It wouldn't take much. But yeah, I hope to do just that for the kids who come to the refuge. Maybe if I'd been

The Harlequin Reader Service® — Here's how it works:

Accepting your 2 free books and gift places you under no obligation to buy anything. You may keep the books and gift and return the shipping statement marked "cancel." If you do not cancel, about a month later we'll send you 6 additional books and bill you just $4.47 each in the U.S., or $4.99 each in Canada, plus 25¢ shipping & handling per book and applicable taxes if any.* That's the complete price and — compared to cover prices of $5.25 each in the U.S. and $6.25 each in Canada — it's quite a bargain! You may cancel at any time, but if you choose to continue, every month we'll send you 6 more books, which you may either purchase at the discount price or return to us and cancel your subscription.

*Terms and prices subject to change without notice. Sales tax applicable in N.Y. Canadian residents will be charged applicable provincial taxes and GST.

If offer card is missing write to: The Harlequin Reader Service, 3010 Walden Ave., P.O. Box 1867, Buffalo, NY 14240-1867

NO POSTAGE
NECESSARY
IF MAILED
IN THE
UNITED STATES

BUSINESS REPLY MAIL
FIRST-CLASS MAIL   PERMIT NO. 717-003   BUFFALO, NY

POSTAGE WILL BE PAID BY ADDRESSEE

HARLEQUIN READER SERVICE
3010 WALDEN AVE
PO BOX 1867
BUFFALO NY 14240-9952

Do You Have the LUCKY KEY?

PLAY THE *Lucky Key Game*

and you can get

FREE BOOKS and a FREE GIFT!

Scratch the gold areas with a coin. Then check below to see the books and gift you can get!

YES! I have scratched off the gold areas. Please send me the **2 FREE BOOKS** and **GIFT** for which I qualify. I understand I am under no obligation to purchase any books, as explained on the back of this card.

336 HDL DVF7   135 HDL DVGN

FIRST NAME   LAST NAME

ADDRESS

APT.#   CITY

STATE/ PROV.   ZIP/POSTAL CODE

2 free books plus a free gift   1 free book

2 free books   Try Again!

Offer limited to one per household and not valid to current Harlequin Superromance® subscribers. All orders subject to approval. Credit or Debit balances in a customer's account(s) may be offset by any other outstanding balance owed by or to the customer.

Visit us online at www.eHarlequin.com

DETACH AND MAIL CARD TODAY!

(H-SR-02/04)

© 2002 HARLEQUIN ENTERPRISES LTD.
® and ™ are trademarks owned by Harlequin Enterprises Ltd.

more conscious of setting a good example when Felicity entered her teens, she'd…'' His voice trailed off and he shrugged. ''Jenny thinks I'm a fool for not knowing they invaded my house whenever I was on business trips. God knows how many bashes Felicity threw that she probably patterned after the cocktail parties I hosted for clients.''

''Are you saying you threw wild parties in front of her?''

''Not wild, exactly. But in Hollywood, people in the industry tend to bring designer drugs with them to cocktail parties. I didn't use, but what if I missed noticing that a client left something lying around? I generally had my parties catered, and I left the cleanup to their staff. I thought nothing of keeping a stocked bar. Frankly, it never dawned on me that my baby sister would sneak food and booze for herself and her friends. Yet Eric said as much. And I obviously made it easy, always shelling out money whenever Felicity asked for it.''

''If you're guilty of anything, Linc, it's not realizing that your sister grew up sometime while you weren't looking. You loved her. However, you need to accept that she not only grew up, but made some bad choices in the process.'' Miranda moved closer, and her jacket front brushed his thigh.

Linc's head shot up. Hearing his name—his first name, which she'd rarely used—fall softly, compassionately, from her lips startled him. An anguish he couldn't abolish compelled him to set his beer aside and reach for the woman offering him compassion and comfort. He wrapped her in his arms and buried his face in her short curls. His heart sped up when she stepped closer, slipping her narrow hips between his thighs. Time slowed as he breathed in the light, lemony scent he'd come to associate only with her.

Randi seemed to hug him back as tightly as he hugged her. She felt *right* to Linc, who didn't stop to consider how little he really knew about the woman he clutched against his fractured heart. At first he was only aware of the comfort she so willingly gave. But, little by little, comfort was replaced by sexual yearnings.

Linc fought the urge to bring her closer, while at the same time he was bombarded by a voice that said to push her away.

It'd been too long since he held a woman. And she felt so good under his exploring hands. Slim hips. Narrow waist. Heat radiating through a threadbare T-shirt. They warmed each other.

His lips, now buried in her springy dark curls, blazed a trail to her ear. One taste, and his mindless quest led to her temple, then her cheek and finally met her mouth in sweet satisfaction. His hands worked their way beneath her shirt and found that her skin was soft and bare. The lips he continued to kiss uttered enticing, breathless sounds that would spur any man's urges into overdrive. Especially a man who'd done without female companionship for as long as Linc Parker had.

He felt the flash of heat at several points of contact and vaguely knew his legs had gone numb with the lethargic heaviness invading his lower body.

Miranda still tried to grapple with how they'd gone from a rational discussion of Linc's life in Hollywood to this...this...mind-boggling assault on her senses.

It occurred to her that she ought not to let him touch her so intimately. But the more his slightly sandpapery fingertips moved over her flesh, the more flesh she wanted to bare for him. His thumbs brushed back and forth over the aching tips of her breasts. Once before, when a would-be lover's tongue had invaded her mouth, she hadn't liked it and had pulled back in alarm. With Linc, there was no sense of fear, and she didn't feel invaded. She felt...out of breath, excited, wanting more.

Linc slowly drew back to take a deep breath and to get his bearings. Sanity returned like a load of concrete dumped on his head. What was he doing? He sprang away suddenly and got a good look at her shiny wet lips, her mussed hair and passion-drugged eyes. A shaft of moonlight haloed her face and hair. For a moment, Linc thought her dark curls had turned platinum before his eyes. She was exquisite. And familiar enough to trigger a distant memory. Then a cloud drifted across the face of the moon, and he blinked several times, unsure of the fleeting metamorphosis.

"Linc?" She opened her eyes and cocked her head to one side. Registering his dazed expression, she stepped back and adjusted her shirt. In fact, she shivered and closed her jacket over her still-tingling breasts. "My dad would say you look like someone walked over your grave." She made an odd, choked sound. "Was kissing me such a bad experience?"

His eyes narrowed. "I'm sorry I got carried away. But you shouldn't have to fish for compliments. I should think you'd know the answer. Kissing you was anything but a hardship."

Ashamed of a neediness that was the antithesis of the Miranda Kimbrough she used to be—the woman she was searching for—she lowered her gaze. "I'll say good night. It's late. And a rancher's life begins at dawn."

Linc caught her sleeve. "You say that with the conviction of someone who knows. Someone who's been there, done that. Is the man you're running from a rancher? Did you tease him out of his mind like you're teasing me? Is that why you're on the lam?"

"No. No. And no again." Miranda deftly disengaged his hand from her denim jacket. "Are you angry because you hate having shared a piece of your life with me? Painful history you'd rather no one learned about? Too bad, Parker. I know, and it moved me to hug and kiss you back. It happened. I won't apologize. But it doesn't give you the right to analyze me. Or criticize me."

Despite the flush staining his cheeks, Linc persisted. He wanted answers, dammit! "I didn't invite you here. You came pretending to be someone you're not. Who are you exactly? And what do you want from me?"

Her eyes filled with tears and her lower lip quivered. "I can't tell you who I am. I thought we'd settled that, Linc. Please believe I'd be honest with you if I could. I want…" She licked her lips and implored him through a film of tears. "I want shelter. That's all. If you can't harbor me on those terms…well, like I said before, I'll leave. You can tell the others anything. Make up a story about me. You've already done that in your mind, I think."

"Dammit to hell!" Linc swiped a hand through the air and said through gritted teeth, "I don't want you to leave."

"What *do* you want? Tell me. I've never been good at reading between the lines."

His chin drooped and he sank back against the porch railing. "Let's keep the status quo until after Thanksgiving. That's when the new director from Social Services is scheduled to pay the ranch a visit. I don't know what she'll ask, but she's bound to want information on everyone I'm harboring. I'll give you until then to decide what to say. Just remember—I want Felicity's Refuge to be on the up-and-up. It's the least I can do to honor the person my sister might have been."

"That's approximately five weeks," she said thoughtfully. "Thank you for that, Linc."

"I don't want your thanks. I want you to trust me, to let me help you. I have connections. You may think Hollywood is all fluff. Most people do. But it's big business. Very big business. I have plenty of experience in solving my clients' problems—legal, financial, whatever. Let me stop this jerk from harassing you."

Miranda was oh-so-tempted to dump her self-made troubles on Linc's broad shoulders. But she thought of Wes Carlisle, who was probably as well placed in Nashville as Parker was in Hollywood. And Wes happened to be the man who had her chained to a contract even Houdini couldn't escape. Briefly she considered what Linc had said about wanting this ranch, Felicity's Refuge, to be above reproach. She'd take the five weeks he offered. Maybe then she'd put out feelers to see if Wes would let her go.

Fat chance. After running into that life-size cutout of herself in the window of a small-town record shop, Miranda knew that if she was found here, Linc's name and ranch would be virtually destroyed by a vicious scandal.

"Randi." Linc pursed his lips and altered his tone. "I've been thinking about what you said regarding Cassie and Wolfie needing to get back to school. I'll find some time tomorrow to deal with it. Will you come to town with us and help me buy them clothes? I hate to spare the time, but…you don't happen to have a valid driver's license, do you?"

She shrugged. "I do. But not a California license. Anyway, I left it behind."

"I see. But you can take the test and get one here, right?"

She looked sad as she shook her head. "I can't, Linc."

He shut his eyes and rubbed the bridge of his nose.

"Then we'll all go, I guess, and call it another supply run. The boys can use jeans, boots and gloves, since I'm asking them to work around farm machinery. I noticed that you and Jenny keep wearing the same things, too."

Miranda wanted to protest against his buying her anything. It wasn't right, considering she had a fortune sitting in Tennessee. The best she could do, however, was mutter, "I'll pay you back one of these days, Parker. As soon as I get on my feet."

"Lassen County has a college. Most California colleges offer satellite courses for the major universities. As good as you are with children, you ought to consider getting a degree in social work." He massaged the back of his neck. "I don't mean to interfere in your life, but given what we've recently observed, the need for more good people in the field is certainly there. And it might help you with your dilemma."

Miranda met his eyes. "My dilemma?"

"Yeah. Help you deal with—you know—the jerk. Social workers must run into a lot of domestic-violence cases."

"I said it wasn't like that," she said tiredly. "It's more…" She stopped midsentence.

"More what?"

"I guess you could say it's more like breaking out of an unbreakable contract," she said lamely. "Really, Parker, I wish you'd quit trying to psych me out. I promise I'll have my life organized before the new director, Mrs. Bishop, shows up here."

Linc pondered her words a moment as Randi whistled for the dog, opened the door and disappeared. "Hey," he called, then tried again. "Hey, there's not a contract written that doesn't have loopholes somewhere. *Any* contract can be broken."

The door slammed. He wasn't sure whether or not she'd heard him. He wondered what kind of contract she was talking about. Live-ins didn't sign prenups that he was aware of, and Linc couldn't think of another type of contract that would make her take such drastic measures.

He knew that trying to figure her out would keep him awake, so he might as well hang out here on the porch. Or better still, make another circuit of the property. Grabbing his beer can, he swung off the porch.

CHAPTER NINE

ALL THROUGH BREAKFAST Miranda felt Linc tracking her every move. She supposed he hadn't liked being brushed off last night. It'd probably stung his ego. Men who looked like Lincoln Parker, especially those in his income bracket, were used to crooking a little finger and having women fall all over them. But a man needed more than looks and money to hold Miranda's interest. He needed to be a lot like her dad. Humble, possessing a keen sense of humor, good at heart. That cowboy thing again.

Parker could kiss, though. Miranda gave him that. If her situation had been different, that alone might tempt her to delve beneath his ever-changing surface.

She hated being judged on superficial attributes, so if she was free to explore an honest relationship with anyone, the sparks they'd engendered last night would certainly be a place to start. Walking off, leaving him standing alone in all that glorious moonlight, had been damned difficult. Smart, however. She needed to avoid being alone with him in the future. That was the wisest course of action, she thought, feeling a weight shift as he stopped eyeing her and stood, ready to leave.

Scraps started barking. "Well, boys," Linc said, "guess we have company. I assume it's our tractor and other implements being delivered. If you're finished eating, grab your jackets and let's go help them unload."

Miranda resisted an urge to dash out with Jenny and the

younger kids to see what they were getting. She calmed the barking terrier and stayed behind to clear the table. Once that was done, she set about making lunches for the boys and Linc, who'd obviously changed his mind again about enrolling the kids in school. He'd said nothing about that or replenishing supplies. She felt oddly relieved.

Busy assembling meat and cheese on the bread slices she'd laid out on the counter, Miranda didn't hear Jenny come in until the girl spoke right behind her.

"What tune are you humming, Randi? It's got a catchy beat. But I don't recognize it."

Humming as she worked had been Miranda's method of creating a new song. She hadn't realized she was doing it now. This was the first melody to spring up since she'd left Nashville. "Gosh, Jenny, you scared me. I don't even know what I was humming." Miranda brandished the knife she'd been using to spread mustard on the bread. "Probably some hit we heard on the radio the other night."

Jenny shook her head. "No. I've got a good ear for music." Leaning her elbows on the counter, she whistled a few bars. "It went sort of like that."

Miranda worked hard to look blank. She'd have to be extra careful around Jenny. The girl did have an uncanny ear.

"Did all the equipment get here?"

Jenny nodded and bent to scratch Scraps's ears. "The delivery dude left. Linc and the boys are out there looking at the manual that came with the tractor. Eric's showing off like an idiot, 'cause he's the only one of the entire bunch who's ever set foot on a tractor. You'd think he invented the plow, for heaven's sake."

"What's his story, Jenny? I hate to pry, but Eric has a huge chip on his shoulder."

Jenny set Scraps down, washed her hands and began counting out plastic sandwich bags. Miranda wasn't sure if the girl would talk about her friend. But after a few moments, Jenny said, "Eric's mom was a dirt-poor migrant worker. His dad, who's half Hispanic, half black, owns a small farm in north-central California. It sits between two big growers who tried everything to run Eric's dad off his land. His mom wanted to take the money they offered, because she hated farming. Eric said his parents fought day and night about it. When he was twelve and his brother, Joe, was nine, their mom up and left. Eric claims that's when his dad became a bully. Every few months they tried to find their mom, and each time social workers hauled them back to their dad and the beatings got worse. At fourteen, Eric ran away to L.A. He's never checked to see what became of Joe, and I think he feels guilty about that."

"Not knowing what became of his brother must be awful."

"Yeah, but Eric's still underage. Technically he'd be sent back to his dad. That's why he avoids cops or anyone who smacks of authority."

"So what'll he do when the woman from Social Services comes to relocate Wolfie, Cassie and Hana? She's bound to want stats on everyone."

Jenny shrugged. "If she makes noises about shipping Eric home, he'll bolt. I hope, since Parker has a license for the shelter and since he's not applying for state aid or anything, maybe she'll leave us alone."

"You think she might?" Miranda hoped Jenny was right. Heaven only knew what would happen if her real identity came to light. Unlike Eric, it wasn't beatings she had to fear. But in his way, Carlisle was a bully, just like

Eric's dad. How many times had Wes said he owned her lock, stock and barrel?

"If you're done with the sandwiches, Randi, I'll take them out to the guys."

"Thanks, Jen. I told Cassie I'd wash and braid her hair this morning. Right after that, I intend to begin cleaning up the living room. The bedrooms and kitchen look almost presentable. But the living and dining rooms still need a thorough vacuuming and scrubbing."

"Can you let Jenny do it?" Linc asked from the doorway, startling both women. "And will you keep an eye on the little kids for a couple of hours, Jen?"

Miranda fumbled the knife she still held, but it was Jenny who demanded answers from Linc.

"Like I said yesterday, I want to go sign Wolfie and Cassie up for classes," he replied. "Since Eric's way more adept at driving the tractor than I am, I'll let him teach the others. This is a good time for Randi and me to run over to the school and fill out the papers needed to reinstate the kids."

Jenny frowned. "Can't you go by yourself? Why do you need Randi?"

"It was her idea. Besides, misery loves company." Linc favored Jenny with a cheeky grin.

Miranda acted nonchalant. "Since they attended that same school in the past, Jen, I doubt it'll take long to enroll them. I'm hoping they haven't missed so much school they'll get shoved back a grade or something."

"It's not as if they won't be bounced again when Social Services moves them to another foster home," Jenny muttered. "Anyway, you know I hate to baby-sit."

Unsure why she blamed Linc, Miranda nevertheless dealt him an accusing glare. "You mean the kids won't remain with foster parents in this area?"

"You're both jumping to conclusions. The welfare office covers a big territory. We should wait and see what Mrs. Bishop has to say about their individual cases before we go making rash assumptions."

Miranda stuffed the last orange in a sack, then washed her hands. She turned to Jenny. "While you deliver lunches to Eric, Greg and Shawn, I'll hunt down Cassie and tell her I'll fix her hair as soon as I get back. Oh, we'd better put Linc's lunch in the fridge. He can collect it later. Jenny, will you keep Scraps inside this morning? I don't want him to get run over by the new tractor."

"You'd better hurry back." Jenny gathered the bags and flounced out the door.

"What bug bit her?" Linc mused aloud.

"You've put her in charge of the little kids again without asking her permission. That's precisely why she ran away from home, you know. Jenny got fed up always having to fill in for her mother." She paused. "I thought last night you said we'd combine a trip to the school with a supply run into town."

"I did. But with Eric being so competent running the tractor, I decided it'd be more efficient to split up the tasks today." Linc pursed his lips. "Are you saying Jenny's not trustworthy? I want to leave the kids in good hands."

"She's trustworthy, but I'll have a word with her first if you'd like."

"Please." He sighed heavily. "Darn, I wish somebody would call about my ad."

"Maybe you're searching for a housekeeper in the wrong place. The city shelters are filled with women down on their luck."

"Drunks and druggies? I don't think so, Randi."

"They aren't all degenerates. But it's your call," she said with a shrug. "How long shall I tell Jenny we'll be gone? You said the boys need boots, gloves and work jeans. And the little kids need school clothes. Cassie just needs clothes, period.''

"I know. I wrote a list of sizes except for you and Jenny. I thought two of us might be able to shop faster than if we all go.'' He handed her his notebook. "If we take everyone, it'll also knock out another full day of work. According to the morning weather report, by Thanksgiving we'll be getting the first of the Pacific storms.''

Miranda lifted her jacket off a peg near the door. "Then let's not waste time. Storms here most likely mean snow, right?''

"I don't know. I've never lived anywhere except Southern Cal. A deluge of rain is the worst I've experienced. How about you? Have you ever driven in snow?''

"A few times. Once a blizzard meant I had to cancel—'' She caught herself and stopped abruptly midsentence.

"Cancel what?'' Linc opened the door and stood aside to let her pass.

She'd been about to say "cancel a major concert.'' Wes had cursed and raged at everyone, including the sky. Secretly Miranda had reveled in the windfall of a day off. Her private bus had been headed for the Catskills, and the near whiteout forced a postponement. She recalled enjoying her forced stay at an obscure motel. Members of her band had indulged in an impromptu snowball fight. Afterward they'd joked around and someone had spiked the hot chocolate with rum. It was the first real fun Miranda had had after losing her dad—which was probably what made the incident stand out in her mind.

"A dollar for your thoughts.'' Linc had noted her pensive silence after she'd pulled on her jacket.

"I was wondering what a blanket of snow would do to your operation here."

"I could function better without it. I'd like to plant crops and bring in the first few cattle and a chicken or two before the snow flies. I'd also prefer to build at least one bunk-house bathroom before the road becomes a quagmire."

"Did you stop to think maybe you've bitten off more than you can chew?"

"Nothing ventured, nothing gained."

"True," she said. "But sometimes nothing's gained by venturing too much."

"Ah, a cynic, I see."

"I'm not a total cynic. But I believe life's better if all things are done in moderation." Leaving him pondering her statement, she went to have a word with Cassie and Jenny.

Linc met her at the SUV and plunged headlong back into their conversation. "Well, I wouldn't have half of what I have today if I'd subscribed to your philosophy of taking life in moderation. I jump into a project with both feet and go full bore. Otherwise, competitors will beat me out."

"Must everything men do be about competition? What's wrong with doing what you do because you love it?"

Linc gave her a sidelong glance. "Have I lost a thread? I'm talking in generalities. Sounds to me as if you're ready to take a chunk out of me for someone's specific trans-gression."

"Sorry. Oh—you just passed a turnoff where a sign said Valley View Elementary School. Isn't that the school we're looking for?"

"From the way Wolfie talked, I thought they rode the bus a lot farther."

"It probably seems a long way to a kid. And depending

on where the ranch is on the bus route, they may take a while to reach the school.''

Linc found a wide spot in the road to make a U-turn. He followed Miranda's directions, found the road and traveled it for a distance. "At least it's paved," he muttered. "Are you sure the sign said there's a school out here in the middle of nowhere?"

"I wasn't until now. Oh, look—to your left." She pointed out a sprawling single-story building with several bike racks and windows dotted with paper pilgrims and turkeys.

"Sure can tell Thanksgiving's around the corner," Miranda murmured as he parked and they climbed out of the van.

Linc studied the artwork as he pocketed his keys. "Can you cook a turkey and all the trimmings?" he asked unexpectedly.

Miranda laughed. "I've never done one by myself. But that's why they make cookbooks. Anyway, there's still a chance you'll hire a housekeeper-cook by Turkey Day."

He yanked on a stray curl peeking over the edge of Miranda's jacket collar. It wasn't until his teasing gesture that she realized how much her hair had grown. Which probably meant she needed to cut it and use another temporary rinse.

Seemingly out of nowhere, Linc asked, "Have you ever thought about going blond?"

Miranda stumbled to a halt. "W-where did that silly question spring from?" she stammered.

Because she'd stopped outside the school's main entrance, Linc did, too. He ran his fingers through her springy curls and watched the autumn sunlight glint off it. "Last night," he murmured, "the moonlight turned your hair…uh…well, never mind.'' He jerked back his hand and buried it in his pocket.

Fear of discovery trapped the breath in Miranda's lungs. If the school bell hadn't rung just then, she decided there was no telling how long they might have lingered there, staring at each other. Luckily the bell spurred Linc to action. He pulled open the door and motioned her through.

She busied herself unfolding a sheaf of papers she'd pried out of Wolfie. Letting Linc lead the way into the office, Miranda shoved the papers into his hands. ''These are apparently the last notices that came from the kids' teachers. George Tucker threw them in the trash. Wolfie said he dug them out later.''

Their arrival was greeted by the school secretary, a Mrs. Banks. ''I remember these children,'' she exclaimed. ''After weeks of nonattendance, we filed their records.'' She walked to a cabinet and pulled out a drawer.

''And no one checked to see why they'd stopped attending?'' Miranda asked.

''Are you their new foster folks?'' The secretary gave them the once-over.

Linc leaned his elbows on the counter and smiled engagingly. ''It's a long story. You're probably aware the area Social Services department is in upheaval until the new director comes on board. By the way, I'm Lincoln Parker. I bought the ranch where these kids live. They're temporarily under my care until Social Services determines where to place them. For their sake—and I'm sure you'll agree—I feel it's best to resume their education ASAP.''

''Mercy, I do agree, Mr. Parker.'' Clearly Linc's winsome smile had flustered the woman. So much so that she searched for and found the permanent record cards without further chitchat.

''I see Wolfgang Schmitt and Cassandra Rhodes need

booster shots. You'll have to get them done within the month.''

"Cassie's real name is Cassandra?" Miranda stood on tiptoe so she could read the card. Mrs. Banks discreetly covered the pertinent information.

"I'll just need your name and phone number in place of George and Lydia Tucker." The woman sniffed inelegantly. "I hope you see that the children attend school more often than their last caregivers did, Mr. and Mrs. Parker."

"Oh, we're not married. I'm his cook," Miranda supplied sweetly. If possible, the secretary's disdain increased.

Linc listened to the byplay with interest. "I've listed my home and cell numbers," he said. "And I can assure you the kids will be here more often and they'll be clean and well-fed."

"That's commendable," the woman said stiffly. "Unwanted children who fall through the cracks frequently get left behind academically."

"Wolfie and Cassie aren't unwanted," Miranda said, no less stiffly.

"That may be true. But they certainly looked as if they were."

"Not anymore. Which reminds me." Miranda snapped her fingers. "We're heading out now to buy their school wardrobes. We don't want them singled out. Can you tell us what the other kids here are wearing?"

"Have a look." The woman raised the window blind behind her and pointed to a nearby playground. Both Linc and Miranda pressed forward to see.

"Holy cow," Linc said in a stage whisper. "They're wearing every manner of dress. How will we ever choose correctly?"

Miranda pulled his notebook from her pocket and began

writing. "I'll jot down a list. You get a bus schedule, Linc."

By the time they gathered the new student packets and said good-bye, Mrs. Banks had warmed only minimally.

"Phew," Miranda said on the way to the parking lot. "She wasn't the friendliest person I've ever met."

Linc laughed. "She tried her best to get your last name on the forms. Just out of curiosity, why are you so determined not to give it out, Randi?"

"To avoid being traced. I thought we had this conversation, Parker."

"Why would anyone look for you at an elementary school?"

She sighed. "I doubt they would. On the other hand, anyone might have access to school records. They're official documents, you know."

Linc studied her profile as he helped her into the passenger seat of the SUV. "How long are you willing to live in the shadows, Randi? Tell me who's making you so afraid. I'll gladly have a talk with the bastard."

"No!" Miranda's voice rose. "No," she said again, a little more calmly.

"All right, all right." Linc stroked her upper arm, his eyes darkly concerned. "You can't run forever. Someday you'll have to trust someone to protect you. I can be that person."

"You agreed to give me until after Thanksgiving, Linc. What's changed?"

He turned his lips into her palm and felt her shiver with...exactly what, Linc wasn't sure. If he could be sure it was desire rather than fear, he'd have no qualms about raising the heat. But the way things stood, he merely sighed. "My word's my bond, Randi. Let's just go to town and get the items on your list."

She sank gratefully into the leather seat. Neither spoke until Linc pulled into the parking lot of a department store in a nearby town. Not Susanville. Miranda had missed seeing the name of this place. But she was glad when a survey of the main street didn't reveal any record stores.

"Shopping will go faster if I take the list for the boys and you buy for yourself and the girls," Linc suggested.

"How will I pay?" She panicked for a moment.

"Here, use my credit card."

"Linc," she drawled, "they won't let me sign your name."

"Right, and we've already established that you won't sign yours. Is your first name even Randi?"

His snide tone landed like a well-thrown punch. He'd set her up, she thought angrily. His comment about the credit card was just another way to bring up the subject of her name. Her identity. "My dad called me that," she said, gritting her teeth. "Hey, look, this store has central checkout. How long will you need to choose for the boys? I can probably fill my list in half an hour."

"A woman who can shop for clothes in half an hour is every man's wildest dream. Marry me," Linc sang out, clutching his heart.

"Ha, ha!" She ripped the list in half and slapped the top half into Linc's hand.

True to her prediction, she whipped through the girls' department in nothing flat. She took longer buying boots and sneakers. She all but raced down the last aisle in order to beat Linc to their appointed meeting place.

He arrived several minutes afterward, looking totally frazzled. "Damn, but you did win the race."

She attempted to appear bored. "Oh, were we in a race?" She hoped it wasn't evident that her heart still galloped like crazy from her last fifty-yard dash.

"Okay, show me what you bought. I'll bet you weren't as generous as I was."

As they compared items, it became evident that she'd outbought Linc two items to one.

"I concede. You're the better shopper."

It was small as compliments went, but Miranda was as pleased as if he'd handed her a gold medal. It was probably because nothing she did ever pleased Wes Carlisle, she mused. He always wanted more, wanted different, wanted better.

Miranda couldn't believe Linc forked over his credit card without batting an eye at the staggering sum. Another area in which Wes was a control freak. Even though *she* earned the money, he harangued her constantly over every nickel and dime she spent.

"Thanks from all of us, Linc," Miranda said quietly as they exited the store.

"You're welcome. I hope the kids like what we bought. Now I'm wondering if we made a mistake in not bringing them."

"I believe I can safely say not one of them has ever been given anything half as nice in a long, long while."

"Except you. You strike me as a woman used to wearing designer duds."

Miranda's eyes widened. "What makes you say that?"

"The way you walk into a room, Randi. Like a queen." He opened the hatch of the SUV to stow their bags. "I'm betting you're no stranger to money."

"Sadly, money doesn't guarantee happiness." There was such a tremor in her voice Linc just stared at her.

He tossed in the last sackful of jeans and slammed the door. "You intrigue me. Comments like that only pique my interest more."

"Why?"

Linc locked the back and removed the keys. He didn't know why she got under his skin, dammit. Or maybe he did. He'd grown up in a shallow town. And he'd spent his adult years dating women who came out of that pool. If he had to label Randi, he'd use the word *genuine*.

And yet...Randi had secrets. Her past was a mystery. So for all he knew she might *not* be genuine at all. Irritated by his seesawing feelings toward her, Linc wrenched open the passenger door. He stood stiffly aside and let her climb in by herself.

Miranda had hoped he'd suggest stopping for coffee before going home.

He didn't.

The first ten minutes of the drive were completed in total silence. Miranda saw that Linc was brooding again. "How many head of cattle are you expecting?"

"Not many."

"Enough to feed ranch residents?"

"No. Enough to give city kids a taste of what it's like to take care of something—someone besides themselves."

"Oh. I know you mentioned planting crops. I've forgotten what."

"Walnuts, citrus and olives. That's it for now, except for enough potatoes, carrots, peas and beans to supply our kitchen with fresh vegetables in the spring."

"Hmm. I read an article about planting tomatoes in a pot inside a deep hole. It protects their foliage and keeps them from freezing or getting scorched, depending on the climate you live in."

Linc gave her a sharp look. "Why would you read agriculture articles?"

"Is there a law against it?"

"I'll wait and plant our tomatoes in April, when it warms up."

"Fine!" She slumped in the seat and crossed her arms.

In spite of his efforts to ignore her, Linc's lips twitched. Hell, she was *impossible* to ignore. "I don't know a damn thing about farming," he admitted. "I'm learning as I go. I really could use some tips. Last night, when I should've been poring over farming literature, I spent my time thinking about kissing you."

Her mouth fell open. Turning red, she sat up and faced the side window. "I...uh...don't know what to say."

"Speechless at last, huh?" Relaxing, Linc planted an elbow on the window ledge, then threw back his head and roared with laughter.

"I'm far from an authority on farming," she said. "I was on a bus in Arizona when I read the piece on planting tomatoes. My dad swore by the *Farmer's Almanac*. But as a part-time farmer in Tennessee, he grew a little tobacco, not walnuts or olives."

"Tennessee?" Linc leapt right on that slip. "So that's where you came by your Southern accent?"

Miranda could have bitten out her tongue. She'd been so careful to avoid personal details in case someone got too nosy and ultimately tied her to the missing Nashville star. "As I said, Dad was on the road a lot. Actually, the farm seems a lifetime ago. I remember I loved what time we did spend there, though."

"Was your dad in sales?"

"Um... Hey! Look at that truck you pulled in behind. He's turning down our lane." She scooted forward. "Your cattle, I'll bet."

"Damn! The man I bought them from promised not to deliver until next week at the earliest."

"Your life's full of surprises, Parker." He scowled at her, but at least she'd forestalled his questions about her father's occupation. The truth would be out if anyone suspected her dad was Doug Kimbrough, lead guitarist for the once-famous Great Smokies bluegrass band.

Unexpectedly, an acute wave of nostalgia tore through Miranda's heart. There were so many great memories mixed in with the more recent bad ones. Wesley Carlisle had, in his greed, ruined something that had been joyful and good.

Miranda was glad the hubbub over the steers and the clothes Linc had bought meant no one was likely to notice her melancholy mood.

The little kids and Jenny were ecstatic as they opened sack after sack.

"Randi, I've never owned such pretty shirts and pants!" Cassie exclaimed.

"Me, neither," Wolfie admitted, his voice quavering. He hooked a skinny arm around his sister. "Now me and Hana are gonna look like normal kids. Thanks, Randi."

Miranda discreetly brushed a tear. "You need to thank Linc. I may have helped pick stuff out, but he paid the bill."

"Is Mr. Linc Santa Claus?" Hana asked in a tiny awe-filled voice.

Jenny chuckled. "Christmas is almost two months away, short stuff. I really doubt some fat old dude in a dumb red suit can top this, though."

Miranda noticed Jenny kept stroking a fringed paisley shawl shot through with gold and silver threads. "I knew you'd like the shawl," Miranda said. "I took it right off a mannequin. They had it teamed with the black crop top, tied around a pair of hip-hugger jeans. The smaller flowered scarves—well, I'll show you girls how to tie them in a cap over your hair. I saw some girls who had them on. They looked really cool."

"Can I wear one now?" Cassie's hazel eyes glowed.

"Sure, sweetie. Tonight, after supper, we'll sneak off and have our own fashion show." Miranda began removing price tags.

Jenny jumped in to help. "While the guys are outside ooh-ing and ahh-ing over a bunch of dumb cows, let's all go wash our hair." Her excitement was infectious.

Cassie, wearing new jeans and a kitten-soft shirt, lamented with a sigh, "I sure wish Mr. Linc would let us stay here forever."

Miranda's thoughts drifted in that direction, too.

It was Jenny's pragmatic admonition as they trooped into the bathroom that threw a damper on hope. "Sooner or later, everything good gets ruined. It's better if you don't wish for too much, kid. Then when you get kicked in the teeth, it doesn't hurt so bad."

Miranda lifted her soapy head from the sink, feeling a need to stand up for Parker. "It's not fair to blame Linc for rules and regulations he can't control. Don't forget he didn't come here with the notion of being a foster dad."

"But he's the one who phoned Social Services," Jenny said after a toss of her still-wet hair. "He could've left well enough alone."

Miranda would have said more, but Jenny switched to another subject—one that practically stopped Miranda's heart. "Hey, look at the color washing out of your hair! I guess I've never been in the bathroom when you put in a rinse before. Rats, Eric's right again. He bet me five dollars black isn't your natural color. What is?"

Standing still, letting soap drip into her eyes, Miranda might have answered had she not caught sight of a flash of blue at the door. Blinking rapidly, she realized Linc lounged in the doorway, listening to every word. Her breath lodged in her lungs as she remembered that he'd also commented on her hair color, too.

Her throat closed at how great he looked with booted ankles crossed and thumbs casually tucked under the buckle of a wide leather belt—as if he was a born cowboy, instead of a brand-new one.

To avoid answering, she turned on the cold-water faucet and ducked beneath it. If nothing else, the frigid water shocked some sense into her. Linc struck her as a man who hated duplicity. Hated lies and liars. And at the moment, her life was one massive lie.

Taking care to wrap a towel around her head until she had a chance to see how much of the rinse had washed out of her hair, she finally acknowledged Linc. "Could you please knock before entering a bathroom? We've been trying on clothes. I'm pretty sure privacy's an issue that'll be high on Mrs. Bishop's rules, Parker."

He unwound his lanky body and backed guiltily from the room. "I just stopped in to pick up my lunch and to ask what time you'd planned supper."

Miranda tugged at the wet front of her T-shirt. Hana had splashed her, and she'd elected to forgo changing until she'd finished her hair. Clearly Linc's interest was divided between thoughts of supper and hunger of another type. She hoped Jenny hadn't observed his masculine response. But not much escaped the teenager.

Sure enough, Jenny jabbed Miranda with an elbow. "You'd better tell him the cook's not on the menu."

Linc's gaze flew to both their faces. At that point, Miranda wasn't sure who was the more crimson, Jenny, Parker or her. Under the circumstances, she thought she threw a fairly good block. "Come on, Jenny, we should at least try to act mature. And Linc, getting back to your question, I'd planned supper for seven. Late enough so you farmers won't lose any daylight, but early enough for Wolfie and

Cassie to get to bed at a decent hour. Remember, they're going to school tomorrow.''

"Tomorrow? Really?" Cassie spoke from behind Linc.

He sprang aside to give her wheelchair access. Scraps lay curled contentedly in the child's lap.

"That's right, kiddo." Linc bent to scratch the head of the yawning dog. "Mrs. Banks at your school promised to try and put you and Wolfie in with the teachers you had before the Tuckers made you drop out."

"Yippee! I *loved* Mrs. Sullivan. I think Wolfie liked Mr. Wall, even though Wolfie says he doesn't like school."

"Maybe he will if we help him catch up," Linc said. "I guess we'll have to see, won't we?" He watched her nod. "Okay, since that's settled, duty calls. I'll let you ladies get back to making yourselves beautiful." His gaze swung to Miranda, this time definitely lingering on the towel hiding her hair.

She grabbed the towel with both hands, as if that protected her against his prying eyes. But her movement only brought his eyes to her breasts. Almost immediately, he left. Not fast enough, however, to keep the heat from stealing into Miranda's cheeks again. She also felt her heart begin to pound. Luckily, Jenny had already turned aside to wipe steam off the foggy mirror.

Miranda knew she and Linc would have to be much more careful about publicly displaying their attraction to each other. She'd come too far in this charade to let out-of-control hormones screw things up for her now. Her chance at ever having a normal future depended on continuing to evade Wes Carlisle's efforts to find her. At least until she figured out what to do.

CHAPTER TEN

DAYS FLOWED into weeks. Life at the ranch fell into a satisfying routine for Miranda. Outside the kitchen window, freshly plowed fields slowly filled with almost-straight rows of spindly walnut and olive trees. Seed grain had been cast across the allotted acres of rich-smelling earth. As Miranda set about baking pumpkin pies and tarts for the next day's Thanksgiving holiday, she reflected on the numerous changes around the ranch.

One positive note: the first bunkhouse now had indoor plumbing. The boys had wasted no time staking claims on beds in the more private quarters. Eric, Shawn, Greg and Wolfie had all moved their belongings. Just yesterday, she and Jenny had hung green-plaid curtains to match the bedspreads. The place looked masculine and amazingly improved.

Three new teens had shown up one day, three weeks after Cassie and Wolfie returned to school but had packed their bags and left a few days later. None of them was willing to work. They were a surly trio, and Miranda had been only too happy to see them go, as had the others. Except for maybe Linc. He honestly thought, now he'd set his mind to it, that he could turn every kid's life around. He'd been dejected following the teens' departure, and Miranda knew he considered them another failure, ranking just below his perceived negligence as a brother.

The only thing that roused Linc from his latest funk was

Wolfie and Cassie coming home with fantastic report cards. Which was the reason Miranda was baking pies and preparing turkey stuffing in advance of tomorrow's holiday. The older teens planned a party in the bunkhouse tonight to celebrate Wolfie and Cassie's success.

They'd put Jenny in charge of decorations. That freed up Miranda to cook, while Linc and the boys planted the last batch of olive trees.

On their most recent supply outing to Susanville, Jenny had been secretive in her purchase of decorations. The boys were afraid she'd go overboard with crepe-paper streamers and balloons.

Even if she did, Miranda had no objections. She was in a mood to celebrate, because there was something else she learned in Susanville. The cutout of her at the record shop had been replaced with one of Justin Timberlake. And her CD, produced after she'd left Nashville, had been relegated to its rightful place among myriad other country recordings.

Feeling freer, she'd stopped at the local library and read several prominent newspapers. Not one word in any of them about her disappearance. At last, it seemed, she was yesterday's news.

With that weight gone, she'd stopped coloring her hair. Only yesterday, Jenny had trimmed off the last remnants of her black rinse. Except for the fact that her hair was pixie short, when Miranda looked in the mirror, she saw her true self again.

She'd caught Linc checking her out in a new way, too, a sexy way that left her stumbling about in a haze. At times, though, she worried that the intensity with which he studied her meant he was still trying to place her, figure out who she was.

The last thing she'd done in town, without telling the

others, was to register for night classes in sociology at the college, beginning in January. Now she was trying to work up the nerve to tell Linc. Her breathing got shaky whenever she imagined how he'd react to the news that she planned to stay on at the ranch after the deadline he'd set for her to either leave or come clean about her real age and identity.

Linc had pressed her often enough to open up. Of course she still continued to hesitate, in spite of the fact that they'd grown closer in the past few weeks. He was always mindful of how much she kept to herself whenever they sat and talked in the evenings. It had become their habit to share coffee and conversation in the kitchen after everyone else had gone to bed.

Furtive good-night kisses had become standard. Yet Linc didn't rush to cross the invisible line to greater intimacy. Miranda had no doubt that her half-truths were to blame.

Linc filled her head day and night. Because he'd come to mean so much to her, she wanted them to take that next step. If they didn't, she was afraid he'd lose interest altogether. In many ways he was an impatient man. She'd gleaned that much through their discussions of his work with some of Hollywood's top stars. A case in point was how quickly he'd leapt into building this refuge. Yes, Linc Parker charged through life at full-throttle—but he expected results.

Smiling at Hana, Miranda said, "Would you like to sprinkle cinnamon and sugar on these pumpkin tarts?"

"Yes, please." The girl, who'd blossomed verbally in the past weeks, hopped down off a green stool Linc had bought her on one of their excursions into town. He joked that Hana and Scraps had turned into Randi's twin shadows. It was true. Miranda had to take care where she stepped or risk landing on one or both.

As she slipped Hana's tarts into the oven, Linc opened the back door and Miranda glanced up. Her ready smile died. "Linc, what happened...? Come sit. Ooh, there's so much blood." She ripped off a handful of paper towels.

He stumbled in and dropped into a kitchen chair. Blood dripped from his right temple, down his cheek, spilling onto his shirt and even the floor. Hana grabbed Scraps and shrank into a corner as Miranda again asked what had happened.

"We were pulling the last sled loaded with olive trees out to the north orchard when the cable attaching the sled to the tractor snapped. It coiled back like a sidewinder and popped me good," he said, warily touching two fingers to his cut.

Miranda batted his hand away. "Stop! Your hands are covered with dirt."

"It's clean dirt," he said. But nevertheless he let his hand fall to his lap.

Sinking to her knees, Miranda rummaged in a lower cupboard. "I know Jenny put one of the first-aid kits you bought in here. Ah, got it." She backed out, red-cheeked but triumphant. She'd soon ripped open several sanitary gauze packets and used them to blot the blood. "It's a jagged, ugly wound. You're going to have a black eye and I'll bet a king-size headache. You probably need stitches, Linc. It's really deep."

"How deep? This is the afternoon before a holiday. There won't be a doctor in his office by the time we drive into town."

"That's why hospitals have emergency rooms."

"No. No hospital. They let my sister die. Tape me up. I'll heal."

She dabbed some more, all the while speaking reassuringly to Hana, who'd started to cry. In Linc's ear, Miranda murmured, ''I can apply a butterfly strip, but it'll still scar.''

''Do it,'' he growled. Feeling her cool hands on his skin, Linc stared woozily at inviting breasts precisely aligned with his eyes. He fought an urge to bury his already aching head in their softness. Just then, Miranda warned him, ''Get ready. This is gonna hurt.''

''Shit!'' *Hurt* was an understatement if Linc ever heard one. Whatever she poured over his temple stung like hell. He grabbed her hips with both hands and hung on tight as wave after wave of pain all but tore off the top of his head.

As the spinning kitchen began to slow, her amused voice penetrated his mental fog. ''Linc, are you still with me? If you don't turn me loose, there'll be two of us sporting bruises tomorrow.''

''Oh.'' His hands sprang free. ''Sorry.'' He spoke automatically, but his fingers itched to latch on to her denim-covered hips again. Miranda and the room smelled of cinnamon and pumpkin spice. Homey scents. For the first time in his life, they gave Linc a sense of peace and serenity in spite of the haze of pain.

She gnawed her lower lip and gazed worriedly down at him. ''That's the best I can do with what's in the kit. I've managed to slow the bleeding, I think. But it hasn't stopped.''

''Believe it or not, it feels better. Thanks.''

''Give me your shirt and jacket. If I soak them in cold water right away, the blood should wash out. I was just fixin' to toss in a colored load, anyway.''

Linc stripped off his jacket, then his shirt. He'd forgotten to undo the buttons on the sleeves, so he couldn't pull off the shirt. Miranda bent to work the buttons free. Despite all the weeks they'd shared a house, this was the first time she remembered seeing Linc shirtless. He was tanned and well muscled, with nicely rippled abs. She realized it wasn't just heat from the oven making the sweat pop out on her brow.

Her throat and mouth were dust-dry. She fumbled the job of getting him out of his shirt—probably because she'd fantasized so often about doing this very thing, only in the privacy of his bedroom. She, of course, still shared quarters with Jenny, Cassie and Hana.

His voice rumbled near her ear. "I'm not much help."

What would he do, Miranda wondered, if she kissed one of the flat brown nipples peeking out from whorls of light-brown hair?

Then she happened to lift guilty eyes and saw that his were smoldering. His thickly lashed lids fell, but not fast enough to hide what was going through his mind. The same thought that was going through hers.

Her lips parted in invitation. A second later, Linc's hands spanned her waist and he wedged her between his thighs.

Then two things halted what promised to be a really steamy kiss. Scraps broke free of Hana's clutches. The terrier knocked over Hana's stool with a loud crash that sent the child into full-blown hysterics. And the oven timer went off, announcing the tarts were done.

Linc and Miranda sprang apart as if shot out of a cannon. She grabbed pot holders with hands that shook.

He tried to quiet the dog as he swung the sobbing child onto his lap. Damn, his head was splitting now from all the noise. "Can't you at least shut off that damned buzzer?" he snapped at Miranda.

She did, but not before unloading the oven.

Hana saw the treats and at once turned off the spigot of

tears. She hopped off Linc's knee and reached for the hot cookie sheet.

Miranda swung her up and out of danger scant seconds before the girl would've been burned. "Honey, we need to let those cool." Dangling Hana awkwardly over one arm, Miranda waved a pot holder over the steaming cookie sheet. Only then did she think to shut off the timer. That was when she discovered Linc and Scraps had departed.

Greg stuck his head in the back door. "Where's Linc?"

"I taped his cut and he left. He didn't come back out to work?"

"Nope. Eric sent me to tell him we've fixed the winch. Did he go see a doc?"

"No. Let me check in his room. And hands off the tarts and pies while I'm gone." She'd seen Greg drooling over the pumpkin confections.

Rushing down the hall, she paused to listen outside Linc's door. When she heard nothing, she tapped and opened it a crack. He sat on the bed shaking analgesic tablets into an unsteady hand.

"The boys are worried about you. Frankly, so am I."

He swallowed four of the pills without water and recapped the bottle. "Tell them to take a break. I'll be okay if I rest a minute." He kicked off his boots and fell back on the pillows.

Miranda walked over and covered him with a robe that lay on a nearby chair. "Are you feeling dizzy?" She turned on the bedside lamp and made him look her in the eye.

"Don't tell me you were a nurse in another life?"

"No, but when you're on the road as much as we were, guys get hurt."

"What guys?" Linc's dark eyes locked with hers.

Saying *the guys in my band* rose to the tip of Miranda's

tongue. She made a great save, mumbling something about her dad and his farming crew right before she plunged Linc's room into darkness again. Her response wasn't really logical—why would her father travel with his farm workers?—but Linc was probably too disoriented to notice. Damn, it was hard to remember to hold her tongue, when by nature she'd always been an open person.

At the door, she hesitated and turned back. "It's not good to sleep after a head injury, Linc. Rest for a while. I'll look in on you at regular intervals. The boys will be glad for the time off. Did you remember tonight is Cassie and Wolfie's party?"

"No. Tonight? Well, I bought them each a set of pencils and had their names engraved on them. It's not much, but they've come so far I wanted to commemorate their progress. The pencils are on top of my dresser. If you have time, would you wrap them? Oh, maybe we don't have any wrapping paper."

"Are you kidding? With Christmas a little over a month away? I bought variety packs of wrap and an assortment of bows. I've even begun my holiday shopping."

Linc grimaced. "Christmas. I always had a secretary handle my gift list."

"You're kidding."

He shook his head, then sucked in a deep, gasping breath.

"Forget Christmas for now," she told him. "Get better, and I promise I'll help you choose what to get everyone. I won't *buy* the gifts for you, though. Shopping is three-quarters of the fun at Christmas. The little kids are already so excited they're bouncing off the walls."

"Randi…" His pensive call stopped her again. "Wolfie, Hana and Cassie may not be with us at Christmas."

Miranda's heart sank. She'd grown very attached to

them. And she knew the girls prayed nightly that they'd be allowed to stay at the ranch. "But...you just said they've come so far."

"I know you think nothing's going to change. It will, though. Eric's already antsy to get back to the city. And I've never made a secret of the fact that the little kids don't fit my agenda of providing a shelter for teens." The frown knotting his brow clearly worsened his headache.

Miranda didn't want to add to his pain, so she withdrew, closing the door gently. The little kids belonged here. This was their home. She'd work on Linc. After all, Christmas was the season of miracles.

"Greg," she called, "Linc's resting. He said for you guys to knock off. Go wash up. After lunch we'll help Jenny decorate the bunkhouse."

"Hmm. Maybe we'll finish the planting. We heard on Eric's radio that we may get snow flurries tonight or tomorrow. I know Linc hoped we'd have all the trees in before the storm hits."

"He said Eric's getting itchy feet."

"Yeah. Shawn thinks Eric's nuts. The rest of us aren't in any hurry to leave."

"Including Jenny?"

The dark-haired boy shrugged. "She'll follow Eric. They're convinced we're gonna see our names in neon lights next year."

"I hadn't heard anyone talking about becoming rock stars in quite a while."

"That's all Eric talks about when Linc's not around. The man doesn't like us to play rock tunes. Or even mention it. Linc flat out hates any music except classical."

A chill struck Miranda. "Hate's a strong word, Greg."

"Then you haven't heard his lectures whenever the subject of us performing comes up. Parker detests everything about the music industry.''

She turned. ''Uh…I have to boil giblets and cube the bread for our turkey dressing.''

''Gotta tell you, Randi, those pies look bad.''

''They do?'' She spun and frowned at her counter full of golden pies and tarts.

The boy laughed. ''Bad means good, Randi. What universe have you been living in? I thought we all came off the same street.''

''Of course. Silly me. It's the Southerner in me, Greg.'' She exaggerated her drawl. ''We say things plumb different down South.''

He retreated, still eyeing her dubiously. Enough so that Miranda vowed to keep a closer watch on her tongue. Even if she relented and revealed her age to Mrs. Bishop next week, she hoped she might keep the truth from the other kids a while longer. She didn't know why, other than that they had such dim views of adults.

Four times during the afternoon and early evening, she tiptoed into Linc's bedroom and shook him awake, asking him to count the fingers she held up in front of his bleary eyes.

''I brought you some soup,'' she said the last time. ''Homemade beef barley.''

He struggled to sit up. ''Is this lunch?''

She glanced at the clock beside his bed, then back at him with a worried expression. ''You slept through lunch and supper, Linc. The others have gone to the bunkhouse to start the party. Do you feel like walking over there?''

He raised himself onto one elbow and blinked at the steaming bowl Randi offered him. ''I've never slept that many hours straight in my life.'' He touched a hand to his bandaged head and winced.

"Still hurt?" she asked softly.

"Feels like hell. Like a jazz drummer going crazy in a too-small nightclub."

Miranda cocked an ear. She, too, heard a low, steady thrum-thrum. Eric must have cranked up the sound on the radio he'd recently purchased. Unless she missed her guess, Greg was pounding on his drum pad. He was saving up to buy a full set of drums. She steadied Linc's bowl and made a mental note to tell the kids to turn down the volume.

"I wrapped the pencils and put them back on your dresser. Maybe after you eat, you'll feel like popping in to hand them out. Wolfie and Cassie are flying high. After I finished the pies, I baked and decorated a cake. I gather the cakes they got for their birthdays, when and if they got them, weren't frosted, let alone decorated. It's so easy to do with the canned stuff, and they were absolutely thrilled."

Linc accepted the bowl and shut his eyes, drawing in the steam. "Can you stay a minute, or do you need to go?"

She sat next to him on the bed. She'd sat on beds with men before, but her heart had never tripped over itself as it was doing now. Miranda and members of the band often rehearsed in ten-by-twelve hotel rooms or on her bus. This was different. Linc Parker affected her in a very different way.

"Randi, earlier I could tell you'd wanted me to be something I can't for Wolfie, Hana and Cassie. I can't be their rock."

"Like it or not, Linc, you already are."

"I've tossed them a bone or two, as any humane person would do. They need more. They need someone who'll stick by them through thick and thin."

"They need food, shelter, clothing and a few hugs. Oh, and a clean place to lay their heads at night. You've given them all that, Linc."

He dipped the spoon in his soup before responding. "They need unconditional love. I don't...can't love them like that."

Miranda placed a hand on his knee. "Why can't you love them? Are you saying they're not lovable kids?"

"No. God, no!" He almost dropped the hot soup, but caught the bowl in time. "I just..." He shrugged and wouldn't lift his gaze. "Some guys aren't cut out to be family men."

"Are you afraid? Is that it? Because of what happened to Felicity?"

His gaze did lift then, and the truth of her words lay dull and heavy in his eyes. "I loved Felicity. She obviously couldn't tell. I won't risk someone else getting hurt because I lack...emotional connection." He shoved the bowl into her hands, fell back and flung an arm across his face. "Forget it, Randi. The subject's closed."

She clung so tightly to the spoon and bowl, her fingers ached. So did her heart. For the children. For Linc. And for herself. A man who couldn't find love in his heart for three homeless waifs probably had no room there for her, either. "You know what, Linc? You can wallow in the pain of losing Felicity for the rest of your life. And this ranch will end up being nothing but a shrine. A meaningless gesture to her name. If that's all you've built here, I'm sorry for you." She stood, and with trembling hands, set the half-finished soup on his nightstand. At the door, she ventured one quick glance over her shoulder. He hadn't moved a muscle.

She hesitated, but only because she wondered whether she ought to take his gifts to Cassie and Wolfie. But it would be a futile act coming from anyone other than the man who'd cared enough to buy them the personalized gifts. A man who nonetheless claimed he couldn't love these children. She stalked out and down the hall, not bothering to shut his door.

Maybe she'd have to rethink staying here. In fact, rather than stick around for the grilling she'd surely get from Mrs. Bishop, why not pack her bag and light out after tomorrow's dinner? She had a bit of money tucked away, thanks to Linc's wages. Turkey leftovers would get her through several days on the road.

Slinging a jacket around her shoulders, Miranda ran blindly toward the bunkhouse. She wished she could as easily bar Linc from her heart as he seemed able to bar her from his. Her and the kids.

A cold north wind had blown up. Greg's predictions of snow on Thanksgiving might come to pass. The prospect left Miranda reconsidering her plan of moments earlier as she walked in on a party in full swing.

The noise level rocked the rafters. Eric's radio/CD player blasted at top decibels—a rap tune by Nelly. She'd heard him sing on the American Music Awards. The song segued into another with a female vocalist.

As she'd suspected, Greg sat cross-legged on the floor, banging sticks on his drum pad. Eric reclined on one bed, strumming his electric guitar, which he now had attached to small but powerful speakers. Jenny, dressed in a long satin skirt and a black cotton sweater that Miranda had helped her find at Goodwill, belted out the words, along with the lead singer.

Miranda stood, still clutching her jacket. Jenny had a pure voice, and that shocked her. Listening to the group, she'd have to say they had talent. But that didn't mean they'd make it in the business. So much more went into being a star than talent. There was the matter of financial backing. Of making good demos and getting them in front of the right people at the right time. But success certainly began with talent.

The CD ended. The kids noticed her as Shawn popped in another disc. Greg called a greeting and waved her over with a twirl of one drumstick.

"Hey, how'd we sound? Eric thinks we're ready to take Hollywood by storm. 'Course, I've gotta get a real set of drums first."

Shawn pulled the tab on a can of cola. "What kept you? I've had a hell of a time holding back from your cake."

Jenny danced across the room doing a quick shuffle and a few finger snaps. "Give her a plate of chips and dip. We've got beer in the cooler," she whispered near Miranda's ear. "We won't bring it out until the munchkins toddle off to bed and after Linc puts in his appearance. Where is he, do you suppose?"

"Beer?" Miranda gasped. "How? When? Linc will have a hemorrhage. Not one of you is old enough to buy or drink liquor."

"Well, neither are you."

Miranda cringed and almost came clean then and there. But Jenny winked. "Actually, Wolfie gave us the suds."

"Wolfie?" Miranda felt as if she'd stepped into another reality.

"Yep. Wait'll you see the cool caves the kid showed us. Wolfie has one of the chambers fixed up as a regular hideout. The middle room is warm and dry. He's stashed food, blankets, even lanterns. Said he snuck supplies out from under George Tucker's nose. That's why he has beer. Tucker kept a well-stocked fridge. He drank dark malt— Eric's favorite. Not mine." She made a face.

"Jenny, I wish you hadn't told me. We have no idea

when Mrs. Bishop is liable to show up. If she finds us with beer, you know what that would do to Linc's license. She'd pull it so fast his head would swim."

"That's what's so sweet about the caves," Eric said, butting into their conversation. "Parker doesn't know they exist. Once he and the kids hit the sack, we'll move our party on out there and you'll see how cool a setup it is."

"Eric, I don't know." Miranda looked and sounded worried.

"Don't be an old poop," Jenny said. "Who're we gonna hurt? That old broad's not gonna show up tonight."

Another song exploded from the player before Miranda could admonish them a second time. Greg went back to pounding his drum pad. Eric grabbed Jenny and twirled her into the middle of the floor to dance. A moment later, Shawn set his plate aside and reached for Miranda. But she noticed the envy and longing that crossed Cassie's thin face. And she realized Wolfie was attempting to teach Hana how to dance.

"Uh, Shawn, thanks for the dance, but why don't I cut the cake while you give Cassie a spin around the room?" She nudged him hard.

"Cassie? But...but..." the boy sputtered.

"Tilt her chair back on two wheels and hold on to the steel arms. Just circle the floor a few times. I imagine she's left out of most activities at school. It must be really rough at her age. I'd do it, but I think it'd mean more if you took her."

Greg, who tended to see the world with more compassion than his companions, dropped his drumsticks and stood. He soon had Cassie smiling and giggling as loudly as Hana. From her vantage point behind the refreshment table, Miranda was able to stand back and enjoy the pleasure on all their faces. What a difference, she thought, between this night and the night they'd arrived at the ranch. The little kids had been sad, frightened and unkempt. The teens, exhausted and half-starved.

If only Linc could see them now. Even a man as cynical as he was would have to break an arm patting himself on the back. She smiled, imagining how pleased he'd be.

A sudden movement near the door caught her attention, pulling her eyes from the dancers. There stood the man she'd been daydreaming about, and he looked anything but pleased. His mouth formed an angry slash below flared nostrils as he bellowed, "Turn off that hideous crap." Grasping both sides of his head, he lost his hold on the gifts Miranda had painstakingly wrapped earlier.

Eric whirled. It was Jenny who leapt to switch off the sound. Shawn stiffened, moving closer to Miranda. Greg eased Cassie's wheelchair to the ground, while Wolfie hugged Hana protectively under one arm.

All the good things Miranda had reflected on only seconds ago fled in a single unhappy heartbeat.

"I didn't sink my hard-earned money into this bunkhouse to give you kids a stage for this...this outrageous music. I thought I made my rules clear from the get-go." Linc's hard eyes sought out and impaled Miranda from across the room. "I expected better of you, Randi. You, who said I'd erected a meaningless shrine to my sister. Shrine denotes someone died. She did. And why? Because I never had the guts to say she didn't have talent. But I *am* telling all of you. You sound worse than...than the mating call of a hundred bull moose combined with two dozen banshees. Not one of you has what it takes to succeed. So pack it in. Go to bed. You can thank me for my honesty tomorrow when we give thanks for having a roof over our heads to block out the snow."

"It's snowing?" All except Miranda and Cassie made a mad dash for the door.

"It is!" Jenny squealed. "Wow, I've never seen snow coming down before."

Randi bent to pick up the gifts Linc had dropped. She handed them to Cassie and Wolfie. As she went to call the others back to watch the kids open their presents, she heard the door to the main house slam and realized Linc had gone. She was so angry at him she wanted to shake him by his ears. "You know, Linc's wrong. I heard you guys. You have talent."

"Yeah, right!" Eric flung his guitar back into the case.

Greg slid his drum pad into his backpack. "Even if we do, it's a cinch we ain't gonna improve if we can't practice. The man couldn't have spoken any plainer. We've gotta figure out which we want more—a career, or food and shelter."

Miranda raked a hand through her short hair. "He's hurt, remember. He's not even aware that you finished planting the last field. Tomorrow he might change his mind."

"Hardnoses like Parker never back down," Eric spat.

Miranda gave up. "Come on, Hana and Cassie. I have to get up early to put a turkey in the oven. I'll come over here tomorrow afternoon and help with cleanup."

Jenny's cheeks were pink, and snowflakes still sparkled in her long dark hair. "Felicity didn't die because she lacked talent. She was insecure because she could never measure up to Parker's expectations. I say we show him we're tougher than that. So we can't practice in his bunkhouse. We can sing and play at the cave."

"Yeah!" Eric shouted. "Let's go."

The others rallied, except for Miranda. She watched them pack up and trudge off into the already snowy hills, declining their invitation to follow. Her hands tightened on Cassie's wheelchair. "Kids, lying is never wise. Lies nearly always come back to haunt you. About this cave, though—maybe we'd better keep it our secret for now."

"Until Mr. Parker's in a better mood?" Cassie whispered.

"Maybe longer," Miranda said with a sigh.

Back at the house, she helped the girls into their pajamas, then sat between their cots and read, as had become a nightly ritual. Tonight she chose a silly story about birthday clowns. It had stunned her to learn that no one had ever read to Hana. Neither she nor Cassie had owned a book until Miranda began buying Golden Books at the grocery store. Hana loved storytime. Already she recognized simple words like *cat* and *fish*. The hardest thing had been making her understand that there wasn't any need to sleep with the books under her pillow. That no one would steal them while she slept.

Tonight, both girls yawned profusely before Miranda closed the book and turned out the light. Almost immediately, they nodded off, and Miranda tucked the covers around their shoulders. The excitement of the party had taken its toll.

On them, but not on her. She worried about Linc, and wondered if she ought to look in on him. She also worried about the teens who'd gone to the cave. She wasn't their keeper, and yet if anything happened to one of them while they tramped around out there in the storm, she'd blame herself.

Reclining against her pillows, she tried composing lines for a new song that had been kicking around in her head. But she hit a snag. In the middle of fluffing her pillows for about the hundredth time, she thought she heard a door open and close. Were Jenny and the boys back this soon?

She tucked an arm under her head, deciding she'd pretend to sleep.

A minute or two slipped by without the bedroom door opening. Her restlessness made Cassie stir and moan. Climbing out of bed, Miranda covered the girl again. Then she felt around the dresser and found a book she'd checked out of the library. A guide to social services in California. She'd fix a cup of tea and read until she got drowsy. With luck, the dry nature of the material would do the trick.

There was a light on in the kitchen. Miranda thought she'd shut them all off. Entering the room, juggling her book while tugging up red fuzzy slipper socks that she wore with her San Francisco Giants nightshirt, Miranda skidded to a dead stop.

Linc Parker sat at the kitchen table holding a raw sirloin steak over one eye. He reared back guiltily and offered a self-conscious grin. "You were absolutely correct in your prediction. I have a doozy of a black eye." He let the steak slide down to rest on his cheekbone, exposing a puffy, purple eyelid. All around his eye were interesting rainbow shades of pink, violet and chartreuse.

"Does meat really work?" Miranda bent down for a closer inspection. "Isn't ice the treatment doctors recommend?"

Linc shrugged carelessly. "This is my first black eye. I remember reading somewhere that football players use raw steak."

Dropping her book, she went straight to the freezer and pulled out a blue ice pack. She removed the ruined steak. "What a waste. Or maybe I can cook it and feed it to Scraps."

"He was just here looking hopeful. By the way, why are you up and roaming around this time of night? Or did you hear me and come to claim a piece of my hide?"

Flopping the steak into a frying pan, which she then put in the fridge, she eyed Linc darkly. "Why would I do that?" she asked as she wrapped the blue ice pack in a kitchen towel and carried it to him. "Hmm, maybe a kiss will make it all better. That works with the kids." Grinning, she brushed a feather-light kiss across his swollen lid before gently closing off his vision with the ice.

"I can't believe you'd kiss me after I acted like a first-rate jackass tonight."

She loved his groveling. "You don't look like a donkey—no pointy ears. A toad, maybe? I've kissed a few of those in my time. But…you don't fit that description, either. I've got it! Not a toad, a frog." Flopping down opposite him so their knees touched, she rested her elbows on the table and delivered a sexy growl. "I dub you a princely frog, Lincoln Parker. My princely frog."

Miranda leaned forward as she waited to see if he'd play along and kiss her, as she'd so often dreamt.

The old kitchen wall clock ticked off the seconds. Miranda was afraid he'd leave her sitting there like a fool. And maybe she *was* a fool to be so charmed by this complicated man. After all, he had acted like an ass earlier, just as he'd said.

As the fingers of his right hand turned icy from holding the pack, Linc's heart thumped like a landing helicopter. His one good eye made a heated circuit of Randi's tense compact body, and he had to swallow the saliva gathering in his mouth. Even with her tousled blond curls, silly red socks and totally unsexy flannel nightshirt, she was a huge turn-on. X-rated pictures began to flip through his aching swollen head. And other parts of his body swelled to match, taking his mind off his injury.

Damn, wasn't the woman aware of the effect she had on him? Linc didn't know and he didn't care. Wanting to be her princely frog and definitely not wanting her to kiss any more toads, he wrapped his free hand around the back of her sweet, sweet neck and closed the distance between their mouths.

She sighed contentedly as their lips met. The kiss was hot and long and satisfying.

After the kiss ended, they rose by tacit agreement, hand in hand, and she turned off the lights. And in the darkness, while snowflakes built outside on his windowsill, together they found warmth and passion in his bed.

CHAPTER ELEVEN

MIRANDA STIRRED, and in the greenish glow of the digital clock on Linc's nightstand, she smiled at his relaxed features. Surprising, since their lovemaking had been a lot like riding out a typhoon in a rowboat.

His eye didn't look so bad in the semidarkness. With both arms flung above his head, he slept like a carefree child. Although, with his sculpted arms and deep chest muscles, grown harder in the past weeks of backbreaking ranch work, he was all man. Definitely all man.

She hated leaving the warm cocoon of his bed, and she shivered in the cold room the instant she slipped from beneath the covers. Miranda wished with all her heart that she could burrow into Linc's side and stay until morning. Their stolen moments had been all she'd dreamt of and more.

Linc could have taken what she offered in the slam-bam-thank-you-ma'am method of her last experience, with someone who'd professed to love her. Linc didn't lie about that part, either. And yet, he'd certainly made her feel cherished. For one thing, he'd looked after the practical matter of protection. For all her sophistication, she hadn't given it a thought. Linc remembered. And he'd had to dig through his dresser drawer to find a buried box of condoms.

Miranda tugged her nightshirt over her head, then was moved to kiss her fingertips and brush them softly over his lips. Even in sleep, he sighed and nibbled at them. The fact that he only belatedly remembered having condoms and wasn't readily able to lay his hands on them said a lot about the man.

The singers she knew, and their band members, carried suitcases full of economy packs along on tours. She used to shake her head over their lack of emotion, of real caring. With Linc, she'd felt cared for. He hadn't rushed. He'd given her ample opportunity to say no. And as they'd cuddled afterward, he'd shared a rare piece of himself. He said that working with ambitious rising actresses had left him jaded and not altogether trusting of women. Despite Miranda's secrets, he felt she was principled.

She spared a last longing glance at his motionless form as she hurried from the bedroom, refusing to think about where they went from here. Or *if* they went from here. This might be their one and only time together, and she'd put it in her storehouse of wonderful memories.

Outside the door to the bedroom she shared with Hana, Cassie and Jenny, Miranda hesitated before entering. According to Linc's bedside clock, it was scarcely past midnight—the witching hour, she thought with a smile. Had Jenny returned from her outing? Miranda doubted it, or else the younger girl would've gone searching for her missing roommate.

Indeed, Jenny's bed hadn't been slept in.

The little girls were fast asleep, though. Scraps's nose peeked out from under Cassie's comforter.

Miranda padded softly across the room and pressed her nose to the window. The snow had stopped falling, although the clouds still hung low. The only light visible shone from a bulb Linc had installed at the peak of the barn gable. It cast gray murky shadows over the blanket covering the ground.

Pleasantly tired but still not sleepy, Miranda debated between going back for the tea she'd never had a chance to drink or taking a shower. Either would give her reason to wait up for Jenny. The shower won. The only problem with it was that her flowery soap washed away Linc's scent. She took a deep breath and shut off the water, superstitiously hoping this didn't mean she'd washed him out of her life forever.

It was the first time Miranda had let herself think about the future. Yes, tomorrow was Thanksgiving. Yes, they'd all seemed excited over the prospect of experiencing their first traditional holiday in a long time. The very first time for some, like Hana, Shawn and Greg. Others, herself included, had some good memories. Suddenly Miranda found herself wondering how she and Linc would act around each other at breakfast. The morning after...

Partially wrapped in a towel but struggling to shove damp legs into sweatpants she'd dragged from her closet in the dark, Miranda heard a light tap on the door. Linc coming to see where she'd gone?

It wasn't Linc but Jenny. "Whatcha doin'?" the girl asked, bringing in the cold. In fact, her sneakers were wet and muddy, as were the bottoms of her jeans.

Miranda finished pulling on her sweats. "I couldn't sleep and I was thinking about coming to find you. Is everything okay?" She leaned close and sniffed, trying to detect if Jenny smelled like beer.

"We didn't drink. Randi, the cave is incredible. We jammed the whole time. The acoustics there are...magic." She hugged herself. "You should hear how great we sounded. I can't explain. Oh, but you don't know anything about music. Forget it. I'm going to bed."

Miranda watched her trundle off, humming happily.

Wouldn't they be surprised by how much she did know about music?

Changing her mind about staying up, she went to bed thinking about the cave. No sooner did she lie down than dreams of Linc replaced all conscious thought.

Too soon her alarm blared in the still-black room, eliciting groans and complaints from the others. "It's okay," she said groggily. "Go back to sleep. I have to get the turkey ready and put it in to roast."

Jenny sat up. "I have to go feed the livestock."

"Isn't it Eric's turn?" Miranda lowered her voice so as not to disturb the kids.

"I said I'd trade with him." Jenny yawned. "Last night he was fired up to write. The notes just flowed. It's the best stuff he's ever done."

"I wasn't aware he wrote songs."

"Not words. Just melody. He hears it in his head. I wish I could put words to his music, but I don't know how."

"Songs are poetry. Hey, I noticed there's a poetry class at the college beginning in January. Why not sign up for it?"

"How do you know that?" By now they'd dressed and left the bedroom.

"I picked up a course catalog. Actually, I'm planning to take two classes. I want to find out what it'd be like to help kids like Wolfie and the girls. So I'm taking Intro to Child Psychology and Beginning Sociology."

"How will you get there? The college is miles away."

Miranda screwed up her face. "I've decided to ask Linc if I can take the driving test. Then maybe he'll let me use the SUV in the evenings. If you had a class on the same night, I'm sure he'd agree."

"But...to get a license you have to, uh, like give your full name and address."

"I have a name, Jenny. And I'll use this address. What do you say?"

"I'll ask Eric. He's afraid if anyone in authority knows our last names, the cops might show up and ship us home."

"That's why Linc started this refuge, Jenny. To help kids who couldn't go home again. You know, you'll have to supply a name to the Social Services director."

"I'll think about it, okay? Is Randi your real name, then?"

"Sort of. It's Miranda." She said it hesitantly to test the waters. When Jenny's expression didn't change, she went for broke. "My name is Miranda Kimbrough." She expelled a breath, feeling lighter for her admission. What she didn't realize was that Linc had emerged from his room and lurked in the shadows behind them.

"Miranda," he said in a gravelly voice that made both women jump. "That's nice. Very nice. It fits you," he said, looking rumpled from sleep as he walked toward them, buttoning the cuffs of a long-sleeved flannel shirt.

Unprepared to see him yet, after the wondrous hours they'd spent making love, Miranda reeled at the sight of him. In worn jeans, Western-style shirt and scuffed square-toed boots, he really was the image of a cowboy. She didn't dare meet his eyes.

"Ugh, Linc, your face could pass for modern art," Jenny gasped.

Miranda did glance at him then. Sympathy rushed through her until Linc brushed off Jenny's comment with one of his own. "Looks worse than it feels. And my headache's gone. To tell the truth, I feel on top of the world." His good eye settled on Miranda as his declaration brought splashes of heat to her cheeks.

"Well, uh...the turkey awaits me in the kitchen. Jenny,

weren't you heading out to feed the stock? Will you gather the eggs while you're at it?"

"Okay. What time are we having Thanksgiving dinner?"

"Around two o'clock, if that's okay with everyone," Miranda said. "No one mentioned a preference, and that's when we always ate at home. Linc, will you carve the turkey?"

"I've never done it," he said, "but sure. There's probably directions in that cookbook I saw you looking at yesterday. Come on, Miranda, I'll follow you to the kitchen. One of us needs to make a pot of coffee. I don't think well without caffeine."

Miranda marveled at how easily her real name rolled off his lips. But she'd rather he didn't use it all the time. She still had the hurdle of Eric—the real authority on musicians.

"If you see the boys, tell them I made cinnamon rolls for breakfast, along with fresh fruit. Makes for an easy meal when the rest of the kitchen is messed up with holiday fixin's."

"Fixin's?" Linc teased as he turned her toward the kitchen and spanned her waist with familiar hands. "I'll bet you don't realize how many times you say you're fixin' to do something."

"Are you implying I talk funny?"

"Not at all." He grinned. And the minute they rounded the corner that hid both of them from Jenny, he moved his hand to the back of her neck and tugged her up on tiptoe to receive a kiss that was almost a sigh of relief.

Jenny's loudly spoken goodbye had him awkwardly releasing Miranda. She sank onto her heels, her brain too scrambled to return Jenny's farewell. Linc called out for both of them.

"How are you this morning?" he asked Miranda with a thoroughly male smile. "Why did you leave without waking me? Moreover, why didn't you stay?"

"You know why. I share a room with Jenny and the kids. How would it look? They all believe I'm Jenny's age, for pity's sake."

"Right! That always slips my mind." He drew back and stumbled over his words. "You *are* twenty-six? I mean, with that haircut you look about sixteen." He blew out a breath. "Hell, of course you're a woman," he said expansively before she scorched him with a frown. "After last night, that much is plain."

"I'd think, after last night, you'd trust me at least to tell the truth about my age," she snapped, flicking on the kitchen lights.

He began to respond, then clamped his lips together and strode straight to the coffeepot. Her name, as well as her face, now capped by blondish hair, kept niggling at the back of his mind. Like he was missing an important piece of a puzzle.

"Given our start, there's no hope for us, is there?" she said in a strained voice. "There'll always be a part of you that wonders about me, Linc. I might as well chalk last night up to a nice interlude."

"It felt like more," he said, drawing water for the coffeepot. "But—" he shrugged "—I've been burned by women I knew a whole lot better. Considering what's at stake with my project and all, I shouldn't have let things go as far as they did. It's just the attraction between us that had been heating up for weeks. Last night was…great," he said softly. "Damn, I'm not saying another word. I don't like that fiery look in your eye."

Miranda put her hands to work preparing the turkey. It was awhile before she was able to ask anything calmly.

"Linc, I'd like to take the driver's test. Jenny and I want to register for some college classes. Shawn's expressed an interest in getting his GED, too."

"Hey, that's good news. Shawn said something about it in passing. I thought it was probably one of those fleeting wishes all kids make. What about Eric? That kid is sharp. He's a whiz with machinery. He could do so much more with his life."

"Eric's a holdout. So you're okay with us going ahead with these plans? We'd need your SUV probably two nights a week. Classes start at six. On those evenings, I can fix a casserole. Someone will have to get Cassie and Hana ready for bed, though."

A look of concern crossed Linc's face. "I haven't given up hope of hiring a housekeeper. Perhaps Mrs. Bishop can help me find someone. I don't think she'll let me expand my operation without household assistance. Of course, baby-sitting the younger ones won't be an issue by January. She'll remove them from here right away, I'm sure."

Miranda straightened from shoving the huge turkey into the preheated oven. "Before Christmas? You think she'll take them before then? Oh, no, Linc!"

Linc's steady regard unnerved her.

"That'd be perfectly awful," she rushed to say. "This is the only home they know. We're their *family*, Linc. They've responded so well to us. I guarantee that holidays without family are absolutely awful." Tears glossed her eyes as she watched his shoulders stiffen. He poured a cup of coffee and walked out of the room.

She didn't see him again all morning. At about nine, the boys and Jenny came in for breakfast. "Hey, Randi," Shawn called. "Will you fix a couple of cinnamon rolls and a thermos for Linc?"

She looked startled. "Is he going somewhere?"

"Nope. We're gonna start cleaning out the second bunk-house. He knows the plumber can't get down the road with his equipment while it's snowing, but he says if it's clean, the woman who's evaluating him can at least see its potential." Greg issued his last statement around a mouthful of gooey roll.

Miranda figured she knew what was behind Linc's sudden need to ready the second bunkhouse. He didn't want her near his bedroom. Why that depressed her, she couldn't say. Deep in her heart she knew her time here at the ranch was limited. One day she'd have to go back to Nashville and face Wes Carlisle. She'd been thinking about an off-hand comment Linc had made a few weeks back. He'd said there wasn't a contract that couldn't be broken. She wished she could ask him more about that without spilling her guts.

While exhaustion had allowed her to walk away from her life without a thought for her future, now that she'd recovered somewhat, she saw how much she'd given up. A house, a hefty bank balance and friends who must be worried sick. But she wasn't ready to see any of them yet. Maybe six months down the road. If Linc let her stay and go to school, the college would uncover another of her falsehoods. They'd discover she already had a liberal arts degree. But a semester of specialized classes would help her counsel kids like Jenny and the others. If she wanted to do anything more involved, she'd have to do a master's program in social work.

Jenny pulled out Hana's green stool and sat at the counter. "Shawn came out to the barn and said Parker agreed to us taking classes. You must've been persuasive, Randi, er, Miranda. I told the others your name," she said shyly. "I hope that's okay."

Miranda glanced at the ring of faces. Not seeing any

recognition that could unmask her, she shrugged. "Like I said before, what's in a name? I answer to most anything."

Eric tossed her the first curve as she poured juice. "When you take your driver's test, Randi, can I tag along?" He puffed out his chest, warding off curious stares. "You heard Parker say he might buy a truck so there'll always be a vehicle here. If I had a current license, maybe he'd let me drive to town sometime."

"Hey, great, Eric. Why can't we all get licenses?" Miranda asked.

"If there's a second car," Wolfie said, picking at his fruit, "can I sign up for soccer? Coach asked me the other day. He saw us kicking the ball at recess."

Shawn, who'd started out the door with Linc's food, turned back. "Soccer's not till spring, right?" At Wolfie's nod, Shawn said, "It won't be Linc's worry then, kid. You'll be living somewhere else."

The older boy caught Miranda's glare. "Well, it's not nice to string kids along," he muttered. "I hated when my old man dangled a carrot under my nose. We all know the old broad from the county won't let 'em stay with Parker, especially if he's the only adult taking care of us."

Cassie began to sob, which set Hana off. Wolfie's lower lip trembled as he tried to soothe his sister.

"Good going, Shawn baby," Eric sputtered. "Happy Thanksgiving."

Shawn left, slamming the door, leaving the others to deal with the fallout.

Four hours later, Linc sat at the head of the table, having done a passable job of carving the bird while studying the cookbook. "Why all the long faces?" he asked, making a survey of the table. "The storm's blown over. Snow's melting. Our table is groaning with good food. Am I missing something?"

"Shawn shot off his mouth and stirred up the little kids by saying the social worker's gonna move them." Greg and the others glared sullenly at their friend, who'd already dug into his mashed potatoes and gravy.

He scowled back. "Why are you pissed off because I call a spade a spade?"

"Cut the swearing," Linc warned. He was uncomfortable because the three smaller kids had turned to him with wide frightened eyes. "Can't we just give thanks that we're together today?"

"My sentiments exactly." Miranda reached out to the kids on either side of her and clasped their hands. "If everybody will show some manners and stop stuffing your faces, we'll say grace. My dad always said collective prayers have a better chance of being answered."

With that none-too-gentle nudge, they all dropped their forks and joined hands.

Miranda waited for Linc to speak. But he stared back at her with a panicked expression. *You do it,* he mouthed. She lowered her eyes and began in her soft sweet drawl, "Our heavenly Father…" She made up her prayer, mentioning each person by name, giving thanks for what they had and what they'd been given. She talked about the beauty and bounty of the land and the importance of family, whether the family you were born to or one you created. She finished by thanking Linc for his generosity.

Only Cassie whispered, "Amen," when Miranda ended her prayer. The others took longer to release hands.

Jenny broke the silence. "That sounded cool, Randi— should we be calling you Miranda all the time now?"

"Either is fine. I even answer to 'Hey you,'" she said with a feigned laugh.

Eric didn't rush to eat. He studied Miranda, finally stating, "I think what Jenny meant is that your prayer sounded like a song. A hymn, maybe."

"That's what I did mean," Jenny piped up. "Or like a poem."

Miranda almost choked on her first bite. The last thing she wanted was to have them connect her to songwriting. She managed to gather her scattered wits fast enough to counter Eric. "Jenny said you spent the night concocting a tune. Must've fried your brain. A prayer is just a prayer, guys. Now eat. If you'd spent all morning hunched over a hot stove, you'd want everyone to enjoy the meal instead of talking." She made a show of passing cranberry sauce one way and steamed vegetables the other.

It worked to keep them occupied. The meal got back on track and conversation meandered down other avenues.

When everyone was finished, Shawn stretched and yawned. "That was the best meal I've had in years. I'm so stuffed I'm sleepy. Mr. P, do we have to go work in the bunkhouse again?"

Linc leaned back and patted his stomach. "This is a holiday. Other than feeding the stock, there's nothing we absolutely have to do. Anybody interested in football? I think there's a game on TV."

Except for the little girls, excited chatter rose as the boys argued about the teams. They all pushed back their chairs and stampeded for the living room.

"Hey," Miranda called. "Are we forgetting house rules? The cook doesn't have to do dishes, remember?"

Greg blocked Jenny's exit. "What do *you* know about football?" he challenged.

"Nothing," she admitted. "But I mucked stalls, fed animals and gathered eggs this morning so Eric could work on his tune. I deserve a holiday like anybody else."

Miranda saw she'd created an opportunity for a typical

sibling battle. Even though they weren't siblings, the family setting encouraged that kind of relationship. "Look, I'm sorry I said anything. I really don't like football. You go on. I need to arrange leftovers in the fridge, anyway."

"I'll help," Linc volunteered. "Even if you don't want to see the game, with two of us working, it'll cut your time in half and give you some free hours to yourself."

No one else wanted Linc to assign them to kitchen duty, so they lost no time in pulling a disappearing act. Miranda heard the bantering around the TV, yet the tension between her and Linc stretched almost to the breaking point. Surreptitious glances from his direction gave her the feeling he wanted to say something to her. She assumed it had to do with last night and dreaded facing what would surely be a stream of regrets.

Finally she turned and accosted him. "You're dying to say something, Linc. So spit it out."

"You read me too well." He shook back a lock of hair that fell over his forehead. "I just want to explain again that I can't keep the little kids, Miranda. I…can't," he said in a rough voice. "You have to stop believing in miracles."

That was what Miranda had expected. But still, it tore a piece out of her heart, because they wanted so badly to stay, and she wanted them to. "I know Cassie needs expensive medical care," she murmured. "And there aren't any kids their age here to play with. But…but…" She felt the tears well up and looked away from the refusal she saw forming in his dark eyes.

"Believe me, they'll be better off with someone who knows more about children, who can guide them past all the pitfalls and problems. If I was that person, Miranda, Felicity would still be alive."

Miranda turned to object to his self-recriminations. But

like smoke, he'd disappeared from the room. She wiped down the table and counters, her mind starting to build a song—an ode to Linc's sister. The stanzas tumbled into place. Skirting the kids lounging on the floor around the TV, Miranda slipped into her room. She took a journal out of her drawer and set down the words swimming through her head. Sometimes would-be songs stalled before verse three. This one wrote itself.

When she'd finished, she shut the book and rubbed her aching shoulders. Too bad no one, least of all Linc, would ever hear "For the Love of Felicity."

ON THURSDAY the week after the holiday, an aging Jeep Wagoneer slogged through a sheet of rain and pulled in next to Linc's Excursion. The school bus had delivered Wolfie and Cassie at the road a scant ten minutes before.

Miranda, gearing up to take her driver's test in spite of the less-than-pleasant weather, had driven out to collect them, since Linc was helping the contractor rough in a bathroom in the second bunkhouse.

"Hey, somebody just drove in. I don't recognize the car." Jenny spotted the Jeep from her perch on a ladder. They'd bought decorations yesterday, and the boys, under Miranda and Jenny's expert tutelage, had cut down a Christmas tree they were about to trim.

Greg cupped his hands around his eyes to peer out a window blocked by the tree. "Could be the contractor's assistant."

"It's almost dark," Miranda said. "Why would someone come to assist him when he's about ready to leave for the night?"

"Dunno." Greg stepped back. "A delivery for Linc, maybe? We're too far off the beaten track to get a door-to-door salesman."

They all laughed and returned to stringing lights. "You have too many lights on the right side," Shawn told Jenny as the doorbell chimed. It was the first time any of them had heard the bell, so it took a moment to realize what it was.

Once they settled that it was, indeed, the doorbell, Hana ran into the hall and flung open the door.

They heard a woman with a high voice speaking to Hana, and Miranda knew instantly who their visitor was— Mrs. Bishop, the dreaded director of Social Services. Her stomach tumbled end over end and bile rose in her throat. Grabbing Wolfie's arm, she hissed into his ear, "Go out through the kitchen and get Linc. Tell him *she's* here."

"Who?" the older boys chorused.

Eric made the connection first. "The dragon lady from welfare. Great. Just great. Their timing always sucks." He threw down the string of lights he'd been winding around the tree. "She's here to wreck our Christmas. I told you guys we shouldn't bother with this tree-trimming crap."

They all looked stricken, none more than Cassie, who immediately began to wail.

Miranda hugged the chair-bound girl and handed her a tissue. "I know her timing stinks, hon. But please dry your tears. If she sees you crying, she'll think the worst. Come on, y'all, put on a happy face." Miranda smoothed back her short hair and took her own suggestion. She pasted on a smile before moving to the door. Hana clung to the knob, gaping at the stick of a woman dressed in undertaker black. *Brother!*

The woman studied Miranda without smiling. She shifted a large briefcase to her left hand, stepped inside and extended a business card. Miranda wasn't surprised to read the name Evelyn Bishop, followed by a string of letters denoting her degrees. Below her name it proclaimed she was indeed Director of Social Services in this part of Northern California.

Pocketing the card, Miranda swept a hand toward the living room. "Please, won't you have a seat? Someone just went out to the bunkhouse to get Linc, er, Mr. Parker." Miranda wanted to bite her tongue for calling him Linc. She caught hawk-eye Bishop's swift intake of breath.

"Is Mr. Parker sleeping at this time of day, for mercy's sake?"

"Sleeping?" Miranda blinked. "Oh, no. He's working with a contractor on the second bunkhouse. They're building a bathroom like he did for bunkhouse one."

"Children sleep in a bunkhouse where there's currently no bathroom?"

"No, ma'am. I mean, yes, ma'am. I mean, no one sleeps there," Miranda said, flustered. "If you'll sit down, I'll go make coffee. It'll only take a jiffy. Oh, would you like a cup? I'm sure Parker will want one." Dang, now she'd disrespectfully called him by his last name.

"Coffee would be nice, thank you. I've recently moved here from the Mojave area. This rain seeps right through a person's bones." The woman glanced around the room as if cataloging all the faces, especially Cassie's red, swollen eyes. Before she perched on the edge of a chair and snapped open her briefcase, a second gaze swept the pile of decorations and the partially trimmed tree. She calmly put on a pair of glasses and extracted a yellow legal pad and pen. Seemingly oblivious to the hard stares, she began to write.

Jenny scurried into the kitchen on Miranda's heels. "She's even more uptight than the counselor who used to come to my mom's house. I'll bet she's listing every fault she's found in the living room."

"Well, she ought to have seen it before the improvements.'' Miranda poured water in the pot and after adding grounds, she pressed the start button, surprised to see her hands shaking. ''Do you suppose the boys made their beds this morning? Maybe one of us ought to check.'' She grabbed the backdoor knob, only to have the door thrust inward, all but knocking her off her feet.

Linc swept in with Wolfie at his heels. He was covered in sawdust from head to toe, and windblown and rain-soaked to boot. ''Sorry, Miranda. I didn't mean to hit you with the door. Wolfie tells me there's a woman here. Mrs. Bishop, I presume. I thought she'd phone first. Where is she and what's she up to?''

Jenny jerked a thumb to signify his quarry was in the living room. ''So far, she's writing a book. Just kidding.'' Jenny grimaced. ''But she's writing more than asking questions. I think she's waiting for you.''

Linc stripped off his gloves and used them to dust off his shirt and pants.

Miranda waved at the flying particles. ''Couldn't you do that on the porch? You want her to think I'm a lousy housekeeper?''

''Of course not. Why are you pitching such a fit?''

''Maybe because your Mrs. Bishop looks like a witch. If something looks like a witch and acts like a witch...chances are she *is* a witch.''

''Shh.'' He clapped a hand over Miranda's mouth. The feel of her soft lips against his fingers sent a crash of excitement to his groin. *Dammit, not now.* If the Bishop woman did have a burr under her saddle, this was the last thing he needed her to see—him with a hard-on for a young woman supposedly in his custody. Especially as the other kids still considered her a peer. Boy, oh, boy. He saw now what a mistake he'd made in not making Miranda tell them sooner.

Wheeling, he slapped his gloves on his hip and stalked from the room.

Miranda didn't know what had happened just now, but she knew something had. As the coffee gurgled its last, she delayed checking on the boys' beds. Instead, she poured two cups and motioned for Jenny to bring cream and sugar.

They reached the living room in time to hear Mrs. Bishop demand to know why Linc had collected all these children without benefit of a state license.

He removed a folder holding several papers from a bookshelf. "I have a license. Ted Gunderson from the Oasis Foundation left me theirs. He told my representative that your predecessor agreed to let me use the balance of the time on their contract. Subject to your inspection of my facility, of course."

She didn't even glance at the certificate. "You know that paper is worthless. My receptionist told you Oasis lost their service agreement over a year ago."

Linc didn't quail under her stern gaze. He slapped the folder shut. "Your office offered me no help in obtaining a license in my own right."

"Well, Mr. Parker, until you have a valid operating license, you're not supposed to shelter anyone on state welfare rolls."

"I'm not." Linc's mouth quirked ominously. "That's the hell of it. Oasis walked away and left three of their former residents. I was told your office has no welfare records for Wolfie, Hana or Cassandra. No one ever checked on them when Oasis was ordered to cease and desist. Wolfie and Cassie didn't attend school for eight months, and not a soul asked why. In Wolfgang's case, the houseparent had him chopping wood and running errands ten hours a day. And if the boy hadn't cared for

Cassie and Hana as well as he had, I would've found them even filthier and more malnourished. As it was, they were borderline. But there was nothing borderline about the condition of the house—it was a disgrace. I'm prepared to deal reasonably with your office, Mrs. Bishop. I doubt you want the local press to get hold of our story. This county's welfare service record is iffy at best.''

"Be that as it may," she sniffed, "I can't be held accountable for things that happened prior to my tenure here."

"Oh, but I'm responsible for not being aware of things I wasn't told about? Things I took in good faith?"

Evelyn Bishop sank back against the chair cushion. Looking up, she accepted the cup of coffee Miranda offered her. "Thank you. Where, uh, is your house mother? Would it be possible for her to oversee the children elsewhere while we conduct business? I believe the young woman who invited me in mentioned a bunkhouse. Could they go there? It sounded as if one's under construction, but the other is fully operational. Am I correct in assuming that?"

"You are. Your mistake is in thinking I have a house mother. Or any employee, for that matter. I've run an ad in the local paper for weeks. Not one person has phoned or come in to answer the ad. And your office was zero help there, too, I might add."

"No woman on board?" Her mouth opened and shut. The coffee cup wobbled in her hand. "Why, that's totally unacceptable! The children…the children cannot stay here a moment longer."

"No," they all cried at once. "We don't wanna go."

The older boys formed a chain in front of Wolfie, who clasped Hana and Cassie to him, as he'd done the day Linc first showed up at the ranch.

Mrs. Bishop and Linc stared at each other, both steely-eyed. Linc took a bracing swallow from the steaming mug. "You have a court order giving you permission to remove them from my care?"

"What?" the woman sputtered. "Those three are wards of the court. I'm authorized to take them into protective custody at any time of the day or night."

Linc dropped his chin and pinched the tight muscles in his neck. "Then you found documents proving Wolfgang and Hana Schmitt and Cassandra Rhodes are in your system? The others came here from Southern Cal. I'm quite confident they've never been on your rolls."

The Bishop woman averted her eyes, but not before Linc saw a degree of uncertainty. Feeling more magnanimous toward her than at any point since he'd walked in, he sank into an adjacent chair. "For the kids' sake, it behooves us both to try and work together. If you ask them, they'll tell you they have food and warm beds now. You'd take them tonight and you'd place them where?"

Her shoulders slumped and she shook her head. "Frankly, I don't know." Removing her glasses, she rubbed tired-looking eyes. "At the moment, our computer shows no vacancy in any of our foster homes. None. The situation in this county is dire."

"I suggest, then, that you leave them where they are for the time being."

Miranda thought her heart would burst with joy when Linc added, "We can set an appointment to meet again. I'm thinking…maybe the week after Christmas?"

The director sipped her coffee. No one breathed until she set down the mug, rose and extended a hand. "Fine. Let's say the Friday after New Year's? Ten a.m. in my office. I promise, Mr. Parker, I will have done my home-work on every one of these children by then." Then, like a threatening black cloud, she departed, leaving sunny smiles behind.

CHAPTER TWELVE

WHILE NO ONE at the ranch, except possibly Linc, was anxious to see time pass and bring the dreaded meeting with Social Services in the new year, the kids did look forward to celebrating Christmas.

"This is the first time I've ever had my own money and could actually buy gifts," Jenny confided to Miranda one afternoon when the two had driven into town by themselves, ostensibly to register for college.

"Don't go overboard. We have to stretch our funds to buy for eight people."

"Eight? Oh, you're including Linc?"

Miranda frowned. "Well, sure. If it wasn't for him, this Christmas wouldn't be possible for anyone." She'd never make an issue of it to Jenny, but Miranda sensed that Linc was getting into the holiday spirit himself. From unguarded remarks he'd made during the minutes they grabbed alone, she'd gotten the impression that nothing was ever made of the holiday when he was a boy. As a kid, he'd been left to fend for himself over Christmas while his actress mother skied the Alps or gambled at Monte Carlo. And apparently his grandmother, the one who'd raised Felicity, considered Christmas just another day.

According to Linc, he gave Felicity a check each Christmas so she could buy what her friends received as gifts from their parents. Big deal. Miranda gathered he'd shelled out money any time the girl asked. But then, she knew he was a generous man.

Jenny interrupted Miranda's ruminations. "It was good of Parker to give each of the little kids twenty bucks so they could buy us gifts. I heard you offer to help them *make* gifts. Since Linc bought that sewing machine, you've been zipping up curtains and bedspreads like mad. How come you know how to sew? I thought you were really little when your mom died."

"I was. But my dad hired female tutors to travel with us when he was, uh, on business. They didn't only teach me academics. The women had hobbies. Sewing, painting and handicrafts. Most of them hung out with me after the lessons, so I did whatever they were doing."

"That sounds like a neat way to live. I couldn't even keep up with my core classes in school. My mom kept me out so often to take care of my younger brothers and sisters. And there was never money for extras. But she managed to buy booze and cigarettes. She always had a boyfriend we fed, too," Jenny said bitterly. "None of them were remotely as nice as Parker."

"But you want better for your own kids when you have them, right?" Miranda stopped on their walk into the college administrative office. "That's why you should get your GED and prepare so you aren't dependent on a man to support you. Don't you want to look at requirements for the GED, as well as sign up for a continuing-ed poetry class?"

"I suppose. But I'm never having kids. No way."

"Oh, Jenny. Someday you'll change your mind."

Miranda needed to steer her friend elsewhere, to keep Jenny from seeing the transcripts that had arrived last week from Tennessee. Requesting them had been risky, but Miranda hoped school wasn't something that would occur to

Wes Carlisle. She counted on the fact that he knew almost nothing about her, other than her ability to write and sing songs. His lack of caring about the people he had under contract was another thing Miranda despised about her manager.

Jenny wandered off to read class brochures while Miranda met with her counselor. Even then, the chance of being found out stressed her out so much that Miranda thought again about revealing her age to the younger girl. The truth would surface, anyway, at the meeting with Evelyn Bishop.

But no opportunity presented itself. Miranda and Jenny parted ways in town, each heading off to do her private Santa business. Conversation on the drive home centered on the holiday. They had a heated debate as to whether Santa should arrive Christmas Eve or Christmas morning and finally agreed to let Linc decide.

That evening, after the others had turned in, Linc and Miranda met in the kitchen for coffee and to chat about their day. It had become a ritual each looked forward to.

Linc sipped coffee and thumbed through the college catalog. "You're really staying on, then? I wasn't sure you would."

"I told you the other night I planned to stay."

"I know. But that was before Mrs. Bishop dropped in. By the way, she phoned today. She ran their routine check with the California department of motor vehicles, and it gave your real age. Apparently Eric told her you were seventeen. She called to ask if I'd like to have a police background check done on you."

Miranda's blood backed up in her veins. "Uh, did you request one?"

"No! As if I would." He reached over and lightly skimmed his knuckles along Miranda's tense jaw. "I said you'd been truthful with me. I also informed her you were all that kept this household running at the moment. I let her know I paid you and Jenny a fare wage for chores. She was impressed but shocked, I think, when I said you two had gone to register for college classes. Although she scoffed about Jenny signing up for poetry."

"Did Mrs. Bishop find problems involving any of the others?"

"As you'd guess, she didn't have any report on Greg. She's in possession of several on Eric's checkered history as a habitual runaway. Shawn's definitely not eligible for state benefits. His dad's worth ten mil or so, she said."

"Money doesn't make a man a good person."

"I know that. So does she. It's..." Linc hesitated. "Mrs. Bishop has the authority to send Jenny back to her mom. Apparently Jenny is sixteen, not seventeen."

"Oh, Linc. Her mom's an alcoholic and maybe a...hooker. The state took the other kids away. Why would she send Jenny back? From something Jenny said about her mom's revolving boyfriends, I'd worry that she could be in danger."

"I can't help that, Miranda. The director has rules to follow."

"You *could* help. Go to bat for Jenny, like you stood up for keeping the little kids the other night. If you don't, Jenny and Eric will run again. They'll be back living hand-to-mouth on the streets."

"Whoa! Wait a minute. I intervened that night when Mrs. Bishop came without phoning, but it doesn't make me a guy who'll buck the system for no reason. I've explained why Wolfie and the others can't stay indefinitely. They need real parents. You said yourself that Cassie needs vigorous medical intervention. I hope you're prepared to hand the kids over at our next meeting."

Miranda's lower lip quivered. "How can you be so cruel? We can get Cassie medical help. Have you forgotten the school nurse had me make doctor and dental appointments for the kids at a clinic where she said they'd gone before?"

"I know, but if anything significant's to be done for Cassie in the way of surgery, she'll need easier access to doctors and hospitals."

"But the kids trust us. They're comfortable here. Sure, Eric and Jenny may still talk about hitting the big time and joke that your connections in L.A. could open doors, but it's mostly talk. Shawn's content. And Wolfie just plain looks up to you, Linc."

Linc's jaw tightened. "I never asked him or anyone to look up to me. I said from the start that I wasn't the man to raise kids. The screwed-up role models I had for parents have never made me a good bet. And don't even *think* of asking me to help Eric and Jenny break into the entertainment business. It's no place for kids their age. Good God, it killed Felicity." His eyes begged her to understand.

She didn't. All her heart felt was a horrible ache. Deep sadness for the children, yes. But also for herself and Linc, who was so afraid to risk his heart. How could she ever reveal the facts about her past after listening to his views regarding her profession? That knowledge hurt badly.

Lately they hadn't slipped off to Linc's bed to take solace in each other's arms. Tonight, however, without a word, they dumped their coffee, turned out the lights and held hands as they trod silently to the master suite.

They rarely talked during these encounters, for fear of alerting the kids. This time they shed their clothes with a kind of reckless abandon. Miranda hoped that if she gave him her all, Linc would feel and accept her love. She thought Linc Parker had known so little love. And yet, she'd never known a more considerate lover.

Tonight, even sensing her haste, he lay facing her, doing nothing except stroking her skin. Eventually she relaxed and began to explore the taut muscles of his back. Only then did Linc close the gap between them to kiss her.

They were slow, methodical kisses that had heat pooling in her belly. Miranda couldn't think when he kissed her like this. She couldn't think about her shady past or her troubled future. Murky lies blended with partial truths as she curved a leg over Linc's hips and accepted his hardness deep within her. Kissing him desperately, accepting and storing up everything she could get.

Linc had immediately realized something was different about their lovemaking that night. As always, he hated sneaking around. He hated knowing Miranda purposely muted her expressions of need and muffled her joyous cries of release. His guilt increased tenfold with each stolen moment. And yet he felt helpless to deny either of them this pleasure. He wasn't a man who indulged in whims, but Miranda had become his addiction. And yet if he'd learned anything from living and working in Hollywood all those years, it was that addictions were never good.

Holding her close, he tasted tears on her cheeks and lips. He was too scared by the thought of losing her to question why she was crying. Not tonight. Maybe not ever. He hugged her tighter, as if holding her would make the world go away. Silently he vowed this had to stop until he was in a position to offer her more than clandestine moments. He swore he'd stay awake until it was time for her to leave his bed. But he fell asleep—shortly after he pulled the comforter up to cover their cooling bodies.

Miranda wrapped her arms around him and fought heavy eyes for as long as possible. She was afraid of falling asleep and spending the night with him, even though she'd love nothing better.

With a sigh, she slid out of the warm bed and dressed quickly, making every effort not to gaze down at him. In the greenish glow of the light spilling across the bed, his face looked different tonight. Harder. Less relaxed. These secret sessions were taking a toll on both of them.

Stealing from his room, softly closing the door, it struck Miranda that tonight they'd both been pretending. Pretending their exchange in the kitchen hadn't altered their feelings. Pretending the changes the new year was going to bring wouldn't affect their relationship—when, in fact, nothing could or would remain the same.

Her mind and heart were so preoccupied with Linc that at first Miranda didn't notice anything amiss when she opened the door and tiptoed into her room. She was digging her nightshirt out from under her pillow when she suddenly whirled on Jenny's bed.

It was empty. Not only empty, but clearly never slept in. The spread hadn't been turned back and there was no indentation in the pillow.

She ran to the window and checked on Linc's SUV. She practically groaned with relief to see it parked in its usual spot. What had she expected—that Jenny and Eric had run away?

She wasted several minutes debating waking Linc. But perhaps Jenny was at the boys' bunkhouse, rehearsing. Eric had talked about them all singing Christmas carols before opening gifts.

Confident that must be the case, Miranda shrugged into a jacket and tiptoed through the kitchen to collect a flashlight. She left the house via the back, as the front door tended to squeak and she didn't want to worry Linc needlessly.

The bunkhouse was dark and she held her breath. Aware that they never locked the door, she went in and shined the flashlight around.

Shawn stirred in one of the lower bunks. "Eric?" he called. "Izzat you?"

"It's Miranda," she whispered. "Jenny's not in her bed."

Shawn sat up and yawned. "Her, Eric and Greg are at the cave. Eric's getting antsy about staying here. He doesn't trust the Bishop broad."

"What's Mrs. Bishop got to do with them going to the cave?"

"They're trying to put together new tunes. Hoping it'll get them noticed by a recording company in San Francisco, since they didn't get anywhere in L.A."

"But...I thought you were part of their band."

"Nah, I discovered I like ranching better. Linc's been square. I'm banking he won't let the old crow ship me home. The others think he'll give us up as fast as bad vomit. But I was sick and tired of the way we were living. I want to stay here and see what the olives look like hanging off the trees we planted." He shrugged. "Anyway, Greg's a natural musician. I'm not."

Miranda chewed her lower lip. She wished she had some insight into what Linc would do if Mrs. Bishop pushed him. "Their band is far from ready to interest a talent scout."

"Maybe," mumbled Shawn. "But they've got cash now to cut a demo. Felicity paid for a couple last year—they turned out really bad, though."

Miranda decided to find the cave and make her own judgment. "Shawn, will you take me to the cave? Right now, I mean," she added when he fell back on his pillow.

"Hell, Randi, I can't find my way at night. The path's as dark as a witch's—"

"Shush," she warned, realizing Wolfie was awake and that he lay listening to their exchange.

"I'll take you," Wolfie croaked. Sitting up, he reached for his boots.

"No. Goodness, I can't ask you to do that. You have school tomorrow."

"My alarm's set for two so I can go get 'em, anyway. It's one o'clock now, but what the heck. I'm awake." He yawned.

Seeing he'd been sleeping in his shirt and jeans, Miranda accepted his offer. If nothing else, she'd chew out Eric and Jenny for involving Wolfie in their deception. Had they no sense? she fumed, practically running to keep up with the boy, who'd set off along a faint trail leading into the hills.

"How often have they interrupted your sleep for this?" she demanded, puffing like a steam engine as the grade grew steeper.

"Mostly they go right after I get home from school, while you're helping Cassie with homework. I go get 'em when you're done helping me with mine. We're always back by supper."

"Well, yes, or I'd have noticed. Or Linc would've. Where does *he* think you all disappear to?"

"He thinks we're studying."

In the distance, a dog began to bark. Or maybe it wasn't a dog. Miranda sped up, falling into step with the boy. "Is that a coyote?"

"It's Scraps," he told her. "Jenny said he wouldn't stay on Cassie's bed tonight. She said you and Linc were in the kitchen talking about those college classes. Jenny didn't dare turn him loose, 'cause she said you'd notice she was gone.''

"Which I did, anyhow. Did she think I'd stay up all night, for heaven's sake?"

"She said you and Linc sit in the kitchen and talk for hours every night."

Miranda flushed. She didn't know anyone had seen. She might have probed more intensely had Wolfie not stopped, pulled aside a wet shrub and pointed to a dark hole in the side of a hill. Somewhere in the muffled interior, Scraps had begun to really set up a frenzied barking.

Wolfie stuck his head in the opening and gave a shrill whistle. Once Miranda's heart stopped pounding and her breath quit coming in short spurts, she could hear music drifting out. It vanished suddenly.

"Come on. Follow me," Wolfie said.

She placed a hand on his shoulder, since stepping into the interior left them in total blackness. Little by little as they walked, she saw light filtering from somewhere ahead. They passed through two caverns before Wolfie made a sharp left turn and, like magic, a large area opened up. Five lanterns threw flickering shadows up granite walls, revealing the teens and the dog seated on a colorful array of blankets. All glanced up and glared at the intruders.

"You're early," Jenny accused.

But Eric caught sight of Miranda. He yelled at Wolfie, "What in hell are you doing bringing Randi here?"

"I insisted," she said, shielding the boy. "I discovered Jenny's bed hadn't been slept in. I might not have worried if you'd left me a note saying where you were."

"I wanted to," Jenny said sullenly. "Eric thought you'd blab it to Linc. We knew he'd freak out."

"What makes you think I'd tell Linc?"

Jenny and Eric laughed as if on cue. "You two are joined at the hip. Beats me what-all you got to talk about with a dude his age," Jenny said. "Eric thinks there's probably more than talk going on. You'd better watch yourself, Randi. Felicity told me her brother only dated the hottest chicks from the movies. There's only one reason a guy like him would take an interest in somebody your age."

Miranda opened her mouth to tell them her real age. But they'd never trust her again if she did. Crouching down, she scratched Scraps behind the ears. "Thanks for your concern, but I can take care of myself. Shawn told me you'd put together a possible new act. Since I've come all this way, why not let me be your first audience."

Clearly uncomfortable, they hemmed, hawed and shuffled their instruments. Miranda thought they were going to refuse. After a long-drawn-out silence, Eric motioned for Jenny to make room for Miranda and Wolfie on one of the quilts.

Then Eric strummed a few chords on his guitar to indicate the range for Greg, who'd settled a battery-operated keyboard on his lap. Jenny smiled and gazed down at her hands.

Miranda was pleasantly surprised by Greg's ability to play the keyboard. Eric, she knew, could do wonderful things with a guitar. Jenny's voice and range had improved with practice. Together the three of them sounded quite professional, and that impressed Miranda. They were better than good, considering their primitive surroundings.

With regard to those surroundings, Miranda listened closely for echoes, the bane of songwriters who picked out tunes on pianos at home. What she heard was music as clear and pure as if they were playing in an acoustical room. At the end of the number, she was moved to clap.

"Wow, you guys, that sounded great! Do another number."

Pathetically eager to show off, they plunged into a medley of current hard-rock hits.

Miranda did more than listen for echoes. And she'd swear there wasn't a single wrong note. Growing excited about music for probably the first time since walking offstage, she found herself gesturing animatedly after the last note died away.

"You're fantastic! But according to Colby Donovan—he's Nashville's leading sound man—performers need something fresh, something different, if they hope to cut a demo and get noticed by anyone in the business."

Three sets of eyes pinned her. Only Wolfie didn't stare at her, and that was because he'd fallen asleep with Scraps in his arms and his head on Miranda's lap.

Fearing at once that she'd goofed, she tried to recover. "I, uh, read that in a country-music magazine once."

"We're not aiming for the country market," Jenny pointed out.

"Maybe you should. Your voice is perfect for the new, crossover country songs. Look at the singers who've risen to the top of both charts," Miranda said.

"Probably this Donovan guy is right," Eric agreed. "Only, we don't know anybody in Nashville or L.A. or San Francisco. Did this Donovan say no one ever makes it with a demo of current hits?"

Miranda was afraid to offer much more detail. She gave a half shrug. "The article did mention that written permission's required to cut most songs already on a tape or CD. Your best bet is to use something you write yourselves. If a producer likes what he hears, he might toss in a backup trio. Maybe a banjo, a regular guitar and a few blended background voices.'' Fearing she'd said too much, she added, ''That's what the article said, anyway.''

Greg leaned on his keyboard. ''How do you get permission for old songs?''

''You have to pay, stupid,'' Eric snarled. ''Big bucks.''

Jenny nervously rubbed her hands up and down her thighs. ''Maybe we ought to call it quits for tonight. Eric, can you hitch a ride into town with Miranda next week when she takes the kids to the clinic? The library will have information on song rights.''

''Good plan.'' Miranda gently shook Wolfie awake. Scrambling up, she tucked Scraps inside her jacket. They all laughed at how widely the small dog yawned.

When the girls were back in their room, Jenny pestered Miranda some more. ''You write poems. Have you written one Eric could set to music?''

On the other side of the room, Miranda froze. ''Poems? Me? What are you talking about?''

''I've seen you madly writing in a lined notebook you stuff in your dresser drawer at night. You left it out one day when you went to help Hana with her bath. I a-accidentally saw a piece you wrote about Felicity. I only read the last few lines, but it was so beautiful it made me cry. I figure you probably wrote about other emotional stuff. If not, I bet you could write a love song. Audiences go wild for love songs.''

Miranda had written a few possibles, any one of which she could develop. But her songs were meant as country ballads. How would her words sound in a rock arrangement? ''Jenny, I write what comes from my heart. It's deeply personal. I'd feel…funny, hearing anybody sing what I've written.'' Which was true. She'd always sung her own material. If she messed it up, she had only herself to blame.

"Promise you'll think about it, at least."

"Okay, I will. But my first obligation is to help Cassie, Hana and Wolfie finish making Christmas presents." Miranda crawled under her covers.

"I know. Listen, if you don't want to share something you wrote, could you maybe teach me how to write? I've got a ton of ideas, I just don't have the education to pull any of them into a song."

"That's why you're taking a poetry class. Nobody taught me, Jenny. I open my head and my heart. I write exactly what I feel." She frowned, adding, "Oh, you know I took a couple of music intro classes. You could, too."

"Hmm. Well, what I read was gut-wrenching. If Parker heard it sung, he'd cry, I bet. G'night, Randi. It felt good knowing you thought we sounded okay."

They'd sounded better than okay. Ironically, they had what Colby liked to call the Nashville sound. Miranda lay awake for hours, fearing she'd opened a Pandora's box.

Beginning the next day, she divided her free time between helping the little kids paint T-shirts for everyone for Christmas and trekking out to the cave to oversee the musicians' budding careers; she'd even written a song for them, hoping to move the group in a consciously country direction. Guilt dogged her footsteps. She was torn between Linc's disdain of the industry and the fact that her friends had real talent. What weighed heaviest on Miranda was the knowledge that in today's market, it took more than talent to break in. It took a brilliant demo, a good marketer to shop the demo around and contacts to get off the ground at all. She had contacts she dared not use, unless she wanted her idyllic life here to be over.

Eric loped up to her as she entered the cave the next afternoon. "Hey, Randi. The lyrics you came up with after supper are so hot! I'm pretty sure I can set them to music.

We're so excited, but I've gotta tell ya, with stuff this good, you could probably sell it for a tidy sum.''

She shrugged off his enthusiasm and turned to Wolfie. ''I missed you at our craft session. Cassie said you'd decided not to make, uh, the same thing they're making.'' She lowered her voice, not wanting to give away the children's secret.

The boy leaned closer. ''A friend at school, Ricky Padilla—his mom makes cool belts and wallets. She'll charge three bucks apiece for the material. And she'll show me how to put buckles on if I go home with Ricky a couple of nights. She said I can stay over, but could you pick me up after supper, Randi? Hana's way better, but no telling how she'd act if I skipped coming home one whole night.''

Miranda ruffled his hair. He'd filled out into a handsome kid. ''Sure, sport. Any day but Wednesday. That's our doctor-and-dental appointment day.''

He screwed up his face. ''Cassie's scared. She said doctors hurt her when they straighten her legs to check her hips and knees.''

''I'll go in with her.''

He nodded solemnly. ''I reckon nobody's ever done that before. Will you do that for Hana, too? I tell her it's probably not right for me to stick around during her exam.'' He shook his head. ''She doesn't understand why I get embarrassed.''

''You're a good brother, Wolfie. The best. But yes, I'll stay with Hana.''

WEDNESDAY ROLLED AROUND, and Miranda loaded the kids in the SUV. She waited for Eric. Instead, Linc came loping out of the house.

Miranda slid out from under the steering wheel and

passed him the keys. "Are you driving them to their appointments, instead of me?"

"I told the other kids we're both going. I promised Mrs. Bishop. She has it in her head that they're my responsibility, however temporary."

"Then she's found their files?"

"No. And it frustrates the hell out of her. She hasn't been able to raise anyone at Oasis, either. They missed their court date, apparently."

"But she's authorizing the children's medical care today?"

"I'm paying for them, Miranda. I figure it's the least I can do."

"Oh, okay. Is Eric coming? He wanted to go to the library."

"I thought he was, but Jenny said he changed his mind."

A couple of hours later, Miranda would have loved a picture of Linc's face when the clinic nurse presented him with the bill. Or maybe he was only stunned by what she said, which was, "Dr. Wyeth thinks you and Mrs. Parker have worked wonders with these kids. Last time the school nurse brought Wolfgang in, he was malnourished. And it's commendable of you to tackle Cassie's problem. The doctor hopes he can find a specialist to take her case, as he mentioned to your wife." The beaming nurse wrote *paid* on the bill and handed the top copy to Linc.

Miranda jostled his arm and whispered, "I explained to Dr. Wyeth that you're only Cassie's temporary guardian. And I'm not Mrs. Parker," she added for the nurse to hear. "I'm Linc's, uh, housekeeper."

Miranda snatched Hana up and balanced her on one hip a moment before turning away, her temper simmering. The nurse knew their situation; Miranda had made it clear to the doctor. But the woman had been eyeing Linc as they went from room to room. Now Miranda had handed her an opportunity to make a play for him.

He didn't linger, however. He sauntered into the waiting room after Miranda. "What was that all about?" he asked as they went down the block to the dental offices.

"Flirting. Nurse Carstairs was flirting with you. Don't tell me you missed her batting her baby blues in your face."

"Hmm, I must have. Anyway, I don't see why you're annoyed with me."

She eased out a long sigh, speaking so the kids wouldn't hear. "I'm not annoyed with you, Linc. It's more that I made my escape from my old life with a noose around my neck. Day by day, as I get more comfortable here, I feel it tightening. None of how I feel is your fault. But I'm sure Mrs. Bishop is going to expose me to the others for the fraud I am. I said I'd stay on, but the teens may vote me out. I can't even say I'd blame them."

He slid a bracing arm around Miranda's shoulders and pulled her against his side. A light rain had begun to fall. One of the many things Linc found appealing about Miranda was that she didn't mind getting dirty or wet. "I stand by my offer to help you get out of the fix you're in, sweetheart, whatever it is. All you have to do is point me in the right direction and say the word."

Miranda gazed at him through lashes clumped together by tears. She hoped he thought they were wet from the rain. She was awfully afraid she'd gone and fallen in love with Linc Parker. And no matter which way she sliced the pie that represented their mixed-up lives, he only considered her a friend and sometime lover.

There was a larger question looming in her mind: could she stay on after Mrs. Bishop dropped her bombshell?

Since love didn't seem to be a word in Linc Parker's vocabulary, maybe it wasn't an issue at all.

Twice in the week before Christmas, Dr. Wyeth phoned the ranch. He'd managed to arrange an appointment for Cassie to see a neurologist and an orthopedic surgeon in Sacramento. Both fell after Linc's scheduled meeting with Mrs. Bishop.

"I'll see that Cassie gets to her appointment, regardless," he promised the doctor. "Even if Social Services finds Cassie's file and places her in a foster home. Will either of these doctors operate pro bono or whatever you MDs call charity cases?"

Miranda cocked an ear to follow Linc's half of the conversation on Christmas Eve. She was on her hands and knees, tucking the last gifts under the tree. Their rain had turned to snow again. Because Wolfie and Cassie were now out of school on holiday break, they'd all begun to feel housebound.

Hana ran through the living room screeching at the top of her lungs. Cassie wheeled full tilt after her. Their shouting caused Miranda to miss Linc's final exchange with the doctor, but it sounded as if he was worried about possible costs. If only she could access her money, she'd pay Cassie's bill. It just wasn't fair that a sweet child remained immobile because the welfare department refused to pay for her surgery.

"Girls, what's the problem?"

"Hana has my gingerbread man." Tears streamed from Cassie's pretty eyes. "She already ate hers, even though Wolfie said she was s'posed to wait till after supper. Hana knows I wanted to leave mine on a plate for Santa Claus."

Miranda crawled over to the girl and rose to dry her face. "Honey, I have plenty more gingerbread men. I made two whole batches after you girls went to bed last night. After supper I thought we could decorate a few and hang them on the tree. But we'll save enough for Santa. Cross my heart.''

"Okay.'' Cassie sniffed a few more times and flung her arms around Miranda's neck. "I love you, M'randa. Hana and I pray every night that you'll get to be our new mommy.''

"Oh, hon.'' Miranda swallowed the lump in her throat. "Just you saying that is the nicest Christmas present anybody could ever give me.'' Smiling sadly, Miranda climbed to her feet. "Girls, go see if Wolfie will run the train Linc set up in the bunkhouse last week.'' He'd bought it as an early Christmas gift—and Miranda suspected it was also something he'd always wanted himself. "I have to go make our Christmas Eve lasagna,'' she explained.

The girls scampered off to find their jackets, and Miranda discovered Linc had hung up the phone. He watched her, an odd expression in his eyes. "You're so good with the kids. I wish Felicity had had someone like you in her life when she was growing up.''

Miranda crossed to him and rose on tiptoe to brush a kiss over his lips. "I'm sorry she's not with you this Christmas, Linc. I overheard you asking your friend John Montoya to put a wreath on her grave. If it wasn't snowing so hard, I'd suggest you fly to Hollywood and deliver the wreath yourself. I could've handled a few days alone with the kids.''

"I know. I did mention it to Evelyn Bishop and she had a conniption. Like it or not, rules for running a facility like mine are spelled out in a licensing handbook. She sent me a copy. So far I've only read the first half.'' He made an exasperated face. "She put a rush order on a new license agreement for me, but if I'd known then what I know now, I probably wouldn't have opened a teen refuge.''

''Why? We all think you're doing a wonderful job.''

''According to the manual, I can't let kids come and go at will. When they arrive, I send a report to the county. It's my duty to keep monthly logs on anyone under nineteen until they're formally signed out of my care by Bishop or another caseworker. If I let anyone leave without going through the proper process, it's a black mark against me and my facility. If a kid dislikes it enough to want to leave, they do something like an exit interview. Too many of those aren't good, either.''

Miranda patted his arm. ''Everyone here seems happy, don't you think?''

''Maybe—but you're the one who brought up the possibility of Eric and Jenny going back to L.A.''

''I did? When?''

''The night you tried to convince me I'm good daddy material.''

''Ah, now I remember. That was the night Mrs. Bishop called. Don't worry. I think the kids have figured out that they've still got a lot to learn before they cut a demo record.''

His brows drew together. ''They should forget the hell about that and concentrate on learning a worthwhile occupation. Now, what were you telling Cassie about lasagna?'' He rubbed his stomach. ''I finished painting the new bunkhouse bathroom today, and it's made me hungry as a bear. Wolfie said we'd better be prepared for the little girls to not sleep well tonight. He said they're keyed up about Santa.''

''They are. And not just the little kids, either. None of them have had a holiday to remember for a long time, if ever. Christmas meant so little in their homes, Linc. No matter what happens with the children after the appointment with Mrs. Bishop, I hope they'll look back on these last few weeks and remember the spirit of giving.''

"If so, they'll have you to thank. Speaking of spirit, will you be moved to visit me tonight? You've been so busy lately," he said, toying with her earring. "I know you've been working with the kids to make gifts, but where do you disappear after they go to bed? Some nights the house has felt...well, downright empty.''

Miranda choked and made a show of coughing into her hand. If Linc had any idea she was at the cave helping Jenny, Eric and Greg with their music, he'd come unglued. "Tonight's not a good night, Linc. As you said, Cassie and Hana are sure to be extra restless.''

He looked disappointed. She felt the same, but had decided she wasn't cut out for a life of deceit. Now she just had to find a way to break the full truth to Linc. If he didn't explode, she intended to ask his advice on getting out of her contract with Wesley.

Supper that evening was a huge hit. The dining room rang with laughter. Everyone, including Linc, helped decorate and string the gingerbread men. It was after midnight when the kids finally settled down.

Miranda had made cranberry coffee cake to serve for breakfast. Even though the house was as ready for Christmas as anyone could possibly make it, she worried that they'd all feel let down after opening the meager, mostly handmade gifts.

Sometimes that happened when people built things up in their minds.

EVEN THOUGH HANA had gotten little sleep, Miranda wasn't surprised when at the crack of dawn, the little girl shook her awake, shouting, "Santa came. Cassie and me went to look, and the gingerbread men on the plate are all gone.'' Her eyes rounded. ''And Santa left snowy footprints all over the carpet.''

Miranda bolted out of bed and dove into a sweatsuit she'd laid out. Dang, she'd forgotten to hide the gingerbread men. ''They're gone?'' she demanded stupidly, letting herself be tugged into the living room.

Linc! He had to be responsible for the piles of new presents and for the empty plate and the floury bootprints that led from the door to the tree. Outside, the snow had stopped falling. A pale sun rose and diamond sparkles rimmed the tracks the older boys were making as they ran from the bunkhouse to the back door. The little girls weren't the only anxious members of the household.

''You play Santa,'' Miranda urged Linc after everyone had found a comfortable place around the tree. Although he shook his head and hung back, they forced him to take part.

There were dolls and doll clothes for the little girls. Sweaters and necklace-and-earring sets for Jenny and Miranda. Leather jackets for the boys, who were totally flabbergasted. All they could do was stroke the supple leather.

Miranda had given the boys cowboy hats, and the little girls pink fuzzy slippers. She gave Jenny a poem and a small vial of real perfume.

When Linc went to open Miranda's gift to him, she held her breath. The plaid wool shirt was nothing to write home about, but how long, she wondered, would it take him to discover the special gift she'd tucked into one of the pockets?

Not long, as it turned out. He removed the tiny square package, and in typical male fashion, ripped off the foil wrap. The others cracked up laughing when Linc removed a small, sterling-silver frog with a gold crown on its head.

He didn't laugh as he nervously turned the frog over and over in his big hands. Until their eyes met across Hana's bright curls and Miranda knew he was recalling the night she first called him her princely frog, she worried that her gift had been a failure.

His slow sexy grin declared his pleasure. And Miranda could tell by his eyes that no one had ever given him a more personal or meaningful gift. Her heart did a happy leap in her chest. Maybe, just maybe, everything would turn out well in the new year....

CHAPTER THIRTEEN

New Year's Eve and Day came and went quietly. Around midweek following the last college bowl football game, Jenny sat at one end of the kitchen table sorting out photographs she'd taken with a camera Shawn and Greg had gone in together to buy her for Christmas.

Miranda occupied the opposite end of the table, sewing flannel nightgowns for Cassie and Hana out of material she'd found to match the fuzzy slippers she'd given them. Scraps napped at her feet and she had to keep scooting him off the foot pedal.

"Why do you always throw up your hand or turn away when I go to take your picture?" Jenny complained.

"I hate seeing spots for an hour after a flash goes off."

"If that's not an exaggeration, I don't know what is. The spots hang around for a minute at best." Jenny opened a second photo packet. "Boy, this is a great shot of Linc and the guys, all in boots, leather jackets and Stetsons. They look like real cowboys. Come see the one you took of us in the cave, singing. We do look sorta like a country band."

"I think so," Miranda said with a small amount of pride. "You guys have softened your image and added a bluesy sound to your music."

Jenny twisted a lock of her long hair. "Greg kind of resembles Neal McCoy. Randi, do you think country fans would accept Eric's ethnic mix?"

Miranda thought of Charlie Pride. "Ethnicity is irrelevant, I think. Fans react to the music. Country fans are more loyal than fickle hard-rock listeners. The fact that you're all nice-looking is a plus with younger fans in any market. Let me see those pictures." Miranda stopped sewing, started to rise, when *pow*, a dazzling flash went off in her eyes.

"Gotcha!" Jenny cried triumphantly.

"Honestly, Jenny, grow up." Irritated, Miranda stalked to the stove, poured a mug of cold coffee and set it in the microwave.

"Caffeine's a drug, you know." Jenny wagged a finger. "It's probably what's making you toss and turn half the night lately. You sit here with Linc and drink too much caffeine."

Miranda rolled her eyes. "I'll grant you it's not good to drink a pot a day like I used to when I practiced long hou...er, stayed up studying." She caught her slip and set down her mug with a gigantic sigh. "Jenny, next week you'll probably find this out from Mrs. Bishop, so I'd rather be the one to tell you. I'm not your age. I'm twenty-six. I've studied music *and* other subjects in college."

Afraid to meet Jenny's eyes, Miranda inspected her last seam. "In two months I'll, uh, be twenty-seven."

"I kinda thought you might be a *bit* older than us, but twenty-seven? Why— Oh, I get it. Did Shawn's dad hire you to spy on him? He tried that once, but Eric and some others caught on and roughed the jerk up."

"No, Jenny, my deception has nothing to do with you or the boys. I, uh, had to disappear. I can't explain why. Please, will you take my word for it?"

Jenny stared at her so long that Miranda sewed a seam crookedly and had to rip it out. "Really," she pleaded, flexing her fingers in the half-finished gown. "The day I met you and found Scraps, I so badly needed friends. You've all been that and more. Friendship's not about age. It has to do with respect.''

"Does Linc know? He does, doesn't he? That's why he looks at you differently than he does me. Well, if you told *him*, I don't see why you couldn't have told us.''

"Linc guessed early on,'' Miranda said with a wry twist of her mouth. "And Mrs. Bishop found out from a DMV check she did. Outside of a few added years, I'm the same me, Jenny. I've asked Linc to let me stay at least a while longer. He needs me to cook until he finds someone else. And I need more time…to…to… I just do. Can you accept that I just have to figure out some stuff about my life?''

"I suppose,'' Jenny said with a shrug. "I never understood why someone with your looks and brains hung out with us, but now I see. It's cool, I guess.''

Miranda watched Jenny gather her pictures and leave the table. A wariness had come over her. In her heart Miranda didn't believe Jenny felt "cool'' about the news. That concerned her, but she didn't know what she could do to alter the course of events now. She felt glad to have the truth out in the open. Sitting down again, she returned to ripping out the botched seam.

But after supper, it was really noticeable that the teens excluded her from their jam session at the cave. That hurt, but in time, perhaps they'd come around. Miranda understood that they felt betrayed. And she *had* duped them. But even if she could do things over, she'd travel the same path. She didn't see any alternative.

"The kids were quiet as mice during supper,'' Linc remarked after everyone had gone, and only he and Miranda remained in the kitchen. "Do you think they're anxious about our meeting with Bishop tomorrow?''

"Aren't we all? Actually, they're mad at me, Linc.

Well, maybe mad's too strong a word. I told Jenny how old I really am this morning. I'm sure she went straight to the boys. I think they're all feeling a bit betrayed.''

He rocked back in his chair and hooked his thumbs through his belt loops. "I suppose they're in the bunkhouse sulking. I'm sorry, Miranda. Is there anything I can say to them to help your cause? Hell, can you add anything to what you've told me?''

Miranda didn't think the kids were in the bunkhouse but had gone to the cave. She definitely didn't want Linc stumbling in on their makeshift soundstage. Then her reputation would be shot in all quarters, except maybe with the little kids.

"No, and no again. They need time to adjust to the fact that I'm more a gen X-er than a gen Y-er.''

He grinned devilishly. "I'm glad you're gen X.''

She would have delivered a smart retort but Hana came running into the kitchen with Cassie wheeling after her. Both girls were dressed in their new pink nighties and wore their matching pink slippers. They looked angelic.

Hana threw her arms around Linc's waist. Cassie hung back, as the younger girl exclaimed, "Look, Mr. Linc, Randi turned us into princesses. But she said we hadda thank you, 'cause you paid for the 'terial.''

"Material," Cassie corrected primly, smoothing her delicate fingers over the satin bows Miranda had sewn down the front of each nightie.

Linc snapped forward so fast his chair legs hit the floor, scaring Scraps. Over Hana's fierce hug, Linc gazed helplessly at Miranda. He didn't seem to know what to do with the clinging child.

Miranda mimed that he should squeeze Hana back. So he did, if clumsily. Then Miranda jerked a thumb toward Cassie enough times that Linc caught her drift and hauled

Cassie's wheelchair closer. "You girls are definitely the princesses of this ranch. I'm happy to have been of assistance, but Miranda made you beautiful. Don't you think she deserves the biggest hug?"

They easily transferred their affection, nearly bowling Miranda over in their enthusiasm. "M'randa, come read us a good-night story," Hana begged.

"Tonight's my turn to feed and water livestock. Maybe Linc will read to you." Snatching her jacket off the peg by the door, Miranda called Scraps and they bounded out on a *whoosh* of cold air.

Linc turned wary eyes to the two little girls, recalling Felicity at the same age. She'd been such a happy kid, always badgering him to play with her or read a book. When had she changed into an unhappy young adult? If he hadn't been so absorbed in his career, could he have saved her? He had been well connected in the L.A. music scene. So she didn't have talent; in his estimation, not all of his clients did, either. No, he thought harshly, he wouldn't feel bad about wanting something better for her.

That was all in the past. Now he couldn't help wondering what the future held for these two little girls. Anybody who read the Sunday papers had to be aware of the deplorable record of welfare systems all over the country. One article had stated that too many kids in foster homes were abused. Chances for Cassie, Hana and Wolfie weren't good. Even as he mustered a smile and stood to follow them, a fist of doubt plowed into his gut. But what could he do, dammit? His mission wasn't to take on the world, but rather to try to save a few misguided teens who might be headed toward his sister's fate.

He sat awkwardly between the girls on one of the cots, after having lifted the birdlike Cassie out of her confining chair. Linc saw the size of the book she grabbed and fought panic and dismay. "Somebody bought you a set of the Little House books by Laura Ingalls Wilder, I see," he muttered, opening the one titled *On the Banks of Plum Creek.*

"Miranda did. She or Jenny reads us one chapter a night," Cassie informed him. "Miranda lets me read one, too. But she has to help with the big words, 'cause I don't know 'em all. Tonight, you don't hafta let me read."

As she spoke, her huge dark eyes lifted to Linc's, and he melted like butter in a skillet. "Darlin', I'll be glad to help you sound out the hard words." He cleared his throat, then sat up straighter when two warm little bodies slipped under his arms and snuggled down, one on either side of him.

For some time after he'd tucked them in for the night and crossed the house to his own room, their predicament preyed on his mind. Allowing them to stay on at the ranch indefinitely was out of the question. But he had the funds to see that Cassie received surgery, if surgery would let her walk again. As he flopped onto his bed, his thoughts jumped backward. Doling out money hadn't helped Felicity. However, his sister had never needed anything as straightforward as surgery. She'd needed love he'd failed to give. Love he didn't know *how* to give, dammit!

The next day, after Linc and the others collected Cassie and Wolfie outside their school and all headed for the meeting with Evelyn Bishop, he noticed the nervousness permeating the SUV's interior.

"Kids, relax. We're going to an office to talk, not face a firing squad." He wasn't able to tell if his joking had alleviated their concern or not.

The meeting started off badly and went downhill from there, largely because the director cut right to the chase. "Jennifer, you are only sixteen. Your mother petitioned the Los Angeles court and has regained custody of your next-younger brother and sister. You were also named in the order. I've called to confirm, but unless the judge gives permission for you to remain at Mr. Parker's facility, the state will return you to your rightful residence in the next couple of weeks. Eric, Greg, I've made new files on you. Shawn's not eligible as I explained to Mr. Parker. Neither is Miranda, of course. Really, at twenty-six, you should get a job," she said, favoring the younger woman with an unblinking stare. "On the brighter side—Lincoln, I've found you a housekeeper."

Getting up, she skirted her desk and went to the door. "Dolores, will you send in Mrs. Phelps?"

Everyone in the room tensed. The wait was short. A jolly-looking woman with short gray hair entered the room. After introductions, the potential employee said to Linc, "I've raised five children of my own, but I'm too proud to go live with any of them. My husband died after a lengthy illness. He needed me to care for him, so I lost my job as a grocery clerk. Now, it seems, everyone thinks I'm too old to do that job anymore. Oh—" she waved a hand "—they don't come right out and say so because it'd violate antidiscrimination laws. All the same, they hire someone younger. I'm healthy and I love kids. A position that provides room and board plus a small salary is exactly what I need to get back on my feet."

"I've checked her references," Mrs. Bishop said. "They're impeccable." She folded her hands atop the files that lay on her desk.

Linc felt manipulated by the director, who hadn't forewarned him about this latest development. He realized with sinking heart that hiring the Phelps woman meant his cozy evenings with Miranda would end. If Miranda stayed, she, Jenny and the little girls would have to move to the second bunkhouse. He was well aware he'd put off suggesting the move, but had been unwilling to admit precisely why until now.

He fiddled with the Stetson he'd removed and set on his knee. This was in the best interests of the refuge. He'd been concerned about Miranda's ability to manage college and her household tasks. Climbing to his feet, he extended a hand. "Mrs. Phelps, you're hired. Do you have a car, or shall I provide you with transportation?"

"I have a car. When should I report for duty, sir?"

"We're informal. Call me Linc," he said, mulling over her question. "Is Monday all right? That gives the kids and me this week to make a few adjustments at home." Releasing her hand, he stood watching as she smiled at Mrs. Bishop and the children, then left the room.

Mrs. Bishop, clearly pleased with herself, picked up a pen and shoved a sheaf of forms across the desk at Linc. "You kids and Miranda may go into the foyer. There's juice in our vending machine. Mr. Parker and I need to discuss his license and how our benefits relate to each of you. We won't be long."

Linc dug out his wallet and handed around dollar bills. The troops promptly filed out the door, except for Wolfie. He walked straight up to the director's desk. "You never said nothin' 'bout Hana, Cassie and me."

The woman reddened. "Well, I...that's one of the things I have to discuss with Mr. Parker. Run along now, Wolfgang. Go wait with the others." She busied herself straightening files until the boy had closed the door fully.

Linc read and signed the license agreement, then glanced up. "What about them? I take it you've found foster homes?"

"Uh...no, I'm afraid not." She steepled her fingers, worry lining her face. "I'm sure it's only a matter of my finding time to unearth their old records and then make home visits to all the families currently utilized by the department. I know you're anxious to unload the children as fast as possible. Unfortunately, at the moment my hands are tied.''

Linc scowled. '''Anxious to unload them' isn't how I'd put it. That sounds so cold. Poor kids—it's their futures I'm concerned about.'' He took a breath. ''So essentially they're still in limbo.''

''Yes. Of course, their greater welfare is at stake. I heard from Dr. Wyeth, who examined Cassandra. He indicated you've requested orthopedic and neurological evaluations of her leg and spine. I'm afraid I can't authorize such an expense yet.''

''I didn't ask the state to pay. I told Wyeth I'd take care of the bills.''

''Yes, but…he and I think you're not aware of future liability. Out-of-pocket expenses could amount to hundreds of thousands of dollars, Lincoln.''

''How can you weigh mere money against the possibility of a kid maybe walking again? The bastard who ought to pay is the guy who threw her down those stairs.''

Mrs. Bishop paled slightly and raised one hand to her mouth. ''I hadn't heard how she came to be incapacitated. I'm sorry. She told you what happened, then?''

''Wolfie did. Cassie's mom's boyfriend is doing time. So is her mother, I gather. Dammit, she's such a tiny little thing. She deserves to have a family who gives a shit about her, if you'll pardon my French. Can't you expedite this process, Mrs. Bishop?''

''I'll do what I can. But I make no promises. I've put a provisional addendum on your license relative to housing the three children until adequate placement is procured. I think you're a good man, Mr. Parker. I hope you'll be able to control the older boys after I arrange to remove Jenny and return her to L.A. I read body language fairly well. Eric and Jenny especially are not happy about my adjudication.''

"Do you know if Jenny's mother has cleaned up her act? She's obviously no saint.''

"Our L.A. office will conduct a home visit before she's sent back, of course.''

"Good. Otherwise, I'd want to intervene. Is that it for now?'' Linc lifted his hat.

"Uh...we, uh, have both avoided mentioning Miranda Kimbrough. I shouldn't have to tell you it doesn't look good for you to allow her to continue living at Rascal Ranch.''

Linc digested Miranda's full name for a lengthy second. "For the record,'' he said, "I've applied to the county asking to change the name of the ranch to Felicity's Refuge. I've ordered a new arch, as well as a sign to post at the highway.''

"Is Felicity the ranch's benefactor?''

"Catalyst. Not benefactor. The investment is solely mine.''

The director raised a dark eyebrow. "Since I have another appointment, I'll end our discussion now. I'll give you approximately a week after Mrs. Phelps comes on board before I make my first unscheduled visit to your facility. I expect by then to have an answer on Jenny Russo. And you, I trust, will have resolved the situation with Melinda, er, Miranda.''

Linc jammed on his hat and gave a curt nod. Mrs. Bishop had made abundantly clear that, to pass inspection, it'd be advisable if Miranda left.

The kids and Miranda all leapt from their chairs as Linc emerged from the office. Miranda wasn't able to decipher his poker face, but his long stride and squared shoulders didn't bode well.

Hurrying to catch up, she took Hana by one hand and, with the other, helped Cassie maneuver her wheelchair out the door and down the ramp.

"What's goin' down, man?" Eric asked, running to stay in step with Linc.

"Nothing. For the time being, everything stays as is."

"Jenny stays?"

"For now, yes."

Eric gave a cautious thumbs-up to his friends. "Are you bullshittin'? You talked the witch out of shipping Jenny home?"

Linc flung open the doors to the SUV and turned to lift Cassie out of her chair. "Eric, I never bullshit. I didn't talk Mrs. Bishop out of anything. In agencies like hers, all decisions hinge on rules. She simply doesn't have the paperwork at present to shift Jenny or to place Wolfie, Hana and Cassie. Now you know everything I know."

"So we're going home to wait?" Jenny looked ready to bolt.

Linc handed her up so she could take her usual seat in the center back. "We're going home to prepare for the arrival of our housekeeper."

"Can we go to Nico's for pasketti first?" Hana asked sweetly.

They all blinked. Hana rarely made personal requests. Her asking for spaghetti, which she'd never been able to pronounce, broke the tension.

Linc smiled as he buckled her into a seat. "If you're not careful, kid, you're going to turn into pasketti. But, okay. We'll stop at Nico's and celebrate hiring Mrs. Phelps, shall we?"

"Don't wanna," Cassie announced, crossing her arms

and poking out her lower lip. "I like Randi best." And with that, she burst into tears.

Linc's heart skidded south. Damn, he'd dreaded this discussion, especially in Miranda's presence. Yet Cassie had given him an opening. "Kids, hiring Mrs. Phelps shouldn't come as any big surprise. You knew from day one that I'd posted an ad for a cook-housekeeper. Miranda and Jenny have kindly filled in. But their college classes start on Monday, so Mrs. Phelps's timing is really good."

"That means we won't earn any more spending money," Jenny wailed.

As Linc backed from the parking space, he glanced over his shoulder at the white-faced girl. "Not true, Jenny. Mrs. Phelps won't be feeding the livestock or collecting eggs. And with opening up the second bunkhouse, she'll need assistance tidying up."

"We're moving into the other bunkhouse?" Jenny didn't sound as if that was welcome news.

Informing Miranda had been what Linc dreaded, and now it was out in the open. He peered at her in the rearview mirror. Faint lines pinched her forehead. Linc sucked in a breath and held it, half expecting her to…to what? Object to the loss of their nightly chats, some of which led to stolen hours in his bed? She'd hardly mention that in front of the kids. And Linc felt awful for dumping the truth on her in such an awkward manner. "Here's Nico's," he announced unnecessarily. "Looks like there's a wait. The parking lot's full. What do you suppose is the occasion?"

"Maybe lots of people hired housekeepers," Wolfie muttered.

"More like half the households in town are tired of holiday leftovers," Shawn suggested. "I'm ordering a big plate of cannelloni with meat sauce."

Miranda laughed. "I've been getting creative with ways

to camouflage turkey. Would you believe I considered making turkey spaghetti tonight?''

Everyone but Hana made gagging noises. ''I like pasketti with anything.'' Her generous acceptance caused Miranda to lean over and hug her.

Having located a parking place, Linc pocketed his keys. He glanced back in time to see Miranda and Hana's curly heads and big smiles, their faces pressed cheek to cheek. The sight rocked him and made him question his earlier acceptance of Mrs. Bishop's edict. The director had let him know that he should say goodbye to Miranda, and he thought he could do it, however reluctantly. Now his resolve to comply with his license requirements seemed to spin upside down. He no longer had a clear perspective on that or anything else.

Above all, he needed space—and time—to figure out what to do about his growing feelings for Miranda.

THE REMAINDER of the week and over the weekend, Jenny moped. She let the others move her most cherished belongings into the bunkhouse, which wasn't like her.

Miranda did her own chores and Jenny's without a murmur. She understood that her friend was hurting over the likelihood of being returned to a home that represented only hopelessness.

''You can't tell me she'll ever change,'' Jenny said bitterly on Sunday afternoon, when she finally consented to discuss her mother. Jenny, Miranda and the boys had slipped off to the cave to try to cheer Jenny up with practice. But it was Miranda who kept attempting to draw Jenny out of her gloom by suggesting they write a new song for the group. One that might help alleviate her anxiety.

'''She'll Never Change.' That's a fantastic title.'' Miranda flipped to a clean sheet in the notebook she always carried. She wrote a few lines and asked Eric to strike a chord on his guitar. He set aside his tape player. He'd turned the tape over after the group's last song. Their habit was to tape two or three numbers, then play them back and come up with changes to make them better.

Miranda hummed a few bars. Standing, she paced and sang what she'd written, motioning with a finger for Eric to follow along on his guitar. Miranda was concentrating so hard, she failed to see that the others stopped in their tracks to gape at her.

Even Shawn, who rarely joined them for these sessions anymore, moved closer and listened raptly.

But the instant Miranda finished the stanza, she sat down again and scribbled another one. She continued the process until she had what would pass for an entire song. "Okay, let's try this from the top, guys."

Her companions remained silent until Miranda grabbed Greg's keyboard. "This is the sound I'm trying for, Greg. Pay attention. See, this is how I'm hearing the chorus in my head."

"So what are you now, a friggin' music teacher?"

Miranda stiffened and snatched her hand from the keys. Too late. Eric sprang up from his seat. "With that voice range, you should be on stage. We all know Jenny's got natural ability. But you, Randi, you've had voice training or I'll eat my guitar, strings and all."

"Get real, Eric. It's these great acoustics in the cave. They're phenomenal."

"How would you know 'phenomenal' acoustics unless you've hung out in a lot of sound studios?" Eric grabbed the book away from her and began to play the part she'd written for his guitar. He stopped abruptly, clapping a hand over the sound hole, stilling the vibration of the strings.

"I'm savvy enough about music to know this is professional stuff you've written."

Miranda yanked back her book and stumbled to her feet again. "Quit making such a big deal out of nothing, or you can do without my help. This is about your trio sounding good. It has nothing to do with me."

All four of the others eyed her speculatively, but no one countered her or agreed with her assessment.

She folded her arms over her notebook and ducked from the chamber into the main cave passageway. "One of us should head back to the house. I think Linc's getting suspicious when we all disappear together. Finding time to practice will be even harder once Mrs. Phelps shows up tomorrow."

"Who cares if Linc's suspicious?" Eric said. "We're not hurting anyone or anything being out here. He's pretty much said farm work won't get under way again till spring."

Miranda poked her head back into the chamber. "True, but that doesn't mean he wants us jamming. I've never met anybody so down on the entire music business as Linc. He blames his sister's love of music for her death. I, for one, like it here at the ranch. I don't intend to rock the boat, so I'm just telling y'all. After today, I'll be too busy with my class assignments to spend time with you out here."

"You mean you've got a bad crush on Linc," Jenny accused her. "You don't want him blaming you for encouraging us."

Miranda tossed her head. "So what if I like him? We're both adults and we're both single."

"How does anyone know what to believe about you?" Eric sneered. "You say you're single, but how do we know? You let us think you were our age, for crying out loud.''

''Believe whatever you want,'' Miranda returned wearily. ''I refuse to be drawn into one of these high-school bitch sessions. I'm going back to the house to finish hemming the curtains for Mrs. Phelps's bedroom.''

She heard their hushed conversation begin moments after she withdrew. But nothing was distinct. Miranda decided there would be more harm than gain in speculating about what they said after she left.

Supper that night was an almost silent meal. Thank goodness Wolfie and Cassie felt like talking about upcoming school projects, or Miranda wouldn't have known how to handle the long pauses.

Linc, it seemed, was lost in his own thoughts. He had little to add to the erratic conversation. Nor did he appear to notice anything amiss with the boys and Jenny. As he pushed back his chair and excused himself from the table, he turned to Miranda. ''What time do you and Jenny need to leave for class tomorrow night? I'm asking, because sometime between when Mrs. Phelps arrives and you take off, I need to run into town and overnight some papers to my business partner in Hollywood.''

''Can't you fax them?'' Miranda asked, without thinking it wasn't her place to question Linc's activities.

''No. I need to transfer joint funds. I, uh, realize I haven't been paying attention to the falling stock market. I've been consumed by the ranch. I want to shift some personal stocks, as well. That requires my notarized signature. I'll also go and see Mrs. Bishop, and she can update me on some of the other details she and I discussed last week.''

No one had to be told one of those other details was

Jenny's status. Another was the placement of the younger kids.

Subdued, Miranda gave Linc only what he asked for. "Our classes begin at six. We need to leave here no later than five-fifteen."

"Good. I'll make sure I'm back by then. And I'll see that you have a full tank of gas."

"Thanks. With Mrs. Phelps taking over meals, I can be ready to roll in no time. Jenny, too, I guess."

"Actually, I'm thinking of signing a withdrawal form tomorrow night," Jenny said. "Linc shouldn't have to pay for a class I probably won't get to finish."

He paused at the door. "We're not sure you'll be extradited, Jenny, or whatever it is they call sending you home. It's quite possible the judge may decide it's better for you to stay here. That's one thing I intend to bring up with Mrs. Bishop. But I can hardly suggest she tell a judge you're thriving and attending school, if a day later that's not true."

"Okay. I'll wait to see what the dragon lady says. I think you can still get part of your money back if I drop out before the second class."

"Answer me this," Linc said. "Are you happy here, Jenny? Until lately, I'd thought so."

She looked startled. "Maybe I don't know how I'm s'posed to feel."

"You and Eric go walking in the woods a lot." Linc smiled when they exchanged glances. "Yes, I've seen you. It's not that I object to exercise or fresh air, but the rest of you seem to invest more time and interest in the welfare of the ranch."

Eric rammed his hands in his pockets and hunched his shoulders forward, drawing his chin down. He said nothing to suggest to Linc that they were really going to the cave.

"You think we don't take an interest and the others do?" Jenny asked.

"Well, Miranda cooks, sews and teaches crafts to the little girls. Shawn's showing Greg and Wolfie how to ride horses in exchange for Wolfie teaching him to fish. You've all been here two months, yet you and Eric still seem…restless."

"We're musicians, man," Eric growled. "All you have on your CD or on TV is the crap they play at rich folks' weddings or funerals."

Linc didn't find his remark amusing. "I don't know that the classical greats like Chopin, Beethoven and Tchaikovsky would appreciate having their work termed *crap,* but I get the picture. I'd frankly hoped exposure to works of the great composers might broaden your musical appreciation."

"Not likely," Eric said, throwing back his shoulders.

"Okay. We'll agree to disagree about music. Otherwise, is the ranch meeting your needs?"

Jenny and Eric flashed a look of confusion between them. "Yes," they said simultaneously. "I do some things with the kids," Jenny added. "In fact, I bought some cool sequins in town today. I was planning to help Cassie and Hana glue them around the bottoms of their jeans."

Linc nodded, about to ask a further question, but the room emptied so fast, Linc blinked—and he discovered himself alone with Miranda for the first time in days. She was rinsing dishes and arranging them in the dishwasher, which should not have been sexy. But there was something about her flyaway blond bob and the curve of her elbow, coupled with the bow of her slender neck, that moved Linc to cross the room, take her in his arms and kiss her hungrily.

Water dripped down the back of his shirt as Miranda

clasped his shoulders. Her heels rose two inches off the ground when she stretched up. It wasn't until they were both breathless and he finally broke away that she slowly drifted back to her feet. "What was all that about?" she asked huskily.

"I felt like it. And it felt good. Damned good."

She gazed up through her lashes and smiled. "Here I thought you were getting ready to replace me in your bed with Mrs. Phelps."

Swinging her aloft, Linc threw back his head and laughed. "That's what I love about you, Miranda. You make me laugh. If you asked anyone who knew me in Hollywood, one thing they'd tell you is how serious I am."

He set her down gently. Although she remained a bit dizzy and drunk on the fact that he'd said he loved her, however casual the declaration, she ached for the man who had nothing in his life to laugh about.

Linc bent and once again kissed away all her thoughts. "Swear to me," he said, "there's no reason I'd ever have to let you leave here."

He'd turned so serious that Miranda just wanted to say or do something to bring back the laugh lines in his tanned cheeks. She poked a finger in his ribs. "Any man who'd say that to a frazzled woman with dishpan hands is either proposing marriage or off his rocker."

Grinning, he shoved a finger in the watch pocket of his too-tight jeans and pulled out an eye-popping square-cut diamond set in either white gold or platinum. The flash of the gemstone in the overhead light nearly blinded Miranda. She was certain her jaw dropped a good six inches.

The ring said so much, and yet she had to deal with a surge of nausea. Linc was aware she still held secrets inside. Oh, how she wanted to accept everything he'd humbled himself to offer her. Yet how, in good conscience, could she commit herself to this man—or anyone? What about the mess she'd left behind? The far-reaching conglomerate of Misty subsidiaries, two homes—one in Nashville, the other the Kimbrough homeplace in Cumberland County. To say nothing of a newly released CD, money sitting in two banks and an apparently unbreakable contract with Wesley Carlisle.

Linc's hopeful smile began to fade. He pulled back the ring. "Is that a flat 'no way in hell' I see in your eyes? Or does your hesitation represent a maybe?" He sighed. "I've been thinking about this since our visit with Mrs. Bishop. I know I'm springing it on you. I bought the ring one day when I went into town for feed. The fire in the stone reminded me of you."

She cleared her throat several times and covered his hand with a shaking one of her own that was still damp and now cold as ice. "I *want* to say yes, Linc. If only you knew how badly. You, the ranch, what you're trying to do here—it all speaks to needs I feel strongly about."

"Then say yes, Miranda. It's a simple word." He reached for her trembling left hand and uncurled her third finger enough to slip the ring up to her knuckle. "If you want me and all this ring stands for, take it. Even if you need time to get rid of the excess baggage we both know you came with, I'm willing to wait."

She swallowed the lumps that threatened to choke her. "I do have an albatross hanging around my neck, Linc. I promise you that what's here—you, school, a home—they're the things I want with all my heart."

Not letting her go on talking, in case she begin to think of reasons for turning down his proposal, Linc drew her to his chest. In one deft move, he slid the ring past the resistance of her knuckle and sealed their loose promise with another kiss.

This time when the necessity to breathe broke them apart, her hands roamed up and down his shirtfront and tears of happiness stood in her eyes, rivaling the sparkle of the diamond. "Is our engagement a secret?" she murmured. "Or dare we go public?"

He framed her smile with his thumbs. "As far as I'm concerned, we can broadcast it to the world."

"Does that mean you'll tell Mrs. Bishop?"

"Uh…why not?"

"Well, then, what if the kids ask us for a wedding date?"

"We'll say the date hasn't been decided. If you're in agreement, we can tell them that no matter what happens in the future, they'll all be invited to attend."

She nodded once, twice, then whirled him around the room until both of them were laughing and completely winded. All the problems she'd left behind still hung over her, but in Linc's arms, none of them seemed important somehow.

CHAPTER FOURTEEN

THEY TOLD THE BOYS about their engagement first and received a so-so response. Miranda expected more in the way of congratulations from the girls. Hana, while not completely sure what engagement meant, couldn't stop touching the ring. Cassie brought her hands to her thin chest. "My prayer tonight is gonna be that when Miranda and Mr. Linc get married, they'll be foster folks to me, Wolfie and Hana."

Linc shifted uneasily. "Uh, instead, Cassie, pray that the new doctor you're going to see can help you walk again."

"Okay. Hana, let's pray for both."

The littler girl bobbed her head.

Jenny didn't even get up from where she sat with sequins and glue gun spread out around her. She may have muttered congratulations, but Miranda wasn't positive.

"Should we let them get back to their project?" Linc asked after their anticlimactic announcement.

Miranda nodded and walked him out of the bunkhouse, then pulled his head down to her level and kissed him hard.

"Coming back with me?" he cajoled, tugging on her hand. "Or maybe we'd better abstain from now until the wedding."

"That's probably best, Linc. I'd better see what's up with Jenny. Her lack of reaction really surprised me."

"If you find out and there's anything I can do, give a yell." Linc lifted Miranda's left hand, brushed a thumb over the stone, then pressed a kiss to her palm. Reluctantly, he walked toward the main house, but kept turning back to smile foolishly at her.

Miranda hugged her jacket around her shivering body. It crossed her mind to run after him and suggest celebrating their engagement in his bed. Resisting the urge, she turned and went into the bunkhouse.

That was when Jenny decided to have her say. As Miranda closed the door behind her, Jenny clapped loudly and slowly. "Con…gra…tu…lations! Now I see what coming to the ranch was all about for you."

Miranda's fixed smile fled. "Excuse me?"

"I finally get it—you being older but pretending to be one of us. It's obvious how you know so much about music, but had to hide it. I don't know where you first saw Linc, but this was all an elaborate plot to follow him here and end up with that rock on your finger."

"You are so wrong! I swear I'd never heard of him until we arrived here."

"Like, right," Jenny jeered. "I didn't fall off a cabbage truck."

"It's the truth, Jenny. The day you and I met was my first time ever in L.A."

"And you expect us to buy your story about reading some article that gave you all your huge amount of knowledge about music? Get real!"

Miranda realized Jenny wasn't going to let up unless she fed the girl's curiosity. As she sat and pulled on her pajamas, Miranda said, "I told you my dad traveled a lot on business. Well, his business was playing guitar in a pretty famous country band. Nearly all of them died in a plane crash." Tears filled her eyes. "I…still can't talk about it."

"Gosh, I'm so sorry, Randi. Shoot me for being such a

bitch. I guess you'd pick up a lot about the business if you went to gigs with him."

"I wasn't stringing you along when I said you guys have talent, Jenny. You're young, but with hard work, I honestly believe you can succeed. Make no mistake though, it's a rough, tough business."

"It's all Eric and I have ever wanted to do. For Greg, it's something to keep his mind occupied and off the fact that he hasn't been able to locate his biological dad. For Eric and me, it's a passion." Obviously feeling bad for the way she'd attacked Miranda, Jenny got up and gave her an apologetic hug.

Miranda willingly let the subject drop. She sat cross-legged on the floor and helped decorate the bottom edges of the little girls' jeans for the next hour.

Later, as she heard Cassie's prayers, Miranda wished Linc hadn't acted so unnerved by Cassie's suggestion. Why was it so outrageous? Fostering the kids would ensure consistency in their lives. And they'd have a good home. She made a mental note to at least discuss the possibility with Linc. Together they would be good parents.

The next day didn't look promising for a heart-to-heart chat. The morning started with a sick horse and the early arrival of Mrs. Phelps. Linc headed for the barn, leaving the housekeeper to Miranda and Jenny. "I've phoned the vet," he called back over his shoulder. "Point her my direction when she pulls in."

By the time the vet arrived, treated the horse and left, Linc had to dash off to town. If he didn't, not only wouldn't his papers get notarized and make the overnight courier, but he'd never get back in time for Miranda and Jenny to make their night classes. "This one-vehicle situation is the pits," Linc grumbled to Miranda. "The first free minute we have after today, we need to see about buying a used pickup.''

''I agree.'' Miranda trailed him outside to pass him the grocery list she and Mrs. Phelps had drawn up. ''The surgeon's office phoned, Linc. They had a cancelation at ten tomorrow and are willing to do Cassie's initial workup then.''

''So soon? Wow, I'm glad you told me. I'll move funds from savings to checking while I'm at the bank today.''

''I want you to go with me to the appointment,'' she said.

''We'll see.'' He brushed a kiss across Miranda's lips before climbing into the SUV. Glancing up, Linc noticed Mrs. Phelps staring out the window. ''Hey, did you tell the housekeeper that you and I are engaged?''

''No. I didn't know how to bring it up. And I thought maybe it should come from you, since you're her employer.''

He smiled. ''I think you'd better go tell her now. I'll break the news to Mrs. Bishop. Otherwise, if Mrs. Phelps reports to the director that I kissed you, the dragon lady—as Jenny calls her—may jerk my license before I get there.''

Although she felt odd introducing the subject to the older woman, Miranda did as Linc requested.

''I'm glad you told me, dear. I didn't mean to spy, but I saw that send-off.'' Her eyes twinkled a moment, then dulled. ''But does your good news mean I'll soon be without a job?''

''He and I haven't discussed a wedding date. Frankly, being engaged is so new to us both, I don't even know if Linc believes in long or short engagements. Plus, I have some business to attend to that will necessitate going out of town for…a while.'' She chewed her lip, knowing this was something she needed to sit down and discuss with Linc.

That afternoon it was Jenny, not Miranda, who was pacing the porch in the drizzling rain, anxious for Linc to get home. The teen flew down the steps the minute he parked, and pounced on him before he'd unloaded the sacks of groceries piled in the back seat. "What did she say?"

"What did who say?" Distracted, Linc shoved two bags full of produce into Jenny's wildly waving arms.

"Mrs. Bishop. You said you'd find out what she heard from the judge."

"Oh, that. They didn't connect. He's had prostate surgery apparently, and his cases have been postponed for two weeks."

"So I'm just hanging on until he gets well? Now I don't know whether to drop that poetry class or stick with it."

"You're registered, so go. Say, Jenny, did I get any phone messages today? Do you know if my partner, Dennis Morrison, called?"

She shrugged. "Mrs. Phelps had me and Randi scrubbing bathrooms and the floors in both bunkhouses today. The woman's a neat freak. We tried to tell her the bathrooms are new and that we'd only just moved into our bunkhouse after giving it a thorough cleaning. But I guess I shouldn't gripe. Now I've *earned* my week's wage."

"Yeah. Hey, let's not stand in the rain talking about money." He grimaced. "My banker in town chewed my ear off enough on that subject today."

Miranda stepped out onto the porch, zipping her jacket and juggling her purse and book bag. "We've gotta run, Jenny, or we'll be late for class. There's Wolfie coming up the walk. Have him carry those groceries inside for you."

Linc sidled past her, trying to flatten his heavier sacks,

but asked her the same question he'd asked Jenny. "Did Dennis Morrison phone me today?"

"The only call I took was from Cassie's surgeon. Oh, and the vet called back to see how the roan was getting along. Who's Dennis Morrison?"

"My business partner. Dennis took on my client contracts when I came here. We agreed he'd pay me five percent of the fifteen they pay. He's been paying by automatic deposit, but I discovered at the bank today that I haven't received the last two. And when I went to transfer funds from the office savings account he and I share, the bank manager I've worked with for years in Hollywood said Dennis blew up at him and closed the account. I left messages on Dennis's voice mail, and gave him my cell and the ranch number. He's probably out of town. Sometimes we have to meet prospective clients on a movie shoot."

Miranda started to let the screen shut, but she grabbed it and propped it ajar. "Didn't he need your okay to close a joint account?"

"Apparently not. But don't worry about it. I've worked with Dennis since we got out of college. We'll straighten things out."

"Oh. Well, I guess you'd know way more about that stuff than I do. I remember you said any contract a person makes can be broken. I was wondering how."

"Well, by hiring a crackerjack financial lawyer." He dropped a kiss on her rain-wet nose. "Marriage isn't that kind of contract, sweetheart. But if you're worried, we can discuss signing a prenuptial agreement." Chuckling, he ducked in out of the rain. "Have fun at your first class, but you'd better take off. I don't want you speeding, especially in this rain. The roads are slick."

She blew him a kiss. "Knowing you worry makes me feel warm and fuzzy." If she expected Linc to laugh at that, she was mistaken. Instead, she heard him greet Mrs. Phelps and immediately ask her if he'd received a call from Dennis Morrison. Linc sounded worried to Miranda. Still, he'd assured her that he and his friend and partner would work out any problem. And he'd given her something to think about concerning her own situation. Could she find and hire a suitable lawyer?

"Wolfie," she said, passing the boy, "Mrs. Phelps said she'd see that Cassie and Hana get a story before they go to bed. But since she's so new, the girls might feel better if you tucked them in. We'll be home around eight-thirty. I know Hana is nervous about staying alone in the bunkhouse."

The boy grinned. "It's been nice not having to rock her half the night. One time filling in ain't gonna kill me, Randi."

"You're a good kid. But what have I told you about saying *ain't?*" Miranda shook a finger at him. When he responded, "Yeah, yeah, yeah," she didn't press the point; instead, she reacted to Jenny's urging her to "get the lead out!"

They arrived on time and their classes went well. "I learned so much in just one night of my poetry class," Jenny said as they pulled out of the parking lot. School dominated their conversation all the way home. Since the rain had turned to sleet, it was after nine when they pulled in. The house was dark except for Linc's room.

"I need to give Linc his keys," Miranda said, stepping up onto the porch.

"If the light doesn't wake the kids in the bunkhouse," Jenny said, "I think I'll do my homework. Will you be long?"

"No. I'm tired, and Cassie's appointment in Sacramento is early tomorrow." Miranda headed for the house.

Treading lightly down the hall, she tapped on Linc's door. She assumed they'd discuss her class and grab the chance to neck a bit. But he was on the phone, involved in serious conversation. She heard him say "John" a couple of times, and knew he hadn't reached his partner, Dennis.

Linc excused himself to the caller and covered the mouthpiece. "Just drop the keys on my dresser, Miranda. I'm talking to John Montoya."

She nodded. Slipping from his room with a waggle of her fingers, she heard Linc curse in connection with Dennis Morrison's name. Softly closing the door, it struck Miranda again that Linc could be having trouble with his partner. Money trouble. And yet, if Linc wanted to involve her, he would. Didn't she have financial worries of her own? Those bank accounts she couldn't access?

She simply had to clear her conscience—dredge up the nerve to come clean with Linc. Maybe tomorrow. He'd be her captive audience on the journey between the ranch and Sacramento.

"I CAN'T GO with you to see the surgeon," Linc snapped the next morning as Miranda questioned the suit and tie he wore to breakfast. Not that he didn't look fantastic dressed that way. He did. He looked…yummy.

But Miranda, who had dark circles under her eyes from staying awake half the night figuring out how to explain her past to Linc, gaped at his tone. "You're Cassie's temporary guardian, Linc. The surgeon's staff won't take my word for anything. Besides, I distinctly recall you telling me Mrs. Bishop expects you to go to their appointments."

"I can't help it. I have to fly down south. Down and back in one day."

"What's more important than Cassie's health?"

"You're asking me to compare apples and oranges."
He shoved a wallet and keys into his slacks pockets. Then
he pulled Miranda into the hall and out onto the porch.
"Don't mention anything to the others. John Montoya says
nobody in the office has seen Dennis in two weeks. It's…
He has total control over my investments as well as over
my clients' funds."

Miranda gripped his arm. "Oh, Linc. Does that mean
you're—?"

"Broke?" he interrupted harshly. "That's a worst-case
scenario. I'm sure there's a good explanation."

"Should I cancel Cassie's appointment?"

"No. I want her out of that damned chair." Removing
his wallet, he peeled off several hundred-dollar bills and
handed them to Miranda. "Mrs. Phelps said you can use
her car today." Sliding his arms around Miranda, he held
her close for a few moments.

She clung, her mind whirling at the frightening possi-
bilities suggested by Linc's admission. She'd followed him
outside with the intention of blurting out the truth of her
past. Now she didn't want to add to his burden. Her situation paled in comparison to his. "No matter what, Linc,"
she murmured, "we have each other."

Her voice was so fierce he drew back and swept a finger
down her nose. "The way you sound, I believe you'd sin-
gle-handedly save me if need be, Miranda."

"I would, Linc. If helping you or the kids lay within
my power, I definitely would."

"Drive carefully in the city. I'll see you tonight. I'll be
back in time for supper."

Fog had rolled in, replacing last night's sleet. Miranda
stood shivering on the porch, watching Linc's departure
until the SUV disappeared in the mist.

She dressed, careful to appear as professional as possible. For Cassie's sake, she wanted the surgeon and his staff to take her seriously.

Miranda had always been a good driver, but the trip into the city in dense fog was precarious. It didn't help that silent tears rolled down Cassie's cheeks the entire journey. "Honey, what's wrong? Don't be afraid. They won't do any surgery today."

"I'm afraid the doctor will say he can't make me walk again." Cassie sniffled.

And since she couldn't promise one way or the other, Miranda swallowed any response.

The exam went better than she'd hoped. The surgeon walked Miranda back to his lab and showed her Cassie's X-rays. "It's beyond me why this child's hip amphithrosis hasn't been corrected before now. Her GP indicated the spine was involved. It's not. We're in luck—it's all ball-and-socket displacement. At most we're looking at three days in the hospital and four to six weeks' recovery, followed up by physical therapy. I can provide you and her guardian with therapy exercises to do at home."

Miranda couldn't contain her joy or the tears streaming from her eyes. "Then all Linc, er, Mr. Parker has to do is schedule Cassie at the hospital?"

"My staff will set a date. Stop and see my nurse. She's preparing a sheet of instructions and a cost estimate. I predict we'll have Cassandra out of that chair by the end of March, depending on when we get her on the surgery schedule."

Miranda supposed that meant it depended on Linc's ability to pay half the charge up front and the other half on dismissal. For that reason, Miranda was reluctant to get Cassie worked up over the exciting news. She was sure she hadn't imagined Linc's worry this morning about his finances.

Nevertheless, she planned to tell him about the surgeon's verdict as soon as they got back to the ranch. The very last thing she pictured was that she'd beat Linc home—or that she'd find Mrs. Phelps wringing her hands. "Eric, Greg and Jenny are gone," the woman cried. "Oh, mercy me! They've run away."

Miranda did her best to calm the woman and the other kids.

"Tell me again, Mrs. Phelps. What happened?" she asked once they were all inside.

"The phone rang. I had my hands full dishing up stew for lunch, so Jenny answered. She started sobbing. I heard her say that Linc had assured her some judge wasn't going to take cases for two weeks. I deduced the caller was Mrs. Bishop. Apparently, she told Jenny the judge wasn't coming back at all and his replacement has ruled that Jenny should be returned to her mother as soon as possible. Next thing I know, my lunch goes begging. And except for Shawn, the teens pack up and clear out."

"They must have said *something* more to you. Or to Shawn. Given you some indication of where they planned to go."

"Not to me. Shawn's a nice boy, and he's very upset. If they confided in him, I believe he'd tell us."

A weary Linc banged into the house, stripping off his tie. He, too, was taken aback by news of the exodus. "Did you call Mrs. Bishop afterward? No? Good! This could put three black marks against my license. As if my life hasn't gone to hell enough today. Mrs. Phelps, you're the adult I left in charge. Why didn't you tell them they couldn't leave until Miranda or I got back?"

The housekeeper burst into tears. "I tried, Mr. Parker. Kids today, they're not like they were in my day. That girl called me an interfering old b-bitch."

Miranda shielded the housekeeper. "Linc, you're not being fair."

He turned to Shawn. "Did they have money?"

"Eric and Greg had saved some wages. I'm not sure how much, Mr. P. Greg did try talking Eric and Jenny out of this. But they've got it in their heads that the new songs Miranda helped them write will open doors that were closed before."

Linc swung around and glared at Miranda. "What's this about songs? You *helped* them in this idiotic quest?"

She didn't quail under his obvious fury. "They have talent, Linc. And they're determined to be in the business with or without anyone's approval. So, yes, I provided some positive direction."

Snorting in disgust, Linc wrenched his cell phone out of his jacket pocket. "How far can three kids get on foot? Was no one aware that they're *my* responsibility? I'll phone the state police. Surely they'll pick them up before they can get far."

Miranda settled Hana and Cassie in the living room with a children's video while the rest of them sat at the kitchen table in virtual silence, waiting for a call from the cops. At one point, Miranda haltingly told Linc how Cassie's appointment had gone. He made no comment until she mentioned the bottom-line cost.

He glanced up at her, misery overflowing his dark eyes. "Tomorrow you'll have to call the surgeon's office and halt proceedings. My good buddy Dennis seems to have skipped the country with all his assets and mine. According to my lawyer, the only thing that'll save me from being held accountable is a document the law firm drew up giving me a two-year interval from all business activities."

"Oh, Linc, that's awful! He cleaned you out?" Miranda

got up and knelt at his side. She cradled his hand against her face until he pulled away.

Propping his elbows on his knees, Linc vigorously rubbed the heels of his hands over his cheeks and eyes. "John Montoya warned me. I should've listened. Thank God I paid cash on the line for all the improvements I made to the ranch. The truth is, Miranda, including what's left in my private account, I'll need every cent the state will pay me to look after Eric, Greg and Jenny if I'm to have a prayer of hanging on to the ranch until we market our first crops."

Miranda slipped the big diamond ring off her finger. "Here, Linc. Sell this. Add it to what you need to pay bills." She still had those earrings sewn into the lining of her jacket, and now she mulled over how to offer him those, as well.

"Absolutely not!" he exclaimed, sitting up straight and squaring his jaw. "This is my problem to handle." He worked the ring back onto her finger.

She'd have argued further, but Linc's cell phone rang and they all hovered, waiting for him to relay what the police said.

"No firm leads yet," he murmured after clicking off. "But the sergeant seems confident that three kids sticking together will be fairly easy to spot. Miranda, we can't let this upset Cassie and Hana. Will you take them to the bunkhouse and act as if nothing's wrong?" He turned to Shawn and Wolfie. "Guys, we'll split the daily chores. I'll go change out of my suit and meet you in the barn. This was Eric's day to feed livestock and refurbish stalls with the fresh hay."

"You're asking us to carry on as usual?" Mrs. Phelps ventured.

"The sergeant said that's best. He or someone from the

department will update us twice a day. Those kids are street savvy. According to police, digging them out if they've gone to ground is a matter of receiving tips. Technically, they can't put out an APB until after twenty-four hours."

At the end of five days, however, the word from the police was that there was still no word.

That very afternoon, Mrs. Bishop showed up unannounced. "I'm here to take Jenny Russo to the bus. The county of her residence has finally paid for her ticket home. Please have her pack her things," she told Mrs. Phelps.

"Oh, my." Mrs. Phelps appealed to Miranda, who sat at the table reading her child psychology textbook.

"Didn't Linc let you know that Jenny, Eric and Greg took off the day you broke the news to Jenny on the phone?" Miranda dropped her book.

Linc and Shawn had the misfortune of entering the kitchen via the back door just then, trailed by Hana. They were just in time to take the brunt of Mrs. Bishop's wrath.

"I'm not attempting to defraud the county," Linc tried to say. "We're doing everything possible to locate the kids and bring them back. Just give me another week before you file a negative report that will affect my license."

"Can you tell me why I should do that, Mr. Parker?"

Linc removed his hat and shrugged out of his heavy jacket. "Shawn was the last to speak with the kids. He's quite certain our budding musical trio plans to cut a demo CD and shop it around among the music producers. I have extensive contacts among that crowd. I've put out the word in L.A. The minute they show up, we've got 'em."

Mrs. Bishop plunked down her briefcase, knocking Miranda's book to the floor. "I suppose I can give you another week, as they've obviously been gone one week already without my being any the wiser. But I'm warning

you, if they don't put in an appearance by then, I want
your word that you'll go to L.A. and see those music people yourself. I don't like lost children on my watch.''

"Nor do I," Linc said, gazing uneasily at the little kids
crowding around the table. "With Mrs. Phelps and Miranda here to look after Shawn, Wolfie, Hana and Cassie,
I can go earlier. How's the day after tomorrow?''

Miranda sat chewing on her pencil eraser, listening intently to Mrs. Bishop. She felt she had to interrupt. "Linc,
what if they're not in L.A.? What if they've gone to Nashville, instead?''

He and the director spun around. "Nonsense," Linc declared, slicing a broad hand through the air. "Jenny and
my sister only ever talked about rock and heavy metal.
Neither would be caught dead listening to stuff coming out
of Nashville.''

Miranda thought they might, especially since she'd seen
fit to remold their style. But without spilling her story in
front of that hateful woman, she was left alone with her
suspicions. Just last night, Miranda had discovered that
Jenny had torn a number of pages from her journal. Among
them were several finished songs, including the one Miranda had titled, "For the Love of Felicity.''

Quietly closing her book and leaving Linc and the director to plot between themselves, Miranda retired to the
bunkhouse. Tomorrow, she decided, she simply had to find
a way to get in touch with old contacts in Nashville and
make some discreet inquiries.

As luck would have it, the opportunity presented itself
at midday. Shawn and Linc were exercising the horses.
Mrs. Phelps had gone to pick up Cassie and Wolfie at
school, after which she planned to go shopping in town.
Hana, who'd come down with a head cold, had fallen
asleep on the couch, Scraps curled in the crook of her arm.

Miranda went to the kitchen phone. She dialed Colby Donovan's number from memory. Her hands shook, and she almost couldn't speak when she heard her music arranger answer.

"Colby," she finally croaked. "It's Miranda. Uh... Misty," she added.

"I'll be damned." The man whistled through his teeth. "So those three kids were telling the truth when they said you told them to look me up. I told Rick Holden I didn't know whether to believe them or not, even though a couple of the songs they sang had the ring of your work. Girl, where in hell are you? Wes...well, we'd all given you up for dead."

Miranda cleared her throat. "Colby, if you were ever my friend, don't tell Wes you've heard from me. I'm phoning about those kids. Their leaving here has caused a guy I care a lot about a heap of trouble. Are they all right?"

"Yeah, they're fine, I think. I liked their sound." Miranda heard him flipping pages. Then he said, "I knew I'd set them up with a time to sing for Rick and a couple of other scouts. This Friday at one. Now that I know for sure those are your tunes, everybody will want to take a closer listen."

"I don't think they're ready to launch, Colby. For old times' sake, would you do me a favor and give me their address? My...friend can come get them, or he can have the local authorities do it."

"They in trouble with the law?" Colby sounded hesitant.

"Only insofar as they're wards of the court and, as such, are under the guardianship of Lincoln Parker. He's the owner of Felicity's Refuge, where they live."

"This refuge, it's like a detention center or something?"

''More like a halfway house for homeless street kids. It's a great place.''

''You work there? What in the hell happened to you, Miranda? Is this about a man?''

''Colby, I'm not telling you anything more. You of all people know how Wes pressured and pressured and pressured me. Suffice it to say, I'm not coming back. I'm deliriously happy here. In fact, I'm engaged to be married.''

''No kidding? That oughta break the hearts of what's left of your band.''

''What do you mean, left of them?''

''Sullivan and Marker retired. Mickie and Dakota split. They grab backup gigs occasionally. You hurt a lot of people when you took off like that, babe.''

''That's been my only regret, Colby. But I really had no other choice.''

''Your dad never woulda slunk off in the night, letting down his friends and fans like you did. He woulda duked it out with Wes.''

''You know Wes never would have released his goose that laid the golden egg.''

''I'll grant you Wes is a major dickhead. I wasn't happy when you signed with him. But he has you under a bona fide contract.''

''A lifetime contract, Colby?'' was all Miranda said.

''Well, then you've gotta prove he's a dickhead. Instead of running away, you coulda hired a lawyer to clean his clock. It ain't right, what you done and how you done it.''

''You think it was an easy decision? I tried to talk to you, Colby. And frankly, you weren't much help. Ultimately, Wes drove me to it. But what about Eric, Jenny and Greg. Will you let me know where they are?''

''I'll think about it. Give me a number where I can reach you.''

"Goodbye, Colby. Since you won't help, I hope you'll at least steer my young friends to a manager other than Wes Carlisle." Feeling her heart pounding and her head spinning, Miranda hung up on her father's onetime best friend.

For the rest of the afternoon and evening, she agonized over having broken her silence.

After supper, she hung around the house until ten or so, waiting for Mrs. Phelps to go to bed.

Linc realized that Miranda wanted to speak privately with him. The night he'd given her the ring, he'd promised himself he wouldn't take her to bed again until she was legally his wife. But as sure as God made little fishes, tonight he planned to break that promise.

Half an hour after Mrs. Phelps closed her bedroom door, Linc folded his newspaper, touched a finger to his lips and held out a hand to Miranda, who fidgeted, pretending to do homework.

"Linc," she whispered as he coaxed her down the hall. "We need to talk. Seriously," she added. Yet from the moment he shut them inside his room and wrapped her in their first real romantic embrace in at least a week, Miranda's resolve to confess her sins flew straight out of her head.

Need and greed drove Linc as he practically ripped the buttons off his shirt. He certainly lacked his usual finesse in getting Miranda undressed.

She didn't mind. It was as if she hoped that touching him, feeling him deep inside her, would drive out the fear that haunted her. A fear that once she'd revealed her secret, she'd lose Linc's love.

"I love you," she whispered over and over.

"I've neglected you," he murmured into her hair when they were too spent to do anything but hold each other.

"Unlike the kids, Dennis, the big dummy, left a paper trail any first-year detective could follow. If he hasn't lost everything in the Grand Caymans, it looks like I may be able to recover part of my clients' money—and my own."

"That's wonderful, Linc." Miranda wedged a small space between them and stared into his beautiful face. "About the kids...Eric, Jenny and Greg." She licked her lips, and Linc cut off her flow of words with a series of kisses that made her eyes roll back in her head.

For the next twenty minutes, Miranda forgot she'd been planning to tell him what she knew of the kids' whereabouts. By the time she remembered, Linc had flung one arm over his head and fallen fast asleep.

She toyed with the idea of waking him, if for no other reason than to unburden her soul. At the last second, she slipped from his bed to dress, swearing that she'd spill out every last detail in the morning.

Unfortunately, her alarm failed to go off. Or else she'd failed to set it when she tiptoed to her own bed in the bunkhouse. The morning began in a panic, with Wolfie pounding on the bunkhouse door, shouting, "Cassie, are you dressed for school? The bus'll be at the end of the road in ten minutes."

Miranda sat up and grabbed her clock. "Wolfgang," she yelped, "tell Mrs. Phelps we overslept. You can either take the bus, or I'll run you and Cassie to school as soon as we get her dressed and she has a bite to eat."

"I'll wait," he said, his voice fading as he trudged away.

Miranda scurried. She was flustered and out of breath by the time she ran into Linc leaving the kitchen just as she and the girls entered it. "Where are you going?" She grabbed his arm.

"Seems we both missed setting our alarms last night." His slow, sexy smile caused her face to flame.

"I...uh...desperately need a word with you, Linc. Can you ride along when I drive the kids to school? We'd have time to talk on the trip home."

"Can't. Today's the day Shawn and I have to fertilize the olives. The weather's finally passable. And tomorrow, remember, I'm going to L.A. again."

"I forgot. It'll only take five minutes, I swear. So when I get back, will you give me that long at least?"

"Sure. If it's that important, Miranda, you know I'll make time."

She left, feeling an impending sense of doom that went beyond what she imagined Linc might say about the latest in her long line of deceptions. He was aware she'd withheld part of her past. And after their closeness last night, in her heart, she sensed their love had risen to a new level. Then why was she so jittery? Like her, Linc would be relieved to have all her secrets out in the open.

Lingering in the circular drive where she'd let the children out of the car, Miranda snapped on the radio and spun the dial to her favorite country-music station. They happened to be playing a number from the last album she'd cut. Shock paralysed her. If the cars waiting in line behind her hadn't honked in irritation, Miranda doubted she would've been able to put the SUV in gear. She'd gotten out of the habit of hearing herself singing on the radio.

The song ended, and a discussion by two disc jockeys ensued. One said, "Listen to this. Rumors out of Nashville last night suggest that Misty's manager might soon have her back in circulation."

Miranda gripped the steering wheel so tightly, her knuckles blazed white. What did they mean? Obviously Colby had talked. Damn him!

She clenched her teeth all the way to the ranch. A terrible fear gripped her. Until she turned down the lane and saw a big dark-blue car angled parallel with the porch. Both front doors to the car stood open. Once she drew nearer, Miranda saw Linc standing on a lower step. Above him on the porch were Wes Carlisle and Rick Holden, his right-hand flunky.

Her heart tumbled end over end. What little breakfast she'd swallowed that morning now threatened to come back up. For a brief panicked moment, she considered slamming the SUV in reverse and fleeing again. Then Colby's accusations reverberated in her head. He'd said her dad would be ashamed of her for taking the coward's way out. Gritting her teeth to keep them from chattering, Miranda pulled into Linc's usual parking space. She hesitated only a moment before throwing open her door and stumbling out.

Linc saw her first. He charged down the path and grabbed her shoulder in a painful squeeze. "When were you going to tell me that you're a goddamned country-western singing sensation? Hell, I should've made the connection. You looked familiar. And why not? Your picture was on the front page of every paper. If I hadn't been ass-deep getting things in order so I could come here, I would've remembered."

Miranda licked her dust-dry lips. "Last night, I…uh… got distracted, Linc. I was going to tell you."

Linc flinched as if he'd been slapped. "Why doesn't that surprise me? All you starlets are the same. You sleep your way to whatever you want."

She did slap him then, and though her fingers stung, she felt better for having wiped the sneer from his face before she paused to rub the spot where he'd gripped her arm.

Linc raised a hand to his cheek, but let it drop. "You

know how torn up I was over Felicity's decision to get involved in that rotten business. I would've forgiven you anything else, Miranda. A string of husbands, a police record, whatever. But I can't forgive that you hid the fact you're part of a world that killed my sister."

She knew that. It was what had kept her from telling him the truth before. "I understand," she said in a voice thick with pain. Even though her hands shook and her fingers were damp with perspiration, she pulled off his ring and pressed it into his palm. "Eric, Jenny and Greg *are* in Nashville. I'll do everything in my power to send them back to you, Linc."

Sidestepping him, she walked up to the two men who hovered in the background. "As you know, I got out of Nashville with next to nothing. It won't take me long to pack." She was relieved that everyone left her alone to pull together her meager belongings. Saying goodbye to the sobbing distraught Hana almost proved to be Miranda's undoing. "Hana, I'll leave you Scraps. Please…take good care of him."

Shawn stepped in for the suddenly absent Linc and pried the weeping child from Miranda's arms. He scooped up the whining dog, who knew something was wrong.

"We'll m-miss you," he stammered. "Take care of Eric and company. I plan to tell Linc he oughta give them their chance."

Miranda ripped a page from the notebook in which she'd written the songs that were now in Jenny's hands, and scribbled. "Here's my Nashville address, Shawn. Be good to Linc and take care of the little kids. Tell the dragon lady if it's the last thing I do, I intend to see that Cassie gets her operation." Shoving the address in his shirt pocket, she turned and slid into the back seat of the over-size luxury car.

Whatever they might have planned, the two men already seated inside apparently thought better of lambasting her. They drove to the airport in Sacramento with no one saying a word. Miranda didn't let on that she was no longer the grieving girl Wes Carlisle had strong-armed into a one-sided contract. Thanks to Linc Parker, she was now a woman. A woman who knew what she wanted out of life.

CHAPTER FIFTEEN

MOST OF WES CARLISLE'S employees recognized the difference in their star performer from the moment she set foot in the recording studio. Wes wouldn't admit that it was any more than her shorter hair, which he professed to hate. Not until they'd been home a week and he was paid a visit by Miranda's newly hired team of attorneys.

"I've got a binding contract she signed a decade ago," he bragged, tossing the document across the desk at the men.

"She was underage and reeling from her father's death. This won't stand up in court and I think you know it. No contract is lifetime, Carlisle."

"She owes me. She walked out and left me holding the bag on a string of sold-out concerts. Here's my lawyer's card. You talk to him about restitution for that."

"Our client's aware that you released a full CD of new hits and rereleased her old songs after she left. In other words, you capitalized on her disappearance."

"So what the hell does she want?" Wes slammed a fist on his desk. "All she ever told me she wanted that I didn't let her have was a damned vacation. She's been gone three months. Isn't that vacation enough?"

"She wants out of the business. But she's prepared to give a final tour that will include several brand-new songs she's written. These are her conditions." One of the lawyers tossed a single sheet of paper onto Carlisle's copy of Miranda's contract.

The man drew the paper slowly toward him. "Who the hell are these West Coasters she wants to open for her?" He listened as Rick Holden said the trio were the kids Miranda sent to get in touch with Colby Donovan. "Hell, you know what it'll take to book these specific ten cities before the end of April? Are you kiddin' me? And she wants her percentage of the take to go to that ranch she was livin' on? I already heard from our banker that she shelled out eighty grand on surgery for a seven-year-old kid by the name of Cassandra Rhodes." Wes clamped his mouth around an unlit cigar, and let the air slide from his lungs. "She's insane. Maybe I'll have her committed."

Several long moments went by. Finally he growled, "I'll consider this offer on one condition. I wanna hear this warm-up trio and also have a listen to Misty's new so-called hit tunes. I don't hafta do any of this, you know."

"Yes, you do," the older lawyer in Miranda's team said. "If you want the last profits you'll ever get out of her."

The youngest of Miranda's three lawyers lifted his briefcase and set it down hard on Wes's desk. "Here's a demo she and the trio have put together. The original is being held by Colby Donovan, in case you have some bright idea about releasing it without Ms. Kimbrough's authorization."

That last comment deflated the manager's final bit of bluster. He snatched up the disc and the business card the lawyer set atop it. Rising, Wes curtly opened his office door and motioned them out. "I'll be in touch. The kid knows damned well a tour like this isn't booked at a moment's notice."

The last attorney through the door paused. "It'd serve you well, Wes, to remember our client isn't a kid but a woman raised in the industry. She's very aware that her name is on the tongue of every disk jockey in the country right now. My firm tried to talk her out of letting you promote this tour. She could go to anyone in town and achieve the same—or better—results. But she feels guilty for running out on you the way she did. Her words, I believe, are that she's her father's daughter. And Kimbroughs don't back out on a deal."

Wes's response was to slam the door in the smiling lawyer's face.

A MONTH LATER, a thinner, sadder-eyed woman than the old Misty sat across from one of her lawyers in a dark pub. "This calendar seems to be in order." She read over a set of documents the man had produced after she gave the dates her approval, and glanced up. "You're absolutely sure there's no way the owner of Felicity's Refuge will ever find out this donation's from me?"

"Your anonymity is assured. I assume you know Mr. Parker is in a considerable bind, both personally and financially, at the moment?"

"Personally?" Miranda's head shot up.

"Yes, our sources tell us the loss of three kids in his caseload reflects directly on his ability to administer his teen refuge. I understand he's also involved in litigation trying to extradite his business partner from the Cayman Islands. So far, it looks promising. What I can't figure out is why you're bent on helping the guy out with an influx of cash on the one hand, and yet on the other you're petitioning to adopt three other children who at present serve as Parker's only source of revenue."

Miranda sighed. "He never wanted them to live at the

ranch. If the area's director of Social Services ever finishes her evaluation and finds their records, she'll be removing Wolfgang, Hana and Cassie from Linc's care, anyway. The accounting firm you recommended has gone over and over my investment portfolio. They assure me that if I never produce another CD but only write songs for other singers, I still ought to be free of money worries. Even if I raise three kids on my own.''

''I doubt you'll always be on your own, a beautiful talented woman like yourself.'' The man snapped his pen shut and shoved it into his pocket.

''Thank you, but my heart belongs to someone who can never love me back. Are we finished? I promised some friends I'd take them to dinner as a way of celebrating their first recording contract.''

The man gathered his papers, drained his drink and dropped money on the table to cover the tab. ''We at Dickson, Lawrence and Todd are pleased to serve you in any way we can now or in the future, Ms. Kimbrough. If you'd like to secure my services forever,'' he added with a grin, ''my kids would kill for tickets to your first and, I might add, sold-out return engagement in Nashville.''

The corners of Miranda's mouth quirked. She relaxed— something she hadn't allowed herself to do until then. ''Give me their names. I'll have seats waiting for them, and for you and your wife.'' She covered her eyes with dark glasses and sealed their bargain with a firm handshake.

Not ten minutes later, Miranda entered a well-known Nashville restaurant. Stripping off the glasses, she perused the crowd. Eventually she found and waved at a trio of familiar faces. ''What's this I hear about you three signing a lucrative deal with the biggest label in the business?''

she teased, hugging them one after the other, each fighting over the right to be first in line.

"As if you don't know we owe it all to you," Eric said, reveling in his new image. "You gave us the confidence we needed."

"You and Colby Donovan," Jenny added. "Until we met him and learned he was your dad's oldest friend, I imagined he was your love interest. Before Linc, that is."

Looking shocked, Miranda sat and thumbed open the menu. "I used to think Colby kept an eye on me because he felt guilty about being sick and missing the gig that night the band's plane crashed. I know now he's a true friend of mine. You should've heard him rake me over the coals for the way I dropped out of life. He lectured me exactly the way my dad would have done." She gave a trembling smile. "But like I said, we all made mistakes."

Jenny stilled Miranda's nervous fingers. "We're set to give you hell tonight for running out on Linc. Shawn says Linc misses you a lot."

"He could've stopped me from leaving with Wes and Rick anytime simply by asking me to stay. But hey, that's all water under the bridge. We're here to celebrate your good fortune. Please don't ruin it by making me cry over Lincoln Parker."

Eric fiddled with his water glass. "We think you should tell him we'll be performing in L.A. and San Francisco. That would open the door to let him back into your life. It'd be like the way you helped me find my brother Joe and let him back into my life. Everybody knows people can say stuff in the heat of the moment they don't really mean. Linc knows it, too."

"He said he'd never forgive me. And I slapped him. Me, who abhors violence." Miranda twisted her napkin around her fork, sounding bleak. "Today, my lawyer

pointed out that I'm stealing food off Linc's table by petitioning to adopt Wolfie, Cassie and Hana. How many
times can a woman dump on a guy before he's truly had
enough?''

Greg frowned. ''You're not dumping on him. Colby said
everything you make on this tour goes to help Linc keep
the refuge open. As well, he said you shelled out for Cassie's surgery.''

''Some anonymity!'' Miranda exclaimed. ''I made that
arrangement in strictest confidence.''

''Yeah, well, Carlisle is blabbing it all over Nashville.
Colby thinks your old manager wants everyone in town to
believe you've lost your marbles.''

Eric touched his glass to Miranda's. ''It's having the
opposite effect. From what we hear, people applaud you
for finally wising up and dumping the bastard.''

''Be that as it may, I don't want any of this to get back
to Linc. I really doubt he wants any help from the likes of
me.''

The waiter came to take their order while Miranda was
still trying to extract promises from the kids to remain
absolutely silent on the subject.

THEY PLAYED the first nine cities on the tour to packed
audiences and rave reviews. Only San Francisco remained.
Miranda found the circuit drained her energy, although it
revved up her warm-up group.

Fifteen minutes before her last-ever concert was set to
begin, Miranda unfolded and reread a letter sent to her law
firm by Cassie's surgeon. It'd caught up to her in Chicago.
The operation arranged by Mrs. Bishop had gone flaw-
lessly, the document said. Cassie was already recovering.
She was still at Felicity's Refuge. Folding the letter, Mi-

randa clutched it to her breast for a moment before tucking it back in the bottom of her makeup case.

Staring in the mirror, she repeated a prayer she always said before going on—at least during every performance during this particular tour. That once this final show ended, the next good news would be that the state of California was authorizing her adoption of Cassie Rhodes and Wolfgang and Hana Schmitt. And oh, in addition, a silly terrier named Scraps.

"Five minutes, Ms. Kimbrough."

Miranda picked up her guitar, the one her father had bought her when she first began to sing. When occasionally performing with his band had given her such joy.

She fluffed blond hair that had grown several inches. Taking a deep breath, she fell in step behind her escort, hired to guide her to a stool set in the center of a darkened stage. Another of her requirements for this tour: banning the use of the mist canisters. She was Miranda now, not Misty.

As the curtain lifted and the lights came slowly up, she began to softly play and sing. She started with a medley of old hits. After each song, the ripple of clapping grew to a crescendo.

She thought, oddly enough, that tonight she'd come full circle from the moment she'd left the stage in Nashville and put in motion a chain of events that changed her life forever.

Heat from a single overhead spotlight warmed her bare shoulders. For this show she'd chosen to wear a simple brown tank top, teamed with a long, cream-colored skirt. A wide leather belt banded her narrow hips and matched hand-tooled cowboy boots—the pair Linc had bought her one snowy afternoon that now seemed almost a lifetime ago.

A hush fell over the crowd as the space lengthened between the last medley and this, Miranda's final number. She turned the microphone down, telling the audience, "This number isn't on your program. It's a special song I'm only singing on my farewell tour. It will never be recorded. I wrote it for a…good friend. And it's about love everlasting."

She cleared her throat, lifted her chin and launched into the soulful ballad, knowing this was the absolute last time she'd ever publicly sing "For the Love of Felicity."

She poured out the words about a young boy forced to grow up too fast. Of responsibility thrown heavily onto youthful shoulders. Of the man he'd become, who thought the best he could do for his kid sister was to earn a lot of money and give her the best of everything. Opportunities of a lifetime.

As always, Miranda felt the tears begin to slide down her cheeks, and she quavered a bit before digging deep to manage the last stanza—about a teenage girl's inability to cope with rejection outside the realm of a loving brother's protection. And of his love, a love so great that at her unthinkable death, his monument was to build a refuge for her lost and lonely contemporaries. A memory that would live on in Felicity's name and always in the brother's heart.

The stage went suddenly black and the velvet curtain fell, making a soft *swish* in the silent auditorium. As had happened in every other city on the tour, the audience drew in a collective breath. When they released it, there was no whistling or stamping, but a reverent standing ovation that followed the singer into the wings.

Miranda felt limp. Utterly drained. With one hand, she staved off anyone in the troupe who might trail her to her dressing quarters.

She dropped heavily onto the stool in front of her

makeup mirror. She covered her face and wept for all that Linc had lost and all that she had lost. She'd offered up this song, this final declaration of her love, but she knew that as soon as she got home, she'd hold a match to the music and lyrics of Felicity's tribute and never sing it again.

Someone tapped on her door. She wasn't ready to greet anyone who might've been given a backstage pass. But then again, she was, after all, a performer. A Kimbrough. Straightening, she smudged away the trail of tears and called, "Come in. It's unlocked."

The door swung inward by inches until, when fully open, it revealed her visitor. Miranda's instinct was to hide. Or to run and throw herself into his arms and beg for his mercy.

Linc Parker stood there, hesitantly rolling his hat around and around in his broad hands. The hands she loved to feel on her skin.

"Hello, Miranda. The, uh, kids are waiting down the hall. They're champing at the bit to come see you. Wolfie, Hana, Cassie and Shawn."

"How did you know I was here in San Francisco?" She clenched her fingers tightly in her skirt. Did he have no idea what it cost her to see him?

"Eric sent tickets, said it was their concert. He didn't say a word about opening for *your* show. So none of us knew until I bought a program for Cassie."

"How is she?"

"Great. She's on crutches, but she's coming along fine. I'll, ah, let you see them soon. I needed a minute alone with you, Miranda. To say how thoughtful you were to write that song for Felicity and…for me."

"As of tonight I'm retiring the song. Well, I'm retiring, too. From the stage."

"I figured that was the case. Mrs. Bishop phoned last night. She said you're adopting the kids." He crushed his hat and swallowed hard. He was forced to blink rapidly and glance away. "It almost kills me to think of losing their laughter. Of course, I thought I was prepared. But after you left…"

"I didn't file for adoption to hurt you further, Linc. I can give them a good home."

"Can you?" He walked toward her, his eyes like burning embers in the low light.

"Y-yes. I love them."

"I thought if you and I agreed on anything, Miranda, it's that kids who've been kicked around the way they've been need both a mom and a dad."

She shut her eyes and rubbed her forehead. "I can't give them that, Linc."

"Yes, you can."

Opening one eye warily, she realized Linc had tossed aside his hat. From the inside pocket of his suit jacket, he removed the ring she'd returned to him the day she left the ranch.

For what seemed like an eternity, they stared at each other. "I'm sorry for hitting you, Linc."

"I deserved that. I'm sorry I let you go. I've missed you so damned much. And I want you back. Back in my home. Back in my bed. Full nights. Every night."

With a guttural cry and a smile through a fall of tears, Miranda slowly extended her left hand.

Linc's breath mingled with an eruption of happy shouts at the open door. Wolfie's voice rose above the rest. "Linc, did you tell her the cops got your partner back and we ain't broke anymore?"

Miranda helped him work the cool band onto her finger, even though neither of their hands was steady. When the ring sat in its rightful place, she curled her other hand possessively over it. Only then did she peer around Linc to look at the invaders.

Soon, all eyes were wet with tears of joy. Cassie led the band of well-wishers into the room. Her small crutches made dimples in the commercial carpet, but she took every step on her own. Hana, Wolfie and Shawn gave Cassie her space. They were followed closely by Jenny, Eric and Greg, who lit up the dim dressing room with their beaming smiles.

A host of white-jacketed caterers surged into the room and began filling two tables with food. "Hey!" Miranda protested. "You've got the wrong room."

"No, they don't," Jenny said. "This is how we hoped tonight would end. Eric, Greg and I owe you guys so much. This is the least we can do, 'cause we're hoping there'll be rooms for us at the ranch whenever we're not on tour or recording in Nashville."

Linc stripped off his tie and stuffed it in his jacket pocket. Bringing out his hand, he wore a strange look on his face. He opened his fingers, and on his palm sat the silver-crowned frog Miranda had given him for Christmas. "How did this get in my pocket?"

"I put him there," Hana admitted, shocking them all by her bold revelation. "M'randa read Cassie and me a book about a frog prince who turned into a man and married a princess. She said they lived happily ever after. Nobody's been happy since M'randa went away. Not even Scraps. Wolfie said I shouldn't tell that we were gonna see her tonight. But…I thought if Mr. Linc had the frog prince, maybe he'd kiss M'randa and then we could all live happily ever after, too."

Linc swung the child up into his arms, then leaned close to Miranda and bestowed on her a kiss that held all the promise one kiss could express. "Yep," he said, giving Hana a wink when he'd straightened. "I feel your magic working, all right."

Holding out her left hand, Miranda waggled it a bit so everyone could see the flash of her diamond. "Voilà! Magic."

"All right!" Jenny flung her arms out and did a gyrating dance across the room. "We've got success, a lotta love and a family in the making. I'd say that's something to celebrate!"

"Good deal. Now can we eat?" Shawn said loudly. "I'm starved."

Linc hooked an arm around Miranda's waist and they laughed.

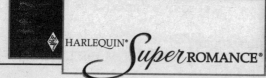

HARLEQUIN *Super*ROMANCE®

Nothing Sacred
by Tara Taylor Quinn

Shelter Valley Stories

Welcome back to Shelter Valley, Arizona. This is the kind of town everyone dreams about, the kind of place everyone wants to live. Meet your friends from previous visits—including Martha Moore, divorced mother of teenagers. And meet the new minister, David Cole Marks.

Martha's still burdened by the bitterness of a husband's betrayal. And there are secrets hidden in David's past.

Can they find in each other the shelter they seek? The happiness?

By the author of *Where the Road Ends,* *Born in the Valley* and *For the Children.*

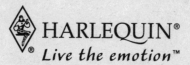

HARLEQUIN®
Live the emotion™

Visit us at www.eHarlequin.com   HSRNSTTQ

HARLEQUIN® *Super*ROMANCE®

**Sea View House in Pilgrim Cove offers
its residents the sea, the sun, the sound
of the surf and the call of the gulls.
But sometimes serenity is only an illusion...**

Pilgrim Cove

Four heartwarming stories by popular author
Linda Barrett

The House on the Beach

Laura McCloud's come back to Pilgrim Cove—the source of her fondest childhood memories—to pick up the pieces of her life. The tranquility of Sea View House is just what she needs. She moves in...and finds much more than she bargained for.

**Available in March 2004,
The House on the Beach
is the first title in this
charming series.**

*Available wherever
Harlequin books are sold.*

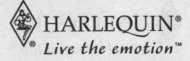

HARLEQUIN®
Live the emotion™

Visit us at www.eHarlequin.com

HSRPC1

HARLEQUIN *Super*ROMANCE®

Five brothers share the bond of family, but little else.

The *Luchetti* **Brothers**

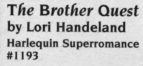

The Brother Quest
by Lori Handeland
Harlequin Superromance
#1193

If anything ever happens to me, go to 445 Briar Lane, Wind Lake, Minnesota.

Colin Luchetti's brother, Bobby, has disappeared, and the only clue is a cryptic message sending Colin to Wind Lake. What he finds when he gets there is unexpected—a day-care center complete with kids, a runaway guinea pig and Marlie Anderson, the owner. Colin needs to unravel the mystery for his family's sake, but can he do it without falling for the woman his brother loves?

Available March 2004 wherever Harlequin books are sold.

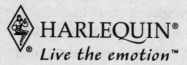

HARLEQUIN®
Live the emotion™

Visit us at www.eHarlequin.com

HSRLBBQ

eHARLEQUIN.com

Your favorite authors are just a click away
at www.eHarlequin.com!

- Take our **Sister Author Quiz** and
  we'll match you up with the author
  most like you!

- Choose from over 500
  author **profiles!**

- Chat with your favorite authors
  on our **message boards.**

- Are you an author in the making?
  Get advice from published authors
  in **The Inside Scoop!**

- Get the latest on **author appearances**
  and tours!

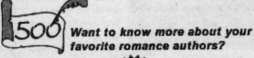

*Want to know more about your
favorite romance authors?*

Choose from over 500 author profiles!

**Learn about your favorite authors
in a fun, interactive setting—
visit www.eHarlequin.com today!**

INTAUTH

If you enjoyed what you just read,
then we've got an offer you can't resist!

Take 2 bestselling
love stories FREE!

Plus get a FREE surprise gift!

Clip this page and mail it to Harlequin Reader Service®

IN U.S.A.	IN CANADA
3010 Walden Ave.	P.O. Box 609
P.O. Box 1867	Fort Erie, Ontario
Buffalo, N.Y. 14240-1867	L2A 5X3

YES! Please send me 2 free Harlequin Superromance® novels and my free surprise gift. After receiving them, if I don't wish to receive anymore, I can return the shipping statement marked cancel. If I don't cancel, I will receive 6 brand-new novels every month, before they're available in stores. In the U.S.A., bill me at the bargain price of $4.47 plus 25¢ shipping and handling per book and applicable sales tax, if any*. In Canada, bill me at the bargain price of $4.99 plus 25¢ shipping and handling per book and applicable taxes**. That's the complete price, and a savings of at least 10% off the cover prices—what a great deal! I understand that accepting the 2 free books and gift places me under no obligation ever to buy any books. I can always return a shipment and cancel at any time. Even if I never buy another book from Harlequin, the 2 free books and gift are mine to keep forever.

135 HDN DNT3
336 HDN DNT4

Name	(PLEASE PRINT)	
Address	Apt.#	
City	State/Prov.	Zip/Postal Code

* Terms and prices subject to change without notice. Sales tax applicable in N.Y.
** Canadian residents will be charged applicable provincial taxes and GST.
  All orders subject to approval. Offer limited to one per household and not valid to
  current Harlequin Superromance® subscribers.
  ® is a registered trademark of Harlequin Enterprises Limited.

SUP02   ©1998 Harlequin Enterprises Limited

HARLEQUIN *Super*ROMANCE®

Alouette, Michigan. Located high on the
Upper Peninsula. Home to strong men,
stalwart women and lots and lots of trees.

NORTH COUNTRY
Stories

Three Little Words
by Carrie Alexander
Superromance #1186

Connor Reed returns to Alouette to reconnect with his grandfather
and to escape his notorious past. He enlists the help of Tess Bucek,
the town's librarian, to help teach his grandfather to read. As
Tess and Connor start to fall in love, they learn the healing power
of words, especially three magical little ones….

Available in February 2004 wherever Harlequin books are sold.

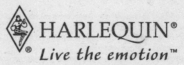

HARLEQUIN®
Live the emotion™

Visit us at www.eHarlequin.com   HSRNCTLW